I sat as if to SAY something
but could not [barcode]
the waiting
It comes like my cat
    Saidy she demands
    Attention
Attention I can not or will
    not not keep bound
    like the coffee ceremony
    water spilling to my cup
    sacred brew that arrests

    my view
I wait for no one
    my dog lies crumpled
    these many years
And I plant to make a
    pond above his bones
    to trickle his name
        from me   make that plan

To have feared something
  beyond my everyday
  and do nothing
Am I becoming this

Tales
from the
Great Turtle

I have hunted down a turtle
  I saw too ~~too~~ slowly exposed on the
Road
Had to go back and place him
  in a more congenial spot
Whether he liked it or not
  ~~It~~ was a long time ago
He was good sized and I
  ~~feared~~ I would never
  run across him or his
  ever again.
Will that ever happen to
  my black widows.

Tales from the Great Turtle

EDITED BY PIERS ANTHONY AND RICHARD GILLIAM

TOR

A TOM DOHERTY ASSOCIATES BOOK ■ NEW YORK

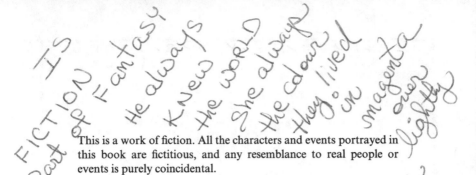

This is a work of fiction. All the characters and events portrayed in this book are fictitious, and any resemblance to real people or events is purely coincidental.

TALES FROM THE GREAT TURTLE

A Tor Book
Published by Tom Doherty Associates, Inc.
175 Fifth Avenue
New York, N.Y. 10010

Tor ® is a registered trademark of Tom Doherty Associates, Inc.

Design by Lynn Newmark

Library of Congress Cataloging-in-Publication Data

Tales from the great turtle / Piers Anthony and Richard Gilliam, editors.
    p.   cm.
  "A Tom Doherty Associates book."
  ISBN 0-312-85628-8
  1. Indians of North America—Mythology—Fiction.
2. Fantastic fiction, American.   I. Anthony, Piers.   II. Gilliam, Richard.
PS648.I53T34   1994
813'.01083520397—dc20   94-28985
                                        CIP

First edition: December 1994

Printed in the United States of America

0 9 8 7 6 5 4 3 2 1

Copyright Acknowledgments

Contents

My STOMACH makes the sound of a cat always not but when I'm listening

Tales
from the
Great Turtle

How to pass on an open page is sometimes beyond me - but after an inadequate can do the trick. Like this alpha... of its own. A wiggle of It has a little Exactly what it is akin plastic not quite a squeak. Phoebe

Introduction

When the dirt comes loose from the rocks and they're being pitched there anywhere and my hole — Brown Enick

This is an anthology of stories by or about American Indians, which the editors hope will help publicize the culture, history, and concerns of Native America while entertaining general readers. Richard Gilliam is an experienced anthology editor who has done most of the work on this volume and whose presence needs no explanation. But what am I, Piers Anthony, doing here? I am known for funny fantasy, and for my personal notes in my books, but I have done very little editing of anything. In fact I tend to regard editors as warts on the fair face of literature, little better than reviewers or used-car salesmen.

I understand that cruise ships may have two captains: one for show, the other for work. (For this volume, perhaps the analogy should be the Peace Chief and the War Chief, but this is not a matter of war and peace.) The show captain dresses impressively and looks great as he moves around the ship, seeing to the comforts of the passengers and answering their stupid questions with wit and charm. He also entertains them at dinners, presides over special events, and will pose for pictures. He is fair-spoken, and is a reassuring presence. Meanwhile the work captain is actually running the ship, getting grubby as he fixes glitches, cussing as he gives emergency orders, stinking of sweat and oil. The last thing he wants is an idiot passenger in his way. But it is because of him that the ship gets where it is going on schedule, neither colliding with an iceberg nor running aground. Perhaps on occasion the two captains change places, and then Captain Show turns grim and businesslike while Captain Work becomes pretty and affable; both are qualified to do whatever job needs doing. Well, for this voyage, uh, volume, I am Cpn Show and Richard is Cpn Work. I do the introduction, my publisher has the book, and it is hoped that my reassuring presence will attract enough readers to make the volume a success. Meanwhile Cpn Work has to do the dirty job of going through nearly a million words of submissions, rejecting most, to select the best stories for publication. Oh, yes, I read the top ones too, but I don't have to break hearts by turning down entries; Cpn Show prefers to pretend that nothing ever founders.

Apart from that, what are my qualifications to participate? Mainly that I wrote the novel *Tatham Mound,* wherein I animated the bones found in a Tocobaga burial mound found near where I live in Florida, trying to show how it was with a vanished culture. This put me on record as a serious historical novelist with an interest in Native American history. I don't pretend to be expert in the subject, just to have sympathy with those I believe the European invaders wronged. I would like to see their concerns get greater recognition. As we planned the anthology, there was a powwow in the vicinity; Richard went, but I did not. I'm a workaholic who hates to lose a day from writing, but on reflection I realized that it was more than that. When I researched and wrote *Mound* I developed a deep respect for the lost cultures, and the characters came to life for me in a special way. I simply did not care to see what has become of the descendants of their cousins who survived the destruction of their way of life. The notion of diluted, sanitized, or invented traditions does not appeal. I'm not interested in seeing a faked up "Ghost Dance" or in buying "native" trinkets produced for tourists—or in a pow wow catering to white folk. Perhaps in my ignorance I wronged the event, but I preferred simply to stay clear. What I desire is gone beyond recovery: the original, untainted culture, fulfilled by the people who lived before the white man's plagues killed perhaps nineteen of every twenty. I wish I could go out, perhaps as a spirit, and visit the Peoples of the One Fire, so called because each year all their blazes were extinguished and then started anew from the lone sacred fire. But their fires in my neighborhood were doused long before I existed. So I can visit them only in my imagination, whose most tangible expression is in my fiction and that of others—as seen in this volume. It may not be physically real, but at least it hints at what is spiritually real.

Once we had the contract for the anthology, my co-editor asked me to contribute a story to it. This was problematical, because I have always looked askance at editors who run their own work. Isn't that a conflict of interest? Besides, I didn't have a suitable notion for such a story. But he was insistent, so I took it under advisement—and one day, reading *Archaeology* magazine, I saw a discussion of a truly ancient American myth. There was my notion. So I wrote my story and sent it in. Then Co-ed suggested that my story lead off the volume. Ouch! I already have enough trouble dodging the slings and arrows of outrageous fortune in the form of potshots from critics; that seemed foolhardy. Still, if I am to judge the merits of the stories of others, shouldn't I try to demonstrate my own ability in this respect at the outset? I have contempt for those who critique the merits of others, when they don't evince any equivalent abilities themselves; that may not be quite parallel to what the Whiteskins did to the Redskins, but it's suggestive. Thus my story is in the pot with the others, and subject to the same cynosure.

At any rate, I believe we have good stories here, and it's a decent anthology. Here you will discover the past and future and alternate realities of Native America, the devious ploys of Coyote the Trickster, the concerns of talking animals, and the pervasive role of magic. Why should a young woman dump her baby in her father's junkyard? What has a tapestry to do with foiling evil? How can one fool a hungry skeleton? What happened to Mount Rushmore? Where is the Valley of Day-Glo? How does the fantasy of Native America differ from that of other cultures? These stories will provide a notion. Meanwhile, I hope that Co-ed's afterword and notes on the authors contribute to your appreciation, and that you find the volume worthwhile, regardless of your affinity with the American Indian tradition. There are things here to entertain you, and things to think about.

Piers Anthony
January, 1994

Headwaters
∎∎∎∎∎∎∎∎∎∎∎

Tortoise Shell

Piers Anthony

He was a young man, handsome, well muscled, and possessed of a clear awareness of the world around him. He came from afar, for his tonsure and tongue were strange, and he seemed to have no destination. Often he slept in trees, but he would accept a bed of pine needles in a lodge if invited, and perform some useful service in exchange. Sometimes a maiden would invite him to her bed, and he would accept that too, but would explain by means of signs that he could not remain beyond the night. This saddened many maidens, for he was of amiable disposition, a fine lover, and seemed to be an ideal marriage prospect. He gave no name and accepted no reward for favors, other than food and lodging for one night.

One maiden appealed to her father, who was a warrior of local prominence, and he braced the stranger. They spoke in signs, and their dialogue was approximately this:

"Youth, I would speak with you."

"I am honored to converse with you, Father." For this was the courteous address for an elder man, by a youth of either gender.

"My daughter regards you well, and so do I, though our acquaintance has been only a day and night. I would have you marry her, and be one with our tribe."

"I would like that, for your daughter is beautiful and you are bold. But I must not stay."

"Why is this?"

"I am a man of dishonor, stripped of my name and exiled from my tribe. I may not return or settle elsewhere until I have accomplished two significant things. I am therefore not eligible to join you and your lovely daughter, much as I would like to do so."

There was a pause, for this was serious news. "For what great crime was this punishment imposed on you?" the father asked at last.

"I spoke sacrilege. I doubted the story of the First Father and the Tortoise Shell."

The father was taken aback. "You were indeed insolent! I can see that our cultures differ from each other in many respects, and surely many of our beliefs are not the same, but we too honor that story and know it to be true. The very sky asserts its validity. What are the two things you must do?"

"I must perform a truly selfless act, and I must achieve belief in the validity of that story."

The father nodded. "This is appropriate, for surely it was the arrogance of ignorance that led you to this folly. When you accomplish it, return here; perhaps my daughter will not yet have married elsewhere."

"I thank you for your tolerance, Father. But tell her not to wait, for though I shall strive to accomplish the first, I fear I shall never succeed in the second. I have had to advise other maidens of this."

The father was angered by this continuing presumption of perspective, but held his temper, for he had initiated the dialogue. "Perhaps if you will accept some guidance . . ."

"I will listen with respect, Father, but I am unable to compel my own belief."

"It is this: go south from here, to the place of the red slope. There you may find what you seek."

The young man bowed his head. "I thank you, Father, for this advice. I will go there." And he turned and proceeded south.

Actually this advice was similar to other suggestions he had received in the course of his travel. Thus he had come generally south, proceeding from tribe to tribe. The description of the place had varied, but there did seem to be a destination that others felt could help him. He hoped they were right, for it was painful to be cut off from the respect and association of others. He was surviving well alone, but his great desire was to be accepted, to marry well, and to know the security of the support of a good community.

He walked for a day, and spent the night in a tree overhanging a quiet river. He speared a fat fish for his breakfast, apologizing to its spirit for depriving it of its body, and walked on south. After several more days he came to a hill that was covered with red flowers, and knew this was the place.

On that slope was a lodge, and in the lodge was an old man. His body was lean to the point of emaciation, and his skin was pallid. It seemed that he would die before long.

"Allow me to fetch some food for you," the young man said, augmenting his words with signs so that he could be understood.

The old man made a weak signal with one hand: "It is no use. I will die anyway."

But the young man went to the field and foraged for beans and a gourd, and went to the nearby river and dug out some clams, and brought these and fresh water to the lodge. He made a fire and prepared a good meal for them both.

While they ate, they conversed. The old man was called Sky River. He had traveled widely once, and knew something of the young man's tongue, so soon they were able to talk as well as sign. That was just as well, for it turned out that the old man was almost blind, and could hardly see the signs. "Who are you, and why do you help one who can do nothing for you in return?" Sky River inquired.

The young man explained about his exile and lack of a name. "I help you because you need help," he concluded. "I would not care to let you die without comfort when I could prevent it."

"I thank you for this help, but it is a wasted effort, for I shall die within two days anyway. My grandsons were killed in battle, and my granddaughters live in other villages, so there is no one to maintain me. It is best simply to let me expire alone, sparing yourself the mischief of the presence of my spirit."

The young man knew what he meant. Spirits, newly freed from their bodies, could be jealous of the living, and strike at any person they encountered. It was therefore best to be elsewhere when a person died. Nevertheless, he persisted. "I have little to lose, and you have great need, so I will help you regardless. What more may I do for you?"

Sky River made a second objection. "If I had my wish, it would be to die in our sacred place, so that my spirit will have the company of the spirits of those I have known in life. But that place is far from here, and difficult to reach even for one in health and unburdened. It would have been a struggle for both of my stout grandsons to paddle me there."

"I will take you there, so that you may die in peace."

"This is a very generous offer, but you can not do this, for only a man's own kin may take him there. The spirits of the sacred place would destroy any other men who intruded."

The young man was silent for a time, considering. Then he had a new notion. "I will adopt you as my grandfather. Then I will be your kin, and the spirits will allow me to bring you there."

"That would be risky," Sky River said, "because the spirits might not recognize the adoption, and would slay you regardless. In any event, you owe me nothing, for I have given you nothing. Spare yourself this thankless chore and go your way with my thanks for what you have already done for me."

"Some risks need to be taken," the young man said. "I hereby adopt you as my grandfather, if you will accept, and I will do for you what a grandson does for his honored ancestor."

Sky River smiled with bemusement. "I accept, of course, and truly you are one I would have been glad to have had naturally. As you have no name, I will exercise the prerogative of my relationship and call you Blank."

"But I can accept no name until I—"

"I have given you no name, merely a temporary designation of nothingness for my convenience. You may discard it when I am dead."

The young man smiled. "I see that you are versed in manners. I will use that designation for now. Where is the sacred place, and how may I transport you there?"

"I have an old canoe, almost as near death as I am. It may endure for this final journey. But I think I can not guide you there, for I can not see well enough to tell one stream from another. We shall have to have help."

"Who will help us?"

Sky River considered. "I once did a favor for the little child of the priest, Sweet Grass, and she said she wished to return it. Perhaps this is the occasion. The spirits should not bother the priest's girl."

So Blank picked up Sky River and carried him to the old canoe, and then paddled him downstream to the village of his people. The old man was fatigued by the effort and fell asleep, so when they arrived, Blank beached the canoe and left him there in shade. But as he sought to enter the village, a warrior challenged him. "Who are you, and what are you doing with that sick old man?" he signed.

"That man is Sky River, my grandfather," Blank signed in return. "I am taking him to the sacred place to die. But I must ask the priest's little child to guide us, because I do not know the way and my grandfather can not see to guide me."

"What little child?" the warrior demanded.

"He called her Sweet Grass. He thought she might do this for him."

The warrior stared at him with a new appraisal. "How can you be Sky River's grandson, and we do not know of this?"

"I adopted him this day."

"And what of his obligations?"

"I will settle them."

"And what of his enemies?"

Blank stood up straight, putting his strong hand on his good stone knife. "I will fight his enemies."

The warrior nodded. "I will tell Sweet Grass." He departed, and Blank waited.

Soon the warrior returned with a small figure swathed in a voluminous feather cloak. "Here is the priest's daughter," he said gruffly, and stood back.

Blank faced her. "I regret asking such a favor of a child, but I must take my grandfather Sky River to the sacred place before he dies, and I need guidance. He thought you might be willing to help."

"What do you know of these matters?" she signed, her large eyes shining within the shroud of the hood.

"I know nothing of anything. Only that I must get my grandfather there as soon as I can, for he is failing."

She studied him a moment. "And you will settle his obligations and fight his enemies?"

"I will stand for his honor, in the manner of his kin. What needs to be settled?"

"And if the settlement is arduous?"

"Kin take no note of difficulty. I will settle it. He will die in honor." He touched his knife again.

Sweet Grass glanced at the village warrior, and nodded. He turned away, no longer standing ready to protect her from possible harm. "I will guide you," she said.

"But what of his obligations? His enemies?"

"There are none. Sky River is well respected. We merely wished to know your sincerity."

So the villagers had not quite trusted a stranger, and had tested him. That was reasonable.

They went to the canoe. Sky River was awake now. Sweet Grass went immediately to him. "Grandfather, why did you not tell me you were failing?" she asked, taking his gaunt hands in her tiny firm ones. She did not use signs now, so Blank had only a vague notion of her specific words, but her manner told him much. "I would have come to you."

"Ah, is it you, precious child?" Sky River asked, gratified. "I would not put this burden on you. But with a strong grandson to paddle me there, I think I can make it to the sacred place before I die."

"Of course you can," she said. She lifted his hands and kissed them. "And of course I will guide you. You know I love you."

"I know it," the old man agreed. "Now, maybe—"

"Do you really think it can be?" she asked.

"I do not know. But I think it is possible."

"Then rest, grandfather, and we shall get you there." She got into the front of the canoe, and Blank shoved it carefully into the water and got into the back.

Sweet Grass pointed upstream. Blank paddled vigorously, for there was a fair current and he had no help. In some tribes, women paddled canoes as well as men, but it seemed not here. In any event, a child would not have been able to help much.

Sky River sank back, staring at the sky. It was clear that his vitality was weakening; he could die before nightfall. Yet he did not rest. "Sweet Grass, my grandson does not know of the love between us. May I tell him?"

The girl turned, still shrouded in her cloak so that only her hands, feet, and eyes showed. She did not speak.

"You spoke in my tongue," Blank said. "She does not understand."

"Ah, yes." The old man spoke in his native tongue, and now the girl reacted. She said something, and turned to face forward again. "She agrees," Sky River said. "So I will tell you that I won her heart by telling her the tales of the sky. She knows and loves them all, and will share their truths with coming generations. She swore she would marry me when she was grown, but of course that was foolishness. She must not marry a failing old man."

Blank smiled through the exertion of his strenuous paddling. "Why not? Is it not a woman's right to marry whatever man takes her fancy?"

"But she is not just any girl, and will not be just any woman. She is the daughter of the priest. She will marry the next chief of our tribe."

"Oh, an arranged union," Blank said. "I hope for her sake that he is a good man."

"I am sure he will be. It is not arranged; this is our way of designating the next chief without strife. She may marry any man, in or out of our tribe. That man will be the next chief."

Blank was surprised. "She chooses the next chief? By marrying him? That I have not heard of before."

"The truths of the sky are eternal, but the customs of tribes differ, as is proper. Her father trained her to choose well. The man she marries will be worthy, and the tribe will accept him and prosper. That is our way. Do you question it?"

"No," Blank said hastily. "I am bound to respect your way, for now I am kin to you. I was merely surprised."

"And of course there will be time," the old man said, "because our present chief remains healthy. Only when he dies will Sweet Grass's husband be chief. So there has been no hurry, and she has time to grow up and choose wisely, and to educate her husband in our ways before he comes to represent us. So it has ever been."

"It is an interesting way to do it," Blank said. "And surely as good as any other."

"But you can see how foolish it would be for her to marry me,"

Sky River continued. "I will die long before the present chief does. So I turned her down, though I love her like no other girl. But she has persisted, and has sought no other man. This is the favor she wishes to do me, as I long since lost my wife."

"But she is a child!" Blank said, surprised.

The swathed figure glanced back, but remained silent.

Sky River smiled weakly. "But she believes the myth of the First Father and the Tortoise Shell. Do you know it?"

"Of course," Blank said, somewhat briefly, because the forceful paddling was tiring him. "That is the story I questioned, so I was exiled from my tribe. I told you that."

"So you did; I remember now. May I tell Sweet Grass your situation?"

"It is no secret. I still do not believe."

The old man spoke to the girl. She turned again, and regarded Blank somberly from under her hood. Then she pointed to the side: it was time to diverge from the main stream to a tributary.

Blank guided the canoe to the lesser stream. But here the current was swifter, and he had to work even harder. He was an expert canoeist who had won races, but this was more of a challenge than he had anticipated. His muscles were beginning to hurt, and he was panting. But he had to keep paddling hard, because otherwise the canoe would be carried back down to the larger river, and the old man would not reach the sacred place in time.

"Do you believe that the First Father is the god of green growing things?" Sky River asked.

"Yes," Blank gasped.

"For so it is written in the sky," the old man said.

"Yes."

"Do you believe that he ages and fades every year, even as do the green growing things?"

"Yes," Blank gasped again.

"And that each year he must be taken by canoe to the Place of Creation, following the great river in the sky?"

"Yes." The world was clouding, and Blank saw nothing but the canoe with the old man lying in its center and the cloaked silhouette of the girl sitting at its prow. His muscles simply could not operate much longer.

"Where he is then reborn from the cracked shell of the giant tortoise?"

"That—no," Blank wheezed.

Then the girl pointed to a small landing place beside the stream. Relieved, Blank used his last strength to propel the canoe there, and fell back, exhausted. It was well that he did so, for the canoe sank as soon as they left it.

But Sky River would not relent. "Why do you believe so much, and not the rest?"

"Because—" Blank paused to fetch in some more breath. "Because man is born of woman, not of a tortoise. Each creature brings forth only its own kind."

"But the First Father is not a man. He is a god. Gods are not bound by the rules of men."

"But then the First Father should not need to die or be reborn," Blank argued, his breath returning.

"Yet that is the god's way. To renew the seasons. We know it is so because it is written in the sky."

"Possibly," Blank said, not caring to argue. That could only alienate him from the man he was trying to help.

"Now you must carry me to the sacred place," Sky River said. "It is not far."

So Blank marshaled his remaining strength, picked him up, and followed Sweet Grass along a path through the forest. They came to a glade with a stone pedestal formed from a boulder. He set Sky River on the stone, as directed. It was rounded and cracked, but solid enough to support him.

"Now it is done," the old man said. "I thank you, grandson, for your valiant labor on my behalf. A lesser man could not have completed this journey, and a less constant one would not have tried. You have favored me as I favored my own adopted grandfather, many summers ago. I die with satisfaction." He closed his eyes and died.

Blank stared at the body. It seemed to waver, and a haze rose from it and wafted toward him. He breathed, and the haze entered him. He felt strange, yet exhilarated.

Sweet Grass faced him. "You have done a great service," she said. "Knowing of no reward."

"I did only what was right to do," Blank said. "I am glad he died in the manner he wished to. A man's death is a special thing."

"But he did not die," she said. "He is reborn from the crack in the shell."

Blank looked. The body lay on what he now saw was an enormous tortoise shell. The vapor might have come up through the crack. "But—"

"Now he has joined you, without displacing your own spirit," she continued. "And you are heir to all that is his."

"But I sought nothing from him!" he protested. "I was trying to do a selfless act."

"You succeeded. You have given him your good young body. You receive all that is his. Including his name. I welcome you back to youth, Sky River."

"But I am not—"

"How is it, then, that you understand me, when I am speaking the tongue you did not know before and my hands are still?"

It was true. He understood her perfectly. He realized that what he had taken to be a vapor was the spirit of Sky River. It was spreading through him, adding its nature to his. Now he saw or remembered Sweet Grass as she had been when he told her the great ancient truths of the night sky, and received her foolish yet wonderful declaration of love. His gifted or recovered name derived from the sky he interpreted: the great milky river that crossed it every night, forever changing orientation and aspect, but constant throughout. "But you as a child—that was ten summers ago!" he exclaimed, feeling his dawning or returning love for the precious girl.

"Indeed it was," she agreed. "I think you have not gazed upon me lately." She flung off the feather cloak and stood revealed as the lustrous young woman she had become. "You are heir also to my love. Now I can marry you, Sky River, for you are young enough." She stepped into his embrace. "And you will be chief."

He would be chief. That was just part of the favor she was returning. But she had had to wait for her change of age—and his. He held her, savoring the realization of the whole of it. He had thought it could not be, until the good-hearted young warrior had come. The one who sought no reward, knowing nothing of the true relation between the sky and the world, or of the special conventions of this tribe.

"Now do you believe in the First Father's rebirth from the cracked shell of the tortoise?" Sweet Grass inquired mischievously.

"Now I believe," he agreed. "Now I am whole."

AUTHOR'S NOTE:

This is a new story, really a fable, but it is based on what may be the oldest story in the world. When mankind came to the Western Hemisphere perhaps twelve thousand years ago, much changed. He encountered a massive wall of ice, and then the geography of a new set of continents, and new animals and plants. He hunted many of the larger creatures to extinction and had to adjust his lifestyle. He learned to forage widely, and then to grow his own food. He settled and developed villages and then cities. He became literate. He developed the world's most accurate calendar. But through it all one thing never changed, except in its own special recurring ways: the sky. The patterns of the constellations were there every night—the same ones he had seen in the Old World. And so the old myths persisted, for their truth alone was unchanging.

One of these was the story of the First Father's annual rebirth from the cracked shell of a tortoise, symbolizing the harvest cycle. When maize (corn) was developed from a wild Mexican grass and became overwhelmingly important as a staple food, he became the god of maize. This myth is recorded on a Mayan stela dating to 3114 B.C.E., more than five thousand years ago. But the myth itself predates maize, going back as far as twenty thousand years—to the time when mankind was still in Asia. The Great Turtle or Tortoise may stem from the night sky of that time, when man tried to make sense of the enormously complicated world his sophisticated mind perceived. It remained because it could be verified at almost any time, at almost any place in the world. Today we call its constellation Orion's Belt: the three bright stars highlighting the back of the tortoise shell, next to the place of creation, beside the enormous sky river we now call the Milky Way. The significance of that tortoise shell is still understood by the surviving Maya of today. It is part of a larger framework of myth that relates the stellar patterning of the night sky to the features of ordinary experience.

So my story, whose geographic and temporal and cultural details are fuzzy, represents a reenactment of a kind of a most ancient myth, with the old man named after that greatest of all rivers, and the priest's daughter named after the increasingly important crop: sweet grass, or maize. Because it *is* a story, reality and fantasy comfortably intertwine. Perhaps the old man really was a god, testing the young candidate's power of body and spirit, and rewarding him with all he had ever desired. Or maybe the girl knew Blank's language, and chose to speak it only when she decided to recognize in him a spirit worthy of the title of Sky River. It does not matter. To the Maya, and surely to other peoples, astronomy was part of cultural reality; the image of the stars was the truth of human relations. A person who did not accept this was denying reality.

Where and when might such an episode have occurred? In the Americas in the past twelve thousand years.

Where There Are Hummingbirds

Anna Kirwan-Vogel

I am called Ch'hupalolil, Sips Flowers. My husband's village was Blue Rock, which is known for the powerful currents and rapids thereabout, and for the great numbers of hummingbirds that come to the flowers among those misty ravines. It is known also for being the country of many a large jaguar, which I affirm, for thus did my family's fate change forever.

My husband, Nine Feathers, Kukun Bor, the father of my son, was the best hunter in Blue Rock. He could find deer even in the worst seasons, but he was too contented a man to watch always for the Lords of Death. So when the weather dried up one year and Kukun Bor nonetheless caught a big buck which hadn't lost all its fat yet, they sent a jaguar to rob his full smoking stage.

I'd been wife to this man for nine years, I can see the way it was. Kukun Bor argued with the jaguar over the deer he'd brought down, for he was proud of his take that day. He was never one to give up our fair share easily. Well, the cricket may make war on the Lord of Death, but he may not count on winning.

Everyone had been eating together under Turtle's roof, and I didn't notice the dogs' barking for a while. Kukun Bor had gone to get meat for our neighbors. Even when I knew something was wrong and we went out to look, I did not see him at first, for he lay among the shadows out beyond the gray heap of maize cobs. It was our son who found my husband's corpse under the clump of papaya trees. That was where the jaguar gave up his cruel game and left Kukun Bor.

I tell you, to this day I have not forgotten his mouth and the strong pillar of his throat, like the corner post of a new house; or his belly, hard as sapodilla wood, with the navel so deep I could fit my thumb in up to the quarter-moon of my nail. Woe to me! Many were the sweet parts of him I never saw but when he was alive. The jaguar was the last to taste them.

My life fell into nightmare, then, for I feared the jaguar now must love me too well. That's how the stories say it is, and the only one of the Old Ones who would come to me, through all the hours of that night, was the Hanged Goddess. But she came with her whispered songs, her sad melodies that dangled and twisted like lianas, and I heard her calling me to come out under the trees.

I'll tell you something about the women in my husband's village. They did not know my mother and my father, who lived many days' hunt from there; and the women of Blue Rock were quick to sweep out bad luck. Not one of those women talked to me to fill my ears against the Goddess's coaxing. They bathed my face and hands and combed my hair, but I thought that night it was like the washing of the dead, like the way we washed Kukun Bor; they knew I would be leaving Blue Rock, one way or another.

The men kept my son, Chan Bor, Nine Sky, at the edge of old Owl's mat all that night, lest in my grief I treat him like a toddling infant again, when he was already old enough to pin lizards with his reed spear. Owl's wife, Yellow Bean House, and the rest of those leather-eyed women—they held me away from my son, and gestured to me to keep my silence so the jaguar would not hear whose house I was in, and bathed my face until I could not feel my own unspilled tears to know how they burned.

So frightened were the people of the village that the jaguar would come back in amongst our homes, Owl was persuaded to invite the King's Guard into our midst. It is more usual for the community to try to avoid such close contact with officials from the great stone houses—especially officials with weapons of war about their persons. But we'd paid our tithes faithfully, Owl said, and we were entitled to ask for protection. It was not as though we were in a season of exceptional harvest, with wealth to hide from shrewd, temple-sharpened hungers. What we had, they wouldn't want, anyway.

When the Guard detachment came, it was the very smallest it could have been: four spearmen—two slaves serving two officers. The Guard Captain was high-born and looked experienced, painted red and black like a coral snake. The younger "officer" was just a boy in black paint and white-beaded topknot. When Yellow Bean House told her sister-in-law that the boy was Lord Shield's oldest son, Serpent Jaguar, the Lord Chan Bahlum, I had to take another look through the doorway, to see if the King's son looked different from other people.

I remember now that I wondered on that day, Do they teach them in Otolum to walk that way? Are the royal kin, the Great Hands, taught to stand on purpose so their strange, big, six-fingered hands are displayed like sprawling clusters of brown seed pods? It gave me a strange feeling to watch the Lord Chan Bahlum handling the dogs they had brought. They were very good-looking hounds, but it was eerie to watch them licking his hands, which were handsome enough, but rather monstrous, after all. Maybe we are meant to feel that, when we are in the presence of the Gods' favorites. Everything was terrible to me during those days of nightmare.

The King's heir was built tall and wide, like most of the men of these reaches, but he was still proportioned as though not fully grown. He had a shaft of nose like a whole shock of cornstalks, and his forehead leaned back like a plump ear of pearly black hard-kernel. He had a pretty, pouting lower lip, and he wore green earbobs I would have wanted desperately, had I seen them the week before.

Owl was trying to make a speech about all the misfortunes that had settled on Blue Rock, slipping in remarks about how hard it would be to meet a draft call and what a good thing it was that Pacal, Lord Shield, was so wise about letting the allies know who was in charge. The Guard Captain was polite, but I could see he was really paying attention to his dogs. The Lord Chan Bahlum followed him around the clearing, step for step, fussing at the knots in the leashes and feeling the edges of the spearheads sticking out of the bundle one of the slaves was toting. He was listening to Owl, but, of course, it wasn't the only thing on his mind.

I saw Chan Bor across the clearing. He was holding on to the ear of Kukun Bor's old hound, Raven. One of the prince's dogs, a bitch, trotted over to sniff at them, but Raven is too lazy to fight over anything she can't eat. No one else went anywhere near Chan Bor, and he couldn't see me inside the doorway. I ached for him as if I were looking at my own hand over there, cut off and walking around without me. What must he have been thinking, poor child? He had always been such a little old man, following his father around and giving him advice—"Try it *this* way, Papa, get hold of it *this* way." I was about to call to him, but Yellow Bean House saw what I was up to, and she hustled me back into her smoky lodge.

To tell the truth, I was exhausted with the horror and the emptiness that washes in over the world after you start getting used to the horror. Minute after minute, hour after hour. I hadn't slept all night after we found him, and it was late afternoon by then. I was sitting there rocking back and forth on my heels, trying not to moan, afraid to go to sleep while the Lords of Death might be on my trail. I don't know how long that was—it got dark, it was dark for a long time. But maybe I did go to sleep after a while. Or maybe the dream just came out into the live world, since I was so weak I couldn't hold it off.

■ ■ ■

I thought I was by the river, where the crossing stones are in dry season. But in this dream they were underwater, and red bundles kept coming downstream, bundles wrapped in red cloth. In the dream, I knew they had men's heads and limbs in them, because there had been a battle upriver. The air was very wet and dewy. The bundles kept floating up against the branches trailing in the water, and getting stuck, and I was very worried because I thought it was up to me to get them loose so they could go to the sea. "The sea is waiting," I said to someone standing near me in the dream. "Those men have to go where the shell trumpets came from."

There was one bundle I just couldn't get loose. It was way out at the end of a long branch, and while I was trying and trying to reach it, it turned into a red flower bud, tight closed but deep red. Then I saw a blue-headed hummingbird come up to the flower bud and push its long beak into the flower. The flower popped open like a rattlebox seed pod. It even made a little sound, like a child gasping in surprise, like Kukun Bor when we'd lain together.

And I woke up then. Something in me knew that that jaguar who took him had been killed.

In the morning, I was acting angry with Yellow Bean House and making remarks to her because they were keeping me in their lodge and wouldn't let me go to my son. Owl came in and he said, "You should be quiet, you're talking like a crazy woman, don't you know that? Who do you think is going to put meat on your rack now? Let them kill the jaguar before it makes more trouble. You can do what you want when they go away again, but I'm thinking about planting season. You think someone wants you for a wife? You'd better do what I advise you."

And Yellow Bean House said, "You don't have an uncle here. You don't have a father-in-law or a brother. Your good luck is no more. If you know what's good for you, you will let Owl do all the talking. Owl knows the Lord Daykeeper at the Red Houses."

I had nothing to do. I couldn't grind corn or prepare food because it would have gone bad from my touching it. My thoughts were going in circles; I was thinking of Kukun Bor, I was thinking of Chan Bor, I was thinking Owl and his wife were so unkind, and then I was thinking, they've lived so many years, they are not sentimental, but they're probably right. And then I would think of Kukun Bor, how he went out for weeks before we were married and strung nets in the bushes along the river.

The nets were made with smooth cotton threads, nothing rougher, and he stretched them near the ripest flowers to catch hummingbirds. When we were married, I had a necklace of the feathers of eighteen hummingbirds, all violet and red and butterfly blue and green as deep water. Deer were not all the quarry he knew. But he did not take too many feathers from any one bird; he took them carefully and from its midline, so that when he released his captives they flew smoothly, humming loudly, rejoicing that he let them go. My necklace was hidden in the rafters of our house, wrapped up with our festival garments and Kukun Bor's mask of the Jaguar-Deer Hero, Lord Yax Bahlum Ceh. If I had been in my own house, I would have climbed up and brought it down, to have something to hold in my hands so they would not be so empty.

One of the slaves came back to the village in the middle of the morning. He was a Zinacantec, I think, his own home even further away than Otolum, and he said the older Lord was snakebit, but the Lord Chan Bahlum, that six-fingered boy, had killed the murderer jaguar. After he told that to Owl, there at the house-cross shrine in front of the door, the Zinacantec came over and stooped down and touched my sandal. I don't know if it is a good thing when a slave treats you with respect, but I'll tell you, right then it was like honey on a cut.

Turtle and Rabbit went back into the south forest with mantles and sleeping mats to fashion a stretcher for the poisoned lord. I went and found Chan Bor, then; at least they could not say the jaguar was listening anymore. When I found him, I bowed to him so he would realize he was the only man in the family now, and I said to him, "Your father was Kukun Bor, the best man in this village. Even the jaguar envied what he could bring down. Everyone else is a coward, now he's gone. Do not you be a coward, Chan Bor. Be brave, so they will remember who begot you." I put my hands on his shoulders, then I knelt down and hugged him to me.

"When I am big, I will hunt jaguars," Chan Bor said. "They will not be safe from me, I promise you."

"Hush," I told him then. "We are the corn of the Jaguar. Kukun Bor will walk with the Growing Gods now, and not the Lords of Death. He will tell them to make rain fall on our corn patch." I did not tell him what Owl had asked: Who would put meat on our rack from now on? He might just as well have said, Who would guard the corn in our garden? Who would root up the weeds around the bean hills? I thought Chan Bor and I would have much to do when planting time came. I still did not see what was happening. I was like a blind woman. The tears those women would not let me feel, they were blinding me.

When the hunting party came back into the village, I would have gone over to them to help with the injured lord. Besides being snake-bit, he had been clawed by the jaguar, and he was very cold-looking, very unwell. The prince had done the killing, but he had not paid the greatest price for it.

Yellow Bean House and all the other wives were standing around like last season's cornstalks, staring and whispering and offering not so much as a dipper of water to anyone. They thought the slaves were to do all that, I suppose. I whispered to Chan Bor to run to our house, because there was a red jar of honey there, and some meal I'd soaked and ground before the night we ate at Turtle's hearth. I told Chan Bor to use the little gourd measure to scoop out two of meal and one of honey, and to put them in the good bowl with the rabbit painted on it, and to fill it up with water and stir it, to make a nice drink for the sick lord. I considered whether he should give it to the Lord Chan Bahlum. I do not know to this day if I thought it might not be allowed, or if I simply lacked the courage I urged my son to practice.

He did not seem so aloof now, the King's son, but talked with Owl as anyone would. Perhaps he was too tired to boast. I heard him say it was a black jaguar, and when he said it, I went and stood by the house-cross of Kukun Bor's house, which had been my house, and I prayed to the Holy Green Cross: *Lead Kukun Bor from this place, his home. Show him the way at the crossroads. Show him to the misty ravines where there are hummingbirds in that world.*

Chan Bor came out of the house with the bowl of corn *atole,* and we went back toward the gathering in the middle of the village. Yellow Bean House and Three Morning Stars came waddling over to us before we got there, and Three Morning Stars put her hand around Chan Bor's arm as tight as teeth. She took the rabbit bowl out of his hand and pulled him away with her, over behind her house, away from the strangers. He was slow to go with her, and I saw the bowl slosh over her hand.

Yellow Bean House was hissing words at me. "They don't need to see a dead man's son. You must come over here with me. Let the Lords see you, now. You're not so skinny, who's going to feed you? Let the Lords see you." Suddenly I understood what she had in mind, what Owl had thought to do about the time to come.

When I was near the young Lord, Owl started to talk as if he were my godfather. "Lord, this is the unfortunate widow. She says she wishes to thank you for protection against the most terrible of killers, the Night Sun whose setting you determined. Wretched woman, she has no father, no brother, no in-laws at all in this country. She wishes to thank you for saving her from the jaguar who knew her scent." I did want to thank him, but I had not told Owl that.

The Lord Chan Bahlum looked me over, and then he looked into my face. I do not think he knew what he was going to do. Is it foolish to think such a thing possible? Now that the hunt was a victory under his feet, he seemed more brave and manly; but I do not think he knew. He opened his mouth as if to speak to me, but then he turned back to Owl. "Her thanks are of value to me," he said politely. *"Your* thanks are of value to me. My Lord my Father bid me say to you, this village of Blue Rock is as my own home. You are as my own children to me."

I would have laughed, a week before, to hear this young cub say such a thing to Owl. Owl is as old as dirt. He is as treacherous as a mudslide, too. I was starting to see that.

"Great and generous are the Great-Hand Lords of the Mats of Otolum," he said now.

The Lord Chan Bahlum suddenly looked relieved. I could see he'd had some idea. "Let it be said thus, let it be thus remembered," he said. "To honor the Great Hands of my Lineage, hear now what I say. The husband of this woman was a skillful hunter. I am told she is a virtuous woman. Let it not be said the Great Hands were empty for her. I killed the jaguar who killed her husband. With my Lord Cousin Flint Hawk, I killed it. Now she will see meat and corn from the Great Hands of Otolum. Let her go to her house and make it clean. Let her see that the spirit of her husband is on his way away from here. I will send people from my Lord Father's household to bring her to the Stone Houses, and she will live with the women of Pacal's house. This is my wish."

Now Owl, that unkind man, looked relieved. Yellow Bean House managed to flop some kind of graceless bow to the young Lord and twist my arm at the same time, and she dragged me away as Three Morning Stars had dragged Chan Bor. I knew then, no one was going to mention Chan Bor to the royal visitors. Chan Bor would not be brought to Otolum with me.

Woe to me! to lose my husband. Woe to me, to lose my only son.

I watched the Lords' canoe slither away on the yellow-green back of the river, and when they were out of sight beyond the big *guacimo* tree fallen across the channel, Chan Bor came up beside me. I turned around, and Owl was walking away with nothing else to say. I followed him and caught up, and Chan Bor came with me—I was holding on to his hand. "Chan Bor," I said, "this is the man who will take you from my care. This is the one who forgets your father was killed by the jaguar while he fetched venison for this one to eat. Old man, who will make *atole* for my son when you have sent me away?"

Owl waved his hand at me as if I were a green fly. No, he didn't want me to land where I could bite him; that was a welt he could do without. "The Good God Yum Kax will give him corn, and I will. My woman will soak it in lime and grind it and cook it." He looked me in the face, then, and I could see his old head doddering a little on his neck, though I don't know if it was age or shame that made him tremble before my anger. "This boy will cut his hair and be a strong hunter," he whined. "He will be a warrior when Blue Rock answers the trumpets with war teams. Your husband saw how the lung fever left us here so sparsely defended. At the Stone Houses there are many boys, and many are slaves. Here, he will do what is needed. He will be like Kukun Bor." I hated to hear his voice on that name. I hated knowing he was speaking wisdom, this once.

I tried to keep Chan Bor near me during those few days. I must have washed his face as often as the dogs barked; in Blue Rock, that was very often. I gave him Kukun Bor's mantle and his game sack and flaying knife, his tumpline and his bird nets. I climbed up under the roof of our old house and brought down the festival goods, head cloths and sashes I'd woven of red and black manta cloth, the separate pieces of the painted wooden mask of Yax Bahlum Ceh, Kukun Bor's gaming kilt, his padded wicker yoke and arm guards, and his black rubber ball.

For myself, I took only my feather necklace. I would have taken the rabbit bowl, but Three Morning Stars had never given it back.

Then I wrapped everything else into two bundles, and pushed them both into a big harvest basket, with the holy-day objects poked far down and the everyday things at the top. I said to Chan Bor, "Wherever you are sleeping, there will be room for this. If anyone tells you there is not room, tell him the spirit of your father's jaguar will come into his field and wait for him. You can use the mantle to sleep in, but it's too long for you to wear yet. You can use the knife. It's the last thing your father touched, and it will always want to feed you."

I showed him how much of the last harvest of corn and beans we still had left, that I would give to Owl and Yellow Bean House. We went out with old Raven and I showed him the honey tree Kukun Bor had found near our field a few months before—a rich hive of the quiet, black *xic* bees with white spots on their wings and no stings. "Don't tell Owl where it is," I said. "When you need something, take some honey to Three Morning Stars: she would eat it all year, if she could. But don't let anyone know where you get it. This will be our secret. Maybe they will start to call you 'the Honey Boy.' "

After we ate some honey, I had to wash his face and hands again.

A Fire in the Heart

Lawrence Schimel

T he sun was nearly asleep in the trees as I left the outskirts of
Tula, walking east. West is holy to Quetzalcoatl, so I went the
opposite way. Maybe that was my mistake; it made it too easy
for him to find me. Quetzalcoatl is the child of Omeoteotl, who created the world and who is duality: both man and woman, good and
evil, and all other sets of opposites in one being.

I did not think of these things when I decided to run away. Otherwise I might have gone north into the mountains or south to Tenochtitlán, and he would not have found me. Perhaps then I could have
broken his prophecy. But I did not; I went east.

I walk mostly during the night when it is cooler. At night the sun
does not stare down on me in anticipation, knowing that it will soon
drink my blood. At night the sun cannot watch where I am going, to
send its priests after me, to bring me back for the sacrifice. At night I
don't see the Quetzal birds, watching me, always watching me, as I
walk east.

When I can see the morning star I stop walking to construct a shelter from branches and a piece of cloth. I work quickly and am hidden
before the star has risen higher into the sky. The morning star is the
eye of Quetzalcoatl, and it is even more important that I hide from
him than that I avoid the sun.

The first night of walking, I do not think of the village or the sacrifice at all. I must move forward, and to think on them will bring me
back a step for every pair I take away from them.

Instead I think of my journey and of the new things I shall find. I
want to see the ocean. They say the water stretches farther than a man
can walk in three cycles of the moon.

When I lie down to sleep after my first night of walking, I dream:

The gods are assembled in darkness to decide who would light this new world. One god steps forward, a wealthy god, dressed in humming-bird feathers and turquoise. He does not think about what the deed entails, dwelling only on the praises he will receive from his fellow gods for its completion, the prestige.

But the gods say that this one god will not be enough to light the world. They call for another volunteer. The gods are silent. No one wants to give up his own life for the good of all.

Finally, the gods call on Nanautzin. Nanautzin is an ugly god, covered in sores and dressed in the most meager of clothes made from woven reeds. Never before has he been worthy of the gods' attention and, honored, he says, "I will do it."

The two gods spend the next four day purifying their bodies.

When the time arrived in which they made their offerings, the wealthy god was a spectacle of ostentation, offering gold nuggets, rare feathers, and gemstones. All Nanautzin had to offer was a bundle of reeds he had woven in a wreath, and some thorns covered in his own blood.

The bonfire lit, the gods look to the pair in anticipation. "Now perform this deed you have promised," they say. "Light this new world that we may see it."

The wealthy god asks, "How am I to do so?"

"Jump into the heart of the flames," the gods reply.

His heart is full of terror, and four times he rushes toward the bonfire, trying to leap into the flames so he will not go back on his word and bring shame upon his head. But he cannot do it.

The gods all turn to Nanautzin, and the honor they gave him by their choice puts courage in his heart. He leaps into the flame, which burns away his life, and he becomes the sun.

Shamed that this poor, ugly god has done what he could not, the wealthy god tries once more to throw himself into the bonfire. Still he cannot do it. All the honor he deserved was given to Nanautzin; all that is left for him is shame and scorn.

There is no sun when I awake, and I am cold.

The second night of walking I reach a town. Everyone knows who I am, though I wear only an old frayed cloth I took to cover me from the sun when I sleep. To pay for my theft I have left the finery they gave me by the bundles of clothes on the riverbank, waiting to be washed. The only thing I still keep of my old life is a small leather bag my father gave me, which I wear about my neck.

They say my mother was killed at my birth. The midwife found three snakes in bed with me. My father killed the serpents and put their teeth in the bag.

The bag is hidden beneath my cloth, and no one but my father knows about it. It is because of my name that everyone knows I am the one who was chosen, the one who was foretold. It has been proclaimed since my birth: Panqutzalizti, holy day of Quetzalcoatl. There is no place for me to go where they do not recognize who I am. So I do not tell them my name. Instead, I rename myself after today, as if I had just been born.

I do not stay long in the town. It reminds me of home and I am not yet ready to think about that. Again, I walk all night and in the morning I dream:

It is the day of the sacrifice and they cannot find me. The priests choose someone to take my place. They must. There is the ceremony.

They choose Four Winds who has lived next to us for many, many uinals. Eleven Moon cries when her brother is chosen. It was not his time. She was not ready. She does not care for the honor of the sacrifice. She does not want her brother to die.

But the priests have chosen him as my replacement, and sacrifice him to the sun. It changes nothing. He is not the one the sun wanted. I am.

There is the sound of great lamentation. Eleven Moon takes the knife the priests have abandoned on the altar and sacrifices herself.

Still, this is not enough to appease the sun. I am the one who was chosen. I am the one who must be sacrificed. That is my destiny.

Only I am not there and the sun dies, falling into the ocean.

There is darkness.

It is still day when I awake, and there are tears in my eyes that are not because of the bright light of the sun, tears like the salt said to be in the waters of the oceans, oceans like the one into which the sun has fallen. I am crying for Four Winds. I am crying for his sister who will mourn him, and the child who must do the chores he once did. I am crying for his parents. I am crying for my own father, who was never allowed to be my father, for I was the chosen one, the one who would be sacrificed. I am crying for my mother who died because she did not rebel against her destiny, who died so that I could fulfill my own.

I clench the bag hanging from my neck in a fist and wonder if I should return home. I feel a sharp instant of pain and open my palm, letting the bag fall back against my chest. A bead of blood wells up on my hand, glowing in the last rays of the sun, opal red or, perhaps, the color of a snake's eyes.

I turn my hand over and offer the blood to the earth, which drinks it greedily. The earth knows I am the one who was foretold. Everyone knows. I have been chosen.

I open the bag and three snakes slither out before I can close it again. They slide over my fingers, their dry scales smooth and cool. They scatter into the underbrush, each in a different direction: one north, one south, one east. I am the one to go west.

Always my choices have been made for me. Nobody ever asked me what I wanted, nobody has ever given me a choice. *They* say I am the one.

Now in the bag are six Quetzal feathers. I do not think about home again and continue walking east.

After the third night of walking I dream of Quetzalcoatl:

He is sitting beneath a tree and seems an ordinary man, wearing a cap made from the skin of a jaguar and a cloak of Quetzal feathers. But I know him for who he is, Quetzalcoatl, a god.

"Sit," he says, gesturing at a spot beside him, under the tree. "Tell me why you are on this journey."

I sit where he has commanded, but am afraid to speak. He waits patiently as I worry. My belly feels as if I have eaten my fill of the sharpest flint shards. As time passes and he does not press me for an answer, I begin to wonder why he is here, asking me questions. He does not seem to need an answer. He is a god; he already knows. But do I? Why am I on this journey?

I am trying to break his prophecy.

But no, that is not all. I am afraid to die, but I am on this journey because I have chosen to take it. It was my decision. For once someone has not told me what I am to do. My life has always been: They say . . . They say . . . It is in the prophecy.

Never did they ask what I wanted.

I did not want to be the one in the prophecy, but I left because I wanted to do something that was my own. Something They haven't said would happen. Something that wasn't in the prophecy.

What am I doing on this journey? What do I expect to do? I have no place to go. Wherever I go they will know me from my name, know what

I have done in denying the prophecy to be fulfilled. I will be the nameless one, born anew each time I enter a town, taking the date of my arrival for my name rather than the date of my birth.

I have no family. Because I am the chosen, I have never had any family. But the village became my family. I was important to them. Now I am alone. Now I have nothing to replace the family I never had.

What am I doing on this journey? I am waiting for Quetzalcoatl to find me and give me the choice of continuing or returning.

I turn to answer Quetzalcoatl, although not the question he has asked, but he is no longer there.

When I wake, I begin walking toward home, walking under the full light of the sun.

The priests give me back my finery, but I am no longer allowed to be alone. Always someone is watching me, so I do not leave again, or try to kill myself. They do not realize I will do neither. I have already had my chance to live in the world outside and I returned. I am dead already.

Always there is a warrior watching, but never my father. He never comes. My guards do not allow me to visit him. I want to tell him I am sorry at least once before I die. I want to say good-bye to him.

But I am not allowed.

The knife shines like a sliver of the sun and I close my eyes as the priest brings it down. My heart constricts, feeling as if it were being squeezed by a hundred snakes.

And then a flash of pain, as hot as if the knife actually were the sun. My heart leaves my body so easily I wonder if, perhaps, it was never really happy there.

My chest is filled with searing, burning, and my body quivers with loss. But I do not think of the pain and it goes away. It is so easy to ignore that I think I must be nearly dead. I am not sure why I am not dead already, but I am not, so I open my eyes. The priest is holding my heart above his head, offering it to the sun. Drops of my blood fall to the ground, and the priest offers these to the earth.

Looking away from my heart, I see my father coming toward me at last. I want to reach out to him, call out to him, but my body will not respond. He reaches out for me, then stops, as if there were an invisible wall blocking his way. He is looking up at the sky, then bows his head and backs away.

I cannot tell if my body still responds to me, but if it does, I am crying. I look up at the sky which stopped my father, afraid that the sun is not content with my sacrifice after all and furious for its interference in the last moment I might have actually been my father's son. There is a darkness on the sun, a spot growing larger as if it were approaching. It is the feathered serpent, flying straight as an *atlatl* toward the altar. This is what stopped my father: Quetzalcoatl himself come to bring my heart to the sun.

But the feathered serpent flies past my heart, which the priest holds high above his head. The serpent flies straight toward me. Its head plunges into the hole where my heart was, and I draw in lungfuls of air as I suddenly remember the pain. It wriggles its feathered body, sliding deeper and deeper into me until there is only the tail flapping back and forth, and then nothing.

When it has disappeared from sight completely, I realize that I am looking down on my body. I no longer feel any pain. I am aloft.

My body bursts into flame as I peer through the priest's fingers, and even though I knew its end was near, I am sad to see it finally over. My body lifts from the altar, hovering for a moment as it folds in on itself, heat exploding outward. I can feel the priest flinch, my vision wobbling, but he does not dare lower his hands or shield himself from the flames. Not now, not in the presence of the god himself.

Again my body flares heat and I feel another constriction in my chest. Only I am no longer in my body, just the heart. Then the heart splits open and I am free, bursting into the air and stretching my coils. The heat radiating from my old body dries my feathers, and I hiss with pleasure as I fly around the globe of fire that once was my body.

As I follow the new sun into the sky I wonder what They will say now.

A Day in the Life
Robin M. Dinnes

The sun rises.

In the Cherokee village of Cowee, the people have already begun their day. The women have this morning's meal of corn cakes prepared and the children are just rising to take their baths in the icy mountain stream.

The leaves are the rich colors of the season of Painted Wood and the village has an air of carefree gaiety. The last white raid has been well over three moons ago.

Growling Bear emerges from his lodge, stretching and yawning at length. He wears only a leather loincloth despite the chill in the air. He is a young brave, only twenty turns of the seasons old. His title, Growling Bear, is new. It is his first title, and he is swollen with pride this morning.

His mate, Morning, is tanning a bear hide. She is smiling, she too is proud of her mate. He has finally completed his journey into manhood—he has proven himself in lone combat with this bear. The meat will be more than enough for her new family in the thick of this coming winter. She feels very fortunate.

Morning looks down at her swollen belly with tender devotion. Her baby wants out, she can feel it kicking harder. The medicine man said that today would be the day. Morning knows that today is the day.

Growling Bear sees his mate and goes to her. She is his only mate, but he is thinking of taking another to help Morning with their first baby. He wants Morning's sister, Rushing Deer, to be his second mate. He smiles in anticipation of surprising Morning with the good news. He will wait until after the baby comes.

Growling Bear squats beside Morning and touches her belly. His thick black hair drops to the ground as he listens to his baby squirm and struggle. Morning grimaces as the first labor pang hits. Growling Bear looks up with concern. "He is ready, Morning. Come." She nods her head in agreement and offers Growling Bear her arm, not missing his hopeful reference to a male child.

In the midwife's lodge, late that afternoon, Morning is deep in labor. She is sweating and moaning in pain and the midwife is chanting a life blessing for the child.

A breathless runner cries from outside the lodge. A white raid. Morning moans again, but this time it is not because of the baby.

In his lodge, Growling Bear quickly gathers his weapons, preparing to fight. He stops at the midwife's lodge to see his mate. He kneels beside the bed and presses her hand to his forehead, silently praying to Grandmother Spider, the lifegiver. Growling Bear's heart aches, Morning must flee from the village now, even though the baby is almost ready. She is burdened, but she must escape before she is too vulnerable. And she must go without the company of the other women and children, for childbirth is sacred and can be witnessed only by the midwife. He strokes her face gently, smiling, trying to be brave for her, then, bidding the midwife go with her, he is gone.

Morning and the midwife struggle toward the forest's edge. They go deeper and deeper into the wood until Morning can no longer stand. How far or long they have traveled she does not know, she knows only that the time is now.

Her son is born in a forest glen beneath a towering oak. Morning is exhausted and lies on the cool earth while the midwife washes the baby in the nearby stream. Morning touches the tree and the grass and the rock beside her, thanking each spirit for her baby's life and safety.

The midwife returns from the stream with Morning's son. And now the two women begin to wonder if it might be all right to return to the village. They are scared, but neither will speak of the raid for fear of cursing the warriors.

The midwife disappears into the wood for a long while. Morning stays in the glen, nursing and soothing her son, trying not to think about being weaponless and alone in the forest with a baby.

The midwife finally returns and says that she cannot hear any sounds of fighting coming from the direction of the village. They decide to return. The trip back to the village seems much longer to Morning.

The day is nearing its end when Morning and the midwife reach the village. There is much activity. Many lodges are on fire, animals are running loose, and some people are apprehensively poking at white bodies. There is much crying. The bodies of some of the braves lie motionless on the ground, others are held in the arms of a sobbing mate. But not only braves lie dead. There are also small children and their mothers who died protecting them—those who did not escape the raid.

Morning looks around in fear. Where is Growling Bear? And Rushing Deer? She sees Rushing Deer and feels relief wash over her, but it does not wash away the fear. Where is Growling Bear? She does not see him standing, and hopes beyond hope that she will not find him on the ground.

She steps carefully among the dead, looking fearfully, hugging her baby close to her. And then she sees what she does not want to see and a flood of tears trickles down her cheeks. Growling Bear's lifeblood runs out of a hole in his chest.

His eyes are open. His body is dead, but his spirit wants to see. Morning silently holds his son in front of him for a long while, until her arms grow tired. Then she puts her finger on Growling Bear's chest and touches her bloody finger to her baby's forehead.

Morning names him Bear Claw, for she knows that Growling Bear's spirit will live on and fight on through his son. She looks up to the sky with tear-blurred, anguished eyes and sees the sun set.

Animal Sounds
Owl Goingback

T he Earth is a great island floating in a sea of water. When all was water, the animals were above in Galun' lati, beyond the arch, but it was very crowded, and they wanted more room. They wondered what was below the water, and at last Dayuni'si, the little water beetle, offered to go see if he could learn. He darted in every direction over the surface of the water, but could find no place to rest. Then he dove to the bottom and came up with some soft mud, which began to grow and spread on every side until it became the land we call the Earth. It was afterwards fastened to the sky with four cords, but no one remembers who did this."

Snapping Turtle paused for effect as he finished the creation story. The children seated before him were as still as stone, their eyes wide with fascination. The medicine man smiled. As a child, he too had enjoyed hearing about how it was long ago, when the animals talked and monsters roamed the land. Back in the days when brave warriors battled magical beasts and hunters stalked . . .

The images in his mind blew away like smoke from a cooking fire. How could he talk of hunters and hunting to children who cried at night from hunger? For almost a month, the hunting parties had returned to the village empty-handed. Gone were the great herds of deer and elk that once roamed the land. Gone too were the turkey, grouse, and raccoons. Even the squirrels and songbirds had left, leaving the forest as empty and silent in summer as it was in the depths of winter.

No one knew why the animals had left. Some thought that the tribe must have done something to anger them. Others speculated that it was a sign that the end of the world was near.

As the food stores dwindled, he had tried every means possible to find a solution to the dilemma. But though he had fasted for days, praying to the Great Spirit for guidance, no answer had been given to him why the animals had left, or how to bring them back. His failure to bring back the animals was seen by many in the village as a sign that his medicine was no longer strong. A few even blamed him outright for what had happened.

Ending his storytelling session with a promise of more later, Snapping Turtle left the circle of children and walked slowly toward the village square. His spirit was heavy and it was all he could do to ignore those who stared at him as he passed.

It is not my fault. I have performed the ceremonies, made all the offerings.

The evening dance was about to begin as he reached the square. Snapping Turtle watched as dancers hurried to tie feathers to their hair and tortoise shell rattles to their legs. There were fewer dancers than in the past weeks. It was not easy to be joyous when your heart was heavy with thoughts of the coming winter and possible starvation. Those who danced did so to ask the Great Spirit to return the animals.

The men entered the dance arena first, led by the warriors of greatest distinction. The night was warm, so many of them wore only a leather breechcloth and moccasins, their arms and wrists encircled with bracelets of copper. Some, however, preferred to dress up completely and wore long hunting shirts of fringed leather, tied at the waist with colorful belts of woven vegetable fibers. A few of the older men had their ears cut and banded with silver, their earlobes hanging down to their shoulders. Most just wore simple earrings of shell.

The women wore dresses, short waistcoats, leggings, and moccasins, all made of leather. They wore their hair long, braided in wreaths, and tied in a knot at the back of their heads. Many wore finger and nose rings. Like the men, almost all wore earrings.

Standing Elk, the village chief, was seated on the west side of the square. Though a warrior of great courage, having obtained the war rank of Man-killer, he liked to sing rather than dance. On the ground before him sat a wooden water drum, made from a hollowed-out section of buckeye trunk. Snapping Turtle was shocked to see Black Raven, a young medicine man from one of the lower towns, seated next to the chief.

Why does Black Raven sit next to Standing Elk—in my spot?

Anger and humiliation shot through Snapping Turtle. He felt his face redden. Did this mean that Standing Elk also believed him too old to carry out the duties of medicine man? Apparently it did. Why else would Black Raven sit at his side? Snapping Turtle wondered if Black Raven would also take his place at the council meeting.

Tomorrow night's meeting would be of great importance. If the animals did not return in the next few days, they would have to decide whether or not to relocate the village. If a move was decided upon, it would have to be done quickly, while there was still time to rebuild before winter. Already the leaves on the trees were changing colors.

As he stood there watching, Black Raven looked up. Their eyes locked and the unspoken words flowed between them. There was no doubt in Snapping Turtle's mind that Black Raven planned to challenge him for his position. Furious, he turned away, but not before he saw a smile touch the corners of Black Raven's lips.

Snapping Turtle's cabin was on the north side of the village. Like the others, it was made of a framework of upright poles covered with bark. The roof was also of bark, sealed with clay to make it weatherproof. He flung the door open and entered the cabin. Morning Star, his wife of twenty years, was tending to the cooking fire. She turned to face him as he came in.

"Why are you not at the dance?" she asked. "They will need you to bless the arena."

"I think they have found another for that," Snapping Turtle replied. He crossed to the other side of the room and took down his medicine bundle from where it hung on the wall.

"Who?" she asked.

"Black Raven sits with the chief. I think they will ask him to bless the grounds."

"Black Raven! But he is not even of this village. What does this mean?"

He turned and looked at her. "It means they think I am too old, that my medicine has left me."

"You are two winters younger than I, and I am not old!"

Snapping Turtle smiled. Morning Star had already seen her fifty-second winter, but she was as full of energy as many women half her age.

"No, you are not old," he agreed. "But many think that my medicine is no longer strong, that I am to blame for the animals leaving."

"But that is not true. You have done everything the way it has always been done. It must be something else."

He took down his ashwood bow and quiver of arrows.

"Where are you going?" she asked.

"There is no meat in the village. The children are hungry. I am going hunting." He looped a coil of rope over his shoulder.

"But the hunting parties have not seen an animal in weeks."

"Maybe one will be successful where many fail."

"But it is dangerous, going off by yourself at your—"

He raised his eyebrows. "At my age? But you said I was not old."

"That was before you started talking about going off by yourself."

He walked back across the room. "It has to be done."

"What about the council meeting? Who will perform the ceremonies, offer the blessings? What if someone gets sick, or injured?"

He stopped in front of her and placed his hands upon her shoulders. "You have been by my side for a long time. You know the prayers and ceremonies as well as I do. Few will object if you take my place this one time. If they do, then tell them to ask Black Raven." He kissed her lightly on the forehead.

"When will you be back?" she asked, worried.

"I do not know."

"At least eat before you go."

He eyed the pot of vegetable soup. "I can think better on an empty stomach."

Snapping Turtle turned and left the cabin, closing the door quietly behind him. Though his wife didn't approve, he followed the only path left open to him. He could not sit by and allow his people to starve. Nor could he allow someone to push him aside. Something had to be done.

He left the village and turned north, following the river. A deep silence surrounded him. Gone were the familiar cries of the night birds and the shrill croaking of the tree frogs. Even the hunting call of the great owl was noticeably absent. Nothing moved in the forest. No animals walked the night. He was completely alone. Above him, the first stars of the evening appeared like tiny campfires in the sky. At least the stars had not left. If they had, it would surely mean that the world was coming to an end.

The moon was high in the sky when he turned away from the river. His destination was a nearby mountain whose peak, unlike those around it, was rocky and bare. According to legend, a great battle had been fought on the mountain between Snapping Turtle's ancestors and giant, flesh-eating birds. The fight would have been lost, had not the Great Spirit intervened and destroyed all the birds with bolts of lightning. The lightning also destroyed all the trees, making the mountain bald.

Spirit Mountain, as the mountain was called, was also believed to be the home of powerful spirit beings. Hunters who camped in the area told of hearing voices or seeing strange lights. It was a haunted place. A place to be avoided. But Snapping Turtle had no intention of avoiding it. Maybe the spirits would know why the animals had left.

He didn't reach Spirit Mountain until sunset the following day. Though the mountain's peak was rocky and bare, its base was covered with a thick pine forest. Several animal trails led through the forest. Some said the trails were also used by spirits. But Snapping Turtle doubted that spirits would have need of such paths. Not knowing which one was the best to travel, he chose the trail that looked the most used.

An uneasy feeling settled over him as he started up the trail. A feeling of being watched. He didn't see anyone, but that didn't mean anything. There were lots of places where a man could hide in the forest—behind a tree, under a bush, or even in the deeper shadows. And Snapping Turtle's instincts had been right too many times in the past to ignore them now. If someone was watching, he would not be caught unprepared. He strung his bow and pulled an arrow from his quiver. He was about to continue on, when he heard a whisper.

Snapping Turtle froze. Someone had spoken. Had he not been listening closely, he would have missed it. He only caught a few words, enough to know that whoever spoke was not a Cherokee.

They are somewhere up ahead.

He notched the arrow to his bowstring and stepped off the trail. Snapping Turtle wasn't sure whether it was an enemy or a friend that he heard, but he wasn't about to take any chances. By leaving the trail and moving through the brush, he presented less of a target.

Like a panther stalking its prey, he crept steadily forward. Though he was a medicine man, he was also a warrior and had been trained accordingly. He knew how to move in the forest, where to place his feet as he stepped. Not a sound did he make as he flowed from shadow to shadow, blending in, using the trees and bushes for cover. The trail led to a small clearing. Snapping Turtle circled around it, approaching it from the back side.

The clearing was empty. Nor was there any sign that anyone had been there. Snapping Turtle was certain it was where the voices had come from. But whoever had spoken was already gone. Perhaps they had heard him coming and, fearing a possible war party, fled deeper into the woods. Then again, maybe they knew it was only one man and were setting a trap. He glanced behind him to make sure no one was sneaking up on him. No one was.

Reluctant to expose himself, Snapping Turtle remained where he was and studied the open area before him. The clearing was not a natural part of the forest. It was too free of roots, vines, and undergrowth to be anything other than man-made. In addition, oak trees grew along its edge, evenly spaced apart, while the rest of the trees in the area were evergreens. The old ones must have built the site as a place to conduct tribal business. There were many such ancient places in the land of the Cherokee.

As he stood there, Snapping Turtle again heard a whisper. Louder. Closer. The voice did not come from within the clearing, but from above it. He looked up, expecting to see someone sitting in the trees, but no one was there.

This is very strange. Talking leaves.

And talk they did. Though he saw no one, Snapping Turtle continued to hear voices. Fascinated, he stepped into the open. The whispering grew louder, more frantic, took on an angry tone. It flowed from one tree to another, circled him. Several voices spoke at once, arguing. He had a feeling they were arguing about him.

In the center of the clearing he discovered a small fire pit partially hidden beneath a blanket of fallen leaves. A few pieces of charred wood still remained in the bottom of the pit, though it had probably been a long time since the fire was last lit. Snapping Turtle gathered up a handful of sticks and dried leaves, and soon had a tiny fire of his own burning in the hole. He didn't build the fire for warmth, or to keep the shadows at bay, but to pay honor to any spirits that might be watching. It was his way of saying, "Here I am, come and join me."

Once he had the fire going, he took a seat beside it and filled the blackened bowl of his medicine pipe with tobacco. He lit the pipe with a burning twig and offered it to the Great Spirit, Grandmother Earth, and the four directions. When the last of the tobacco was smoked, he scattered the ashes on the ground and slipped the pipe back into its bag.

No sooner had he finished with his prayers than he noticed a leaf falling from one of the branches above him. He wouldn't have paid much attention to it—after all, it was just a leaf—except that it floated and danced about, as if tossed by the wind, on a night when there was no wind. The leaf also changed colors as it fell, from brown to green to glowing white. Puzzled, Snapping Turtle leaned forward to see where the leaf landed, and was amazed to see it burrow its way into the ground.

What is this? A leaf that acts like a bug.

A few seconds later, a small white stick poked up out of the ground where the leaf had disappeared. Four more sticks quickly joined the first.

Like dancing maidens, the five white sticks twisted, twirled, and bowed, bending low to the earth and then stretching toward the sky. Snapping Turtle was spellbound, for he had never seen such a sight. He was even more astonished when he realized that the sticks were actually the bony fingers of a skeleton's hand.

The fingers opened and closed, tearing at the dirt surrounding them. A wrist came into view, followed by an elbow. A second hand appeared. And a skull. The skull turned his way, looked at him with empty eye sockets.

Terrified, Snapping Turtle resisted the urge to flee and remained seated. He watched in horror as the skeleton pulled itself out of the ground, brushed the loose dirt from its yellowed bones and rotten leather breechcloth, and turned toward him.

"Who have we here?" it asked, speaking in a deep voice.

Snapping Turtle jumped when the skeleton spoke. He hadn't expected it to speak, and wondered how it could, having neither tongue nor throat. But speak it did.

"I am Snapping Turtle," replied the medicine man, trying to control his fear. "My people are the Cherokee."

The skeleton put his hands on his hips and laughed. "Ho, it is known that Snapping Turtles are good to eat. I think you too will be tasty."

Snapping Turtle swallowed hard. He had heard the Catawbas tell stories about cannibal skeletons that lived somewhere in the mountains, but had never thought the stories were true.

"But why do you want to eat me, Uncle?" Snapping Turtle asked, using the title of respect. He felt it was a good idea to be polite to someone who wanted to eat him.

"Because that is what I do," the skeleton replied. "I am Man-Eater, chief of the undead."

While Man-Eater spoke, several more leaves—five in all—fell from the trees. Like the first leaf, they too changed colors and sank from sight upon reaching the ground. And where each leaf landed, out popped a skeleton. The five skeletons, dressed in a similar fashion and every bit as frightening as Man-Eater, formed a circle around Snapping Turtle.

"These are my brothers," Man-Eater said. "This is Woman-Eater, Child-Eater, Baby-Eater, Flesh-Eater, and Bone-Gnawer."

Snapping Turtle greeted each in turn, trying to keep the names straight. It wasn't easy, because they all looked alike.

"Before we eat you, you must tell us why you have lit the sacred council fire, summoning us from the darkness."

"I did not mean to summon you, Uncles," Snapping Turtle said. "I only lit the fire to pay my respect to the spirits of this land and ask for their help."

"And who are you to call upon the spirits for help? Are you a medicine man?"

"Yes," Snapping Turtle replied. "Only it seems that my medicine has grown weak. I have said the prayers for the people of my village, done all the ceremonies, but the animals and birds of the forest have moved away."

The skeletons all laughed, their teeth clicking together. Man-Eater spoke again. "The animals have not moved away. They have been taken."

Snapping Turtle was shocked. "Taken? Taken by who?"

"By Tsul 'Kalu, Slanting Eyes, the hunter god. It is he who has taken all the animals and birds of the forest."

Snapping Turtle was confused. "But why?"

"Slanting Eyes is very greedy. He believes that everything belongs to him. He no longer wishes to share with anyone. He has taken the birds and animals to the place where he lives, on top of this mountain, and hidden them deep below the ground."

"But there are enough deer, turkey, and other animals for all to eat!" Snapping Turtle protested.

"Oh, he does not *eat* the animals," Man-Eater said. "Slanting Eyes is a god and does not need to eat. He just likes to listen to the sounds they make."

"He only listens to them?" Snapping Turtle asked, amazed.

Man-Eater nodded. "That's right. He finds their whistles, shrieks, and roars very soothing. It helps him sleep."

"But if Slanting Eyes keeps all the animals to himself, my people will starve this winter."

"He does not care," Man-Eater said. "Nor do I. Now, all this talk about eating has made me hungry. It is time for us to eat you."

The skeletons closed in around Snapping Turtle.

"But, Uncles, I am an old man," Snapping Turtle argued. "My meat is tough."

Man-Eater laughed. "We do not care. Our teeth are quite sharp." To demonstrate, he snapped his jaws together several times.

Snapping Turtle was in serious trouble. He had to think up something quick or else he was going to be eaten.

"Wait, Uncles," Snapping Turtle said, holding his hand up. "Before you eat me you must help me free the animals and birds."

The skeletons hesitated. "We only eat people. Why should we help you?"

"Because unless the animals return, the people will move away and there will be nothing for you to eat."

Man-Killer motioned for the other skeletons to wait. Snapping Turtle knew his words had them thinking.

"It is your choice, Uncles," Snapping Turtle continued. "You can eat one old, stringy man now, and have nothing to eat ever again. Or you can help me and have lots of people to eat."

The skeletons whispered among themselves in a language Snapping Turtle didn't understand.

"Very well," Man-Eater said at last. "We will help you get the animals back, but you must promise to let us eat you when we are finished."

"I promise," Snapping Turtle said. He extinguished the tiny fire with a handful of dirt, slung his quiver of arrows over his shoulder, and grabbed his bow. Man-Eater waited for him to stand up, and then turned and started on the trail that led up the mountain. Snapping Turtle followed.

They walked single-file along the trail, with Man-Eater in front, followed by another one of the boney warriors, then Snapping Turtle, with the rest of the skeletons behind him. With skeletons in front of him and behind him, escape was impossible. But Snapping Turtle wasn't thinking about getting away—not yet anyway. Despite the danger, he needed the skeletons to help him free the animals from Slanting Eyes. Snapping Turtle had never seen the hunter god, but had heard that Slanting Eyes was a fierce, towering warrior with the body of a man and the head of a deer.

Several hours passed before they finally climbed to where the forest ended. Rocky cliffs, white in the moonlight, rose above them, crisscrossed with shadowy crevices and ravines like the face of an old man. The trail wound its way along the face of the cliffs, but it was extremely narrow in places and often covered with loose rock. They would have to be careful, for one misplaced step could mean disaster.

Almost to the top, they came upon a place where a small spring gurgled out of a fissure in the rocks, crossed the trail, and cascaded down the side of the mountain. The spring was quite narrow and didn't present much of a problem to cross, provided they stepped carefully on the slippery rocks. Therefore, Snapping Turtle was quite surprised when the skeletons scrambled up the rocks to climb above the tiny trickle of water, rather than wade through it.

Suspecting some hidden danger, Snapping Turtle cautiously dipped a fingertip into the steam. The water was cold, not boiling hot, and it tasted like all other water. So what was the danger? Why did the skeletons go out of their way to keep from crossing it? He thought about it for a moment—and came up with the answer.

They may be skeletons, but they are still spirits, and cannot cross running water.

Snapping Turtle smiled. Such knowledge might prove useful. He looked up. The skeletons waited for him on the other side of the spring. He had started to wade across when he heard a peculiar sound coming from the opening where the water appeared.

"Wait. I hear something," Snapping Turtle said. He straddled the spring and pulled a few loose stones away from the opening. The sound was quite clear. It was a blend of different cries, chirps, and whistles. As he listened, he could make out the roar of a panther, the cry of the great hunting owl, and the screech of an eagle.

He pulled his head out of the opening and turned to Man-Eater.

"They're in there, just on the other side of this wall. I can hear them. The animals. All of them!"

Man-Eater nodded. "It is as I have said: Slanting Eyes has hidden them here."

"How much farther to the home of Slanting Eyes?" Snapping Turtle asked, stepping away from the opening.

"We are practically there," Man-Eater said.

They left the stream behind and continued to the top of the mountain. There, nestled amid an outcropping of gray rock, was the opening to a cave. Man-Eater pointed at the opening.

"The home of Slanting Eyes."

Snapping Turtle felt his pulse race. He had never visited the home of a god before.

"Is Slanting Eyes inside?" he asked.

Man-Eater cocked his head to the side, listening. "Yes, he still sleeps. I can hear his snores."

Snapping Turtle listened, and he too could hear a low rumbling, like thunder over the mountains, coming from inside the cave.

"Does someone stand guard while Slanting Eyes sleeps?" Snapping Turtle asked.

Man-Eater shook his head. "He has no need of a guard. No one would be stupid enough to disturb the rest of the hunter god."

Except us, Snapping Turtle thought.

Cautiously they crept toward the opening and peered in. The cave was large, dusty, and bare. Not at all what Snapping Turtle expected the home of a god to look like. Several torches were set in notches along the back wall, their flames bathing the rocks in an amber glow. And there, sleeping upon a bed of woven fibers beneath the torches, was Slanting Eyes.

The hunter god was as tall as three men put together, and as big around as a giant oak tree. He wore a breechcloth made from two buffalo hides, and moccasins of elk skin. His body was like a man's, but his head and neck was that of a mighty buck deer, with a horn rack wider than Snapping Turtle was tall. A necklace of human skulls adorned the neck of Slanting Eyes, while bands of hammered copper circled his arms and wrists. On the floor beside him lay a bow and a quiver filled with lightning bolts.

"See," Man-Eater said, stepping next to Snapping Turtle. "It is as I said, the sounds of the animals lull him to sleep."

It was true. Slanting Eyes snored heavily. Beyond the sleeping giant was an opening to a tunnel that led farther back into the mountain. From this opening came a barrage of animal and bird sounds.

"The sounds come from that way." Snapping Turtle pointed. "The animals are in there."

"We must walk quietly if we are to slip past," Man-Eater said. "Slanting Eyes will not be happy if he awakes and finds unwanted visitors in his home."

Moving as quietly as possible, Snapping Turtle and the six skeletons tiptoed past the sleeping giant. They came so close to Slanting Eyes that Snapping Turtle could have reached out and touched him, had he dared. Once past, they grabbed two of the torches from the wall, and several unlit ones from a nearby stack, and hurried down the tunnel.

The tunnel sloped downward and twisted back and forth like a serpent. It was wide enough that they could walk three abreast, but not wide enough to move a whole herd of animals through it. Slanting Eyes must have brought the animals in by another way.

Coming out of one of the turns, they came upon a large opening in the floor of the tunnel. Snapping Turtle almost fell in it, and probably would have, had not one of the skeletons caught his arm and pulled him back from its edge.

Man-Eater leaned forward and held his torch out over the hole. The amber glow was not bright enough to reveal what lay below. But they could tell from the noise, and the smell, that they had found the missing animals.

"We must get down there," Snapping Turtle said.

"It is too deep. We cannot climb down there," Man-Eater replied.

Snapping Turtle thought about it for a minute and came up with an idea. "Give me your leg bones," he said.

"What?" cried the skeletons.

"Just one each. You will still have one to stand on."

"But how will we walk?" Man-Eater asked.

"You will be able to hop on the other leg. Now hurry, we don't have much time. Do you want to eat me or not?"

The skeletons grumbled and complained, but did as they were asked and removed their legs at the hip. As they did this, Snapping Turtle unrolled the coil of rope he carried and cut it into two equal lengths. Giving him their legs, the skeletons hopped about and tried to maintain their balance. The medicine man wanted to laugh, but didn't.

Removing the feet, Snapping Turtle separated the legs at the knee joint. He then tied the pieces together with the two lengths of rope, spacing the bones about three feet apart. When he was finished, he had a ladder over thirty-six feet long. He fastened one end of the ladder to a large rock near the hole and lowered the other end into the opening.

"How do you know it will be long enough to reach the bottom?" one of the skeletons asked.

"I don't," he replied. "I can only hope that it is long enough. He picked up his torch. "I will go first. If I reach the bottom, I will yell and you can follow."

The skeletons crowded around the opening to watch as he carefully lowered himself from one rung to the next. He looked up as he went. The glow of the torches above him grew smaller and smaller.

He had just reached the next-to-last rung when he felt a cold draft caressing his skin. Pausing, he held his torch out and looked about. The light reflected off hundreds of eyes in the darkness below him. There was a stirring and a few growls as the animals moved back in fear.

"Shhh . . . easy, my brothers. I am here to help you."

He lowered himself to the last rung and held his torch beneath him. The floor of the cavern was only a few feet below. Smiling, Snapping Turtle jumped off the ladder.

The sight that greeted him as he landed was a shock. Never had he seen so many animals in one place. There must have been thousands of them. Bobcat and bear, wolf, fox, and squirrel, they all sat together, watching him, their eyes reflecting the glow from the torch. Snapping Turtle could not understand how predator and prey could sit beside each other so peacefully, unless Slanting Eyes had cast a spell over them to make them docile. Or perhaps the animals had formed an alliance until they returned to their homes in the forest. Did they know he had come to help them?

One thing for sure, some great magic must have been worked to get so many animals together. Snapping Turtle still could not figure out how they had been brought in, unless they had been lowered down the shaft a few at a time.

Snapping Turtle held his torch above him as he walked about. The cavern was gigantic, big enough to hold several villages with space left over. But, enormous as it was, it was so crowded with animals that there was barely enough room to walk around. He wondered what the animals did for food, but then he noticed that the cavern's floor was covered with a thick carpet of moss, already grazed bare in some areas. Apparently the plant-eating animals ate the moss. Maybe the predators ate some of the plant-eaters.

In the center of the chamber, a spring bubbled up out of the floor and flowed toward a far wall. No doubt it was the same one they had seen on the outside.

Curious, he followed the spring to where it passed through the rock wall. To his delight, he discovered that many of the rocks in the wall were loose. Perhaps this was the secret entrance he had been looking for. Maybe Slanting Eyes had sealed it up once the animals were inside. He tugged at one of the rocks. It moved easily. With a little effort, he could probably widen the opening.

Snapping Turtle returned to where the shaft was, and called up to the skeletons above. "Come down now. There's work to be done."

He waited by the ladder while the skeletons climbed down. As the first one lowered itself to the floor, there was a great hissing and screeching from the animals around them.

"Move slowly," Snapping Turtle warned. "If you panic the animals, we will be crushed to pieces."

The skeleton nodded and stepped away from the ladder. The animals closest to it backed up. When all of the skeletons had descended to the lower level, Snapping Turtle explained his plan to them.

"The rocks on either side of the spring are loose. If we can widen the opening, we can free the animals."

"But what about our legs?" asked Man-Eater. "Are we expected to hop about and work at the same time?"

"We still need the ladder to get back out of the cave . . . unless you want to cross the spring to get out."

The skeletons mumbled some complaints, but finally went along with Snapping Turtle's plan. They had agreed to help, and knew that when the animals were finally set free, they would get to eat.

Following Snapping Turtle to where the spring bubbled up out of the ground, the skeletons split up. Half followed on the left side of the spring, the other half on the right. When they reached the wall, they proceeded to enlarge the opening, taking care not to step in the water. Fortunately the work was not very difficult; they soon had the hole widened to several times its original size. Still, it was only wide enough to allow a few animals through at a time. Even then, some of the larger animals would have to squeeze. They kept digging.

As they dug, Snapping Turtle noticed the sky outside growing lighter. It wouldn't be much longer before morning came. The skeletons noticed the sky too.

"Enough!" Man-Eater said. "This hole is plenty wide."

Snapping Turtle stepped back to look. "I think you are right. Now we must get the animals through it."

"And how are we supposed to do that?"

Snapping Turtle scratched his head in thought. "I know. We will frighten the animals. They are afraid of spirits, so you will be able to scare them easily. We will get behind them and herd them through the opening."

"Then let us do it and be done with it," Man-Eater said. "Never before have I worked so hard for a meal."

The skeletons turned away from the opening and hopped around to the back side of the cavern. Snapping Turtle followed them, pausing when he reached the shaft that led to the upper level. Taking hold of the ladder's lowest rung, he watched as the skeletons waved their torches and made terrifying sounds. The animals and birds reacted immediately, fleeing in terror. As they charged toward him, Snapping Turtle pulled himself up and climbed the ladder to the level above.

Reaching the upper level, he quickly untied the ladder and rolled it up. He tucked it beneath his arm and raced down the tunnel, slipping past Slanting Eyes, who still slept, and out of the cave.

He followed the path down the mountain, arriving at the opening as the last of the animals emerged from within. Snapping Turtle watched in delight as the animals ran and crawled down the mountain, disappearing into the heavy forest. Above him the birds formed a giant flock, circled the mountain twice, and flew to the east to greet the rising sun.

As the animals disappeared from sight, he turned toward the opening. The skeletons stood just inside, looking out. By removing the rocks from the wall, they had allowed the spring to widen. A pool of water covered the opening, separating the skeletons from Snapping Turtle.

"You have tricked us!" Man-Eater shrieked, realizing what had happened. "You said if we helped, you would let us eat you. But you lied. You are not a man of your word!"

"I am too a man of my word," Snapping Turtle replied. "Here I am. Come and eat me."

"But we cannot cross running water!" the skeletons wailed.

"You can't? But why did you not say so? Had I known, I never would have come out here." Snapping Turtle cupped his hand to his ear, listening. "But I'm afraid it's too late for me to come back inside. I think Slanting Eyes is waking up."

The skeletons looked around, frightened.

"He is going to be terribly upset when he finds the animals gone and you in their place. I think maybe you will be the ones eaten. But perhaps you can fool him. If you can make noises like those of the birds and animals, he might go back to sleep."

"At least give us our legs back!" the skeletons cried.

Snapping Turtle glanced down at the ladder he carried. "I'm afraid I must keep this. No one will believe my story unless I offer some proof. Feel proud, for this ladder will prove that I am not as old as they say, and that my medicine is still stong. It will hang in a place of honor in the Town House of the Cherokee, and all who see it will know how Snapping Turtle and six evil skeletons brought back the animals.

"I must go now, for it is getting late and I do not want to be here when Slanting Eyes wakes up." With that, Snapping Turtle turned and started down the mountain. He'd only taken a few steps when he heard some rather peculiar noises behind him. He paused to listen, and then laughed.

The noises he heard were animal sounds and bird calls, made by six one-legged skeletons hopping about in a dark cave.

Sacrifice

Alan Riggs

Tacheni pleaded with her mount for more speed as she struggled to raise her arrow into firing position. She could see Motah on her flank, his bow already raised and fixed upon the young prongbuck they had driven from the herd. *Not this time,* she thought as she dug in her heels and let out a loud shout. The buck spooked and veered suddenly, spoiling Motah's shot but presenting a broad flank to Tacheni. In an instant she sighted and let fly. The arrow sank deeply into the antelope's neck, and Tacheni gave a triumphant yell as the beast staggered and fell.

She slowed her horse to a walk as Motah pulled up beside her. "That was unfair," he snapped as Tacheni dismounted to finish the kill. "I had a clear shot."

Tacheni said a quiet prayer, asking forgiveness of the antelope's spirit, before answering her brother. "Then you should have taken it," she retorted. "You waited so long I was afraid you had fallen asleep." *Besides,* she added silently, *I had to make this one count.*

"You know that isn't true," he said. "You were just afraid to lose because this might be your last hunt."

She looked up at him sharply, but there was no taunting in his twelve-year-old eyes, only frank assessment. "You know me too well, little brother," she said. "Already you show the wisdom of a warrior."

Motah beamed with pride at her compliment. "Perhaps we can still hunt together, sometimes, after I have found my vision," he offered tentatively.

Tacheni smiled sadly as she struggled to throw the antelope across her horse's back. "You know Grandmother would never allow that," she answered. There were few capital crimes among the People, but incest was one. It was unthinkable for a brother and sister to spend time alone together after they had both reached adulthood, and she had been bleeding for nearly a year. Once Motah undertook his vision quest, their hunts would end. And he would begin his quest very soon.

"I spoke to Old Nokoni yesterday," he said, as if divining her thoughts. "He believes that my power will be very strong. He says that he will prepare the sweat lodge for me before the winter hunts begin."

Tacheni could hear the pleasure in his voice, but she could not share it. *So soon,* she thought. *Motah will find his power and join in the great hunt, and I will sew beads and tan hides, and the meat I butcher will be killed by someone else's hand.*

And I will find a good husband and raise strong children, she thought. And there was a happiness in that thought, but it was not the joy that she tasted when her arrow found its mark.

"I am sure the great herds will tremble at your approach," she said as she mounted once more. "Though you might have to actually shoot your arrow to drop a buffalo."

"You're just jealous," he said. And the truth of that statement rested bitterly in Tacheni's mouth as they turned for home.

The return went slowly. Despite the success of the hunt, Tacheni was in no mood to press their pace. Motah's exuberant anticipation of his future only called attention to the emptiness of her own prospects. There was no vision quest waiting for her, no guiding spirit waiting to lead her to power. Her service to the tribe would be fulfilled through marriage and child-rearing, but even there her hopes were slim. She was a poor cook, her beadwork was barely adequate, and she hadn't the patience to soften leather properly. No man was going to trust the management of his household to her meager skills. Though she was a first child and considered beautiful, it was generally assumed that she would become the second wife to an aging warrior. Lost in her ruminations, Tacheni scarcely noticed as the twilight deepened into darkness.

Suddenly she realized that Motah was whispering at her nervously. "What?" she asked.

"I said I think something's wrong. We've been riding too long. Do you think we missed the village?"

"You mean the great warrior can't even remember the way home?" she chided.

"I . . . I wasn't paying attention," he admitted. "I was thinking about my vision quest."

As he spoke, Tacheni took stock of her surroundings. She was surprised to find how dark it had become, and even more surprised to find that *she* didn't know where they were.

"It's all right, little brother," she said softly. "I wasn't paying attention, either." As she spoke, Tacheni searched the darkness for familiar landmarks. She thought she could see a faint light flickering in the distance.

"Look," she said, pointing, "that must be a cooking fire. We've only drifted a little off course."

"Hah. Race you home," said Motah, preparing to kick his mount forward.

"Go ahead," she said. "I don't think I'll hurry to find the scolding Grandmother has waiting."

Motah paused, contemplating the reception they could expect for their late return, then relaxed. "A true warrior returns home without haste," he agreed.

Still, they increased their pace slightly. The distant flames seemed to warm their path, and when they got close enough to hear singing, their spirits lifted even further. Until they realized that the language of the singers was not their own.

CRACKLED MAGIC

Tacheni crept forward slowly, keeping her belly close to the ground. Motah was beside her, a look of grave determination on his young face. As they neared the fire, Tacheni recognized the site; they were in a small hollow not far from the tribe's autumn camp. A large fire burned in the center of the hollow, and several figures danced around it, chanting loudly. The air crackled with a powerful magic, and Tacheni could feel the hair on her neck tingle under its force.

testosterone high

The men stopped dancing, and a huge figure stepped into their circle. He carried a pipe in one hand and a great war club in the other. He began to sing and dance wildly about the fire: charging in, swinging his club as if attacking an enemy, then dancing back, turning great circles with both arms outstretched. He danced so close that the flames seemed to wrap around his limbs, and smoke appeared to flow from his arms. His warpaint glowed like fresh blood in the flickering light. Tacheni's heart sank, and she heard a muffled gasp from Motah as he, too, recognized the paint: Morning Star of the Skidi.

Quiet fear

Slowly, deliberately, they retreated the way they had come. Tacheni could hear the grass scream beneath her every movement. Once her hand came down heavily on a small twig and snapped it. The noise seemed as loud as a Spanish rifle, and she nearly cried out, but they were not discovered. The blood still pounded in her ears when they reached the horses, but her fear was turning into quiet resolve.

The Skidi were possessed of great magic. Their priests read mysteries in the movements of the stars. Their knowledge was respected throughout the Great Plain, but sometimes the stars demanded a terrible price for their secrets. Then one of the Wolf People would be driven by a dream to wear the Morning Star raiment. The priests would weave their magic, and Morning Star would go hunting in the plains, hunting not for buffalo, but for a human maiden. No one could resist their hunt, because they were following the demands of the stars. A war party could seek vengeance later, but the hunt could not be stopped. Anyone who interfered was killed, if not by the Skidi warriors, then by the power of the god's anger.

Tacheni put her face close to Motah's. "You have to go warn the tribe," she whispered. "The Skidi won't attack until their ritual is done. There might be time to pack up the village and avoid their hunt."

"We both have to go," whispered Motah.

"No, one of us has to stay and keep watch. If they finish their ceremony early, I can run and give warning."

"Then I'll stay. You warn the others."

Tacheni searched Motah's eyes and saw only firm resolve. "But don't you see?" she whispered. "This might be part of your vision quest. I think you're supposed to carry the warning and prove your valor to the tribe."

She could see his determination wavering. "Hurry," she said, "and be careful. It will be dangerous if they have scouts watching the camp."

That seemed to convince him. Slowly he pulled away from her and mounted his horse. "I'll come back for you," he said.

A sinking feeling came over Tacheni as she watched him disappear into the darkness. She had never lied to him before. The chiefs would not move the village to avoid the hunt. Perhaps some of the maidens would be hidden away, but not all of them. If the Wolf People didn't find their chosen prey, they would exact payment in blood. Tacheni said a quiet prayer, asking her brother's forgiveness. Then she turned and walked resolutely into the hollow.

The Skidi warriors stopped their singing in amazement as she walked into their circle. The two closest to her quickly grabbed her arms and dragged her to Morning Star. There was a great deal of animated conversation. Apparently some of the dancers believed that the power of their magic had called her here to become their sacrifice, but Morning Star was not convinced. He kept pointing toward the sky and waving his hands in negation. The argument showed no signs of nearing an end until a high-pitched war cry cut through the noise.

Tacheni whirled around just in time to see her brother's horse charge into the hollow. Two of the Wolf People moved to intercept him, waving war lances menacingly. But they did not actually attack, and Motah rode right through them. Tacheni could see that his bow was drawn and his aim rested firmly on Morning Star.

"No!" Tacheni screamed as one the Skidi threw her to the ground and stood guard above her.

As Motah drove his horse forward, Morning Star danced around the flames once more. The huge club lashed out, striking the firewood and launching flames and burning brands toward the horse's face. The beast spooked, throwing Motah and racing away from the fire. Motah fell heavily, bow and arrow sliding from his grip. Before he could recover, one of the Skidi warriors snatched up the bow and tossed it into the flames.

Tacheni watched Motah struggle to his feet. The Wolf People were shoving him, waving their weapons at him, trying to chase him away. But he kept trying to reach her. Even after Morning Star began swinging his club in vicious arcs less than a hand's width from his head, Motah wouldn't retreat.

"Run!" cried Tacheni. "Save yourself!"

But he wouldn't leave. Once again the Skidi knocked him to the ground, and once again he struggled to his feet. But this time there was something in his hand: an arrow. He clutched it absently, as if unaware what his hand was doing. Then he gave a sudden yell and leaped for Morning Star. The surprised Skidi could only stagger backwards as Motah completed his attack, but that half-step saved his life. The boy's leap fell short, and the arrow lodged in the huge man's calf.

The warrior yelled in pain and rage as he raised his club one last time. Tacheni's cry, "No. Please," sounded weak even to her own ears: too weak to stop the great club from descending, far too weak to keep it from destroying her brother's skull.

There were no more arguments. Tacheni watched as Morning Star yanked the arrow out of his leg and tossed it into the fire. One of the others brought mounts, and the huge man mounted without even looking at the wound. Tacheni was pulled from the ground and taken to Morning Star, who lifted her easily onto his horse. She sat numbly as they rode into the darkness.

Tacheni took no interest in the journey. Night turned to day turned to night. She sat uncaring, enfolded by the arms that had killed her brother. The few short breaks in their ride did little to ease the weariness of her body and less to relieve the weight on her soul. A dozen times she began in her mind a prayer to Motah's spirit: a plea for forgiveness, a promise of retribution. But each time she was too ashamed to complete the ritual.

Only when they reached their destination did she begin to notice her surroundings. The group crested a small hill and Tacheni saw the Skidi town nestled in the woods near the banks of a broad stream. Tacheni was puzzled. There were no tepees in the village, only ten or twelve huge, earth-covered domes. As her captors started whooping and yelling to announce their triumphant return, people poured out of these buildings and ran to surround them.

The crowd churned about them, jumping and yelling and waving their arms. One by one, the warriors in their group were pulled from their horses and swallowed up in the celebration. Soon only Tacheni and the Morning Star remained mounted. The mob circled and seethed around them, but they were never touched.

Then, in an instant, all sound and motion ceased. The crowd parted, and a man wearing the painted robe of a priest walked slowly through the opening. He was tall, maybe as tall as Morning Star, but thin, almost skeletal in appearance. Skin stretched tautly across his face, pulling his lips back into a mirthless grin. Deep hollows surrounded his eyes, shadowing them even in the morning's light. Within those shadows floated two pits of cold, hard stone.

The man said nothing. He only held out his right hand and fixed his gaze upon her. Tacheni felt his eyes take hold of her as the hawk seizes a hare. Without volition she slipped from the horse's back and walked over to join the priest. As she neared, the man turned and walked back toward the village. She followed, dimly aware that Morning Star had dismounted and walked behind her.

They entered one of the large halls; it was empty of people, but a large fire burned at its center. They circled the flames and stood before an altar on the far wall. The priest took down a bundle of thick fur and unrolled it on the ground. Tacheni stood passively as the Morning Star disrobed. The hawk feathers, the wildcat pelt, the otter-skin collar—one by one, the warrior handed his totems to the priest, and they were bundled in the fur. Then the priest led them back to the fire. For the first time Tacheni noticed that the large warrior was limping slightly, and some part of her was pleased.

The priest tossed a powder into the fire, and thick smoke billowed forth. The smoke surrounded her, filling her lungs, but it did not choke. Instead she felt as if she, too, were becoming smoke: insubstantial, ethereal, dreamlike.

Tacheni was unsure when he had entered, but she became aware of another man moving through the smoke. He wore the totems of the wolf and was circling in and out of the fire. As he danced near, the priest pulled a large blade from beneath his robe and plunged it into the wolf's chest. The man fell to the ground, blood spurting into the

she too was becoming smoke

fire. A part of her mind thought that, in that moment, he looked very much like Motah.

The priest pulled out his blade and threw it into the flames. He placed a hand over the wound and started singing in deep tones. Tacheni would have been surprised at the richness of his voice, but she seemed incapable of surprise. She watched without concern as the wound stopped bleeding and color returned to the man's skin. He rose to his feet and continued his approach, moving slowly, cautiously. When he reached Tacheni, he laid one hand softly on her shoulder.

Instantly the clouds lifted from her mind. The wolf's touch was soft but unyielding. He quickly stripped off Tacheni's simple buckskin dress and moccasins. She stood naked while the priest anointed her with pungent oils. Then the wolf dressed her in a fine skirt and blouse. He gave her new black moccasins, a fine robe, and a soft down feather for her hair. Finally he handed her a carved wooden bowl and a buffalo-horn spoon. Then the wolf took her away from the priest and into his own lodge.

Tacheni quickly became accustomed to her new routine. She lived in the wolf's lodge, along with thirty or forty of his kinsmen. Of them all, only she had no chores. Each morning the wolf would wake her and dress her in finery. Then he would lead her to the lodge of the large warrior who had been Morning Star. There, before even their host had chosen, the wolf would take the finest portions of the meal and place them in her wooden bowl. She would eat her fill, using no utensil but the horn spoon, and then they would return to the wolf's lodge.

Throughout the day she was given every luxury. If she showed hunger, the people of the village brought the fruits of their gardens to the wolf, who placed them in the wooden bowl for her pleasure. If she showed thirst, her bowl was filled with fresh water from the stream. She was entertained by athletic contests and children's games and occasionally by exhibitions of sorcery from the Skidi magicians. She was treated better than the chief's own wives, but no one spoke to her. No one but the wolf ever came close to her.

After many, many such days, the routine suddenly changed. When the wolf led her to breakfast, there was no meal waiting in the large warrior's lodge. Confused, Tacheni followed along as the wolf led her to each building in the village, and at each one they found no food prepared. As they left each lodge, its inhabitants exploded in a flurry of activity. Belongings were packed and loaded onto travois, which were hitched to dogs and horses. Large tepees were rolled up and tied for transport. Tacheni's spirit soared when she recognized the preparations: a hunt.

Well before noon, the Skidi were ready to depart. The wolf led her to a small brown mare. It was of poor quality compared to those of her own people, but still healthy. She could scarcely contain her exhilaration as she mounted and joined the procession. The open plains called to Tacheni's spirit. She longed to sleep in a tepee once more, instead of the wolf's crowded lodge, to feel the smooth power of a running horse beneath her, to hear the rumble of the great herds as they ran.

Once the march was under way, hunters branched off to seek game for the trek. The rest of the village followed the trail blazed by the Skidi scouts. In the afternoon they stopped and the women set up camp. As usual, Tacheni had no duties while the rest of the women raised tepees and built cooking fires in anticipation of the hunters' return. The wolf led her to a campsite and motioned for her to dismount. She started to comply, but then hesitated. How could she let this chance go to waste?

She snapped her heels into the mare's flanks, spurring it into a gallop. It was glorious to feel such freedom and power again. She heard shouting behind her. A glance backward showed the wolf and two other warriors riding in pursuit, fanning out to prevent her escape. She laughed. Where did they think she was going? Even if she found her way back to the spot of her capture, her village would long since have moved on to other hunting grounds. No, the only escape she sought was here, in the freedom of motion.

Still, there was no reason not to have a little fun. She broke sharply left, guiding the mare expertly with her knees as she leaned into the turn. She spun in a tight arc and headed back the way she had come, slicing through the line of her surprised pursuers. As the Skidi regained their composure and spun to follow, she turned again. Tacheni led them in a weaving game of catch-the-rabbit, slipping just through their pattern of enclosure again and again. She was aided in this by the fact that only the wolf was actively trying to *catch* her; the others were just trying to block her path with their horses.

A shout from the west cut through her merriment. She turned and saw a large band of warriors heading in her direction at a gallop. They numbered more than a dozen, and soon had her horse surrounded. With a soft sigh of regret, Tacheni reined in the mare and studied the newcomers. Two of them were hunters she recognized from the village, but the rest were strangers. They all seemed to defer to a striking young warrior with three red feathers tied to his hair.

Tacheni's study of the man was cut off abruptly, though, when the wolf rode up beside her. He snatched the reins from her hands and started screaming at her incoherently. Tacheni was afraid he would strike her when a soft question from the feathered warrior cut through

the striking one, ain't it like always

his vehemence. The wolf seemed shaken for a moment, then calmed himself with a visible effort. He spoke rapidly to the newcomer, indicating Tacheni's costume and pointing at the plain where their chase had taken place.

The newcomer looked at her for a moment, then said, "You are of the Snake people?"

Tacheni recognized the name; other tribes named her people for the snake, just as the Spaniards called them *Comantcia.* "We call ourselves Numinu," she said. "It means 'the People.' "

"I am Petalesharo," he said. "I know some of your tongue."

His accent was strange, but Tacheni was thrilled to hear her own language once more. "I am Tacheni," she said, smiling broadly.

Petalesharo motioned that they should all return to the camp, and then moved his stallion into position beside Tacheni's mare. "You led them a fine chase," he said. "Do all of your women ride so gracefully?"

His voice was soft, yet it had a strange, penetrating quality. Each word seemed to grab her and command her attention, and she found herself fighting off a blush at his compliment.

"All of the People learn to ride when young," she said. "But perhaps some women do not find the joy in it that I do."

"I think, perhaps, that many men do not find such joy," he replied thoughtfully. "But we arrive, and I fear the wolf is anxious to get you settled in his camp. Good night, joyful rider, I have enjoyed our meeting."

Tacheni's thoughts raced, searching for the proper reply, but "Good night" was all that came.

The wolf guided her down from the mare, holding the reins this time to ensure that she complied. Then he guided her to the tepee that they would share with his wife and youngest son. For dinner, she was taken to the tepee of the warrior who had been Morning Star. On the way, she found her eyes roving the camp, searching for some sign of Petalesharo but finding none. As usual, the finest portions were placed in her wooden bowl, but despite her exertions she had no appetite.

The morning was cold and gray and bitterly cold. The women broke camp, and once again the hunters left the trail. Tacheni searched and spotted Petalesharo, riding out at the head of his warriors. As she watched the telltale red feathers disappear in the distance, the first flakes of snow began to fall.

They traveled through the day, making camp in the afternoon. This time Tacheni was given no opportunity to ride free; the wolf kept her under close watch. She watched each group of hunters as they returned for the night, but there was no sign of Petalesharo. There was only more snow and a night that grew ever colder.

For four more days they traveled. Each day Tacheni searched for some sign of the feathered warrior, and each day she was disappointed. As the snow deepened, the horses began suffering. Often the women would have to gather shoots or soft bark to supplement their forage. All work was done inside the tepees now, by the light and warmth of the fire. Despite the hardship, Tacheni sensed an air of anticipation in the camp. She soon understood why; a great herd was near.

At the next campsite they were not alone; a vast field of tepees awaited them. Tacheni guessed that there must be three or four villages already here. The camp layout had a space exactly in its center, and the scouts led them directly to it. Their camp went up as usual, though the work was slowed by distractions as men and women from the other villages came to pay respects.

Tacheni felt a rising hope as she surveyed the camp—Petalesharo had to be here. She tried to spot him, but the camp was too large, and the wolf would not let her wander. Still, she held on to the hope. She tried again as she was being led to dinner, but again was unsuccessful. She was still looking over her shoulder as she entered Morning Star's tepee, so the soft voice caught her completely unprepared.

"Good evening, Tacheni, are your rides still joyful?"

Tacheni jumped and spun around, nearly losing her balance. "Pe Petalesharo," she stammered. "Yes. I mean, no. I mean, I haven't been able to ride freely since we last met."

"I have startled you," he said. "I am sorry." But he didn't try to hide his slight smile.

"I am pleased to see you again," said Tacheni. "It is a pleasure to hear my own language."

"Then I am pleased to speak it," he replied. "But please, seat yourself. We will speak as you eat. Until you have chosen your portion, this warrior cannot feed his family. Or his guests," he added, patting his stomach.

Tacheni absently accepted a portion of deer from the wolf as Petalesharo's soft voice filled the tepee.

"I have thought much about you since our last meeting, joyful rider. I have thought that it is a poor thing for a happiness such as yours to be given to Morning Star."

A sudden hope filled Tacheni. She started to speak, but Petalesharo lifted a cautioning hand.

"I am a powerful man among my people," he said. "But I cannot overrule the stars. My father is chief among all men of the Skidi villages, but even he cannot overrule the stars. The Morning Star ritual is a heavy burden for my people. We do not seek it out, but when the dream takes a warrior it must be obeyed. The Morning Star has claimed you, and he will not be denied. But I would know you before you die, so that your joy can be preserved in memory."

Tacheni fought back the tears she felt inside her. She tried again to speak, but her voice failed. "I . . . I don't know what to tell you," she finally croaked.

Petalesharo nodded and looked at her thoughtfully. "The night is cold," he said. "I think that I am in no hurry to return to my camp. I will sit here, near the warm fire, and as long as I stay, you will be welcome to stay also."

They sat in silence for a while, and Tacheni felt as if the Skidi warrior was searching for something within her. Then he spoke again, letting each word fall gently from his lips.

"I have heard our host speak of a brave warrior who fought in your defense," he said.

Tacheni felt the memory of Motah's death swell within her, and again she had to fight back tears. "My brother," she said. "He was only twelve. He had not yet found his power."

"You are wrong," said Petalesharo, but she read no rebuke in his eyes, only concern.

"Rawihu is a mighty warrior," he continued, nodding toward their host. "It would take a valiant boy to do him any harm, but your brother did not fight Rawihu. The warrior he fought was filled with the Morning Star's dream and protected by the Morning Star's totems. No boy could have caused him harm. Your brother found his magic, and it was powerful."

Somehow, that thought gave Tacheni comfort. "Thank you," she said.

Petalesharo smiled. "So, I know your sorrow," he said. "Now you must tell me what hides behind it."

His words worked their way inside her, touching places even the fire couldn't reach. Her awareness became focused on Petalesharo: the way the flames threw shadows playfully across his face, the soothing sound of his voice, the warmth she felt in his conversation. All else faded from consciousness, and she talked. She talked about the childhood games she and Motah had played, and about the jokes they shared with Grandmother. She talked about the riding contests and how Motah shared his lessons of the bow and the hunt with her. She talked about the final hunt that they had shared, and her shame at lying to him. She talked of things she had never shared with anyone, and sometimes surprised herself with the words. By the time she stopped, the fire was nothing but embers.

She felt suddenly embarrassed as she realized that the wolf was still sitting quietly at her side. The large warrior was also there, though his family had long since gone to sleep.

Petalesharo stood and stretched. "I think that the night is not so cold anymore," he said. He started to extend a hand toward Tacheni, but quickly pulled it back. A sad smile crossed his face as the wolf helped her to her feet.

"I thank you, Tacheni, for the gift of your conversation," he said as the wolf ushered her out the door of the tepee.

She was amazed to see the first signs of dawn already lighting the eastern sky. Had she really spoken for so long? She should be exhausted, but instead she was filled with a curious energy. She had not forgotten Petalesharo's words. She was going to die; nothing could prevent it. Yet she was exhilarated, as if a great weight had been taken from her. The ground itself felt alive beneath her feet.

The next days were filled with activity. Hunters worked furiously, driving their horses through the snow to launch arrows into the herd. The women followed close behind to skin and butcher the animals as soon as they fell. Tacheni did not have a chance to speak with Petalesharo again, but she would see him sometimes among the hunters, marked by the flash of red feathers. Then she would imagine that she rode with him, somehow, relishing the speed of the stallion and the power of the great herd. In those moments her fate seemed remote and inconsequential. But she knew it couldn't last.

Soon the travois were filled with meat and skins, and Tacheni knew the hunt was nearly done. The wolf woke her at dawn, as usual. But instead of taking her to breakfast, he motioned for her to mount and follow him away from camp. The wolf led her away from the herd to where another rider waited, his cloak wrapped tight against the lightly falling snow. Tacheni's heart skipped as she recognized Petalesharo. The two Skidi spoke briefly; then the wolf turned and headed back toward camp.

"I have promised him that you will not try to escape," said Petalesharo. "Is this true?"

"Yes," she said.

"Good. I am not needed for today's hunt, and I have decided that I am bored with shooting buffalo. I think that if I ride in the other direction I might find something more interesting to hunt."

With that, Petalesharo wheeled his stallion and rode off. As he turned, a rolled deerskin fell from his horse's back and landed in the snow. Tacheni dismounted to retrieve it, and discovered that it held a fine wooden bow and a quiver of arrows. She gave a cry of joy as she leaped onto her horse and urged her into a gallop. The wind was bitterly cold, but it could scarcely touch the fire that burned inside her.

They did not speak as they rode; there was no need. At times Tacheni could not contain her delight. Then she would run the mare, feeling the glorious power of speed and freedom. Sometimes she would chase Petalesharo; other times he would chase her. Then they would walk the horses, searching for signs, sharing a communication deeper than words. The moment became perfect when they spotted the deer track, still clear in the fresh snow.

It wasn't long before they caught sight of the doe, searching for forage in the snow. Petalesharo motioned for her to wait while he guided his horse cautiously downwind. Tacheni nocked an arrow in readiness and slowly maneuvered her mare into position.

When she heard Petalesharo's cry, she kicked her horse into a gallop. The doe, spooked by Petalesharo's yell and charging horse, fled along a path parallel to her own. She had a brief instant to find her shot before the doe reacted to her and changed course. She didn't waste it. The arrow flew from her bow and struck the deer's ribs, but it didn't penetrate. The head broke off and the shaft bounced harmlessly off the doe's side. Tacheni stared in surprise while the startled animal bounded away.

When she told Petalesharo what had happened to her shot, he simply said, "I know."

"What?"

"I sabotaged your arrows," he said. "I could not let you kill the deer."

"I don't understand." Tacheni said. "Why?"

"I wanted to give you your hunt," he answered. "But you have been chosen by Morning Star. His hand is upon you and upon all things which touch you. If you had killed the deer, the carcass would have gone to waste, for no one could safely use the skin or eat the flesh. Then the doe's spirit would be angry and require appeasing. I hope you are not angry."

Tacheni smiled at his concern. "You have given me a gift beyond all measure," she said. "I am not angry. I think that I have never been happier. I only wish that this hunt never needed to end."

"I, too, wish that, joyful rider," he said. "For more reasons than you know."

Tacheni could see that he was struggling with a strong emotion, so she waited quietly for him to continue.

"I did not join the hunt today, because the villages already have enough food for the winter. Today's hunt was for one animal only—

the animal to be used in the Morning Star ceremony. Tomorrow the tribes will return to their villages, and the priests will begin studying the sky. When the Morning Star burns brightest, you will die."

So soon, thought Tacheni. Yet in some ways the pain she heard in Petalesharo's voice was more terrible than her own fate. She wanted to reach out and comfort him, but that was impossible. She would not spread her doom to him.

"Listen," Petalesharo said suddenly. "You must flee. Take the horse and seek out your own people."

"But I have promised to return," she said.

"No. *I* promised that you would return," he answered. "And when you do not, the wrath of Morning Star will fall upon me. You will be safe."

There was a desperate plea in his eyes, but it was a plea that she could not answer. "No," she said. "No, I cannot do that."

The silence of their journey back to camp was broken only by the wind.

Tacheni sat quietly on the soft cushion while the priests chanted their songs. Occasionally her gaze wandered around the lodge, but nothing had changed. She sat in front of the altar in the lodge which had once been Rawihu's. He and his families were gone now, as were their possessions. Only she and the priests were present.

The tall, gaunt priest was there, with his terrible hollow eyes, and so were sixteen other minor priests. For four days they had been wrapping her in smoke and binding her with their songs of power. They stripped off her clothes and painted her body. Then they dressed her again in new clothes. They took the feather from her hair and gave it to the fire. Then they put new feathers in her hair. Sometimes Rawihu would be present, once again wearing the dream of the Morning Star. And sometimes the wolf would come in and feed her or take her quickly to the river.

Tacheni saw the wolf come through the lodge's entrance, accompanied by the first light of dawn. This time he did not bring food. *So it is today,* she thought. *Good.*

The priests stopped singing. At their signal, the wolf came over and lifted her from the cushion. She saw Morning Star standing by the door, waiting to lead them into the light. The wolf followed Morning Star; she followed the wolf; the priests followed her. The procession reminded her of the long march back from the hunt. On the day the Skidi broke camp, she had searched for some sign of Petalesharo, but there was none. It was better that way. What more could they say?

A soft touch pulled her from her reverie. She became aware that the procession had stopped at the foot of a four-step scaffold. The wolf was gesturing at her, trying to coax her up the steps. Tacheni hesitated. She knew there was no escape, but how could she walk meekly up those steps? She could feel the presence of a thousand other maidens, a vast procession stretching to the past and future, each slowly ascending the steps to her death. No, not to *her* death, to the nameless, faceless death of a Skidi sacrifice: a death, and thus a life, without identity.

No, Tacheni thought. *I refuse.*

The wolf continued his pantomime cajolery, but Tacheni ignored him. She would not enter the next world without her name. She would die, but she would make the death her own.

She started to turn. Immediately she felt the effect of the priest's spells. The magic wrapped around her, gripping her with unbreakable force. She knew that she could not escape those bonds, but she wasn't trying to escape. The spells tried to drive her forward, pressing her toward the scaffold, but Tacheni turned inside the pressure. Slowly, as if moving against a great wind, she spun to face her captors.

She met the eyes of Morning Star and was rewarded with a slight gasp of amazement. Then she turned to meet the hooded gaze of the tall priest. She saw anger there, and a great swelling of power as he fought to bend her to the ritual. But she was unafraid.

"I am Tacheni, maiden of the Numinu," she called out. "And I follow the path of my own will."

As she spoke, she noticed a figure on horseback standing behind the crowd. It was Petalesharo. He sat perfectly still, as if in shock, until her eyes found his. Then he burst forward with a tremendous yell. The villagers scattered before him as he drove his stallion toward the scaffold. He reined in beside her and started shouting at the priests. The tall priest shouted back, pointing to the scaffold and to the Morning Star. Tacheni could not understand their words, but she saw that many of the people were uncertain whom to support.

Then Petalesharo suddenly reached down and grabbed Tacheni, swinging her easily onto the rear of his stallion. He shouted to the priest again and then waited quietly, but no response came. With a shout, Petalesharo kicked his horse forward and drove through the crowd once more. Though there was no pursuit, he urged the stallion to a full run as soon as they cleared the village.

Tacheni wrapped her arms around him, reveling in the sensation. The sudden freedom and the speed made her feel weightless, lifted by the joy in her spirit. She was also intensely aware of Petalesharo's nearness, his back against her chest, his hair in her face, the places where his legs touched her own. She was barely aware of their lessening speed. Only when the stallion stopped and Petalesharo moved to dismount did she loosen her grip.

There was a diffidence in his manner as he helped her from the horse, a strange distance. He did not meet her eyes as he spoke.

"I have discovered where your tribe has made its winter camp," he said. "If you keep to the course I have set, you will find them after three or four days' travel."

Confusion, joy, and pain warred in Tacheni's heart. "You are sending me away?" she said.

"I must," he said, meeting her gaze.

Tacheni saw a pain in his eyes that mirrored her own. "Why?" she asked.

"The priests are wrong," he said. "There is power in the Morning Star ritual, but it is not the power of the god's anger. It is the power of our own fear. I saw that when you turned at the foot of the scaffold. Your bravery was more powerful than the priests' spells. I knew then that the ceremony was evil, that we must never perform it again.

"But my people are still afraid," he continued. "I must show them the way. When I touched you, disrupting the ritual, I focused the power on myself. If the Morning Star is truly angry, then he will take my life. But I do not think that will happen. When the people see that I remain unharmed, they will see that the ritual is untrue."

"Then I must stay also," she said. "My survival will also prove the ceremony false."

Tacheni saw tears swell in Petalesharo's eyes, but his voice remained steady.

"You can not stay," he said. "It is not safe. The priests will not strike directly at me, but you would have no shield from their anger. If I took you for my wife, people would say that I stopped the ceremony only to have you for my own, not because it was untrue. Then they would not give up the ritual. Also, if you stay, you will become a target for those who are still fearful. They will mark you as bad luck, and any misfortune that befalls my people will be blamed on your presence. My heart breaks to see you go, joyful rider, but you can not stay."

The sorrow in his voice was almost more than she could bear. "I must go," she agreed. "But before I do, you must answer me two questions. When you reached out to touch me, daring Morning Star's anger, were you afraid?"

"Yes," he said. "But I could not let you die."

Tacheni moved forward until they were almost touching. She looked into his eyes for several heartbeats, feeling the warmth of his breath on her face.

"And are you afraid now?" she asked.

As an answer, he pulled her into his arms and kissed her fiercely. The wind was cold and the ground frozen, but wherever they touched she felt a desperate, yearning fire. There was no restraint in their union. But if she felt a small amount of pain underneath her passion, then that, too, was perfect.

Tacheni guided the horse easily toward the collection of tepees that marked the winter camp. She was greeted by shouts of surprise and happiness as her family and friends ran to welcome her. To be home once more filled her spirit with a gentle warmth, but her eyes kept wandering to the horizon.

Cherokee Dreaming

Billie Sue Mosiman

F*alling through the space where there is no light, falling for a mil-
lennium, pinwheeling and grasping for earth . . .*

The chief of the peace village in the far south corner of Tennes-
see saw Black Wolf when he was first brought in for shelter from his
wrongdoing. Black Wolf lay comatose on a travois hauled behind a
horse. Heaped over the mindless young man were bearskins, black
and brown. The messenger slid from his animal and, talking in that
reverent way required of men in the presence of an old chief, he said
softly, as if not to disturb the spirits who surely held Black Wolf under
their spell, "This warrior fell during battle with the white invaders
from the east. He was found wandering outside the battlefield with
blood on his hands, talking to unseen beings."

"What did he do so wrong?" Already the chieftain suspected the
truth. It was the blood that told.

"It is said he was seen during the heat of battle nearing the white
chief, the one we had been told to honor, not to kill, so that when we
took him prisoner we might make a treaty. But Black Wolf forgot
himself or he was possessed by the blood from many enemies and so
when he reached the white chief, he drove the point of his spear
through his heart."

"And it was after he knew of his disobedience that he began to see
and speak to spirits?"

The messenger nodded. "It is thought so. As punishment. The
white chief was a famous tracker and hunter who had at other times
been a friend to the Cherokee."

"And did the other warriors want to kill Black Wolf for this?"

"Had I not taken him away quickly, he would be dead. Now there
can be no treaty. More white invaders will come to fight. On our journey here for sanctuary, Black Wolf went into the dream sleep as you
see him now. He has not said a word in two days, nor has he taken
sustenance."

■ ■ ■

An eagle borne on the back of a ray of light streaked through the heavenly void and lifted him on its wings. Oh, my father, have you come to rescue me from evil in this place? And the eagle kept its peace, circling slowly to land on ground as hard as rock, baked by sun, as dry as bone of a dead man bleached by wind and rain . . .

"Take him inside the council house," the peace chief said. Two men helped the messenger carry Black Wolf and lay him by the sacred fire. The chief made sure the savior was given a deerskin bag of maize to sustain him as he returned to the war village, three days distant.

Inside the windowless council cabin, smoke from the everlasting fire rising through the smoke hole in the roof, the chief squatted beside the prostrate warrior and chanted a prayer for his spirit to return. Tonight he would bring the medicine man and ask that a black drink made from holly be given Black Wolf. They must make him sicker before they could save him from the paw of dream-death. If that did not work, then magic must be tried.

The chief reached out and touched Black Wolf's forehead and cheeks. His skin felt as cool as a stone in a swiftly moving stream. The shock of this caused the chief to recoil and hurry from the cabin to find help. He could not wait for the night.

A hand reached out and touched his head, his face, and he jerked back at the touch, fearful enough to lose his heart through his mouth. But there was no one there. Nothing there but the burning light.

All around him stretched a vista barren of tree or hill, bush or river. This must be the place the giant spirit would crush him. He had never seen land such as this. He had wandered far from his moist, shadowed, forest home.

The giant came minutes after he had murdered the great white chieftain. He appeared from among the dead, rising up from the earth as a swirling fog, and pursued him to the woods' edge and beyond, shouting in Cherokee that he had taken one too many lives, he had taken the *wrong* life. And he would pay for this.

This repayment might not be so horrible if only night never descended.

Black Wolf craned his neck and checked the sky for the bright god. There it was, that burning sun that had baked this alien plain and burned away all the water. If it remained, he might find a way back to his own land. But if night came . . . if that void from which he had been tumbling returned . . .

The medicine man of the peace tribe stood over the young man in the council house. He rattled his pouch of quartz, of stones found in deep, rushing waters, of tiny bones from the sacred eagle, and a yellowed tooth from the spiny pig who killed Cherokee last spring. He halted, seeing a vision flitting through the dense air of the one-room structure, and said to his chief, "He has been captured."

"By what or by whom?"

"It is the white chief. His spirit was stolen prematurely. It was not ordained. He will make this one suffer now."

"Can you make the black drink for him?"

The medicine man, taller by a head than the chief, looked down into the old man's eyes. "I can make it and I will, but whatever I do may not recall this warrior to the living. He will battle again, this time with ghosts, and nothing I do can prevent it. This I have seen."

He heard a deep sigh and twisted on his haunches to see who was there, what manner of being might be so concerned about his welfare, but again no one was there; the plain burned steady and even and empty to the horizon, flat and desolate.

Where are you? If you want me, you must make yourself known. I have no weapons, but I will tear out your throat with my teeth, you yellow dog.

"I see you still harbor your bloodlust, that you want to kill anything that moves, even what is already dead by your murderous zeal."

Black Wolf stood and turned around and around in circles, searching for the owner of the voice that came to accuse him. A stagnant breeze lay its breathy hand against his face and chest, drying the sweat there, then moved on to leave behind boiling heat. *I am innocent of these charges! You led your people against my people. For this treachery, I could not let you live.*

"Even when you had been told I was to be spared?"

That was a mistake! My chief never should have asked it of his warriors. You brought war. You had to die.

The ghostly voice joined the wind to moan low over the shimmering blue mirages across the open plains. Black Wolf felt himself alone again. He did not know where to turn. Or how to survive. All he knew was that he was mad and had been transported into the other world. Or he was dead.

It would be best if he were dead.

■ ■ ■

The black drink took a day to prepare. Before it was ready, Changing Sky tried to get sips of water and elk broth down the sick man. Little of it stayed in his stomach. It ran from his slack mouth, and when he did swallow, it came dribbling out in little vomity patches where he lay with his head turned to the side so he would not strangle.

With the chief and high members of council sitting around the fire, smoking the ritual tobacco, Changing Sky propped the possessed warrior's back against his chest. He mumbled prayers to invoke the strong spirits of Deer and Elk and Bear to help him get the black drink past the warrior's throat. It took over an hour, and still half the drink was lost down the poor man's chest, running like rivulets of black mud to mingle with the dirt of the cabin floor.

It did not matter. It would not throw out this demon spirit that had hold of the young man. He would fight it off himself, in the dream-sleep, or he would die before long. His ribs poked against his skin like the ribs in the sides of starving dogs, his pallor grew more pronounced as the hours passed, and his eyes rolled back and forth, back and forth, behind loosely closed bluish lids.

It was late in the night before the black drink began to work. Black Wolf, lying again on the bear rugs by the fire, began to sweat, water rolling off him in sheets, and then he started to retch forth the black bile left behind in his stomach. Changing Sky motioned to the old men to leave the council cabin and leave them alone. If they protested, it was not until they were outside and beyond his hearing.

"I can do little more for you," he whispered to the convulsing husk writhing on the rugs. "I will keep you safe tonight, but tomorrow . . . tomorrow there will be a reckoning. Fight. Fight hard. Win over the monster in your dreams or he will carry you away."

He was no monster when he appeared. He was a giant treading the world, his head in the clouds, his feet shaking the very foundation of the land Black Wolf stood upon.

He bellowed and his cry blew away the sun.

Though sudden darkness rattled Black Wolf deep in his gut and took away his wind, he drew from a well of anger and said, *You will not defeat me! I am not a puny toad beneath your foot. I will not be moved. I will stand my ground until you release me from this bleak crater of emptiness.*

Without the sun to sheath the world, dark was more than a blanket, it was the inside of a mountain, it was Death wrapped around

Black Wolf on every side. Gone was the plain, the forsaken reaches, the hazy blue of the remote horizon.

"Come with me," the booming voice demanded. "Sacrifice yourself before me. Tear out your own throat and spill that cold murdering blood."

I WILL NOT.

"Then prepare to engage me, you sniveling red devil."

Changing Sky held down his charge by straddling him and placing his hands against his shoulders. There was bucking and a wild keening coming from Black Wolf's wide-open mouth. If Changing Sky could have reached it, he would have taken his spirit bag and shaken it at the room to keep the monsters from coming too near. He could feel them moving all around the cabin, circling in; he could smell their decaying spirits and hear their echoing crow caws trying to frighten him.

And he was frightened, though this was not something he ever admitted to the tribe. When monsters came for a person, they didn't care who might be in the way, they could take a man, even a medicine man, and throw him several feet into the air; they could rip the flesh off his bones even as he watched in horrified fascination; they could hold him in the coals of the sacred fire and burn out his eyes. Not to be frightened would be foolish in the extreme.

He began to chant. He called on his ancestors to help him. He felt them rallying, just at the periphery behind the circle of monsters, and he chanted louder, determined to bring them into the fray to protect him. To protect Black Wolf.

Before they were both lost.

"You didn't know I was master of black magic, did you?"

Black Wolf trembled, though he tried to hide that trembling by forcing his hands onto his waist, and spreading apart his legs in a stance of determination. *I do not know what this is, black magic,* he said. *It has no power over me for I do not believe it.*

"I don't believe in your Indian shaman, either, but even now he forces his way between us, trying to hold on to your mangy hide."

Black Wolf blinked in the ultimate darkness and reached out with his mind to feel for the help the giant said stood in the way. He could not feel it, could not see it, but it must be true or he would have already been snatched through the whirlpool of darkness and taken away to the nothing where the Master of Breath gathered the dead.

"I could swoop you up in the palm of my hand and dash you against the hidden sun if . . ."

Changing Sky felt needles of sweat sting his eyes. Smoke from the fire wove its way like a snake around his head and insinuated itself into his nostrils and mouth. He saw his ancestors, called from the Great Beyond where they were at rest, dueling with monsters he saw as clearly as he saw his own hands on Black Wolf's spasmodically jerking shoulders. There were his father and his mother, the papoose on her back with his little brother in it. There were his grandparents, wrinkled and bent, but staggering forward against the tide of evil spirits. There were people from the dead he did not recognize, perhaps his great-grandparents and his great-great-grandparents, all of them throwing up their hands and blocking the progress of things it was difficult to believe existed in the spirit world.

Some of the monsters were soot black and broken and shriveled. Some were the color of heaven, with eyes as large as their entire head shapes. Some were the amber of flame, their many-tentacled arms ending in talons longer than those of the eagle.

"Oh, Great Spirit!" Changing Sky cried out. "Help us now before it is too late."

Black Wolf went to his knees. He could not feel the earth beneath him. It was gone, just as the sun was gone, and the moon and the stars and the home of the people. He bowed his head. Above him loomed the giant. He could not see him, but he smelled his putrid breath and he heard his wild-wind breathing. What manner of man had he killed? Leader of his people, worker of magic, cruel and powerful. It was good he was dead. Yet even in death he was able to reach out and make his killer suffer horrors. *I defeat you,* he said. *I revile you. I place you lower than the beetle who shuffles through waste for its nightly meal.*

"Oh, do you?" the voice rumbled. "Do you think I cannot overcome your shaman? Do you think my magic less than that of your people? Watch while I swallow him whole and then I will grab you up and place you in my gullet along with him. Afterwards, I will spit the two of you out into the nether reaches, away from all that you know."

They were nibbling at his toes and gnawing at his elbows. Changing Sky saw it and tried to consider it an illusion, just another way to frighten him so he would let go of Black Wolf. But he felt it, and the first break in his skin that spewed blood caused him to scream out like a wildcat fallen into a pit, his head thrown back, the muscles of his throat cording, throbbing with his cry. "Beasts! Begone!"

His call caused the village guard dogs to howl. It brought the chief running and the council and half the village. They crowded into the cabin, but began to back out again, leaving a wide berth around where Changing Sky knelt on top of Black Wolf, holding him to the ground.

Startled whispers were exchanged. They could not see the invisible beings doing battle, but they said:

"Look, his feet—"

"And his arms—"

"There is blood on him—"

"Something just tore at his shoulder!"

"It is evil spirits."

Changing Sky rolled his eyes to heaven. A chunk of his flesh had been torn from the top of his shoulder where the bones met. Blood streamed down his arms. It welled and dripped from his bitten feet and calves. He knew that if he moved, if he deserted Black Wolf, the young warrior had no prayer of survival. He was in dream-sleep and unable to protect himself from this hungry onslaught. "Fight back, wherever you are," he commanded, leaning down into the grimacing face of Black Wolf. "Fight back or we both shall meet our master tonight."

Wails rose from the women outside the cabin. Wakened children began to cry. The dogs howled and leaped at the far moon. The men left inside pressed back against the log walls and they were either whimpering at a sight such as they had never seen or they prayed loudly for ancestors to come save the village. Even the chief had stepped back from the bloody mess near the fire and whispered incantations against whatever evil had found its way onto sacred ground.

Black Wolf heard someone tell him he must fight, that if he did not fight, they would both meet the master tonight. He knew this was the voice of truth. He knew he could not cower any longer, trembling and reeling from vertigo whenever he thought about the lost world under his feet, nothing there to support him in the blackness. He stood straight and turned his face up to where he had last heard the voice of the giant.

"I see you rise. Will you find a spear this time to thrust through my heart?"

I need no spear, he shouted. *I need only the strength of my people and the knowledge that you are an evil thing of the night.*

Even before he had finished speaking, Black Wolf lurched forward despite his fear of gravity and nothing to stand upon in the black void. He found he moved forward anyway, just as if he had been walking on land. He moved faster, tucked down his head, reached out his arms to wrestle whatever he found in the dark, be it giant or not. He was Cherokee. He was a mighty warrior. He had killed the leader of men who would shed the Cherokee blood and scatter the Cherokee nation. And he would do it again. This time he would finish it.

The giant's voice came close now, like a thunder against his ear. YOU DARE ATTACK ME WHEN I AM GOD IN THIS PLACE?

Black Wolf shut off his ears to what the giant had to say. It did not matter if this being was a god or if this was his kingdom. The life of this malign spirit must be destroyed before the shaman was killed and before Black Wolf could escape from the dreadful dark.

His head butted against thick, stinking flesh, hard flesh, flesh that yielded little. He wrapped his arms around it and dug in his fingers. *Die! Will you die?*

There was a rending of the void and once more the beam of light from the sun widened the crack until the light spilled over all the forsaken landscape. Black Wolf could see that the giant had shrunken. He was no longer as tall as the clouds and as large as the mountains. He was but a man again, the same man who stood on the battlefield with his long rifle aimed to take down a Cherokee when Black Wolf rushed him.

They wrestled and fell to the hardpan of the plain. The sun now beat blindly down, searing Black Wolf's eyes. He drew back his head and jerked it forward hard, knocking his enemy in the head. The white's skin broke and blood gushed instantly. Black Wolf ground his teeth, fury and the thrill of combat overriding every nerve of his body. He brought his hands up to the enemy's throat and there he clamped them, tightening with all his strength, grunting, being rolled over the sandy ground, the sun winking in and out over his enemy's shoulder as they flipped.

Changing Sky felt the change. Black Wolf was fighting. His face had taken on a hard, dead look and his eyes were not rolling in fear. The monsters occupying the small cabin were losing focus, disappearing one by one.

"Don't let up," he said to the warrior beneath his hands. "Fight him to the end."

■ ■ ■

As he squeezed the life from the marauding spirit who had terrorized him and held him prisoner, Black Wolf felt the world of the bright, shining plain shimmer and thin, the way a piece of cloth grows transparent when wet. His enemy's hands tried to tear him away from his grip, but Black Wolf would not let go now.

The world thinned even more. But the light remained. The sandy ground behind the spirit's back blurred and Black Wolf shook his head to clear his vision, thinking sweat was getting into his eyes, but as he did so he saw that all around them the land was gone and something else was creeping in to replace it. There were walls! Dark, sooty, rough-hewn log walls. And people. His people. It was the peace village where people lived who did not make war. Old men who must have been the peace chief's council members wore long faces and darted their eyes here and there, watching for a signal that they should flee.

He squeezed tighter, his arms aching with tension, his fingers digging deeper and deeper into the spirit man's throat, and suddenly, without the feeling of any movement whatever, Black Wolf found himself on his back, a medicine man looming over him, holding him down on a mat of bearskins near a sacred fire.

Black Wolf nearly wept with relief. He let his fingers fall loose. He blinked, wondering what was real and what was not. Had he overcome the white man's magic in that land of desolation and despair? Had he really?

"You have won." Changing Sky relaxed his grip and sank back on his heels. His blood still streamed and he must take care of that quickly, but he was so tired he didn't know if he would be capable of moving.

"I . . . I . . . dreamed . . ."

Changing Sky shook his head. "Do not speak of evil. I'll send a woman with food for you."

Two men came to help Changing Sky to his feet, and then led him outside the cabin into early-morning light the color of flint.

Black Wolf rolled onto his side and pressed one palm to the ground. Then he reached out and felt the heat from the fire. He ran his hand over the bear fur and buried his face in it.

It was good to be in the world of the people. If he must take sanctuary here in the peace village forever, he did not care. His time of war was great and now it was over.

Years later when he was an old man himself, wrapped in the skin of an elk and wearing the headdress made of feathers from the hawk, eagle, swan, and crane, he told young Cherokee who wanted to move south into Alabama about how some white men possessed black magic and were too hard to kill, even when they were dead. The more he told the tale, the less the younger generations believed it, but Black Wolf persisted, until his final day of breath, to warn his people against congress with the foreign invader.

He hated most that they would have to learn the lesson on their own and that they would not have Changing Sky to battle at their side. To fight monsters, the Cherokee needed not only shamen, but also the preservation of truth and memory.

The Woman Who Loved
a Bear

Jane Yolen

I t was early in the autumn, the leaves turning over yellow in the puzzling wind, that a woman of the Cheyennes and her father went to collect meat he had killed. They each rode a horse and led a pack horse behind, for the father had killed two fine antelopes and had left them, skinned and cut up and covered well with hide.

They didn't know that a party of Crows had found the cache and knew it for a Cheyenne kill by the hide covering it.

"We will wait for the hunter to come and collect his meat," they said. "We will get both a Cheyenne *and* his meat." It made them laugh at the thought.

And so it happened. The Cheyenne man and his daughter came innocently to the meat and the Crows charged down on them. The man was killed and his daughter was taken away as a prisoner, well to the north, to a village on the Sheep River which is now called the Big Horn.

Is that the end of the story, grandfather?

It is only the beginning. This is called The Woman Who Loved the Bear. I have not even come to the bear yet.

The man who carried the pipe of the Crow war party was named Fifth Man Over and he had two wives. But when he looked at the Cheyenne girl he thought that she was very fine looking and wanted her for his wife. Of course his two wives were both Crow women, which means they were ugly and hard. They were not pleased about the Cheyenne woman becoming his third wife. When they asked her name, she told them she was called "Walks with the Sun," so they called her "Flat Foot Walker." But they could call her what they wanted, it did not change the fact that she was beautiful and they were not.

So whenever Fifth Man Over was away from the lodge, they abused the Cheyenne girl. They hit her with quirts and sticks and stones till her arms and legs were bruised. But they were careful not to hit her in the face, where even Fifth Man Over would see and ask questions.

The days and weeks went by and the beautiful Cheyenne wife had to do all the hard work. She had to pack the wood and dress the hides; she had to make moccasins, not only for her Crow husband, but for his ugly wives as well.

Grandfather, I have heard this story before. I have seen a movie of it. It is called "Cinderella."

Is there a bear in "Cinderella"?

No, of course not.

Then you do not know this story. This is a true story, from the time when children played games suited to their years and spoke with respect to their grandfathers. You will listen carefully so that you may tell the story just as I tell it to you.

Now in Fifth Man Over's lodge there also lived a young man, about a year older than the Cheyenne woman, who was an Arapahoe and had been taken as a slave in a raid when he was a small child. He had the keeping and herding of Fifth Man Over's horses. He was not straight and tall like a Cheyenne, but limped because his left foot had been burned in the raid that made him a slave. But he had a strong nose and straight black hair and he spoke softly to the Cheyenne woman.

"These women abuse you," he said. "You must not let them do so."

"I cannot do otherwise," Walks with the Sun answered. "They are my husband's elder wives." It was the proper answer, but she was a Cheyenne woman and they were only Crows, and so she said it through set teeth.

"Make many moccasins," the Arapahoe told her. "Many more than are needed. Hide some away for yourself."

"Why should I do this?" she asked.

"Because you will need them on the trail back to your people."

She looked straight in his face and saw that there was no deceit there. She did not look at his crooked leg.

"You will wear out many moccasins on the trail," he said.

■ ■ ■

When does the bear come in, grandfather?

Soon.

How soon?

Soon enough. It is not time to cut this story off. Listen. You will have to tell it back to me, you know.

Walks with the Sun made many moccasins and for every three she made, she hid one away. This took her through winter and into the spring when the snow melted and the first flowers appeared down by the river bank.

"We will go in the morning for the buffalo," said Fifth Man Over to his wives. By this he meant he would ride a horse and they would come behind with the pack horse pulling the travois sled.

"She should not come with us," said his first wife, pointing to Walks with the Sun. "She is a Cheyenne and has no stamina and will not be able to keep up and will want more than her share of the meat."

"And she is ugly," said the second wife, but she did not say it very loud.

"I will stay home, my husband," said Walks with the Sun, "and make the lodge ready for your return."

"And you will not break any of the pots we have worked so hard on," said the first wife.

"And you will not eat anything till we come back," said the second wife.

With all this Walks with the Sun agreed, though she would have loved to see the buffalo in their great herds and the men on their horses charging down on the bulls, even though they were Crow and not Cheyenne. She had heard that the sound of the buffalo running was like thunder on the great open plain, that it was a music that made the grasses dance. But she kept her head bent and her eyes modestly down.

So Fifth Man Over and his two wives and most of the other hunters and their wives left to go after the buffalo. And the Arapahoe went, too, for he was to take care of the horses along the way.

Grandfather, a buffalo is not a bear, and you promised.

There will be a bear.

Buffalo do not eat bear. Bear eat buffalo. I prefer the bear.

There will be a bear.

There had better be.

■ ■ ■

But the young man returned the long way around, leaving his own horse in the timber outside of the camp. He came limping into the Crow village and the old people said to him, "Why are you here? What has happened to the people?" By this they meant the Crows.

"Nothing has happened to the people. They are following the buffalo. But my horse threw me and ran away and I have come back for another." He went to Fifth Man Over's lodge and saddled another horse and put two fine blankets on it, but not the best, because he was a slave after all. But before he mounted up, he went into the lodge and said to Walks with the Sun, "Now is your time. I have hidden my own horse in the timber down by the creek. You must take a large pot and go down as if for water and you will find it there. Put your extra moccasins in the pot, for should you lose the horse, you will surely need them."

"What of you?" asked Walks with the Sun. "Surely you want to leave here."

"I have no other home," he answered.

"Then you shall come home with me," she said.

"I am poor and I have a bad leg and I am not a Cheyenne," he said. "But I will watch out for you, never fear."

He rode away, but in a different direction from the creek, so that no one would suspect that the two of them had spoken. And Walks with the Sun did as he instructed. Taking a large pot, she put the moccasins in. Then she went to the creek. There she found the horse, saddled, with two blankets. Swinging herself up into the saddle, she began to ride south, towards her home.

I am still waiting, grandfather.

Patience is a good thing in the young.

I am *not* patient. I am impatient.

I did not notice. The bear, though, is coming. In fact, grandson, the bear is here.

Here? Where?

In the story. But you cannot see it unless you listen.

I see with my eyes. I hear with my ears, grandfather.

You must do both, child. You must do both.

Walks with the Sun rode many miles until both she and the horse were tired. So she got off, unsaddled it, and let the horse feed on the new spring grass. Then she resaddled the horse and rode another long time, past the Pumpkin Buttes. There she made camp, but without a fire in case anyone should be looking for her.

In the middle of the night she awoke because of a huffing and snuffling sound and the horse got frightened and screamed like a white woman in labor, and broke its rope. It ran off not to be found again.

And there, near here, with the moonlight on its back, was . . .

The bear, grandfather.
The bear, grandson.

Walks with the Sun spoke softly to the bear, not out of honor but out of fear. "Oh, Bear," she said, "take pity on me. I am only a poor Cheyenne woman and I am trying to get back to my own people." And then, quietly, carefully, she pulled on a pair of moccasins and stood. Carrying several more pairs in each hand, she backed away from the bear. When she could no longer see the great beast, she turned around and ran.

She ran until she was exhausted and then she turned and looked behind her. There was the bear, just a little way behind. So, taking a deep breath, she ran again until she could barely put one foot in front of the other. When she turned to look again, the bear was still there.

At last she was so tired that she knew she must rest, even if the bear was to kill her. She sat down on a hollow log, and fell asleep sitting up, heedless of the bear.

While she slept, she heard the bear speak to her. His voice was like the rocks in a river, with the water rushing over. He said: "Get up and go to your people. I am watching to protect you. I am stepping in your tracks so that the Crows cannot trail you, so that Fifth Man Over and his ugly wives cannot find you."

When Walks with the Sun awoke, it was still dark. The bear was squatting on its haunches not far from her, its head crowned with the stars. Awake, she did not think he could have spoken, so she was still afraid of him.

She rose carefully, put on new moccasins, and began her journey again, but this time she did not run. She walked on until she could walk no longer. Then she lay down under a tree and slept.

You said he spoke in a dream, grandfather.
I said he spoke while she slept, grandson.

Is that the same as *really* speaking?

You are sitting with me on the buffalo-calf robe. Do you need to ask such questions?

In the morning Walks with the Sun awoke and saw the bear a little ways off on top of a small butte. It did not seem to be looking at her but when she started to walk, it followed again in her tracks.

So it went all the day, till she reached the Platte River. Since this was early spring, the waters were full from bank to bank. Walks with the Sun had no idea how she could get across.

She sighed out loud but said nothing else. At the sound, the bear came over to her, looked in her face and his breath was hot and foul-smelling. Then he turned his back to her and stuck his great rear in her face. By this she knew that he wanted her to get on his back.

"Bear," she said, "if you are willing to take me across the river, I am willing to ride." And she crawled on his back and put her arms around his neck, just in front of his mighty shoulders.

With a snort, he plunged into the water.

The water was cold. She could feel it through her leggings. And the river tumbled strongly over its rocky bed. But stronger still was the bear and he swam across with ease.

When they got to the other side, the bear waited while she dismounted, then he shook himself all over, scattering water on every leaf and stone. Then he rolled on the ground.

While he was rolling, Walks with the Sun started on. When she looked back, the bear was following her just as he had before.

So it went for many days, the Cheyenne woman walking, the bear coming along behind. When she was hungry, he caught a young buffalo calf and killed it. She skinned it, cut it into pieces, took her flint and made a fire, then cooked the meat. Some of it she ate, and some she gave to the bear. The rest she rolled in the skin, making a pack which she carried on her back.

Did she feed him by hand, grandfather?

By hand?

Did she hold out pieces for him to eat?

That would be foolish, indeed, grandson. He could have taken her hand off at the wrist and not even noticed. Where do you young people come up with such foolish ideas, heh?

Then how did she feed the bear?

She put it down on the ground a little way from her and the bear walked up and ate it.

Oh.

They came at last to the Laramie River and below was a big village, with so many lodges they covered the entire bank.

"I do not know if those are my people or not," Walks with the Sun said. "Can you go and find out for me?"

The bear went up close to the outermost lodge, but someone saw him and shouted and someone else, an old man whose hand was not so steady, shot an arrow at him. The arrow pierced his left hind foot and he ran back to Walks with the Sun, limping.

"Oh, Bear," she cried, "you are hurt and it is all my fault." She knelt down and pulled the arrow from his foot and stopped the bleeding with the heel of her hand.

When the people tracked the blood trail to them, she was still sitting there, holding the bear in her arms. Only he was no longer a bear, but a young man with a strong nose and straight black hair and a left foot that was not quite straight.

The bear turned into the Arapahoe slave, grandfather?

That is not what I said, grandson.

But I thought you said . . .

Listen, grandson, listen.

Walks with the Sun took the buffalo hide, shook it out, and turned it so the hair side was outward. Then she wrapped the Arapahoe in it to show he was a medicine man. Her people put great strings of beads around his neck and gave him feathers to honor him. Then they lifted him onto a travois sled and, pulling it themselves, brought him into the village.

He never walked as a bear again, except twice, when the people were threatened by Crows. Walks with the Sun became his wife and they had many children and many grandchildren, of which I am one, and you are another. The buffalo hide we are sitting on today is the very one of which I have spoken.

Is that a true story, grandfather?

It is a true story, grandson.

But how can it be true, grandfather? People can't turn into bears. Bears can't turn into people.

Heh. They do not do so today. But we are speaking of the time when the Cheyenne were a great nation and still in the north, when the land was covered with buffalo, and we passed the medicine arrows and buffalo hat from keeper to keeper.

And the buffalo hide, grandfather?

And the buffalo hide, grandson. This ties it off.

What does that mean?

That storytelling is over for the night. That it is time for children to ask no more questions but to sleep. For old men to dream by the fire.

This ties it off, grandfather.

Author's Note:

This story is based loosely on the Cheyenne Mystery Story "The Bear Helper," as retold by George Bird Grinnell in *By Cheyenne Campfires* (University of Nebraska Press, 1971).

Downstream

Man Who Bleeds Tears

R. K. Partain

W hen you lose your name, you become small. When you lose your spirit, you become nothing.

Man Who Bleeds Tears stood in knee-high grass on the knoll that overlooked the burning village. His dark eyes were damp, but whether from the constant wind or from the unrelenting sadness in his bones, he would not decide. His people were gone. Mothers and fathers, children, old people. They lay dead before him in the places where they had fallen, their brown limbs leaking red. Even the dogs had been killed, massacred. He, too, would have died, he knew, had he not been hunting and away from the sprawling village.

Summer dwellings, *ge-tsa'di,* boxlike, made of thick posts swaddled with twigs like baskets covered in clay, burned in great fires. The adjacent winter homes, *a-si',* cone-shaped, some thirty feet in diameter at the base and fifteen feet high, burned with equal passion.

He wished he were dead.

Dead was better than this.

He and the chestnut mare at his side began the long walk home.

Past carefully tended fields of corn and beans and squash, he made his way, heart thrumming harder and harder with each painful step. Two chickens, sole survivors, cackled at his approach and ran away, wings flapping, disturbing the eerie silence of this summer afternoon.

Teeth met teeth in a feeble attempt to keep his scream inside his mouth as he saw the first of them close up.

Say no names, Wind Spirit warned him.

"No names," Man Who Bleeds Tears repeated quietly.

The broken body at his feet belonged to a young boy. No more than ten, this small, dead treasure. His thin chest was painted in blood, punctured. Three times? It was hard to tell. Too hard to tell.

Man Who Bleeds Tears shivered in the bright sunlight as he wondered what this child's last thoughts had been. Had he longed for the safety of his mother's arms? The white path. Or had he stood bravely before his killer, defying the inevitable? The red path.

Did he know Death was upon him?

Eyes as shiny as water-polished stones stared back at Man Who Bleeds Tears.

The boy knew, Wind Spirit moaned. *They all knew.*

Man Who Bleeds Tears forced his unsteady gaze from the boy and looked instead at the larger picture of ruin. Homes smoldered, gray and black smoke rose like confused snakes toward the Sky Land. Bodies. Lifeless. Everywhere. Some burning, flames having caught their clothing. There had been more than two hundred people in this village when he had left three days ago.

His wife was here. Somewhere.

His mother's brother would be here also. The man who, in the ancient tradition of the Cherokee, had raised him from a child, taught him all he knew about hunting, living, dying. Laws.

He looked for the *uku,* the leader of the village, and did not see him. He, too, would be lying in this horror somewhere, Man Who Bleeds Tears knew. Behind the *uku's* house was buried the war hatchet, symbolizing that this village was at peace with its neighbors. Man Who Bleeds Tears should go and dig up the hatchet. Use it to slay the guilty.

He glanced at the end of the village where the *uku's* house stood burning. His gaze snagged something before reaching its intended goal.

Say no names.

A pregnant woman lay in the path, her swollen belly firm and round like a small mound of fertile soil.

The mingled smell of blood and smoke overtook his senses. He wavered. In defiance, he drew in a deep breath.

And his feet were running before he could stop them. Faster. Faster. His hand found his knife, withdrew it before he reached the woman.

Knees slammed into hard-packed dirt.

Tears welled up in his stinging eyes as he tore the woman's shirt away from her cold belly.

. . . *no,* Wind Spirit sighed.

Man Who Bleeds Tears ignored the small plea and drew his blade across the woman's stomach. No blood seeped out from the wound. He could hardly see now, his hands frantic as they searched the cavity.

There! He had the child.

Carefully he pulled the baby from the womb. Slick black hair plastered to a reddened face. Eyes closed. Fists clenched. Dead.

Man Who Bleeds Tears groaned heavily as he clutched the lost future of his tribe to his breast. He was alone now. The last one. Later he lowered the child, a girl, to her mother's arms.

He stood up, wiped his face. The whisper of flame was the only sound he heard now. Even the small river running to the east of the village had lost its incessant voice. Beyond the river, lush hills of green and brown loomed. Hunting grounds. Holy grounds.

Man Who Bleeds Tears knelt at the woman's side and took her small hand into his own. As was their custom, he shook it solemnly, spoke a sad farewell, and stood slowly.

He turned around, ashamed of himself for being so weak, unable, now, to go farther into the village. He would come back. Later. After he had had time to pray for guidance. For strength. He would return and clean the dead, dig the graves, bid farewells. Find his wife. Kiss her lips one last time. Lower her broken body into the . . .

His scream shattered the brittle silence and sent birds flying. Animals ran for cover. The air trembled.

Harmony would be restored! Fulfilling the Blood Law became his sole purpose as his torn heart led him out of the killing grounds.

He followed the slow-moving river. Thick woods of green leaf and gray bark flanked both sides of the muddied water. He walked until the sun was low in the sky, his horse trailing patiently behind him. He came to a place he had known for many years, although he had not visited since his marriage four summers ago.

This place was sacred, or so his mother's brother had told him when he was just a boy and visiting for the first time. Magic could be done here.

It was at the confluence of the great river and a small stream. Clear water from the mountains flowed down the stream and entered the river. Joy came from the stream. It was joining its mother once again.

Man Who Bleeds Tears removed his wooden saddle from the mare and tossed it to the soft, sandy ground. The blanket his wife had made him came off next. This he tossed over his shoulder. Taking his bow, ten arrows, and his knife, he slapped the mare; it ran off down the river. Man Who Bleeds Tears scanned the horizon. Purple skies, laced with pink and ocher. His family on the long march to join the Sky People.

Seven clans of Cherokee: Wild Potato, Bird, Long Hair, Blue, Paint, Deer, Wolf. There had been members of each clan in the village. His own, Wolf *(ani wayah),* had been the largest of the seven. Blood Law required him to restore harmony by killing those who had killed. Substitutes were allowed.

But who had killed them?

Shawnee?

Maybe.

The white-faced intruders?

He'd heard stories of white men killing people for land, for gold, for nothing. There had been talk of a white warrior, Evan Shelby, leader of a large army, who had destroyed the five villages Dragging Canoe had settled.

Who had committed this atrocity?

Who would do such a horrible thing?

He did not know.

He turned from the river and walked into the darkening woods. Not far in, a bramble of mulberry vines hindered his path. Swiping them away with his arm, he entered the small holy place hidden behind.

Night came upon him slowly. He longed for the darkness. The blanket of solace.

You must obey the Blood Law. It was the voice of his mother's brother. Soft, comforting, save for the words he brought.

"But how? Who?"

He sat in a small clearing, not large enough for a man to lie down across. Thick vines and small trees had created a nearly impenetrable wall surrounding him. In the center of the roughly circular area stood an odd-shaped rock. Granite. Petroglyphs, markings in the stone, some older than time, he supposed, were hidden under the darkness. His fingers traced them as he remembered their shapes in his mind. The snake; the bent tree; the name of a baby girl he had never known. Others, too, some of them now mysteries, their meanings lost forever.

The rock was comfort.

The rock was strong.

And it was wise.

"What should I do?" he asked the spirit of the rock.

You cannot kill everyone, he replied.

Man Who Bleeds Tears nodded. He *had* entertained the thought of killing as many as he could get his hands on—anyone, it didn't matter. But to kill wantonly would make him one of the murderers he was obliged to find.

"How do I find these dogs, these killers?" he asked bitterly.

Find the ones with bloody hands.

"Hands can be washed."

That is true.

Man Who Bleeds Tears sat back on his haunches. "Hands can be washed, but not hearts, not spirits. Innocent blood has stained them this day."

He closed his eyes and was immediately flooded with scenes of a happier time. The great ball field to the west of the village, filled with cheering men and women as a group of sixty men played *anetsa*. He remembered the feel of the heavy stick in his hands, his strong legs pounding down the field, the fur-covered ball out in front of him, a horde of rivals stampeding behind him. Sticks, shoulders, even fists were fair in this game. Many a man had been carried off the playing field bleeding that day, some badly.

Whap! And the ball sailed for the goalposts. In between the two sticks.

That point had won the game, which had started two days earlier in conjunction with the Green Corn Dance, the annual celebration of the ripening corn.

Coming back to his pain, Man Who Bleeds Tears felt several rolling down his face. They dropped off his chin, only to burn his naked thigh. He wiped his face harshly. "No tears!"

He will need help with this, his mother's brother said to the spirit of the rock.

Yes, the spirit of the rock replied.

Man Who Bleeds Tears closed his stinging eyes again and focused his will toward the quiet conversation taking place all around him.

We cannot tell you who did this, mother's brother said sullenly.

I know.

"You can tell me," Man Who Bleeds Tears whispered into the night. "I will find justice."

There followed a long silence in which it seemed all three were in deep thought. The spirit of the rock broke the spell.

The spirits of your people cannot help you with this quest. I will speak with Eagle. Perhaps he will help us.

Mother's brother said thank you many times and then departed after telling his sister's son to be brave, true, and patient.

Man Who Bleeds Tears promised he would be all that and more.

Go to the river and wait, the spirit of the rock said. *If Eagle will come, I will send him to you there.*

"Thank you, Father Rock. I will wait as long as it takes."

I cannot promise that he will come. Paint your body black and red, the colors of war. If he comes, you must be ready.

"I will be." He placed five of his arrows and his blanket on the stone as offerings and gained his feet. He made his way back to the river and found his saddle where he had dropped it in the sand. He had made this saddle many years ago from white oak boards and fresh buffalo hides. It was a fine saddle and had served him well. He dug through a side pouch and found his paint. Black and red. Mother's brother had told him long ago to keep his paint close at all times.

Standing in silver moonlight, he removed his hunting shirt, revealing the tattoo of the sun in the center of his chest. Other, smaller tattoos adorned his dark skin. His name was written over his right breast. His accomplishments in battle were etched on his arms. Fine, graceful lines of great artistry detailed his history. He gazed up at the full moon, arms at his sides, head raised, and said a silent prayer for his people and for his own courage.

A screech owl delivered the prayer with a ghostly hoot.

Man Who Bleeds Tears knelt and began the long, slow process of painting his body.

By the time Eagle arrived, Man Who Bleeds Tears had painted his body in alternating stripes of black and red. The only part not covered was his back, which he could not reach. The six-inch-wide bands of paint were drawn diagonally, starting at his forehead with deep crimson red, the bottom of his face covered in black. Neck red. Chest black first, then red, then black. And downward to his bare feet, the slanting lines depicting the speed he wished to find on this journey.

Somewhere in that time a small yet bright fire had begun to burn in his eyes. He stood, wearing only his leather flap and his knife, when the great bird appeared.

Eagle circled high above him, wings outstretched. The bird was as large as a house, and his white head shone against the dark sky. Black eyes stared down.

"No fear," Man Who Bleeds Tears whispered softly to himself as the great bird turned gracefully and swooped down. The sleek dive was silent. Not even the stilled air was disturbed as Eagle landed.

"Spirit of the rock has asked me to help you," Eagle said, his eyes flickering constantly, on the lookout.

"Do you know what happened?"

Eagle nodded. "I saw the carnage. I did not see the act. What do you want from me?"

"Take me through the skies, show me who did this to my people."

Eagle considered him for several moments and then turned his back on him. "We will try."

Man Who Bleeds Tears climbed onto the soft, warm back of the eagle and held on to feathers as large as canoes. Eagle lifted his massive wings and became one with the sky.

Man Who Bleeds Tears watched in awe as the ground fell away from him. His grip tightened; fear tried to steal into his pounding heart. He forced it back. Cold, silent wind brought bumps to his flesh, black hair streamed behind his head.

The river became a black ribbon. Trees became sticks. Mountains became hills. And hills disappeared altogether.

"What are we looking for?" Eagle cried over his shoulder.

"Justice," Man Who Bleeds Tears screamed, the word barely breaking through the howling wind.

Eagle grinned. "Justice is hard to find, my brave friend. We must narrow this down some. We will ask Moon for his help." Eagle did not wait for a response. He turned his wings sharply to the right, flapped them once, and rose suddenly.

Man Who Bleeds Tears found it hard to breath as he and Eagle soared higher and higher into the night. A large, billowing cloud floated ahead of them. Eagle cawed once, folded back his wings, and cut smoothly into it. Man Who Bleeds Tears released his right hand and tried to catch some of the cloud. Like the breath of a ghost, it passed through his fingers; he smiled for the first time that day.

As suddenly as they had entered the misty realm of cloud, they broke through the other side. Bright moonlight lay atop the shadowy hills and valleys of several other clouds, giving Man Who Bleeds Tears the impression that he might actually be able to walk across them.

Eagle continued upward.

At the edge of darkness, Eagle began a slow circling motion. As was the custom, he gave out three sharp yells to announce their presence.

Moon answered, "Hello, Eagle. What have you there on your back?"

"This is Man Who Bleeds Tears. He is in need of our help."

Moon's deep voice carried sympathy with it. "Yes, I know. Sun saw the act, but she will not speak of it. Not even to me."

"Will you light a way for us?" Man Who Bleeds Tears asked.

"Light a way to what?" Moon replied.

"To the killers. To the ones who did this."

"I cannot light the way to mystery. I will show you the way home, though," he offered.

Eagle's back shivered, feathers ruffled. "He must obey the Blood Law! He cannot go home until justice is satisfied."

"I have no home," Man Who Bleeds Tear added quickly.

"That is not true," Moon replied patiently. "You may go to any village, and they will take you in. You are of the *ani wayah* clan, are you not?" He didn't wait for a reply. "There are many in the Wolf clan. You have many family members. Go to them. They would have come to you had the fates been reversed."

"He must obey the Blood Law," Eagle said again, this time sternly.

"Yes, I suppose he must." Moon fell silent for a few moments. Eagle and Man Who Bleeds Tears continued in their great circle.

Finally, Moon said, "I cannot help you, but perhaps Morning Star can. She may have seen something that can lead you toward the right path."

"I cannot go to Morning Star!" Eagle said loudly. "This is as far as I can go."

"I know," Moon said softly. "Man Who Bleeds Tears, are you determined to follow this path?"

"Yes!"

"Then you will have to wait here for Morning Star. Eagle can come back for you later."

Moon slid a long, silver ray out toward his flying visitors. "Come."

Man Who Bleeds Tears studied the shimmering ribbon of light; he could see through it. He would fall through if he stood on it. He was sure of that.

Eagle spoke: "Fear will kill you slower than the fall."

He was right. "Thank you, Eagle," Man Who Bleeds Tears said as he swung his leg over the bird's back and stepped off onto the moon ray. "I have only my knife to offer as a gift."

"Find harmony, that is reward enough," Eagle said, and then disappeared suddenly into the clouds.

Man Who Bleeds Tears stood, nearly frozen with concern, as he watched the great bird depart. He was afraid to move too suddenly.

"I will not let you go," Moon said gently. "Too many have been let go as it is." His voice shook with sadness, Man Who Bleeds Tears thought.

"I will summon Morning Star. It will take her some time to get here. Rest easy now. She won't be long."

Moon's face seemed to dim as if he'd left, yet Man Who Bleeds Tears could still see his pocked countenance. He bent his knees and slowly sat, drawing his legs under himself.

As he waited, surrounded by cold blue night and silent, passing clouds, he thought of what Moon had said earlier. About going to another village. Starting over.

He, like all Cherokee, took his clanship at birth from his mother's clan. There was no such thing as a Cherokee orphan. It could not be. He could go to any village of Cherokee and be addressed as brother. They would welcome him, treat him well, and protect him, if need be.

Then why did he feel so alone?

He missed his wife, for one. Since the grisly discovery he had fought hard to keep her image out of his mind. Had tried even harder to not think of the pain she must have gone through. The sudden fear flooding through her. Her frantic eyes searching for her husband, the man sworn to protect her. The man who was not there when she needed him most.

"Forgive me," he moaned into the night, his eyes misting again.

"Man Who Bleeds Tears?" The gentle voice came from everywhere; it sounded like the tinkling of small bells. He turned and saw Morning Star behind him. She was radiant. White and glowing and warm.

"Yes," he said, standing.

"Come with me." She offered her own beam of pure light for him to stand upon.

"Morning Star will take good care of you," Moon said, his face brightening. "She is very kind."

"Thank you, Moon, for what you have done," Man Who Bleeds Tears said, stepping onto Morning Star's beam. "I have only my knife to offer as a gift."

Moon's face twisted slightly. "Don't thank me yet. It is not finished."

Man Who Bleeds Tears wondered about that statement for a second, but then dismissed it as Morning Star brought him closer to her.

Her exquisite brightness seemed to shine into his flesh, into his bones, even into his tortured soul. She was Woman. The essence of Female. For the first time that day, he felt warm.

"We will look," she said as he stepped off the beam and onto her radiant sphere of hope.

He felt only the faintest sensation of movement as they began traveling west. Through scattered clouds he saw Mother Earth grow smaller and smaller until she was no larger than a stone he might easily hold in his hand.

"Your wife has forgiven you," Morning Star said simply, her voice as sweet as honeysuckle.

His heart ached a little less with the knowledge.

Sun exploded out from behind the far side of the world. Morning Star bid her a good day. Man Who Bleeds Tears screamed painfully, his hands flying to his eyes.

Too late.

Morning Star moved herself out of the Sun's rays and asked, "Are you all right?"

Man Who Bleeds Tears removed his hands from his eyes and opened his eyelids. Nothing. He closed his eyes again and saw a perfect picture of Sun etched inside the black holes.

"I am blind," he said, defeated.

He felt Morning Star's love for him rise up from under his feet and caress him. "I am sorry," she said mournfully. "I did not know Sun's light would hurt you."

"What do I do now? How can I fight when I cannot see!" He fell to his knees, dead eyes scanning the universe.

"This is my fault," she said. "I have done this to you."

"No, it is no one's fault." His hand found his knife. He would plunge it into his chest, end this awful journey, and argue with the gods, if need be, that he tried. Tried but failed.

Morning Star stopped him. "No, do not do that. I will make you into light. Light that can search until the spirits are appeased and justice is found."

"But how can I find justice if I cannot see?"

"You will see."

Yaktu and his son waited for the booming plane to pass overhead. The night sky was clear and bright; stars filled every inch of the velvet blanket.

"There he is!" Yaktu said to his son of eight. He pointed skyward, his finger directed at the comet streaking across the black horizon. "That is Man Who Bleeds Tears."

"What does he do?" the boy asked, his eyes filled with wonder.

"He seeks justice. But he will not find it."

"Why not?" the boy asked, glancing up at his father.

"It's too late. The guilty are dead now, their spirits gone from this earth. He cannot find them. But he continues to search. He was the last, you see. He must search." Yaktu placed his hand on his son's head. "Do you understand?"

The boy shook his head.

Yaktu smiled warmly. "That's all right, you are young still. Remember this, though, as he pursues the guilty, he also watches over the innocent. When you feel alone, empty, when you feel there is no use in going on, seek him. He will listen. And maybe that's what he does best. He reminds us that we are never alone. Come, I will tell you his story."

They began the long walk home. Yaktu slipped his hands into his pants pockets. "Man Who Bleeds Tears stood in knee-high grass . . ."

The Bison Riders

Brad Linaweaver

John didn't care that the toothless old woman was probably out of her mind. He believed the gods to be frugal in their fashion and so much magical ability had been granted this poor woman that she would naturally prove deficient in other areas. What mattered was that her spirit eye was always open, and she was willing to share her visions. He smiled at her wizened face that seemed to float in the greasy smoke rising from her little clay pot that hung over a modest fire.

Maybe the woman could answer his questions and put his soul at ease. If she really had psychic powers she would know that his father wouldn't approve of John's stepping foot on any reservation, much less giving credence to the superstitions peddled by an old woman. From earliest memory John had been told that he was an American first and not to be overly concerned with his Amerind heritage. He'd never thought much about such things until he went to college and met members of a radical political group.

"You're *not* John," one of his new friends had told him. "That's a white man's name. Why don't you show pride and take your real name?"

"But I don't even know my tribe," he tried to explain. "I mean, I have a pretty good idea of which tribes I could claim. . . ." A grimly efficient anthropology student, he had started to construct a possible past. So intent was he on the details of his own lineage that he failed to notice that the young man in front of him was at least seventy percent European in contrast to John's largely Native American physiognomy.

"You're missing the point," said John's interlocutor. "I am Hawk Above the Clouds." Gesturing at the blond coed wrapped around his arm, the young man added, "My friend hasn't chosen her new name yet, but she will."

John admired the woman's strong blue eyes, thought about the situation for a moment, and shook his head in confusion. As if sensing this, she told him, "Oh, it's all right. I'm a Wiccan. We join our red sisters, and brothers, in respecting Nature."

Her boyfriend winced at her choice of words, but to John this seemed a welcome change of subject. Her mentioning of Nature opened a door in him. Suddenly he was talking to her with a greater enthusiasm than he had intended. He told her of how he had spent the previous summer on a dig in one of his favorite regions. He described arriving by jeep through a pine forest, and enjoying the morning-fresh fragrance before venturing out into the flat vastness of the surrounding desert. He told her about the cedars that came after the pines; and the blue-gray mountains on a horizon that seemed to beckon him out into the deep desert, as full of smells and sights and sounds as the woods had been, but more subtle in presentation. She must have noticed how his smile grew and his face turned up almost in ecstasy as he remembered the sand dunes, and the bright colors of red and gold where rock and clay met, and the fierce wind that scoured the otherworldly terrain. He finished with a few words about the sudden storms and the beauty that had clutched his heart.

She had seemed to be listening, nodding now and again at appropriate moments. But when he had spent himself, she simply blinked her perfect blue eyes and said, "What do you think about the tropical rain forest?"

He had never been to the rain forest, never been in South America at all. Neither had she. The conversation meandered down a winding tributary of statistics that neither of them could possibly know firsthand, and then drowned in a lagoon of soggy anticapitalist rhetoric.

John would see a lot more of this duo in ensuing months, as well as other members of their small but vocal organization, NAME (Native American Mobilization Effort). He didn't take NAME seriously at first. His favorite anthropology professor, Dr. Frederick Rae, was a master of sarcasm, especially where student activists were concerned. NAME was made to order for this teacher's brand of wit.

The first time John had met the leader of the organization was when Gray Bear Walking audited Rae's class. The professor was up to the challenge, beginning his first session of the quarter, the way he always did, by shooting a dart into the back wall from his South American blowgun. This got everyone's attention. "You need to learn about tools and weapons before you make up endless kinship charts," he liked to say. He was making his favorite point against armchair anthropologists who never get anywhere near a helping of long-pork, when he noticed the president of NAME in the back row. The professor added a few choice words about xenophobia and ethnocentricism.

soggy antici ipa tion

"White man's rules," came the low, steady voice out of the lean, brown body of Gray Bear Walking.

"And what about science?" Rae wanted to know.

"No such thing," was the reply, as cold as an abandoned campsite. "You want to kill our pride." The professor had smiled at the young man's gift for demagoguery, and moved on. But after class John felt he had to confront the student leader, whose real name was hard to find.

"You can't deny the quest for objectivity," John had said.

"What do you know about quests," the other said, "when you won't even undertake to find out who you are? I pay no heed until you find your true self."

Those words had burned themselves down deep where dreams live. John started dreaming himself into canoes and moccasins; into tepees where the young wife always enters after the husband; into war dances and mortifications of the flesh and staring at the sun until the brain grows hot . . . and you wake up.

Strangely, the people he was meeting through NAME seemed indifferent about any discussions concerning his visions. They were organizing a protest against the university's traditional Indian symbol for the football team. John wouldn't be available to help. He had a vision quest waiting.

A full day and night of driving had brought him to stand before the old woman in her wickiup. As she fussed over her little pot of foulsmelling medicine brew, he reflected on the unlikelihood that Gray Bear Walking had ever heard of her. John had learned about the woman through Professor Rae, always reliable when it came to locating Native American curiosities. (His collection of artifacts ranged from as far north as Canada and as far south as Peru.)

"Tell me your spirit beast!" the old woman cried out, bringing John out of his reverie with promise of greater reveries to come. She enunciated pretty well, he thought, for a toothless hag.

"I don't understand," he answered lamely.

"The animal meant for you," she said, her voice a dull roar in his ears. "If you would journey on the great river, Turtle Father must speak to your spirit self."

"I need you to help me find out, I guess."

"No!" she almost screamed. "You must know first. First! Is it bear? Eagle? Wolf? Serpent? You must tell me." As she harangued him, a thin line of spittle traced its way down her wrinkled chin. The smoke surrounding her head made it seem larger and bulkier, rounder; and peering from the center of that cloud were two red-coal eyes, burning. He recoiled as if from a physical blow. He knew his

Sucking vertigo

animal spirit at last, something thundering across a thousand leagues of dry prairie, exploding out of the dead past with an almost unbearable force of life: the buffalo, the bison.

He told her. She nodded. "We are ready to send you to other self."

"Into the past," he said, sitting cross-legged on the ground.

"No," she answered. "Not this world's past, but your true self's past." He didn't have a clue what she meant, but he figured he would be finding out if he had the courage to drink the horrid brown mixture she was even now offering him from a large wooden spoon. He hoped the brown lumps floating on the surface were nothing worse than mushrooms.

The taste was something like a curry that had gone bad. But he was able to keep it down. He didn't have to wait long for what he assumed were the hallucinations. First there was a burning sensation in his eyes. Naturally he closed them—and experienced acute vertigo. He was having trouble breathing until he was distracted by the not entirely unpleasant experience of something wet sucking its way up his spinal cord until it reached the brain . . . and gobbled it whole.

When he blinked his eyes back into some kind of focus, he was outside . . . in the middle of a great, flat prairie . . . with dry grass whispering in a breeze that wasn't nearly cool enough. He was sitting astride something he assumed to be a horse, but he wasn't fully conscious of the situation and there seemed to be a slight haze surrounding everything. His sense of smell was not impaired, even if he would have liked to avoid the thick odor hanging in the air as if a hundred old carpets had been soaked and then left out to dry in the sun.

"Far Seeing Eye," a voice addressed him, "your father still misses the old ways."

John hesitated as if realizing that the moment he turned his head he would be committed to accept as reality whatever presented itself. He looked. An Indian dressed in the full panoply of war, and with bright warpaint highlighting his scarred features, grinned at him, his head held high against an empty blue sky. The old woman was certainly earning the few dollars John had forced into her gnarled hand. Why, the hallucination was so convincing that John seemed to be comprehending an alien tongue. Although he was studying Native American languages, this one was unknown to him.

Unknown . . . except part of him *did* know it; and he realized that he could speak the language as well. His companion continued speaking: "There's no denying your father was good at the old tricks. My mother says your father was the best at putting on a white wolf's skin and sneaking up on a buffalo. They really had courage in those days. Of course, if I have to be close to one of the great beasts, I prefer my

in full panoply

own mount!" The young man patted the hump that was just underneath an elaborate saddle. John's eyes grew wide as he followed the motion and saw all of the two-thousand-pound monster the Indian was riding.

Then the inevitable question: Just what was John sitting on, anyway? He felt a sudden panic when he saw the broad, brown expanse of the smaller buffalo underneath him. This one probably weighed in at only fifteen hundred pounds. In John's right hand was a fine piece of rope, part of a full bridle that went all the way around the gigantic head.

Where the hell was he? Plains Indians never rode buffalo. They hunted them for food and clothing and even shelter, given how much of the tepee depended on them. Nothing was allowed to go to waste. The bones, horns, hoofs . . . all were used, and the dung was a primary source of fuel. Before the European invasion brought horses, hunting these beasts was considerably more dangerous. He'd heard of the trick with wolf skins. But how could they be riding buffalo, and with such technologically advanced saddles?

Closer scrutiny of his companion's saddle, which was easier to see than his own, revealed horn neck, horn cap, pommel, and even stirrups, but shaped differently than they would have been for a horse. Saddles made him think of horses again. Even as the thought galloped into his mind, he realized that there was no word in this language for *horse*. He heard himself trying to ask the question, but couldn't get past the difficulty of the elusive word. He remembered scraps of phrases and vocabulary from Commanche, Apache, Kiowa, Pawnee, all to no avail.

"What are you talking about?" his friend asked.

"I'm sorry," he managed to answer. "I'm a bit confused today."

"You better get over that before the battle!"

Oh, great. A battle. But he couldn't let that deter him from figuring this thing out. He was sure that the old woman was giving him a dream back in time. Maybe this was a period before the arrival of the white man. But that still wouldn't explain the technological sophistication of these saddles. There were words he could use to ask about the white man. He did.

"Far Seeing Eye," began his friend, whose name he didn't know, "we have always treated your visions with the utmost respect. I learned from you the prayers to the spirit of the buffalo when we must kill him, or when we must feed him the herbs to make him docile enough to ride. But the great battle is before us after weeks of planning in which *you* played a crucial part. Are these new visions a warning? It's too late now for pale men and strange animals to make a difference." As the man spoke, he grabbed the long black elk-skin sash he wore, and held on to it as if to a lifeline.

If only John could call the man by name! Whatever was happening gave him the power to understand but not to remember who he was. Naturally, John assumed he was inhabiting the body of an ancestor. More questions occurred to him but before he could ask them events overtook both young men.

The other gave a war cry at the sight on the horizon. Smoke signals were making a string of white cotton balls against the sky, drawing attention once again to the absence of any clouds. John swallowed hard as the immense beast beneath his legs surged forward. He was keeping pace with his companion, who began to veer slightly to the right. John had been riding horses since he was a child, but they hadn't prepared him for this. He was twisting in his saddle the moment he pulled on the reins, but he managed to hang on.

If he'd thought horses put you far away from the ground, and their hooves were a sound you could feel in your bones, he hadn't reckoned on the thunder made by these incredible animals. He found it hard to believe the creature was made of flesh and blood. Such doubts were soon rendered moot by what was waiting for them at the end of their long ride.

moot by what

Over a rise was a welter of blood and gore, the first battle John had ever seen. But not even the screaming men, the howling beasts, the hacking and stabbing and dying could distract his attention from the spectacle of who was doing the fighting, and how they were doing it. For one mad instant he saw the tableau of war frozen for his edification. Time enough to dive into the maelstrom and wonder if to die here meant to die back in his own world. Time enough to take the bow and arrows slung over his shoulder and make his bloody contribution to the carnage. There was no doubt as to the enemy. He knew them on sight. The only trouble was that he couldn't believe it.

Wielding obsidian-bladed clubs and ornate javelins, attired in gold and jade and yellow parrot feathers, raising a din with conch-shell trumpets and clay whistles, the enemy could be nothing else but Aztec. They had never come this far north. At its height, their empire had stretched from the Gulf Coast to the Pacific, and given their limitations in terms of resources and technology, they had been over-extended before the Spaniards came and destroyed them. They had never been close to having what they were employing in this battle.

They drove massive chariots drawn by half a dozen buffalo. John knew about Aztec gold. Everyone did. The Aztecs had not even prized the stuff except when it was transformed into works of art. Besides vast quantities of gold, they had plenty of wood and copper, but they

had never learned how to make bronze. And yet right now, in front of John, he saw that the armor of these Aztec warriors, and important sections of the chariots, were bronze, impossible bronze!

But the most amazing feature of the chariots was that instead of wheels they rode on helix cylinders, spiraling down a hill, storing energy, and greatly increasing the speed by which they could go up the next hill. They also had a golden, or gold-plated, weapon that shot small arrows in rapid-fire succession. From a distance John had no idea how they worked, but they were silent, which ruled out gunpowder.

And then class was over. John was jolted back into reality, or what passed for reality, as an arrow creased his cheek. The pain was sharp and stinging, and he could feel wet blood trickling down his face. With another whoop of a war cry, his companion hurled himself into the fray. John remembered that his own name in this place and time was Far Seeing Eye. He hoped his vision would make him a deadly warrior. There was another war cry! A few seconds later he realized that he was listening to his own voice.

John had been mediocre at archery before, but this body he was inhabiting knew what to do. While two bow-lengths from the enemy, he was already fitting arrow to the taut string, pulling back, aiming without thinking, and letting it go the moment he was near enough to reach the target. A few seconds later his arrow seemed to appear in the chest of an Aztec warrior, who fell out of his chariot and was trampled into pulp by the buffalo of the next chariot behind him.

John didn't have time to reflect on his accuracy because he had already fired two more arrows. He didn't see what happened to them because a war club grazed his head with sufficient force to knock him from his steed, but he didn't lose consciousness within the dream, or whatever this was. Falling to the ground, he scrambled to his feet, barely noticing a broken rib. An Aztec priest was advancing on him, holding a foot-long flint knife. There wasn't time to retrieve his bow, so he pulled out his own knife and took a fighting stance.

The surprises weren't over for him yet. John never tested his mettle with the priest because one of the chariots came close, very close, and an obsidian club appeared and smashed the bald head of the priest like a rotten egg. John wiped the blood from his eyes, and caught a grin from the commanding officer of the Aztec army. The man looked to be the identical twin of Gray Bear Walking. And then he was gone in the dust, and John had more pressing matters to concern him.

A gang of priests had managed to surround his friend, who had also become separated from his mount. John couldn't tell which buffalo it was, but he was sure that one of their two shaggy beasts was

Aztec pulp   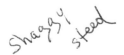   *Shaggy steed*

being attacked by at least a dozen wolves. He hadn't noticed where the wolves came from, but as he saw Aztec foot soldiers seeming to control the animals with whistles, he remembered the words of the old woman about his not being sent back into his own timeline. Whatever world he'd stumbled into, this wasn't in any history text taught by Professor Rae!

The buffalo's eyes had been torn out by the wolves, and now they were working on its legs, ripping into them with a courage equal to that of the great beast itself. But the bravery of a man is always the greatest because he knows his own mortality; and the bravery of the other Plains Indian now called to John, as the priests bore down upon him, eager to cut out his heart and offer it to Huitzilopochtli, their hungry god of the sun.

John got his arms around the priest's thin body, and broke the man's back in a rage. Then he used the body as a shield against the next priest's knife. His comrade rallied at the attempted rescue, and soon the two of them were fighting back to back, and the last surviving priest had run off like a jackal. No matter how stupid it sounded to the other man now, John had to know something.

"Before we die," he said, "I'd like to hear you say your name again, my friend."

"White Owl. I should not have doubted your visions, Far Seeing Eye. We are losing the battle. And this was supposed to be a trap for them."

"What went wrong?"

"Where are the reinforcements? They must have seen the signal."

The conversation was becoming more informative all the time, but it was cut short by the termination of the battle. The two friends were surrounded by a wall of Aztec soldiery. The priest who had been driven off returned, looking more demented than ever, and relishing his second chance. But this just wasn't his day. The officer who looked like Gray Bear Walking stepped down from his chariot and saved the two captives from the carving knife.

"I am Prince Cuauhtekoch," he announced grandly, "and I accept your surrender. You will be taken to our new city where your blood will make a worthy offering."

The priest was obviously disgruntled, and of the opinion that these two should be sacrificed here and now. There seemed to be a protocol covering such matters, and the end of the battle altered the situation. Sacrifices were now to be postponed for proper festival and ritual.

The prisoners were tied up behind the chariots. John hoped the distance would be only so great, or else the captives would not survive to be slaughtered later. Before the great trek began, Cuauhtekoch came up close to John and whispered in his ear, "Your secret agent from Tlaxcala betrayed you, but no matter. He is no longer breathing, and the real traitor will be dealt with later, the one we both love!'' John's expression registered nothing. He wished he had some clue what was going on.

They only traveled a few miles before nightfall, and then the caravan stopped to make camp. Apparently the Aztecs wanted healthy sacrifices. Before the darkness fell, John had an opportunity to study the chariots more closely. Once again he marveled at the technology of this world. They had progressed well beyond the straight-pole arrangement of early chariots. He ached to take one of the mechanisms apart to see how it worked. How unfortunate that his own body was slated for a similar operation.

He wondered what would happen if he slept. He seemed to be tired. Still, he put off sleeping as long as he could. Perhaps he would wake up with the old woman, back in the good old U.S. of A! He still had several thousand unanswered questions to deal with first. One of the Aztec soldiers sang a hymn to the stars and John realized, yet again, that he understood every language spoken here. The words had a haunting quality:

> *We only came to sleep*
> *We only came to dream*
> *It is not true, it is not true*
> *That we came to live on the earth.*

John slept. He did not dream, unless he was dreaming of sleep. And when he opened his eyes to the sun, he was still a prisoner of the Aztecs. They fed the prisoners white and yellow tortillas. The food was actually good. They did not mistreat those who were to be food of the gods.

The poetry from the night before had only been a taste. Aztecs would walk up and down the line of captured warriors, throwing flowers at them and reciting verse. John realized that most of his companions did not speak the Aztec language, but the man whose body he inhabited was apparently an exception before John was ever in the picture (or else the leader would not have whispered to him in Aztec). At any rate, John wondered how the man would have responded to two lines spoken by one of the poets:

> *But our body is like a rose tree . . .*
> *It puts forth flowers and then withers.*

He didn't like the sound of that.

The journey took another two days. They finally reached a city

mourner
blossom

under construction next to a large lake. There was something incongruous about an Aztec pyramid being constructed next to a stand of pine trees. A titanic block of stone was being carved into a giant bowl for what, John was sure, could be no good purpose. A utensil of those dimensions must be intended for the gods, and he didn't doubt what sort of cuisine they preferred.

No sooner had they arrived at the site than Cuauhtekoch gestured for John to be separated from his fellows. White Owl already wore the expression of a mourner at a funeral feast. He looked at John with concern, and hopefully no suspicion. But then what had Far Seeing Eye done, or left undone? So far, John had found it easier to learn about this alternate timeline than to find out anything of substance concerning the man he was supposed to be.

Hands still tied from when he was on the line, he followed the prince and a number of his retinue into the largest dwelling, and one of the few completed buildings. Comfort for an aristocrat appeared to be a high priority. As they entered the rooms, a young girl with blue-dyed hair passed her lord a flower. There was something almost dainty about the way he sniffed the blossom's aroma.

"A charnel-house odor hangs about our places of worship," said Cuauhtekoch with a shrug, "so we develop an appreciation for perfumes and other pleasant scents." Somehow John's sympathy was held well in check. "Oh, come now, Far Seeing Eye, enough of your frowning. I know what you and my sister have been planning. I respect you for it, but she should have known better."

They entered a bedchamber, and to John's surprise all the guards were instructed to leave except one, a man the prince obviously trusted beyond the normal call of duty. "I know you're expecting her," he told John with a wink, "but keep your breechcloth on. Perhaps it's time you should be told that I have enjoyed her in the same way, although years before you came on the scene. She liked me enough to make a statue of me. She's sentimental that way."

The man's manner was so insulting that John felt like taking the risk of slugging him, even though he didn't have a clue to the plots and counterplots that revolved around these people. His expression must have been interpreted as pride and firm resolution by the prince.

"I see that you still love her," he said. "Well, I tell you that I loved Nezaberlcoyotl, or at least his brain. He was as smart as his father, and as great an engineer. I will never forgive your slaying him, but his work was completed before your filthy tribe got its hands on him. His father gave us the chariot, with a little help from that Chinese captain he captured and befriended. Now his son has given us weapons that, when we have mass-produced them, will bring all other peoples under our dominion."

titanic guffaw

"What sort of weapons?" John asked. He really wanted to know.

"Don't play the fool with me," said the prince. "With the new projectile devices and the exploding powders, no one will stand before our might. And after this continent is subjugated, we will explore and conquer the rest of the world. Two oceans! Think of it. Beyond two oceans lie two other worlds, with other races, other blood, an uncountable number of sacrifices for Huitzilopochtli. And Tonatiuh will never tire of hearts, and the sun will never go out when it is fed so well; and our capital of Tenochtitlán will be the capital of the universe, and the eagle will perch on the cactus forever as we will live forever, the greatest race of all times and all worlds. . . ."

John was getting better at recognizing the demagogue style. This one had a glazed look in his eyes, and a certain nervous tension that put John in mind of a certain European tyrant from the first third of the twentieth century, in a world that obviously didn't belong in this particular stream of history. Living up to the name of Far Seeing Eye inspired the asking of impertinent questions, such as, "Do you really believe all that?"

The prince was just taking a deep breath, and he let out a guffaw of surprise. "You are a remarkable man," he said, "even to think of such a thing, much less put it into words. Of course, I admit I'm a politician. I believe what is expedient to believe. But it's certainly better to believe in a world with a purpose than that we are here by accident."

"The world can have a better purpose than your plan for endless bloodletting."

Again the Aztec noble was taken aback. "You show a side of yourself I never imagined," he said. "I always knew you were more than a savage. After all, your tribe may have learned from us how to use the bison for a purpose never dreamed of, but your people had the brains to make alterations and invent new things. If my sister must take up with a barbarian, she did as well as could be expected. But even she would never dream you'd advocate open atheism."

He reclined on the bed, but extended no invitation that John even sit upon the floor. The noble continued to ramble a bit: "As a member of the Eagle Knights, I should have slain you in the most painful way I could imagine. Your blasphemy does not make you the ideal candidate for sacrifice, even as a captive warrior. But no matter. I keep my bargains, and we must be liberal about such things. No one is perfect, after all."

John was getting tired of this. The prince was giving him information, all right, but he couldn't make much sense of it. He could hardly ask the man to tell him everything from scratch as though Far Seeing Eye had become Dimwitted Brain, and needed to be reminded of

tur quoise
hegemony

nearly everything. He needed months to understand this world, and he had a very good idea that his schedule would not be accommodating.

While John had been looking about the room for some method of escape, the prince had produced a turquoise necklace from somewhere and was playing with it. "How my sister loves her trinkets," he said. "I've had to punish her, you know. I've taken away most of what she loves. Which one of you was it who first conceived the notion of taking me prisoner today, and breaking the alliance with—well, you know which tribes are the weakest link in our new hegemony."

Not having the least idea made it all the easier for John to be heroic. "I won't tell you," he said with genuine confidence.

"I admire you," said the prince. "Torture doesn't work on you people because you self-inflict it so often for your rites of manhood. And anyway, you'd say that you were at fault instead of she if it came down to a 'confession.' But I must tell you that she never had any intention of reducing human sacrifice. She's a pious woman. But the two of you would probably have gotten along otherwise. You're both so passionate! My death and your diplomatic skills would have created the first serious challenge to the empire in a long time."

He bounced to his feet and held out his hand as though John were free to take it. "I'll keep my promise," said Cuauhtekoch. "One last night of love for both of you. I still love her in my way. I don't care about the priests and their stupid rules anyway. Her heart will be in the hands of the goddess Tlazolteotl soon enough. And you will feed the sun himself. The two of you make a lovely couple. You're strong and handsome, while she is the most beautiful woman in the world— I'm sure we can agree on that much—with her great, round eyes that look right through you and the light brown color that almost appears to be gold when the light is just right, and her perfect teeth. . . ."

The prince took a deep breath, and shook his head as if clearing it of personal fantasies. John did not doubt that in another minute the man would be offering to join them in the bed of love, and what's tomorrow's sacrifice among friends? One thing was certain, however. John was ready to meet this Native American Cleopatra as he'd never wanted to meet anyone before. His heart was beating faster at the thought of their embraces. The prince might be the scoundrel of all time, but his word-picture of his sister had worked some powerful magic.

Precisely at that moment there was the sound of an explosion, followed by screams. A voice in the corridor was shouting, "The slaves are in revolt. They have the powder!" The next moment a door burst open and a large white packet, with a fuse attached, was thrown into the room. There wasn't time to pull the fuse, much less grab the explo-

word picture *much less.*
magic

sive and throw it somewhere else. Even before it touched the ground, the bomb went off.

For John the experience was not painful at all. When the smoke cleared, he was back in the old woman's wickiup without even a head-ache or a stomachache. He was also very annoyed.

"Is that it?" he asked.

She sounded tired as she said, "Your quest is over."

He was becoming more annoyed. "I don't believe it. I was about to meet the most beautiful girl in the world for a last night of indescrib-able ecstasy."

"Over," said the old woman. "No more."

"But where was I?"

She smiled her toothless smile. "How should I know?" she asked. "Each person's quest is his own."

"You knew enough to say I wasn't going back in . . . normal time, or whatever you said."

"Each quest goes to the important place for him. Goes to other worlds, other possibilities."

The frustration was becoming unbearable. "Then send me back!"

"I can't. You were given last cycle of someone's life. You have re-turned, which means the life is over. You already paid, so you may go now." She hunched over the fire and began fiddling with the three sticks that formed a tripod from which hung her little clay pot. She did not speak to him again.

He took his time driving back, arguing with himself every mile. Frequently he would stop and get out of the car. He would stand there, in the dust, feeling the sun on the back of his neck. The air smelled of rubber and road and gasoline. Sometimes he would walk a half-mile out into the countryside, kicking at rocks and picking up sticks as if he were a kid again. Then he would return to the car and drive some more.

By the time he reached the campus he had come to a decision. He wasn't going to join NAME. He went looking for Gray Bear Walking and found him slapping the blond Wiccan, who was cowering in a cor-ner and not doing a very good job of standing up for herself. John picked up enough scraps of the conversation to get the general idea that Gray Bear Walking thought he had a right to take whatever he thought his due from white people. His victim apparently shared enough of the same viewpoint that she was only halfhearted in making the feminist case. Nor was she doing anything about her assailant's unprotected throat and eyes and ears and groin.

John didn't think very much about the woman's lack of skill in the art of self-defense. He was busy. No sooner did he have his arm around the bastard's throat than he realized he could easily kill the other man. A brief flash of the anger he had felt toward Prince Cuauhtekoch almost turned the tide into a crimson one; but he regained control of himself and simply beat the other man until his face would never be as handsome again. What finally made him stop was the expression on the young woman's face. She had never seen such an explosion of violence before. He hoped she would never do so again.

John decided not to tell Professor Rae that the crazy old woman might not be crazy after all. He kept his vision quest to himself. Except that he let a little of the story, just the least little bit, slip into a letter he felt he had to write:

Dear Father,

You probably wondered if I would ever write you again. It has been hard on both of us since Mother died. I'll always appreciate how supportive she was of my decision to major in anthropology. When you said it wasn't a practical choice, I was sure that you had other objections. I admit I'm more interested in my heritage than you are. I've always felt that you were ashamed somehow of being a Native American. Yet that didn't keep you from marrying a Native American.

I'll always remember your horror stories about dealing with federal Indian agents when you were a boy on the reservation. I'm not saying that you've spent your life in denial. I've never said that. I agree that the greatness of this country is to share the same national identity regardless of who you are or where you come from.

I'm writing now because I've recently had an experience that reminds me that anyone can be an oppressor and anyone can be a victim. You'd think a thought so obvious would never be denied, but apparently it is beyond many people.

On campus we recently had a memorial for all the Native Americans who died at the hands of the Spaniards. I'm looking at a reproduction of Xipe Totec as I write this. He was the god of spring planting for the Aztecs. Priests danced in his honor while wearing the skins of sacrificial victims. The Spanish empire was wrong in what it did in America. But other peoples at other times would be as bad, given the power, given the opportunity. So obvious. So hard for some people to accept.

I hope one day you will be proud of the career I have chosen. I am an American and I am a Native American. I am an individual. And I am your son.

One day I hope to find a woman who will mean to me what

Mother meant to you. I have a deep faith that such a woman is in this world, and I will find her. Wish me well, Father. I wish you nothing less.

                    Love and respect from your son,
                    John

The Old Ways

Ed Gorman

FOR NORMAN PARTRIDGE

T here had been a gunfight earlier in the evening, but then, in a place like this one, there usually were gunfights earlier. And later, for that matter.

The name of the place was Madame Dupree's and it was one of the big casino-drinking establishments that were filling the most disreputable part of San Francisco in this year of 1903. The Barbary Coast was the name for the entire district and, yes, it was every bit as dangerous as you've heard. Cops, even the young strong ones, would only come down here in fours and sixes, and even then an awful lot of them got killed.

The way I got this job was to get myself good and beaten up and tossed in an alley behind the Madame's. One of her men found me and brought me to her and she asked me if I wanted a job and since I hadn't eaten in three days I said yes and so she put me to work as a floater in her casino. What I did was walk around with a few hundred dollars of Madame Dupree's money in my pockets and pretend to be drunk. Inevitably, rubes would spot me as an easy mark and invite me into one of their poker games. Thanks to a few accouterments such as a holdout vest and a sleeve holdout, I could pretty much deal myself any cards I wanted to. Eighty-five percent of my winnings went back to Madame Dupree. The rest I kept. Not bad pay for somebody who'd been raised on an Oklahoma reservation and seen three of his brothers and sisters die of tuberculosis before they reached eight years of age. I'd gotten my memory back and wished I hadn't.

What Madame Dupree didn't say—didn't need to say, really— was that an Indian was a perfect mark because he was held to be the lowest form of life in these United States, even below that of Negro and Chinaman. What rube could possibly resist taking money from a drunken Indian? Or, for that matter, what Indian could resist? You saw a lot of red men along the Barbary Coast, men who'd worked or stolen their way into some money and now wanted to spend it the way white men did. The Barbary was about the only place in the land where no distinction was made among the races—if you had the money, you could have anything any other man could have. This included all the white girls, some of whom were as young as thirteen, though this particular summer a wave of various venereal diseases was sweeping the Barbary. More than six hundred people had died so far. A Methodist minister had suggested in one of the local newspapers that the Barbary be set afire with all its "human filth" still in it. I wasn't sure that Jesus would have approved of such a proposal, but then you never could tell.

Tonight's gunfight pretty much started the way they all do in a place like this.

On the ground floor, Madame Dupree's consisted of three large rooms, the walls of which were covered by giant murals of easy women in even easier poses. As you wandered among the sailors, the city councilmen, the crooked cops, the whores, the pickpockets, the professional gamblers, the farmers, the clerks, the disguised ministers and priests and even the occasional rabbi, the slumming socialites, and the sad-eyed fathers looking for their runaway daughters, you found gambling devices of every kind: faro, baffling board, roulette, keno, goose-and-balls, and—well, you get the idea.

Tonight a drunken rube suspected he'd been cheated out of his money. And no doubt he suspected correctly. He got loud and then he got violent and then as he was being escorted out one of the side doors by a giant Negro bouncer with a ruffled white shirt already bloody this early in the evening, he made the worst mistake of all. He pulled his gun and tried to shoot the bouncer in the side. And the bouncer responded by drawing his own gun and shooting the man's gun away. And then the bouncer threw the man through the side door and went out into the dark alley.

Everybody who worked here knew what was going to happen next. Every bouncer at every major casino in the Barbary had a specialty. Some were especially good with knives and guns, for instance. This man's specialty was his strength. He liked to grab the top of somebody's head with his giant hand and give the head a violent wrench to the left, thereby breaking the neck. I'd seen him do it once and I couldn't get the sight out of my mind for a couple of weeks afterward. The funny thing was he was called Mr. Stevenson because late at night, at a steak house down the street, he read Robert Louis Stevenson stories out loud to anybody who'd listen. Mr. Stevenson told me once, "I was a plantation nigger and my master thought it'd be funny to have a big buck like me know how to read. So he had me educated from the time I was six and a couple of times a week he'd have me come up to the house and read to all his friends and they just couldn't believe I could read the way I did." That gave us something in common. An Oklahoma white man who ran the town next to my reservation put me through two years of college. I probably would have finished except the man dropped straight down dead of a heart attack and his son wasn't anywhere near as generous.

That was how Mr. Stevenson and I were the same, the education. How we were different was his physical strength.

After Mr. Stevenson finished with the rube, I got myself a good cigar and wandered around in my good clothes, weaving a little the way I did to let people know that I was a drunken Indian, and I got pulled into three different games in as many hours. I won a little over four hundred dollars. Madame Dupree would be happy—at least she would be if she'd gotten over her terrible cold, which some of us had come to suspect was maybe something more than a cold. Be funny if one of the owners died of venereal disease the way their girls and their customers did.

Around ten, I saw Mr. Stevenson working his way over to me. He wore his usual attire, a bowler perched at a rakish angle on his big head, his fancy shirt with the celluloid collar, and a sparkling diamond stickpin through his red cravat.

"You catch a drink with me?" he said as he leaned over the table where I was playing.

"Something wrong?"

He nodded. He had solemn brown eyes that hinted at both his intelligence and his anger.

"Five minutes."

"You know that coon?" one of the rubes said after Mr. Stevenson had left.

"Met him a little earlier. Why?"

The rube shook his head. "Scares the piss out of me, he does. I heard about how he snaps them necks." He shuddered. "Back in Nebraska, you just don't see things like that."

I finished the hand and then joined Mr. Stevenson at the bar. As always, he drank tea. He took his job very seriously and he didn't want whiskey to make him careless.

I didn't much worry about things like that. I had a shot of rye with a beer back.

"What's up, Mr. Stevenson?"

"Moira."

"Oh."

There was a group of reservation Indians who had collected in the Barbary over the past two years or so. Maybe a dozen of us, all employed in various capacities by the casinos. One was a very beautiful Indian girl who'd been called "Moira" by the Indian agent where she'd grown up. Mr. Stevenson was sweet on her, and in a terrible way. He'd go through periods where he couldn't sleep; you'd see him standing in front of her cheap hotel, staring up at her window, doing some kind of sad sentry duty. Or you'd see him following her. Or you'd see him sitting alone in a coffee house all teary-eyed and glum and you knew who he was thinking about. Or I did, anyway. I'd gone through the same thing with Moira myself. I'd been in bitter love with her for nearly a year but then I'd passed through it. Like a fever.

Not that you could blame Moira. She was as captivated by another reservation Indian named Two Eagle as we were captivated by her. Did all the same things we did with her. Followed him around. Bought him gifts he didn't want. Wrote him pleading little notes.

Then they got a place and moved in together, Moira and Two Eagle, but word was things weren't going well. He was one of those Indians too fond of the bottle and too bitter toward the white man to function well. Kept a drum up in his room and sometimes in the middle of the night you'd hear it, a tom-tom here in the center of the Barbary, and him yowling ancient Indian war cries and chants. He was fierce, Two Eagle, and he seemed to hate me especially, seemed to think that I had no pride in my red skin or my ancestors. I returned the favor, thinking he was pretty much of a melodramatic asshole. I was just as much an Indian as he was. I just kept it to myself was all.

Only time I ever liked him was one night when I ran into him and Moira in a Barbary restaurant, real late it was, and Two Eagle gentle drunk on wine, and him telling her in great excited rushes about the old religions of ours, and how only the red man—of all the earth's peoples—understood that sky and sun and the winds were all part of the Great God spirit—and how a man or woman who knew how to truly speak to God could then address all living creatures on the earth, be they elk or horse or great mountain eagle, for all things and all creatures are God's, and thus all things in the world, seen and unseen alike, are indivisible, and of God. And he spoke with such passion and sweep and majesty that I could see tears in his eyes—as I felt tears in my own eyes . . . and I saw that there was a good side to his belligerent clinging to the old ways. But his bad side . . .

Moira liked white-man things. Back when she'd let me take her to supper a few times, we'd gone for a long carriage ride by the bay and she'd enjoyed it. Then we went up where the fancy shops were. She made a lot of little-girl sounds, pleased and cute and dreamy.

This was the part of her Two Eagle hated. By now he'd got her to dress in deerskin instead of cloth dresses, her shining black hair in pigtails instead of tumbling tresses, her face innocent of the "whore paint," as he pontifically called it. He worked as a bouncer in a place so tough it might have given Mr. Stevenson pause, and she worked behind the bar in the same place. Pity the man who got drunk and started sweet-talking Moira. Two Eagle would drag him outside and make the man plead for a quick death.

Now that I was over Moira, I didn't especially like hearing about either of them. But you couldn't say the same for Mr. Stevenson. He was as aggrieved as ever, all pain and dashed hope.

"She went out on him."

"Oh, bullshit."

"True," he said. "Few nights ago. They got into a bad fight and he kicked her in the stomach. He didn't know she was just startin' to carry a baby. Killed the baby and nearly killed Moira, too."

"The sonofabitch. Somebody should kill that bastard."

"You haven't heard the rest of it."

"I'm not sure I want to."

"He wants to cut her."

"Cut her?"

"The old ways, he says. What the Indians used to do back when I was on the plantation. When a woman went out on a man like that. You know—her nose."

"That's crazy. Nobody does that shit anymore."

"He does. Or at least he says he does. You know how he is. All that warrior bullshit he gets into."

"Where's Moira?"

"That's the worst part. She thinks she's got it coming. She's just waitin' in her room for him to come up and cut her. Says she believes in the old ways, too."

I shook my head. "That sounds like Moira." I took my pocket watch from my breeches. "I've got some time off coming. I can tell Madame Dupree I'm going for the rest of the night."

"You're tough, man, but you aren't that tough. Two Eagle'll kill you." He showed me his hands. How big they were. And strong. And black. "Fucker tries to cut her, I'll take care of him." He nodded to the front door, his bowler perched at a precarious angle. Sometimes I wondered if he had it glued to his bald head. "Let's go."

We went.

Making our way along the board sidewalks this time of night meant stepping over corpses, drunks, and reeking puddles of vomit and blood from various fights. Every important casino had a band of its own, which meant that the noise was as bad as the odors.

It was raining, which meant the boards were slick. But we walked fast, anyway. Two Eagle had a couple of rooms on the second floor of a livery stable. Moira lived there, too. She'd waited a long time for him to marry her. I figured she'd wait a lot longer.

A drunken rube made a crack about Mr. Stevenson, but if the black man heard, he didn't let on. Just kept walking. Real quiet and real intense. Like he had only one thought in the entire world and everything else just got in the way. Moira can make you like that.

The Barbary looked pretty much as usual, a jumble of cheap clothing stores for drunken sailors, dance halls where the girls were practically naked, and signs that advertised every kind of whore anybody could ever want. There was a new one this month, a mulatto who went over four hundred pounds, and a lot of Barbary regulars were giving her a try just to see what it'd be like, a lady so fat.

Half a block away you could smell the sweet hay and the sour horseshit in the rain and the night. Closer, you could hear the horses roll against their stalls, making small nervous sounds as they dreamed.

We went up a long stretch of outside stairs. The two-by-fours were new and smelled of sawn wood, tangy as autumn apples on a back porch.

Stevenson didn't knock. He just kicked the door in and stepped over the threshold. The walls inside were stained and the floors so scuffed the wood was slivery. She'd put up new red curtains that were supposed to make the shabby room a home but all the curtains did was make everything else look even older and uglier.

Moira, sad beautiful Indian child that she was, sat in a corner with her head on her knees. When she looked up, her black eyes glistened in the lantern light. She wore a deerskin dress and moccasins. The walls were covered with the lances and shields and knives and arrows of Two Eagle's tribe. He liked to smoke opium up here and tell dream-stories about ancient days when the medicine men said that the bravest warriors had horses that could fly. But the toys on the wall looked dulled and dusty and drab. Every couple of weeks he had his little group of Barbary-area Indians up here, Moira had told me once. The last stand, I'd remarked sarcastically. But she hadn't found it funny at all.

"This is crazy shit, Moira," I said. "We're gonna get you out of here before he comes back."

She had wrists and ankles so delicate they could make you cry. She stood up in her red skin, no more than ninety pounds and five feet she was, and walked over to Mr. Stevenson and said, "You don't have no god damn right to come here, Mr. Stevenson. Or you either," she said to me. "What happens between Two Eagle and me is our business."

"You ever seen a woman who's been cut?" I said. I had. The man always took the nose, the same thing the ancient Egyptians had taken, just sawed it right off the face, so that only a dark and bloody hole was left. No brave ever wanted a woman who'd been cut, so many of the women went into the forest to live. A few even drank poison wine to end it quickly.

She looked at Mr. Stevenson. "We don't have no whiskey left."

"So the nigger goes and fetches you some, huh?" he said in his deep and bitter voice.

"I need to talk to Jimmy here, Mr. Stevenson, that's all. Just ten minutes or so."

He brought up his big murderous hands and looked at them as if he wasn't quite sure what they were.

"Rye?" he said.

She smiled and was even more beautiful. "Thanks for remembering. I'll get some money from Two Eagle and pay you back."

"I don't want any of his money," Mr. Stevenson said, and fixed her with his melancholy gaze. "I just want you."

"Oh, Mr. Stevenson," she said, and gently touched her small hand to his wide hard chin. Sisterly, I guess you'd say. She was like that with every man but Two Eagle.

"You don't let him lay a hand on her," Mr. Stevenson said to me as he crossed the room to the door.

I brought up my Colt. "Don't worry, Mr. Stevenson."

He glanced at her one more time, sad and loving and scared and obviously baffled by his own tumultuous feelings, and then he left.

"Poor Mr. Stevenson."

"He's a decent man," I said.

"Kinda scary, though."

"Not any more so Two Eagle."

"I just wished he understood how I felt about Two Eagle."

"Maybe he finds it kind of hard to understand a man who kicks a woman so hard she loses the baby she's carrying—and then wants to cut her nose off."

"He didn't mean to kick me that hard. He was real sorry. He cried when he saw—the baby."

I went over to the window and looked out on the Barbary Coast. One of the local editorial writers had estimated that a man was robbed every five minutes in the Barbary. At least when it rained, it didn't smell so bad.

I turned back to her. "I want to put you on a train tonight. For Denver. There's one that leaves in an hour and a half."

"I don't want to go."

"You know what he's gonna do to you."

Her eyes suddenly filled. She padded back to her corner and sat down and put her head on her knees and wept quietly.

I went over and sat down next to her and stroked her head as she cried.

After a time she looked up, her cheeks streaky with warm tears that I wiped away with my knuckles.

"He caught me."

"It's not something I want to hear about."

"I was so mad at him—with the baby and everything—that I just went out and got drunk. Didn't even know who I was with or where I was."

"Moira, I really don't want to hear."

"So he came looking for me. Took him all night. And you know where he found me?"

I sighed. She was going to tell me anyway.

"Up in some white sailors' room. There were two of them. One of them was inside me when he came through the door and found me."

I didn't say anything. Neither did she. Not for a long time.

"You know what was funny, Jimmy?"

"What?"

"He didn't hurt either one of them. Didn't lay a hand on them. Just stood there staring at me. And the guy, well, he pulled out and picked up his clothes and got out of there real fast with his friend. It was their own room, too. That's what was real funny. By then, I was sober. I tried to cover myself up but I couldn't find my clothes, so I went over and held Two Eagle just like he was my little boy, and then he started crying. I'd never heard him cry before. It was like he didn't know how. And then I got him over to the bed and I tried to make love to him but he couldn't. And he hasn't been able to since it happened, almost a week now. He's not a man anymore. That's what he said to me. He said that he can't be a man ever again after what he saw. And it's my fault, Jimmy. It's all my fault."

I wanted to hate him, or her, or myself, I wanted to hate some goddamned body but I couldn't. It was just sad human shit and at the moment it overwhelmed me, left me ice cold and confused. People are so god damned confusing sometimes.

She laughed. "You and Mr. Stevenson must have some conversations about us, Jimmy."

I stood up, reached back down, and took her wrist. "C'mon now, I'm taking you to the train."

"You ain't takin' her nowhere."

A harsh quick voice from behind me in the doorway. When I

turned I was looking into Two Eagle's insane dark eyes. I'd never seen him when he didn't look angry, when he didn't look ready for blood. He wore a piece of leather tied around his head, his rough black hair touching his shoulders, his gaunt cheeks crosshatched with myriad knife slashes. His buckskin outfit gave him the kind of Indian ferocity he wanted.

He came into the room.

"Why can't you be true to our ancestors for once, Jimmy?" he said, pointing his Colt right at my head. "Cutting her is the only thing I can do. Even Moira agrees. So why should you try to stop it? It's our blood, Jimmy, our tribal way."

"I don't want you to cut her."

His hard face smiled. "You gonna stop me, Jimmy?"

He expected me to be afraid of him and I was. But that didn't mean I wouldn't shoot him if I had to.

And then Mr. Stevenson was in the doorway.

Moira made a female sound in her throat. Two Eagle followed my gaze over his shoulder to the huge black man in the doorframe.

"You're smart to have him around, Jimmy. You'll need him."

Mr. Stevenson came into the room carrying a bottle of rotgut rye in one hand and a single rose in the other. He carried the flower to Moira and gave it to her. Then, without any warning, he turned around and backhanded Two Eagle so hard the Indian's feet left the floor and he flew backwards into the wall. The entire room shook.

Mr. Stevenson wasn't going to bother with any preliminaries.

He went right for Two Eagle, who was trying to right his vision and his breathing and his ability to stand up straight. He'd struck his head hard when he'd collided with the wall and he looked disoriented. Bright red blood ran from his nostrils.

Mr. Stevenson grabbed him and it was easy to see what he was going to do. Maybe he thought that this would ultimately give him his first real chance with Moira, killing Two Eagle by snapping his neck.

"No!" I shouted.

And dove on Mr. Stevenson's back, trying to pull him off Two Eagle.

But it was no use. I clung to Mr. Stevenson like a child. I could not even budge him.

By now he had his hands in place, one on top of Two Eagle's head, the other on the bottom of his neck—ready for the single wrench that would kill Two Eagle.

Two Eagle used fists, feet, even his teeth to get free, but Mr. Stevenson paid no attention. He was setting himself to perform his most magnificent act . . .

Moira shot him once in the side and then raised the gun and shot him once on top of the head. His hair flew off, a bloody black coil of curls affixed to the wall by pieces of sticky flesh and bone.

The funny thing was, he kept right on going, as if he refused to acknowledge what Moira had done to him.

Getting ready to snap Two Eagle's neck—

And then she ran closer, shrieking, and shot him again, and this time not even Mr. Stevenson could refuse to acknowledge what had happened. Blood poured from his ears.

An enraged Two Eagle was now able to bring his hands up and seize Mr. Stevenson's throat, holding tight, choking him, as the big black fell over backwards, Two Eagle riding him down to the floor and then grabbing the gun from Moira's hand.

Two Eagle put the barrel of the .45 to Mr. Stevenson's forehead and fired three times. Didn't seem to matter to him that Mr. Stevenson had died a little while ago.

With each shot, Mr. Stevenson's head jerked upward from the coarse board floor and then slapped back down.

Two Eagle was calling him nigger and a lot of other things in our native tongue.

Then he was done, Two Eagle, pitching forward and lying face-down on the floor, very still for a long time.

I got up and straightened my clothes and picked up my gun from the floor where it had fallen when I'd jumped on Mr. Stevenson.

Moira said, "You two shouldn't have come up here."

"I guess not." I nodded to Mr. Stevenson. "He was trying to help you was all."

"It wasn't none of his business and it ain't none of yours, either."

"I guess he didn't see it that way. Seeing's he loved you and all."

"A nigger," Two Eagle said, getting up from the floor suddenly. "A nigger, lovin' Moira. Maybe you think that's all right, Jimmy, but then you give up bein' a true man a long time back."

And then he went for him. Couldn't help himself. He still had all this fury and it had to light somewhere.

So he came at me, but he was stupid because he didn't look at my hand.

I felt his powerful arm wrap around my neck. I smelled his sweat and whiskey and tobacco.

He pushed me back against the wall.

And that was when I raised my Colt and put it directly to his ribs and fired three times.

He was dead before he hit the floor.

She was screaming, Moira was. That was about all I can tell you about my last few minutes in the room. She was screaming and Two Eagle had fallen close by Mr. Stevenson and then I was running. That's about all I can remember.

Then there was the night and the rain and I was running and running and running and tripping and falling and hurting myself bad but no matter how far or how fast I ran, I could still hear Moira screaming.

Week later it was.

I was back doing my nightly turn at Madame Dupree's, winning upwards of five hundred dollars this particular night, when I saw Lone Deer come in the side door by the faro layout.

She looked frantic. I figured it was me she wanted.

Being's as we were waiting for some liquid refreshments at our table, I got up and went over to her.

When I reached her, she said, "She's goin', Jimmy. Leavin' us. Twenty-five minutes, her train leaves. I didn't find out till half an hour ago myself. Thought I'd better tell you."

"I appreciate it."

I suppose, like Mr. Stevenson, I'd had the idle dream that Moira and I would be lovers now that Two Eagle was gone. I didn't have to worry about any recriminations from the law getting in my way. A dead nigger and a dead Injun on the Barbary Coast don't exactly turn out a lot of curious cops. They're just two more slabs down at the morgue.

I'd figured I'd give it a few weeks and then go see her, tell her how what I did was the only thing I known to do—kill him to save my own life. And then I'd gentle-like invite her out for some dinner and . . .

But that wasn't to be. Not now.

Moira was leaving.

"You'd better hurry," Lone Deer said. And then took my arm and drew me closer. "There's something else I need to tell you."

Less than two minutes later I was running toward the depot. It was crowded and the conductor walked up and down all pompous as he consulted his railroad watch and shouted out that there were only a few minutes left before this particular train pulled out.

I found her in the very back of the last coach. The car was barely half full and she looked small and isolated there with the seats so much taller than she was. Moira. She'd always be a child.

I dropped into the seat next to her and said, "Lone Deer told me what you did."

"I wish she wouldn't have. I didn't want nobody to see me off."

"I love you, Moira."

"I don't want to hear that. Not with Two Eagle barely a week dead. Didn't I betray him enough?"

I'd seen the soldiers drag my grandfather from the reservation one day when I was very young. They were taking him to a federal penitentiary where he would die less than two months later at the hands of some angry white prisoners. I could still feel my panic that day—panic and terror and a sense that my own life was ending, too.

That's how I felt now, with Moira.

"But I won't betray him no more," Moira said. "You can bet on that."

"Is that why you did it?"

"Why I did it is none of your business."

I looked at her there in her black mourning dress and black mourning hat and black mourning veil, a veil so heavy you couldn't make out anything on the other side.

"No man'll ever want to bother me again. I made sure of that."

I was tempted to lift the veil quickly and see what she looked like. Lone Deer had said that Moira had used a butcher knife on her nose and that nothing remained but a bloody hole.

But then I decided that I didn't want to remember her that way. That I always wanted her to be young and beautiful Moira in my mind. Every man needs something to believe in, even if he knows it's not true.

"You got a ticket, buck?" the conductor asked me. Ordinarily, I'd take exception to his calling me "buck," but at the moment it just didn't seem very important.

I leaned over and kissed Moira, pressing her veil to her cheek. I still couldn't see anything.

"Hurry up, buck. You get your ass off of here or you show me a ticket."

I squeezed her hand. "I love you, Moira. And I always will."

And then I was gone, and the train was pulling out, all steam and power and majesty in the western night.

Then I walked slowly back to Madame Dupree's where I got just as drunk as Indians are supposed to get.

Lost Cherokee

Steve Rasnic Tem

ct. 3, 1839:
The old man crouched down before the fire with his grandchil-dren—the elder boy of ten summers and the small girl who had jumped down but six years before—the grandfather's clothing worn, fraying, too thin for the cold as the wagons swung north and away from Cherokee land, his brown turban stained, his eyes filled with the sadness of four family members dead, these children's parents collapsed on the trail, only two of the fifteen lost at each stopover on the Removal, and two others slain by the Unecas, the whites, when they refused to give up their small mines, their nice houses, the well-tended gardens.

"This is what the old men told me when I was a boy." His grandchil-dren drew closer, as this was always his way to begin a tale.

"In the beginning the animals and the land were not friends of the human being. The human being was new, some say created by Coyote, some say by Rabbit, and new things are not always embraced. The human beings lived on a high rise cleared out of the great wood, and they never left there. You see, they were afraid of the great wood where the animals lived. It was dark there, and the ways of the animals were not the ways of the human being.

"Then the animals were not as they are today, you see. The animals were bigger, stronger, more perfect. They spoke the same language as the human being and lived in villages arranged much as our own Chero-kee villages. They had chiefs and clans and councils. Frog was council leader. Rabbit was messenger and led the dances.

"These animals are now gone. Some time ago, so long ago the human beings have forgotten, the animals left this world and flew up to the seven heavens, where they live in Galunlati this very day. These animals we know today then came to earth to be the imitators of these great ones. But these great ones once lived, believe this.

"Long ago, those who would someday become the Cherokee lived among the other human beings in this bare spot on the mountain. One

day, one of these early Cherokees woke up, as from a dream, and knew what it was he must do, that he must leave this place and travel into the wood, that he must make friends of the animals. He also knew the sadness of being alone after this dream; the dream gave him this. And he knew that only the animals could doctor this new pain. He did not understand, then, what he would find: demons, ghosts, and little people, as well as the great animals.

"No one, of course, remembers his name. This was before the time of names. I call him Tsalagi, the ancient name for the Cherokee, which means 'cave people' or 'mountain people.' For this man stood for us all, you see, like our other old heroes such as Oconoslota, Doublehead, John Watts, or Chief Junaluska, who saved that devil Jackson during the Creek wars. The Cherokee have always had someone to stand for them when it was needed. This is Tsalagi's story, my grandchildren."

When Tsalagi woke up that morning a cloud bank seemed but a few feet above his head. He rolled over and gazed at the land about him: he was on the ground outside the bark huts, and the only one of his people awake. He could not understand this, as the sun had already risen, and besides, he had slept in the hut with his family the night before, not outside, exposed to the darkness. He crawled to his knees, climbed to his feet, and found himself ducking as if to avoid bumping his head into that cloud bank. But the cloud bank now seemed farther overhead, circling, and as Tsalagi moved, the cloud moved with him.

He entered the hut of his father and looked around. Everyone was asleep, but such a strange sleep. Their bodies looked stiff, uncomfortable, their breathing so shallow that at first he feared they might be dead. His brothers lay like a pile of young warriors killed in battle with Raven, but Raven had not bothered them since before even his father's time. His sisters and mother lay huddled together. His father slept alone, by the door where Tsalagi had crouched and entered. This startled Tsalagi; his father should have been alarmed, up and ready for battle. But he continued to sleep.

He bent over his father and gently pushed at the old man's chest. Then harder. Finally, forgetting himself, he slapped his father, then stumbled backwards in fright. His father continued to sleep the sleep of the dead. But his flesh was warm, his eyelids fluttered.

Tsalagi went to every hut in the village. Everywhere it was the same. He examined the sky for signs from Yowa and the Elder Fires Above. Nothing. He examined Sun, the creator, but nothing seemed out of place.

Then he saw the cloud again, circling rapidly directly over his head. Was this the sign? He suddenly felt adrift, dizzy, and then found himself with a clear head again, looking deeply into the great wood. And he knew what he must do.

He returned to the family hut for a pouch of food—nuts, roots, berries—then hefted the spear he knew his father intended to give him when Tsalagi became a man. He slipped into his skirt of overlapping bark and feathers. He also took the hollow reed and a few wood-and-feather darts in case the smaller animals allowed him to eat them. He knew his father could always make another, and he did not know if there would be reeds where he was going.

When he emerged the cloud was still overhead, but very soon began to fly rapidly in the direction of the clearing's edge and the border of the great wood. Tsalagi barely kept up. He stopped momentarily at the clearing's boundary, where the human beings had blackened a narrow circle around the village with the flame the Thunder Beings had given them. It was not known what the Thunder Beings meant by this gift—some thought flame still another thing sent to trick the human beings, or a new toy the Thunder Beings wanted to try out on the village first—so since its first discovery in the tree, flame was used only for magic, or for bathing the meat before eating.

Tsalagi looked at the black band before his feet, then searched the sky again for the cloud. It seemed to have stopped just over the edge of the wood, waiting for him. Tsalagi took one cautious step over the boundary; then, when nothing happened to him, he ran straight for the wall of trees as fast as he could.

The cloud was circling madly.

He had never felt so close to things. Branches poked him in the back and ribs and he whirled with his spear ready, then stumbled backwards over fallen logs. He looked about in wonder. The green and blue leaves moved in the slight breeze like countless waving hands.

Tsalagi felt other thoughts brushing up against his own, other voices that always seemed to fall apart into rustlings and drippings and swishings when he tried to make out the words. Sun seemed to have disappeared, and the heart of the wood seemed much like the times when Moon had just come out of hiding. But now and then he gazed hard at the branches overhead, and he could still catch some glimpse of white mist. Knowing that the white cloud was still there somehow reassured him.

The ground beneath him seemed to be rising, which bothered him, as he'd always imagined the ground hidden by the wood to be as flat as the village clearing. He had visions of a great monster stirring out of the fallen leaves and moss, much like the ones he had seen inside his head during the darktime. Great wings knocking him off the world. He shivered and crept up the rise, expecting to flee at any moment from a gigantic upraised claw or beak. He watched his feet, seeing himself stepping into an enormous, watery eye.

He discovered that the farther he traveled from the village the hungrier he became. For some reason he had lost his ability to go without food for long periods. He had good luck with the blowgun, telling the small flock of birds that he must take one of the group, but no more than was needed, and for good purpose. The birds quieted almost instantly, and seemed to rest until he had chosen one of their number. The second day he killed a small lizard with his bare hands, and imagined taking the power of this strange creature within himself. All the next day he felt fleeter of foot, and better able to control his thirst.

As he went farther and farther into the great wood, Tsalagi discovered that not all of the forest was the same, as he had once thought. The trees were of many kinds, the flowers countless. In some places great, twisting vines draped the trees. In others the bases of the trees were surrounded by thick undergrowth and he had to go around, the swiftness of the little cloud overhead not allowing him the time it would take to chop and tear his way through. He thought many times of his family, but they felt as distant as a dream to him now.

One day the cloud stopped him at a wide place in the stream. Tsalagi tried to go on, but the small cloud was persistent, lowering and circling over a small area. He looked into the stream at this point and discovered some whitish objects on the bottom. Examining these, he found he could pry them open at a seam. The gummy flesh inside tasted good.

Suddenly, Tsalagi bolted upright, a feeling like a knife suddenly crossing his secret thoughts. The edge of this knife seemed to trail off into the most shadowed part of the wood behind him. He turned and stared there, unmoving. He barely touched his blowgun, then felt foolish with such a small weapon against such a big darkness, and grasped the end of his spear. He could now see there was movement in the dark, but his eyes were not good enough to see what beast caused this.

Then two yellow eyes, a great orange beak, glistened back in the wood, and that surrounded by a blackness deeper than any of the shadows. Judging from their placement, Tsalagi knew the animal to be two men in height. He was sure this was one of the great animals, the first he had ever seen. He thought it must be Raven, or one of Raven's brothers.

Raven seemed to be traveling in a large circle around Tsalagi, but made no sound, even when crossing the stream. Tsalagi did not know how this could be, but this was one of the great animals, he thought; they could do anything. Every few moments Raven would turn his enormous head and look directly at Tsalagi, straight into his eyes, and Tsalagi would tremble all over.

Raven's movements were so slow, ponderous, and deliberate that Tsalagi didn't quite know what to make of them. He thought Raven must be acting out some sort of plan, dancing some kind of pattern, but he did not know what it could be. And the slowness of Raven's movements made it impossible for Tsalagi to determine whether the giant creature's circle was narrowing.

At last Raven stopped and stared at Tsalagi for a long time. Unblinking. In the dim light Tsalagi could see the sleek outlines of the enormous head, the way the feathers tufted in back and extended over each yellow eye. Then Raven closed his eyes and covered his beak with midnight wings, and vanished back into the shadows.

Some time later Tsalagi heard a woman scream, and sounds of a great struggle a little distance away, where the trees had grown closer together and more tangled. He saw that the cloud had now sped up, the falling sun seeming to turn its outer edges the color of milk with some blood mixed in. Then it stopped over this place, the woman screamed again, and Tsalagi raced forward, snapping branches out of the way, bruising himself against hidden trunks, pulled and clutched at by thin vines and briars. When he reached the thickest part of the entanglement he thrust himself between two large trunks and squeezed himself through. He proceeded like this toward the source of the screams, going as fast as he could, scratching his face, tearing skin and scraping the feathers from his skirt, and all this time not sure why he was doing this. Raven would be there to crush his skull and suck out his thoughts, he was sure.

The woman was no longer screaming when Tsalagi reached the small open place. She appeared relaxed, leaning back and gazing at him. Smooth dark skin, narrow face, white teeth. She wore a white cloth wrapped around her waist. Her breasts were large and full.

It was the woman's barest movement, the way she wrinkled her nose and widened her eyes slightly, that led to Tsalagi's quick movement to the left.

A black hand swung down beside him, striking a large stone near his feet. Sparks flew, a burning smell in the air.

Tsalagi whirled and crouched with his spear thrust forward. He looked around anxiously: the woman, tangled trees, vines, branches, undergrowth, stones. Nothing else? Then his eyes were drawn to the shadows between two large trunks about six strides in front of him. A darker shape within the gray. He stared in confusion as a dark head thrust itself forward.

"Flint?" he said in wonder.

The figure stepped completely out from the trees and stood motionless, legs apart. His skin seemed as dull as unpolished stone, except for an occasional shine where the muscles made hollows or rises in the flesh. Dark as the darktime. At first Tsalagi thought the man was naked, the shadowed flesh hiding his member, but then decided he was wearing a small skirt that was somehow joined to his body almost seamlessly. The same black color, and that moved as he moved. Tsalagi could distinguish nothing about the man's face, the roughness of it reminding him of broken stone, until under what might have been the man's eyebrow ridge two new shiny places suddenly appeared.

Tsalagi stiffened. "Flint," he said again, with more conviction. Flint was staring at him.

The village grandfathers talked about Flint all the time. Tsalagi remembered several stories from childhood. Flint the Terrible, they liked to call him, a very wicked man. He liked to eat people, especially babies and very young children. His father used to warn him that he shouldn't stray too far from the hut or Flint might get him. There were stories that when parents tried to save their children from Flint, he just ate them up too. No one was safe from Flint.

Flint knocked Tsalagi sprawling over fallen logs and stones. Tsalagi moaned and clutched his back. Flint laughed a hollow laugh like rocks rattling inside a gourd. Like an old man, Tsalagi thought.

Flint ran up to Tsalagi, thrusting one massive foot toward his chest; Tsalagi rolled and scrambled for a higher perch. Flint roared behind him and beat at the rocks. The air smelled as if it were burning.

Tsalagi crouched on the first branch of a large tree, just out of Flint's reach. Flint swung one sharp-edged hand against the wood. Chips flew.

Tsalagi could see now that Flint did look much like an old man in some ways, in some ways as old as the village's oldest grandfathers. Great seams ran down Flint's chest and tangled together on his stomach. His neck had a wide crack in it. What might have been hair seemed the same as the rest of Flint, and looked like small broken stones on top of his head. Flint tilted his head up to Tsalagi, and the two shiny places were there again. Tsalagi shivered and leaped to the next tree just as Flint hacked the trunk rapidly in two.

Then the rattling laughter again, and a voice like stones grinding together: *I'll take you, too. I'll eat the woman first, and I'll finish off with you.*

Flint lowered his head and charged the tree. Tsalagi jumped just as the tree flew to pieces and small fires burst out all around his feet.

Tsalagi found his spear on the ground and turned. Flint charged again, but with his head up. Tsalagi threw the spear. The point shattered and the staff fell beneath Flint's thundering feet.

The rough valleys etched into Flint's stomach were clearly detailed for Tsalagi before he tumbled out of Flint's way. Flint stopped short, turned, and stood looking for the small human being.

Tsalagi had Flint's cracked stomach vaguely in mind when he saw the large trunk resting within a sling of vines just above eye level, but later he would not be able to claim any organized or intricate strategy. He was exhausted and frightened; he also thought the vines might carry him to safety. He was too panicked to notice the precariousness of the tangle of tree trunk, branches, and vines overhead. He simply ran madly, leaped, and clung to a vine.

Tsalagi bellowed as it seemed the entire forest was crashing around him. Vines whipped his back; branches tore at his face and arms as they tumbled past. The vine he clung to bobbed and twisted, spinning him around like a spider at the end of a strand.

But as the vine twisted him toward Flint, he saw the trunk falling and striking the unmoving Flint directly in that tangle of stomach seams.

Flint roared, then burst, and hot flint flew all over the wood.

The woman's foot was injured, so Tsalagi had to carry her. She was heavier than he would have thought, and he soon began to wonder whether he must leave her behind. The cloud was overhead again, and seemed to insist that they travel faster. And she was ungrateful; why should he help her?

But again he was impressed by her beauty. Narrow face, white teeth. Raven's eyes, shining. She pushed up against him, and his stomach began to tighten.

Then he looked down at her again, her long face growing longer, her teeth long and sharp, bright light in her eyes . . . she began to laugh, high-pitched and shrill, the way an animal might laugh.

The old grandfather laughed uproariously and slapped both his knees. The children broke their intense, wrinkled gaze and giggled, winked at each other, and stared dreamily into the fire.

"So that's how Tsalagi destroyed Flint. That's what some of the old people who lived long ago said about it. Now some say Tseg'sgin', the human trickster, killed Flint, and others say Rabbit killed him, but I think it was probably Tsalagi."

The little boy turned and asked, "But, grandfather, what about the woman? What was happening to her?"

"Ah . . ." the grandfather sighed with satisfaction. "That was no beautiful woman, children. That was just Coyote, up to his old tricks again.

"Coyote isn't always a coyote, and you can't always describe him. Some call him the Great Hare, the Crow, even Raven. Our own name for him is Tsistu. And some say he's Old Man, Trickster, Imitator, First Born, Changing Person, Creator.

"Coyote doesn't know about good and bad; he just does what he needs to do. But you know, you can't know the land, you can't live with it and be part of it, unless you know Coyote. Coyote helped the Cherokee be friends to the land and the animals . . ."

Tsalagi stood wordlessly as the woman's outline began to blur, then overlap with that of someone else's. For a moment he thought he saw his own father's face in the cloud of bodily and facial features the woman had become, but then her body started to fade out completely. Her eyes grew brighter as the rest of her disappeared, until finally they hung suspended by themselves in midair, all that was left of her.

The two dark orbs fell to earth with a plop.

Tsalagi approached the eyes uneasily, glancing from side to side for any signs of her. He looked up and could not see the cloud, and was instantly filled with panic. Even though he didn't know the cloud's purpose, it had made him feel safe in this mysterious home of the animals.

The wood had grown darker, the shadows back behind the trunks moving forward and closer to Tsalagi. He stopped to look at the eyes. They looked like two pieces of dark stone. He picked them up and rolled them around in his palm.

Suddenly each eye uncurled from within and stood up on eight tiny legs. Two spiders began walking up his arm. Tsalagi yelped and slung his arms to the side to get rid of them.

The cackling seemed to come from every corner of the wood. Tsalagi watched the two eyes scurrying up a tree trunk.

The laughter continued in a voice half-human and half-animal. A bird swooped low and tormented him with this same laughter. A small squirrel crossed his foot, looked up, and opened up with this same laughter. He jerked his head from side to side, frantic, but could see her nowhere. He wasn't even sure what to look for: the woman, or something else.

An old man walked out of the shadows, adorned in a bark-and-fur skirt and a long bulky cape of feathers. His face was painted in whites and reds, with swirls of bright blue on each cheek. He seemed emaciated but vigorous as he strode directly toward Tsalagi. Then he winked, threw up his cape as if it were a pair of wings. He gestured toward the sky, and thousands of tiny bright dots appeared on the blackness.

He turned and stared at Tsalagi. "Well?"

Tsalagi stared at the old man, then at the small dots of light, then at the old man again. He could think of nothing to say.

The old man spat, turned to the sky, and waved his hands again. The tiny points of light began to swirl, then rearranged themselves in great agitation. The old man looked back at Tsalagi. "What do you say now?"

"I don't understand . . . what are they?" Tsalagi answered.

"Stars!" the old man bellowed. "I was mixing them up! How did you human beings ever get to be so stupid? I wish I'd never made you."

Tsalagi gasped. The old man grinned.

"Yes . . . it's true, young human. If not for me, you wouldn't be standing here so ignorant, or having all those strange anxious dreams." The old man drew up his knees and was suddenly sitting in midair. "It was a long, long time ago, but still long after I'd created the earth." The old man eyed the boy sharply. "Yes, I did that, too. See, there was nothing around but water, me, and all these ducks. Just ducks, no other animals. So I told the ducks that it wasn't good to be alone like that. The grebe dived to the bottom of the water and brought some mud up. So I started in the east, and as I traveled I spread the mud around and made the earth—I made it large so there would be plenty of room. Once we had the earth, there would be things who wanted to be there. We heard a wolf howling, so I knew he would be there. Then came the coyote, and the stones. A star came down and became a tobacco plant. A lot of other things happened; I started the whole thing."

Tsalagi sat before the old man in awe. "You did it all?"

"Everything. Didn't take me that long, either."

"And you made the human beings?"

The old man broke out of his trance and looked down at Tsalagi. "I don't need you to remind me that I haven't finished that particular story, young boy." Tsalagi began to smile, but the old man raised his hand. "So far you human beings have been a great disappointment to me."

Tsalagi noticed something wrong with the old man's head. It appeared to be flat on top. He couldn't remember it being flat before, and then it suddenly seemed even flatter. And wider. And wider. The old man's head was stretching out on both sides, narrowing, and then his neck pulled up into this narrowing, then his arms, his chest, his belly, his legs, all drawing up and widening out into a thin line. Bumps began to grow out along the length of this line. These became larger until Tsalagi realized he was gazing at a distant horizon of mountains. He looked around him: the trees were all gone, the plants, the streams, the rocks. Nothing but an expanse of empty, flat land, extending in all directions.

Moments later a large gray shape was approaching Tsalagi from the horizon line, too rapidly. Tsalagi could not understand the swiftness of the movement, and his head began to pound. Long hair, gray and brown, in front. Narrow head and long teeth. A four-legged animal, as tall as two human beings at its shoulders.

Learn the patience of the spider, the leap of the panther . . .

Tsalagi heard this in his head. "Who are you?"

The voice laughed within his head a time, and then Tsalagi realized he was now hearing it aloud, but the animal's lips weren't moving. *Some call me Coyote,* the voice said.

Coyote's lips began to move. "Or Old Man Coyote. But I prefer for you to call me Coyote."

Coyote winked at Tsalagi with one great eye, and then his body seemed to rearrange itself. Coyote appeared thinner now, his legs larger, and he stood as human beings stood. His stiff front legs slowly began to bend and became as flexible as a human being's arms and hands.

An enormous forest tree suddenly burst full-grown from the land before Coyote.

Coyote plucked out his eyes and threw them up into the air above the tree. "This is how I see long distances," he said. Then the eyes returned to his paws when he commanded. "Now you try."

Coyote handed Tsalagi his eyes, and Tsalagi threw them into the top branches of the tree. But they would not come down when he called them. Coyote called, too, but still they would not return.

"I never should have made you!" Coyote screamed, jumping up and down. He pleaded with his eyes to come down, but they remained where they were.

The sun rose quickly in the sky; in but a short time Tsalagi was able to watch it rise to a spot overhead.

The eyes of Coyote began to swell and attract flies beneath the hot sun. Coyote cursed them.

"The day is fading and I still have much I must teach you," Coyote said to Tsalagi. Then Coyote felt the earth, made a hole with his foot, reached in, and pulled out a struggling little mouse. He plucked out one of the mouse's eyes and fitted it into an empty socket. But the mouse escaped before he could grab the other one.

Coyote pawed at the ground until he had dug up a huge mound of earth. The dirt made a face, then a body, and soon a buffalo stood before them. This time Coyote asked permission, and the buffalo gave him one of his eyes. "The buffalo helps me in my troubles," Coyote explained to Tsalagi. Tsalagi knew he'd never seen such an animal as the buffalo, but for some reason he seemed to know all about him.

Coyote could see again, but he couldn't walk straight. The buffalo eye hung outside the socket, it was so big. The mouse eye rolled around inside and often fell back from the hole so he couldn't see out of that one.

After much practice, Coyote tilted his head and walked that way to keep the small eye from rolling out. Afterwards, Tsalagi always saw Coyote with his head tilted. "Follow me . . . and your first lesson is to beware of overconfidence in magics of any kind," Coyote said.

"Stay awake while I'm talking to you!" the voice shouted in Tsalagi's ear. He opened his eyes to the small white cloud and towering trees overhead.

"It's time you faced facts!" the voice cried again, and Tsalagi rolled over and searched for his tormentor. But all he could see was green and blue leaves, dark bark, stones.

"You've a job to do, a quest! Yes, a quest it is!" the voice shouted again, and Tsalagi finally saw the speaker: a filthy black cockroach lying in front of his feet. Tsalagi pulled back in disgust. The cockroach had an enormous, red-painted mouth.

"Coyote?" Tsalagi whispered.

"What does the forest say?" The sound of Coyote's chuckling coming from the cockroach distressed Tsalagi.

"I . . . I don't know."

"The trouble with you human beings is you never listen. I told you my name once before. But there's no time for that."

The old man stood up and waved to the cloud overhead. It began to lower.

But Tsalagi was still staring at the old man. He wore Raven's head over his own. He looked down at the obviously troubled boy. "You must learn to make a friend of Raven, too."

Tsalagi stared at the back of Raven's head, the old man's narrow shoulders, as white mist swirled around them both. The head turned and the dark woman smiled at him with needle-sharp teeth.

"Let us go," she said.

The cloud rose up above the trees, bearing the woman and Tsalagi toward the sun. "Yes, this is mine too," she said without turning, answering a question Tsalagi had been thinking.

Tsalagi was remembering several things he *may* have done with Coyote during their time together, but they could have been dreamed, or Coyote might have just told him about them, he'd never be sure: picking berries from the bottom of a stream; watching as Coyote made one dark and twisting wind after another and sent them marching across the flat land; eating snakes; taking himself apart piece by piece and throwing the pieces through a small hole in a hollow tree; and images of other events he couldn't even begin to put together.

The giant cockroach spoke up. "This is but one possible future, Tsalagi; there are many. The choice is yours."

The high mountain clearing with his village had replaced the sun before them. The cockroach stepped out of the cloud and walked toward the hut of Tsalagi's family. It turned at the halfway point, a tall handsome man with dark, dark eyes, Raven's feathers draped over his shoulders. His voice was somber. "I've but one more tale to narrate for you, young boy."

Coyote entered the family's hut, and it was as if Tsalagi could see through walls.

Coyote told one of Tsalagi's sisters that he was very fond of her and, spreading the Raven's wings over his chest and calmly rearranging his skirt, told the father that he would kill her if she refused to become his wife. Tsalagi's father became enraged and shouted, "You're no good! She won't have you!"

Tsalagi watched as days passed before his eyes. His sister grew ill; he watched her waste away until she was on her deathbed. His father brought in everyone in the village who thought they might have a cure, offering everything he had in exchange, but she only grew worse. They could do nothing. She died.

Tsalagi cried as they wrapped her in blankets and laid her on a raised platform outside the village. An old woman in a black hood came into the clearing and stood beside the platform. When everyone was gone she threw back the hood and Tsalagi recognized her as an older version of the dark beautiful woman. He gritted his teeth. "Coyote!" he cried.

Coyote laughed his old woman's laugh and then called up to the platform, "Get up! Get up!" The body moved on the platform! Tsalagi clenched his fist; perhaps Coyote wasn't so bad after all, just a trickster, a joker.

Then Coyote took Tsalagi's sister to a pool in the sky. There he sang a power song and bathed the body. The girl sat up in the water and Coyote touched her eyes and fixed them so they would open, washed away the smell of death from her body, and put a sweet smell into her breath again.

"I am your husband," Coyote told her. If you ever leave me, you will die again." Tsalagi watched in anger.

It was not long afterwards that Tsalagi's father discovered the desecrated grave site and followed his daughter's trail to the pool in the sky (although Tsalagi knew it wasn't really in the sky—Tsalagi knew this was just Coyote's way of showing him). His father shouted at Coyote. Coyote said nothing.

Tsalagi's father grabbed his daughter, saying, "We are leaving. This one is no good."

"But if I go back he says I will die again," she said.

"This one is always lying," spat the father, and took his daughter away.

Again Tsalagi watched nervously as his sister lay in bed. She would not eat; she went to sleep right away. The next morning she made no sound, and Tsalagi's mother discovered that she was dead once again.

Tsalagi moaned as his father returned to the pool in the sky where Coyote had been watching. Would Coyote kill his father too? But then, Coyote had died many times and been revived by the bluebirds; perhaps he would do the same for his sister. Of course, it must just be Coyote, up to his old tricks again.

"Please come and doctor my daughter," Tsalagi's father said to Coyote. "If you do this you may have her as your wife."

"But I'm no good, remember? After this, medicine men can doctor the sick, but no one will be able to help the dead." Then Coyote laughed his strangest laugh, a laugh like screaming birds. He shrank into a small dark bird and flew away, still laughing.

"I never make promises," the old man told Tsalagi, "but if you do a thing for me, perhaps I will reconsider and bring your sister back to life."

Tsalagi frowned and looked at his hands. For a moment they looked like Coyote's paws and he was afraid, but then they appeared as hands again. "But, Coyote, why do you pull these tricks to make us do things? Why not just ask us?"

"You human beings will only respond to tricks, that's your shortcoming. You do not understand the animal ways."

They were back in the forest again, in a part darker and stranger than any other place Tsalagi had been. Odd sounds broke his thoughts. His body did not feel good.

"All right, Coyote. What do I do?"

"I have a dragon for you, called Uk'ten', that you must kill. But first you will need another weapon."

"I have a spear with a point from Flint. And a blowgun."

Coyote snorted. "Uk'ten' would break those in two. You need Snake. I'll take you where you can find him."

"Why am I to kill this Uk'ten', Coyote?"

"Everyone is frightened by Uk'ten'. You need to make friends with me, with the Thunder Beings who hate Uk'ten'. You human beings need animal friends if you ever want to leave the village and live in the great wood."

Coyote showed Tsalagi how to burn a log until it was almost hollow, then to scrape away the burning parts. This made a vessel that Coyote called a canoe, for traveling the stream—which had now grown much larger—through the wood. The stream would take him to Snake and Uk'ten'. A little of the cloud went with Tsalagi, floating on the water around the edges of his canoe. The rest stayed behind with Coyote, swirling around him until he was completely covered up. The last time Tsalagi looked back before heading down the stream, both had disappeared.

"What did this Uk'ten' look like, grandfather?" The children were agitated, staring into the fire wide-eyed.

"A dragon, children, is many things which never belonged together, suddenly all inside one animal. The darkest of all the dark animals. In all its parts, the forest is as much a part of it as it is part of the forest.

"The old grandfathers had different stories about how Uk'ten' looked, but I believe he was like this: head of a great raven, chest of a buffalo, hips of a giant cockroach, legs of a hare, eyes of a spider, tail of old possum."

The children giggled.

"Don't laugh, children," the grandfather warned. "Uk'ten' was a bad animal, terrible. All the animals, even the great ones, were afraid of him. No one knew what to do, until Coyote thought maybe this new animal, the human being, might kill him since Uk'ten' did not know or understand the human being. But it was a dangerous quest for Tsalagi."

The grandfather settled back to continue his tale of Tsalagi, trying to ignore the wails of those mourning their dead in the other wagons. What could be the future for these children? He hoped they would not hear the wails for at least the short time of this tale.

The place where Coyote had told him he would discover Snake was easy to find. Not long after he had left Coyote, Tsalagi recognized the landmark he was to seek: a huge stump at the bend of the river. He used the long pole he'd cut to steer over to the bank, and pulled his canoe up on shore only a small distance from the stump. As instructed, he climbed up and stood over the many holes at the top. Then he chanted the charm Coyote had taught him:

"Red Lightning! *Ha!* You will be holding my soul in your clenched hand.

"Ha! As high as the Red Treetops—*Ha!*—my soul will be alive and moving over there.

"Ha! It will be glimmering here below.

"Ha! My body will become the size of a hair, the size of my shadow!"

And the next instant a long black snake leaped out of one of the holes and was writhing in Tsalagi's left hand. Tsalagi yelled and struggled with the snake which seemed confused, darting head and tail in opposite directions as if it were trying to stretch itself, making short, tight arcs with the length of its body.

Tsalagi heard Coyote laugh, and the snake suddenly went rigid in his hand, then a sheen crept over the hardened body.

A snapping turtle had appeared on the edge of the stump. It bobbed its head up and down, then said, "Don't just stand there, sharpen it on the top of my shell."

"Sharpen it?" Tsalagi looked at the curious black implement.

"Yes, stupid; it's a weapon."

"Weapon?"

"Sharpen it! Uk'ten' will be here any time; I sent a message to Thunder to lead him here. Snake is a kind of long knife, very hard. It's your only chance against the dragon."

Tsalagi held the long object against the rough surface of Coyote-turtle's back and rubbed it back and forth. The snake had straightened out enough so that it did resemble a long knife, but with a small bend here and there. The rocklike snake head made a good grip.

"Find his underside, some soft place there," Coyote-turtle said, even as he was changing himself into a rainbow-hued fish and flapped back into the stream.

Tsalagi turned, Snake in hand, as a large cloud of mist was settling into the forest floor. Before the mist had drifted away, he could hear the snarls and tearing sounds of a fierce battle.

A large, dark shape, something like a human being's shadow blown all out of proportion, stumbled back out of the mist, followed by the dragon Uk'ten', swinging its great-beaked head from side to side and lashing out with its segmented tail. The dark figure roared: Thunder, as Tsalagi had learned. Then the figure suddenly vanished, leaving the air spotted with small fires that quickly died out.

Uk'ten' seemed to stare at Tsalagi with his enormous spider-eyes, and began advancing slowly toward the trembling boy. Tsalagi raised Snake to ward off the attack.

But the long knife suddenly began writhing in Tsalagi's hands. He clutched the squirming head and snapping jaws tightly, maneuvering his body in a rough circle as Snake attempted to slap his face and shoulders with the tail. Finally Snake pulled free and escaped Tsalagi's grip.

Beware of overconfidence in magics of any kind . . .

Tsalagi hadn't even considered acting without the sword, and at first ran around the clearing while Uk'ten' chased him. He grabbed at a stick and turned just as the dragon had him backed against a large stone, and used the stick to keep the snapping, drooling, venomous jaws away from his face.

Uk'ten' curled his tail from overhead and brought it down against the stone, but Tsalagi had already leaped aside.

Once behind the dragon, Tsalagi reached for a large stone to throw at the raven's head, but once the stone moved, Tsalagi realized it was part of the dragon's foot. He turned and ran for shelter.

Things aren't as they seem sometimes . . .

Uk'ten' roared and twisted around in the undergrowth, crushing plants flat and uprooting small bushes. Enraged, he swung his tail in a blind maneuver, apparently attempting to find the young boy's body, and the great segmented tail crashed through a small tree trunk.

Learn to be resourceful . . .

Tsalagi searched the brush frantically for a stone, a limb, anything he might throw. Without thinking, he found the turtle, picked it up, and threw it at the surprised Uk'ten'.

The turtle shouted, startled, with Coyote's voice as it bounced off the dragon's scaled hide. Uk'ten' swung to find the creature, but Coyote had already turned himself into shadow.

"Observe what happens if you touch his tail, boy. I suggest you avoid it," Coyote's voice whispered in Tsalagi's ear. Coyote materialized behind the dragon, grabbed the tail rather comically, and his arm immediately fell off. Then the rest of his flesh dissolved, leaving a pile of bones behind the dragon.

The dead sometimes are reborn . . .

But then Coyote was beside him, saying, "See how poisonous an Uk'ten' is? See what happens?" before he disappeared once again.

Tsalagi ran to pick up the spear inside his canoe, when he tripped over the turtle which had again materialized. Needles of pain worried his back, and his head seemed to have become a cloud.

Remember to watch your step . . .

Uk'ten' turned and rushed behind Tsalagi. As Tsalagi fell, the dragon tumbled over him, stood upright, and did not see the frightened Tsalagi cowering underneath. Then Tsalagi pulled out his flint knife and began slashing at Uk'ten's soft underbelly.

Uk'ten' bellowed and twisted around even as Tsalagi rolled out and leaped into the brush. There he landed on Snake, who was now stiff and weaponlike again. With renewed confidence the boy stood up and motioned arrogantly at the dragon. After all, Coyote wanted the Uk'ten' slain; he would not betray him now, surely.

The dragon stood and stared at the boy, its head bobbing up and down. Its great legs pounded the forest floor in impatience.

So Tsalagi made the first move, with the long knife Snake feeling rigid and reassuring in his hand. He watched the scales carefully. They made fine armor, he thought. How would he get through? He took a cautious side step to the canoe, the dragon watching him carefully, and retrieved his spear with the other hand. He continued his approach, both weapons raised and ready.

Uk'ten' roared and thundered forward. Tsalagi pushed the great head off with the spear and began hacking at the cracks between some of the scales with Snake. The strange clang the two surfaces made upon meeting bothered him, but soon he could see a thin line of pale liquid seeping between the seams. He hacked and levered with the crooked blade, until finally great rivulets of the pale liquid began to flow.

Uk'ten' whipped his tail around and Tsalagi had to throw himself to the ground to avoid it. He could taste the poison as it passed.

Tsalagi shoved the spear deep into the dragon's neck. The dragon swung its body around and several of its scales ripped into his side. He doubled over with the pain, surprised he hadn't died instantly. Perhaps the poison wasn't the same in every part of the dragon's body.

Uk'ten' attempted to move its great bulk around in order to get a good place to swipe Tsalagi with its poisonous tail. But instead it ran afoul of the shoreline and Tsalagi's canoe. It made one false step into the canoe, then flipped over on its back at the water's edge. Tsalagi ran and positioned himself by the white and tender belly. He looked down at the great Uk'ten', listening to its labored breathing, and slowly raised Snake overhead for a thrust.

You must learn to make friends of Raven, too . . .

Tsalagi gazed into the forest: the great dark head, the yellow beak, the all-encompassing midnight wings . . .

. . . and thrust down with all his strength. It took a long time for the great Uk'ten' to die.

Tsalagi did not see Coyote again that day, nor did he stay around to gloat and fill himself with pride. He climbed back into the canoe to head upriver, already planning the difficult if not impossible journey back to his home village.

He had seen something in Raven's eyes he did not like. He had seen himself, and had shamefully enjoyed that sense of recognition.

You must learn to make friends of Raven, too . . .

And much to his pain, Tsalagi had. He had made a friend of Raven the killer, who enjoys what he destroys.

"But, grandfather, that can't be the end of the story!" the children wailed. "Did Tsalagi have any more adventures? Did he ever see Coyote again? What about his sister? Did Coyote bring her back to life as he'd promised?" They watched the fire anxiously; the old man could tell they'd stayed up too long. They were restless.

"Tsalagi had many more adventures, most of which I will tell you in the future, many of them with that devil Coyote. And remember what Coyote said about promises. No, he did not revive Tsalagi's sister. Those who are dead will always remain so, after Coyote made his decision that time.

"Never believe anything Coyote says. He is complicated, hard to figure. He is an opposite to himself. This, I think, was his big lesson for Tsalagi."

The children fell asleep, and the grandfather sat by the fire and waited for the sleep to overtake him as well. He loved the old stories about Cherokee heroes; he was glad the children did, too. Somewhere, someone was crying. He'd seen them carrying the bodies out of the wagons even as he finished his story. Three more dead. The Ravenmockers were busy this night.

He felt greatly tired, but said a prayer they wouldn't come for him this week, not until he'd finished his tales.

The Kemosabee

Mike Resnick

So me and the Masked Man, we decide to hook up and bring evildoers to justice, which is a pretty full-time occupation considering just how many of these *momzers* there are wandering the West. Of course, I don't work on Saturdays, but this is never a problem, since he's usually sleeping off Friday night's binge and isn't ready to get back in the saddle until about half past Monday.

We get along pretty well, though we don't talk much to each other—my English is a little rusty, and his Yiddish is nonexistent—but we share our food when times are tough, and we're always saving each other's lives, just like it says in the dime novels.

Now, you'd think two guys who spend a whole year riding together wouldn't have any secrets from each other, but actually that's not the case. We respect each other's privacy, and it is almost twelve months to the day after we form a team that we find ourselves answering a call of nature at the very same time, and I look over at him, and I am so surprised I could just *plotz,* you know what I mean?

It's then that I start calling him Kemosabee, and finally one day he asks me what it means, and I tell him that it means "uncircumcized *goy,"* and he kind of frowns and tells me that he doesn't know what *either* word means, so I sit him down and explain that Indians are one of the lost Hebrew tribes, only we aren't as lost as we're supposed to be, because Custer and the rest of those *meshugginah* soldiers keep finding us and blowing us to smithereens. And the Kemosabee, he asks if Hebrew is a suburb of Hebron, and right away I see we've got an enormous cultural gap to overcome.

But what the hell, we're pardners, and we're doing a pretty fair job of ridding the West of horse thieves and stage robbers and other varmints, so I say, "Look, Kemosabee, you're a *mensch* and I'm proud to ride with you, and if you wanna get drunk and *shtup* a bunch of *shikses* whenever we go into town, that's your business and who am I to tell you what to do? But Butch Cavendish and his gang are giving me enough *tsouris* this month, so if we stop off at any Indian villages, let's let this be our little secret, okay?"

And the Kemosabee, who is frankly a lot quicker with his guns than his brain, just kind of frowns and looks hazy and finally nods his head, though I'm sure he doesn't know what he's nodding about.

Well, we ride on for another day or two, and finally reach his secret silver mine, and he melts some of it down and shoves it into his shells, and like always I ride off and hunt up Reb Running Bear and have him say kaddish over the bullets, and when I hunt up the Masked Man again I find he has had the *chutzpah* to take on the whole Cavendish gang singlehanded, and since they know he never shoots to kill and they ain't got any such compunctions, they leave him lying there for dead with a couple of new *pupiks* in his belly.

So I make a sled and hook it to the back of his horse, which he calls Silver but which he really ought to call White, or at least White with the Ugly Brown Blotch on His Belly, and I hop up on my pony, and pretty soon we're in front of Reb Running Bear's tent, and he comes out and looks at the Masked Man lying there with his ten-gallon Stetson for a long moment, and then he turns to me and says, "You know, that has got to be the ugliest *yarmulkah* I've ever seen."

"This is my pardner," I say. "Some *goniffs* drygulched him. You got to make him well."

Reb Running Bear frowns. "He doesn't look like one of the Chosen People to me. Where was he bar mitzvahed?"

"He wasn't," I say. "But he's one of the Good Guys. He and I are cleaning up the West."

"Six years in Hebrew school and you settle for being a janitor?" he says.

"Don't give me a hard time," I say. "We got bad guys to shoot and wrongs to right. Just save the Kemosabee's life."

"The Kemosabee?" he repeats. "Would I be very far off the mark if I surmised that he doesn't keep kosher?"

"Look," I say, deciding that it's time to play hardball, "I hadn't wanted to bring this up, but I know what you and Mrs. Screaming Hawk were doing last time I visited this place."

"Keep your voice down or that *yenta* I married will make my life hell!" he whispers, glancing back toward his teepee. Then he grimaces. "Mrs. Screaming Hawk. Serves me right for taking her to Echo Canyon. *Feh!*"

I stare at him. "So, *nu?*"

"All right, all right, Jehovah and I will nurse the Kemosabee back to health."

"Good," I say.

He glares at me. "But just this one time. Then I pass the word to all the other rabbis: we don't cure no more *goyim*. What have they ever done for us?"

Well, I am all prepared to argue the point, because I'm a pretty open-minded kind of guy, but just then the Kemosabee starts moaning and I realize that if I argue for more than a couple of minutes we could all be sitting *shivah* for him before dinnertime, so I wander off and pay a visit to Mrs. Rutting Elk to console her on the sudden passing of her husband and see if there is anything I can do to cheer her up, and Reb Running Bear gets to work, and lo and behold, in less than a week the Masked Man is up and around and getting impatient to go out after desperadoes, so we thank Reb Running Bear for his services, and he loads my pardner down with a few canteens of chicken soup, and we say a fond *shalom* to the village.

I am hoping we have a few weeks for the Kemosabee to regain his strength, of which I think he is still missing an awful lot, but as fate would have it, we are riding for less than two hours when we come across the Cavendish gang's trail.

"Aha!" he says, studying the hoofprints. "All thirty of them! This is our chance for revenge!"

My first thought is to say something like "What do you mean *we*, mackerel eater?"—but then I remember that Good Guys never back down from a challenge, so I simply say "Ugh!" which is my opinion of taking on thirty guys at once, but which he insists on interpreting as an affirmative.

We follow the trail all day, and when it's too dark to follow it any longer, we make camp on a small hill.

"We should catch up with them just after sunrise," says the Masked Man, and I can see that his trigger finger is getting itchy.

"Ugh," I say.

"We'll meet them on the open plain, where nobody can hide."

"Double ugh with yogurt on it," I say.

"You look very grim, old friend," he says.

"Funny you should mention it," I say, but before I can suggest that we just forget the whole thing, he speaks again.

"You can have the other twenty-nine, but Cavendish is mine."

"You're all heart, Kemosabee," I say.

He stands up, stretches, and walks over to his bedroll. "Well, we've got a hard day's bloodletting ahead of us. We'd best get some sleep."

He lies down, and ten seconds later he's snoring like all get-out, and I sit there staring at him, and I just know he's not gonna come through this unscathed, and I remember Reb Running Bear's promise that no medicine man would ever again treat a *goy*.

And the more I think about it, the more I think that it's up to me, the loyal sidekick, to do something about it. And finally it occurs to me just what I have to do, because if I can't save him from the Cavendish gang, the least I can do is save him from himself.

So I go over to my bedroll and pull out a bottle of Mogen David and pour a little on my hunting knife, and try to remember the exact words the medicine man recites during the *bris,* and I know that someday, when he calms down, he'll thank me for this.

In the meantime, I'm gonna have to find a new nickname for my pardner.

Going After Old Man Alabama

William Sanders

C harlie Badwater was the most powerful medicine man in all the eastern Oklahoma hill country. Or the biggest witch, depending on which person you listened to; among Cherokees the distinction tends to be a little hazy.

Either way, when Thomas Cornstalk finally decided that something had to be done about Old Man Alabama, he didn't need to think twice before getting in his old Dodge pickup truck and driving over to Charlie Badwater's place. Thomas Cornstalk was no slouch of a medicine man himself, but in a situation like this you went to the man with the power.

Charlie Badwater lived by himself in a one-room log cabin at the end of a really bad dirt road, up near the head of Butcherknife Hollow. There was nobody in sight when Thomas Cornstalk drove up, but as he got down from the pickup cab a big gray owl fluttered down from the surrounding woods and disappeared into the deep shadows behind the cabin. A moment later the cabin door opened and Charlie Badwater stepped out into the sunlight. " *'Siyo, Tami, dohiju?''* he called.

Thomas Cornstalk half-raised a hand in casual greeting. He and Charlie Badwater went back a long way. " *'Siyo, Jali. Gado haduhne?* Catching any mice?" he added dryly.

Charlie Badwater chuckled deep in his chest without moving his lips. "Hey," he said, "remember old Moses Otter?" And they both chuckled together, remembering.

Moses Otter had been a mean old man with a permanent case of professional jealousy, especially toward anybody who might have enough power to make him look bad. Since Moses Otter had never in his life been more than a second-rate witch, this included a lot of people.

One of his nastier tricks had been to turn himself into an owl—he could do that all right, but then who can't?—and fly over the woods until he spotted a clearing where a possible rival was growing medicine tobacco. Now of course serious tobacco has to be grown absolutely unseen by anyone except the person who will be using it, so this had meant a great deal of frustration and ruined medicine all over the area. Quite a few people had tried to witch Moses Otter and put a stop to this crap, but his protective medicine had always worked.

Charlie Badwater, then a youthful and inexperienced unknown, had gone to Moses Otter's place and told him in front of several witnesses that if he enjoyed being a bird he could have a hell of a good time from now on. And had turned him on the spot into the mangiest, scabbiest turkey buzzard ever seen in Oklahoma; and Moses Otter, after a certain amount of flopping around trying to change himself back, had flown away, never to be seen again except perhaps as an unidentifiable member of a gang of roadkill-pickers down on the Interstate.

That, Thomas Cornstalk recalled, had been the point at which everybody had realized that Charlie Badwater was somebody special. Maybe they hadn't fully grasped just how great he would one day become, but the word had definitely gone out that Charlie Badwater was somebody you didn't want to screw around with.

Now, still chuckling, Charlie Badwater tilted his head in the direction of his cabin. *"Kawi jaduli'?* Got a pot just made."

They went inside the cabin and Thomas Cornstalk sat down at the little pine-board table while Charlie Badwater poured a couple of cups of hell-black coffee from a blue and white speckled metal pot. "Ought to be ready to walk by now," Charlie Badwater said. "Been on the stove a long time."

"Good coffee," Thomas Cornstalk affirmed, tasting. "Damn near eat it with a fork."

They sat at the table, drinking coffee and smoking hand-rolled cigarettes, not talking for the moment: a couple of fifty-some-odd-year-old full-bloods, similarly dressed in work shirts and Wal-Mart jeans and cheap nylon running shoes made in Singapore. Charlie Badwater had the classic lean, deep-chested, no-ass build of the mountain Cherokee, while Thomas Cornstalk was one of those heavyset, round-faced types who may or may not have some Choctaw blood from way back in old times. Their faces, however, were similarly weathered, their hands callused and scarred from years of manual labor. Charlie Badwater was missing the end joint of his left index finger. There were only three people who knew how he had lost it and two of them were dead and nobody had the nerve to ask the third one. Let alone Charlie.

They talked a little, finally, about this and that; routine inquiries about the health of relatives, remarks about the weather, the usual pleasantries that a couple of properly raised Cherokee men will exchange before getting down to the real point of a conversation. But Thomas Cornstalk, usually the politest of men, was worried enough to hold the small talk to the bare minimum required by decency.

"Gusdi nusdi," he said finally. "Something's the matter. I'm not sure what," he added, in response to the inquiry in Charlie Badwater's eyes. "It's Old Man Alabama."

"That old weirdo?" Charlie Badwater wrinkled his nose very slightly, as if smelling something bad. "What's he up to these days? Still nutty as a *kenuche* ball, I guess?"

"Who knows? That's what I came to talk with you about," Thomas Cornstalk said. "He's up to something, all right, and I think it's trouble."

Old Man Alabama was a seriously strange old witch—in his case there was no question at all about the definition—who lived on top of a mountain over in Adair County, not far from the Arkansas line. He wasn't Cherokee; he claimed to be the last surviving descendant of the Alabama tribe, and he often gibbered and babbled in a language he claimed was the lost Alabama tongue. It could have been; Thomas Cornstalk couldn't recognize a word of it, and he spoke sixteen Indian languages as well as English and Spanish—that was his special medicine, the ability to speak in different tongues; he could also talk with animals. On the other hand it might just as easily have been a lot of meaningless blather, which was what Thomas Cornstalk and a good many other people suspected.

There was also the inconvenient fact that there were still some Alabamas living on a reservation down in Texas, big as you please; but it had been a long time since anybody had pointed this out in Old Man Alabama's hearing. Not after what had happened to the last big-mouth to bring the subject up.

Whatever he was—Thomas Cornstalk had long suspected he was some kind of Creek or Seminole or maybe Yuchi, run off by his own people—Old Man Alabama was as crazy as the Devil and twice as nasty. That much was certain.

He was skinny and tall and he had long arms that he waved wildly about while talking, or for no apparent reason at all. Everything about him was long: long matted hair falling past his shoulders, long beaky nose, long bony fingers ending in creepy-looking long nails. He walked with a strange angling gait, one shoulder higher than the other, and he spat constantly, *tuff tuff tuff,* so you could follow him down a dirt road on a dry day by the little brown spots in the dust.

It was widely believed that he had a long tongue like a moth's, that he kept curled up in his mouth and only stretched out at night during unspeakable acts. That was another story people weren't eager to investigate first hand.

He also stank. Not the way a regular man smelled bad, even a very dirty regular man—though Old Man Alabama was sure as hell dirty enough—but a horrible, eye-watering stench that reminded you of things like rotten cucumbers and dead skunks on the highway in hot weather. That alone would have been reason enough for people to give him a wide berth, even if they hadn't been afraid of him.

And oh, yes, people *were* afraid of him. Mothers hid their pregnant daughters indoors when they saw him walking by the house, afraid that even a single direct look from those hooded reptilian eyes might cause monstrous deformities to the unborn.

Most people, in fact, avoided talking about him at all; it was well known that witches knew when they were being talked about, and the last thing people wanted was to draw the displeased attention of a witch as powerful and unpredictable as Old Man Alabama. It was a measure of the power of both Charlie Badwater and Thomas Cornstalk that they were willing to talk freely about him. Even so, Thomas Cornstalk would have been just as comfortable if Charlie Badwater hadn't spoken quite so disrespectfully about the old man.

"All I know," Thomas Cornstalk said, "he's been cooking up some kind of almighty powerful medicine up on that mountain of his. I go over that way pretty often, you know, got some relatives that call me up every time one of their kids gets a runny nose . . . anyway, sometimes you can hear these sounds, up where your ear can't quite get ahold of them, like those dog whistles, huh? And people see strange lights up on the mountain at night, and sometimes in the daytime the air looks sort of shimmery above the mountaintop, the way it does over a hot stove. Lots of smoke too, that's another thing. I got a smell or two when the wind was right and I don't know what the old man's burning up there but it's nothing I'd want in *my* medicine bag."

He paused, sipping his coffee, his eyes wandering about the interior of the cabin. Lots of medicine men live surrounded by all sorts of junk, their houses littered and smelly, walls and ceiling hung with bundles of dried herbs and feathers and skins and bones and other parts of birds and animals. Charlie Badwater's cabin, however, was as neat as a white doctor's office, everything stowed carefully away out of sight.

"I went up to see him, finally," Thomas Cornstalk said. "Or tried to, but he was either gone or hiding. I couldn't get close to the cabin. He's got the place circled—you know? You get to about ten or fifteen steps from the cabin and it starts to be harder and harder to walk, like you're stepping in molasses, till finally you can't go any farther. By then the cabin looks all rubbery, too, like it's melting. I had my pipe with me, and some good tobacco, and I tried every *igawesdi* I know for getting past a protective spell. Whatever Old Man Alabama has around that cabin, it's no ordinary medicine."

"Huh." Charlie Badwater was beginning to look interested. "See anything? I mean anything to suggest what's going on."

"Not a thing." Thomas Cornstalk pulled his shoulder blades together for a second. "Place made my skin crawl so bad, I got out pretty quick. Went home and smoked myself nearly black. Burned enough cedar for a Christmas-tree lot before I felt clean again."

"Huh," Charlie Badwater said again. He sat for a minute or so in silence, staring out through the open cabin door, though there was nothing out there but a stretch of dusty yard and the woods beyond.

"All right," he said at last, and got to his feet. "We better go pay Old Man Alabama a visit."

Thomas Cornstalk stood up too. "You want to go right now?" he said, a little surprised.

"Sure. You got something else you have to do?"

"No," Thomas Cornstalk admitted, after a moment's hesitation. He wasn't really ready for this, he thought, but maybe it was better to get on with it. The longer they waited, the better the chance that Old Man Alabama would find out they were coming, and do something unusually bad to try and stop them.

Charlie Badwater started toward the door. Thomas Cornstalk said, "You're not taking any stuff along? You know, medicine?"

Charlie Badwater patted his jeans pockets. "Got my pipe and some tobacco on me. I don't expect I'll need anything else."

Going out the door, following Charlie Badwater across the yard, Thomas Cornstalk shook his head in admiring wonder. That Charlie, he thought. Probably arm-wrestle the Devil left-handed, if he got a chance. Probably win, too.

They rode back down the dirt road in Thomas Cornstalk's old pickup truck. Charlie Badwater didn't own any kind of car or truck. He didn't have a telephone or electricity in his cabin, either. It was some mysterious but necessary part of his personal medicine.

The dirt track came out of the woods, after a mile or so of dust and rocks and sun-hardened ruts, and joined up with a winding gravel road that dipped down across the summer-dry bed of Butcherknife Creek and then climbed up the side of Turkeyfoot Ridge. On the far side of the ridge, the gravel turned into potholed county blacktop. Several miles farther along, they came out onto the Stilwell road. "Damn, Charlie," Thomas Cornstalk said, hanging a left, "you think you could manage to live further back in the woods?"

"Not without coming out on the other side," Charlie Badwater said.

The road up the side of Old Man Alabama's mountain was even worse than the one to Charlie Badwater's place. "I was here just this morning," Thomas Cornstalk said, fighting the wheel, "and I swear this mule track is in worse shape than it was then. And look at that," he exclaimed, and stepped on the brake pedal. "I know *that* wasn't there before—"

A big uprooted white oak tree was lying across the road. The road was littered with snapped-off limbs and still-green leaves. The two men in the pickup truck looked at each other. There hadn't been so much as a stiff breeze all day.

"Get out and walk, then," Charlie Badwater said after a minute. "We can use the exercise, I guess."

They got out and walked on up the road, climbing over the fallen tree. A little way beyond, the biggest rattlesnake Thomas Cornstalk had ever seen was lying in the road, looking at them. It coiled up and rattled its tail and showed its fangs but Charlie Badwater merely said, *"Ayuh jaduji,"* and the huge snake uncoiled and slid quietly off into the woods while Charlie and Thomas walked past.

"I always wondered," Thomas Cornstalk said as they trudged up the steep mountainside. "You suppose a rattlesnake really believes you're his uncle, when you say that?"

"Who knows? It doesn't matter how things work, Thomas. It just matters that they *do* work." Charlie Badwater grinned. "Talked to this professor from Northeastern State once, showed up at a stomp dance down at Redbird. He said Cherokees are pragmatists."

"What's that mean?"

"Beats me. I told him most of the ones I know are Baptists, with a few Methodists and of course there's a lot of people getting into those holy-roller outfits—" Charlie Badwater stopped suddenly in the middle of the road. "Huh," he grunted softly, as if to himself. Thomas Cornstalk couldn't remember ever seeing him look so surprised.

They had rounded the last bend in the road and had come in sight of Old Man Alabama's cabin. Except the cabin itself was barely in sight of all, in any normal sense. The whole clearing where the cabin stood was walled off by a kind of curtain of yellowish light, through which the outlines of the cabin showed only vaguely and irregularly. The sky looked somehow darker directly above the clearing, and all the surrounding trees seemed to have taken on strange and disturbing shapes. There was a high-pitched whining sound in the air, like the singing of a million huge mosquitoes.

"You were right, Thomas," Charlie Badwater said after a moment. "The old turd's gotten hold of something heavy. Who'd have thought it?"

"It wasn't like this when I was here this morning," Thomas Cornstalk said, looking around him and feeling very uneasy. "Not so *extreme,* like."

"Better have a look, then." Charlie Badwater took out a buckskin pouch and a short-stemmed pipe. Facing toward the sun, he poured a little tobacco from the pouch into his palm and began to sing, a strange-sounding song that Thomas Cornstalk had never heard before. Four times he sang the song through, pausing at the end of each repetition to blow softly on the tobacco. Then he stuffed the tobacco into the bowl of the pipe. It was an ordinary cheap briar pipe, the kind they sell off cardboard wall displays in country gas stations. In Cherokee medicine there is no particular reverence or importance placed on the pipe itself; the tobacco carries all the power, and then only if properly doctored with the right *igawesdi* words. Charlie Badwater could, if he had preferred, have simply rolled the tobacco into a cigarette and used that.

He lit the pipe with a plastic butane lighter and walked toward the cabin, puffing. Thomas Cornstalk followed, rather reluctantly. He didn't like this, but he would have followed Charlie Badwater to hell. Which, of course, might very well be where they were about to go.

Charlie Badwater pointed the stem of the pipe at the shimmering wall of light that blocked their way. Four times he blew smoke at the barrier, long dense streams of bluish white smoke that curled and eddied back strangely as they hit the bright curtain. On the fourth puff there was a sharp cracking sound and suddenly the curtain was gone and the humming stopped and there was only a weed-grown clearing and a tumbledown gray board shack badly in need of a new roof. Somewhere nearby a bird began singing, as if relieved.

"Asuh," Thomas Cornstalk murmured in admiration.

"Make me think, I'll teach you that one some time," Charlie Badwater said. "It's not hard, once you learn the song . . . well, let's have a look around."

They walked slowly toward the cabin. There wasn't much to see.

The yard was littered with an amazing assortment of junk—broken crockery and rusting pots and pans, chicken feathers and unidentifiable bones, bottles and cans, a wrecked chair with stuffing coming out of the cushions—but none of it suggested anything except that you wouldn't want Old Man Alabama living next door. A big pile of turtle shells lay on the sagging front porch. There was a rattlesnake skin nailed above the door.

"No smoke," Charlie Badwater said, studying the chimney. "Reckon he's gone? Well, one way to find out."

He stepped up onto the porch and turned to look back at Thomas Cornstalk, who hadn't moved. "Coming?"

"You go," Thomas Cornstalk said. "I'll wait out here for you. If it's all the same to you." He wouldn't have gone inside that cabin for a million dollars and a lifetime ticket to the Super Bowl. "Need to work on my tan," he added.

Charlie Badwater chuckled and disappeared through the cabin door. There was no sound of voices or anything else from within, so Thomas Cornstalk figured he must have been right about Old Man Alabama being gone. That didn't make much sense; why would the old maniac have put up such a fancy protective spell if he wasn't going to be inside? Come to think of it, *how* could he have laid on that barrier from the outside? As far as Thomas Cornstalk knew, a spell like that had to be worked from inside the protective circle. But nothing about this made any sense. . . .

Charlie Badwater's laugh came through the open cabin door. "You're not going to believe this," he called. "I don't believe it myself."

"What did you find?" Thomas Cornstalk said as Charlie came back out.

"About what you'd expect, mostly. A whole bunch of weird stuff piled every which way and hanging from the ceiling, all of it dirty as a pigpen and stinking so bad you can hardly breathe in there. Nothing unusual—considering who and what lives here—except these."

He held up a stack of books. Thomas Cornstalk stared. "Books?" he said in amazement. "What's Old Man Alabama doing with books? I know for a fact he can't read."

"Who knows? Maybe got them to wipe his ass with. Ran out of pine cones or whatever he uses." Charlie Badwater sat down on the edge of the porch and began flipping through the books. "Looks like he stole them from the school over at Rocky Mountain. Old bastard's a sneak thief on top of everything else."

"What kind of books are they? The kind with pictures of women? Maybe he's been out in the woods by himself too long."

"No, look, this is a history book. And this one has a bunch of pictures of old-time sailing ships, like in the pirate movies. Now why in the world—"

Charlie Badwater sat staring at the books for a couple of minutes, and then he tossed them aside and stood up. "I'm going to look around some more," he said.

Thomas Cornstalk followed him as he walked around the cabin. The area in back of the cabin looked much the same as the front yard, but then both men saw the blackened spot where a small fire had been burning. Large rocks had been placed in a circle around the fire place, and some of the rocks were marked with strange symbols or patterns. A tiny wisp of smoke, no greater than that from a cigarette, curled up from the ashes.

Charlie Badwater walked over and held his hand above the ashes, not quite touching the remains of the fire. Then he crouched way down and began studying the ground closely, slowly examining the entire area within the circle of stones and working his way back toward where Thomas Cornstalk stood silently watching. This was one of Charlie Badwater's most famous specialties: reading sign. People said he could track a catfish across a lake.

"He came out here," he said at last, "barefoot as usual, and he walked straight to that spot by the fire and walked around it—at least four times, it's pretty confused there—and then, well . . ."

"What? Where'd he go?"

"Far as I can tell, he just flew away. Or disappeared or something. He didn't walk back out of that circle of rocks, anyway. And whatever he did, it wasn't long ago that he did it. Those ashes are still warm."

A small dry voice said, "Looking for the old man?"

Thomas Cornstalk turned around. A great big blue jay was sitting on the collapsing eaves of Old Man Alabama's shack.

"Because," the jay said, speaking in that sarcastic way jays have, "I don't think you're going to find him. Not anytime soon, anyway. He left sort of drastic."

"Did you see what happened?" Thomas Cornstalk asked the jay.

Charlie Badwater had turned around too by now. He was looking from Thomas Cornstalk to the jay and back again. There was an odd look on his face; he seemed almost wistful. For all his power, all the fantastic things he could do, he had never been granted the ability to talk with animals—which is not something you can learn; you have the gift or you don't—and there are few things that can make a person feel quite as shut out as watching somebody like Thomas Cornstalk having a conversation with bird or beast.

"Hey," the jay said, "I got trapped in here when the old son of a bitch put that whatever-the-hell around the cabin. Tried to fly out, hit

something like a wall in the air, damn near broke my beak. Thought I
was going to starve to death in here, till you guys showed up. Tell your
buddy thanks for turning the damn thing off."

"Ask him where Old Man Alabama went," Charlie Badwater said.

"I saw the whole thing," the jay said, not waiting for the translation. Thomas Cornstalk noticed that; he had suspected for some
time that blue jays could understand Cherokee, even if they pretended
not to. "Old guy walked out there mumbling to himself, stomped
around the fire a little, made a lot of that racket that you humans call
singing—hey, no offense, but even a boat-tailed grackle can sing better
than that—and then all of a sudden he threw a bunch of stuff on the
fire. There was a big puff of smoke and when it cleared away he was
just as gone as you please."

"I knew it," Charlie Badwater said, when this had been interpreted
for him. He squatted down by the fire and began picking up handfuls
of ashes and blackened twigs and dirt, running the material through
his fingers and sniffing it like a dog and occasionally putting a pinch in
his mouth to taste it. "Ah," he said finally. "All right, I know what he
used. Don't understand *why*—there are some combinations in there
that shouldn't work at all, by any of the rules I know—but like I said,
what works is what works."

He stood up and looked at the jay. "Ask him if he can remember
the song."

"Sure," the jay said. "No problem. Not sure I can sing it, of
course—"

"I'll be right back," Charlie Badwater said, heading for the cabin.
A minute later Thomas Cornstalk heard him rummaging around inside. The jay said, "Was it something I said?"

In a little while Charlie Badwater came back, his arms full of buckskin bags and brown paper sacks. "Lucky for us he had plenty of everything," he said, and squatted down on the ground and took off his
old black hat and turned it upside down on his knees and began taking
things out of the bags: mostly dried leaves and weeds and roots, but
other items too, not all of them easily identifiable. At one point
Thomas Cornstalk was nearly certain he recognized a couple of
human finger bones.

"All right," Charlie Badwater said, setting the hat carefully next to
the dead fire and straightening up. "Now how does that song go?"

That part wasn't easy. The jay had a great deal of trouble forming
some of the sounds; a crow would have been better at this, or maybe a
mockingbird. The words weren't in any language Thomas Cornstalk
had ever heard, and Charlie Badwater said he'd never heard a song
remotely like this one.

At last, after many false starts and failed tries, Charlie Badwater got all the way through the song and the jay said, "That's it. He's got it perfect. No accounting for tastes, I guess."

Charlie Badwater was already piling up sticks from the pile of wood beside the ring of stones. He got out his lighter and in a few minutes the fire was crackling and flickering away. *"Ehena,"* he said over his shoulder. "Ready when you are."

"You want me in on this?"

"Of course. Let's go, Thomas. *Nula."*

Thomas Cornstalk wasn't at all happy about this, but he walked across the circle to stand beside Charlie Badwater, who had picked up his hat and was holding it in front of him in both hands.

"This I've got to see," the jay commented from its perch on the roof. It had moved up to the ridgepole, probably for a better view. "You guys are crazier than the old man."

Charlie Badwater circled the fire four times, counterclockwise, like a stomp dancer, with Thomas Cornstalk pacing nervously behind him. After the fourth orbit he stopped, facing the sun, and began singing the song the jay had taught him. It sounded different now, somehow. The hair was standing up on Thomas Cornstalk's neck and arms.

Suddenly Charlie Badwater emptied the hat's contents onto the fire. There was a series of sharp fizzing and sputtering noises, and a big cloud of dense gray smoke surged up and surrounded both men. It was so thick that Thomas Cornstalk couldn't see an inch in front of his face; it was like having his head under very muddy water, or being covered with a heavy gray blanket.

Other things were happening, too. The ground underfoot was beginning to shift and become soft; it felt like quicksand, yet he wasn't sinking into it. His skin prickled all over, not painfully but pretty unpleasantly, and he felt a little sick to his stomach.

The grayness got darker and darker, while the ground fell away completely, until Thomas Cornstalk felt himself to be floating through a great black nothingness. For some reason he was no longer frightened; he simply assumed that he had died and this was what it was like when you went to the spirit world. *"Ni, Jali,"* he called out.

"Ayuh ahni, Tami." The voice sounded close by, but strange, as if Charlie Badwater had fallen down a well.

"Gado nidagal'stani? What's going to happen?"

"Nigal'stisguh," came the cheerful reply. "Whatever . . ."

Thomas Cornstalk had no idea how long the darkness and the floating sensation lasted. His sense of time, the whole idea of time itself, had vanished in that first billow of smoke. But then suddenly the darkness turned to dazzling light and there was something solid under his feet again. Caught by surprise, he swayed and staggered and fell heavily forward, barely getting his arms up in time to protect his face.

He lay half-stunned for a moment, getting the breath back into his lungs and the sight back to his eyes. There was hard smooth planking against his hands; it felt like his own cabin floor, in fact, and at first he thought he must somehow be back home. Maybe the whole thing was a dream and he'd just fallen out of bed . . . but he rolled over and saw bright blue sky above him, crisscrossed by a lot of ropes and long poles. He sat up and saw that he was on the deck of a ship.

It was a ship such as he had only seen in books and movies: the old-fashioned kind, made of wood, with masts and sails instead of an engine. Off beyond the railing, blue water stretched unbroken to the horizon.

Beside him, Charlie Badwater's voice said, "Well, I have to admit this wasn't what I expected."

Thomas Cornstalk turned his head in time to see Charlie Badwater getting to his feet. That seemed like a good idea, so he did it too. The deck was tilted to one side and the whole ship was rolling and pitching, gently but distinctly, with the motion of the sea. Thomas Cornstalk's stomach began to feel a trifle queasy. He hadn't been aboard a ship since his long-ago hitch in the marines, but he remembered about seasickness. He closed his eyes for a second and forced his stomach to settle down. This was no time to lose control of any part of himself.

He said, "Where the hell are we, Charlie?"

From behind them came a harsh cackle. "Where? Wrong question."

The words were in English. The voice was dry and high-pitched, with an old man's quaver. Both men said, "Oh, shit," and turned around almost in unison.

Old Man Alabama was standing on the raised deck at the stern of the ship, looking down at them. His arms were folded and his long hair streamed and fluttered in the wind. His mouth was pulled back at the corners in the closest thing to a smile Thomas Cornstalk had ever seen on his face.

"Not *where*," he went on, and cackled again. "You ought to ask, *when* are we? Of course there's some *where* in it too—"

The horrible smile disappeared all at once. "Say," Old Man Alabama said in a different voice, "how did you two get here, anyway?"

"Same way you did," Charlie Badwater said, also in English. "It wasn't very hard."

"You're a liar." Old Man Alabama spat hard on the deck. "It took me years to learn the secret. How could you two stupid Cherokees—"

"A little bird told us," Thomas Cornstalk interrupted. He knew it was too easy but he couldn't resist.

"I used the same routine you did," Charlie Badwater said, "only I put in a following-and-finding *igawesdi*. You ought to have known you couldn't lose me, old man. What are you up to, anyway?"

Old Man Alabama unfolded his long arms and waved them aimlessly about. It made him look remarkably like a spider monkey Thomas Cornstalk had seen in the Tulsa zoo.

"Crazy Old Man Alabama," he screeched. "I know what you all said about me behind my back—"

"Hey," Charlie Badwater said, "I said it to your face too. Plenty of times."

"Loony old witch," Old Man Alabama went on, ignoring him. "Up there on his mountain, doing nickel-and-dime hexes and love charms, comes into town every now and then and scares the little kids, couldn't witch his way out of a wet paper sack. Yeah, well, look what the crazy old man went and did."

He stopped and shook himself all over. "I did it, too," he said. His voice had suddenly gone softer; it was hard to understand the words. "Nobody else ever even tried it, but I did it. Me."

He stared down at them for a minute, evidently waiting for them to ask him what exactly he'd done. When they didn't, he threw his hands way up over his head again and put his head back and screamed, *"Time!* I found out how to fly through time! Look around you, damn it—they don't have ships like this in the year we come from. Don't you know what you're looking at, here?"

Thomas Cornstalk was already glancing up and down the empty decks, up into the rigging and . . . empty decks? "What the hell," he said. "What happened to the people? The sailors and all?"

"Right," Charlie Badwater said. "You didn't sail this thing out here by yourself. Hell, you can't even paddle a canoe. I've seen you try."

Old Man Alabama let off another of his demented laughs. "There," he said, gesturing out over the rail. "There they are, boys. Fine crew they make now, huh?"

Thomas Cornstalk looked where the old man was pointing, but he couldn't see anything but the open sea and sky and a bunch of seagulls squawking and flapping around above the ship's wake. Then he got it. "Aw, hell," he said. "You didn't."

"Should have been here a little while ago," Old Man Alabama chortled, "when they were still learning how to fly. Two of them crashed into the water and a shark got them. Hee hee."

"But why?" Charlie Badwater said. "I mean, the part about traveling into the past, okay, I hate to admit it but I'm impressed. But then fooling around with this kind of childishness, turning a lot of poor damn sailors into sea birds? I know you hate white people, but—"

"Hah! Not just any bunch of sailors," Old Man Alabama said triumphantly. "Not just any white people, either. This is where it all *started,* you dumb blanket-asses! And I'm the one who went back and fixed it!"

He began to sing, a dreadful weird keening that rose and fell over a four-tone scale, without recognizable words. Charlie Badwater and Thomas Cornstalk looked at each other and then back at the old man. Thomas Cornstalk said, "You mean this ship—"

"Yes! It's old *Columbus's* ship! Now the white bastards won't come at all!" Old Man Alabama's face was almost glowing. "And it was me, me, *me* that stopped them. Poor cracked Old Man Alabama, turns out to be the greatest Indian in history, that's all—"

"Uh, excuse me," Thomas Cornstalk said, "but if this is Columbus's ship, where are the other two?"

"Other two what?" Old Man Alabama asked irritably.

"Other two ships, you old fool," Charlie Badwater said. "Columbus had three ships."

"That's right," Thomas Cornstalk agreed. "I remember from school."

Old Man Alabama was looking severely pissed off. "Are you sure? Damn it, I went to a lot of trouble to make sure I got the right one. Gave this white kid from Tahlequah a set of bear claws *and* a charm to make his girlfriend put out—little bastard drove a hard bargain—for finding me the picture in that book. Told me what year it was and everything. I'm telling you, this is it." Old Man Alabama stomped his bare feet on the deck. "Columbus's ship. The *Mayflower.*"

"You ignorant sack of possum poop," Charlie Badwater said. "You don't know squat, do you? Columbus's ship was named the *Santa María*. The *Mayflower* was a totally different bunch of *yonegs.* Came ashore up in Maine or somewhere like that."

"These schoolkids nowadays, they're liable to tell you anything," Thomas Cornstalk remarked. "Half of them can't read any better than you do. My sister's girl is going with this white boy, I swear he don't know any more than the average fencepost."

Old Man Alabama was fairly having a fit now. "No," he howled, flailing the air with his long skinny arms. "No, no, it's a lie—"

Charlie Badwater sighed and shook his head. "I bet this isn't even the *Mayflower,*" he said to Thomas Cornstalk. "Let's have a look around."

They walked up and down the deserted main deck, looking. There didn't seem to be anything to tell them the name of the ship.

"I think they put the name on the stern," Thomas Cornstalk said.

"You know, the hind end of the ship. They did when I was in the corps, anyway."

They climbed a ladder and crossed the quarterdeck, paying no attention to Old Man Alabama, who was now lying on the deck beating the planks with his fists. "Hang on to my belt or something, will you?" Thomas Cornstalk requested. "I don't swim all that good."

With Charlie Badwater holding him by the belt, he hung over the railing and looked at the name painted in big letters across the ship's stern. It was hard to make out at that angle, and upside down besides, but finally he figured it out.

"Mary Celeste," he called back over his shoulder. "That's the name. The *Mary Celeste.*"

Charlie Badwater looked at Old Man Alabama. *"Mayflower.* Columbus. My Native American ass," he said disgustedly. "I should have let those white guys hang him, back last year."

Thomas Cornstalk straightened up and leaned back against the rail. "Well," he said, "what do we do now?"

Charlie Badwater shrugged. "Go back where we came from. *When* we came from."

"Can you do it?"

"Anything this old lunatic can do, I can figure out how to undo."

Thomas Cornstalk nodded, feeling much relieved. "Do we take him along?"

"We better. No telling what the consequences might be if we left him." Charlie Badwater stared at the writhing body on the deck at his feet. "You know the worst part? It was a hell of a great idea he had. Too bad it had to occur to an idiot."

"Nasgiduh nusdi," Thomas Cornstalk said. "That's how it is."

He looked along the empty decks once again. "You think anybody's ever going to find this boat? Come along in another ship, see this one floating out here in the middle of the ocean, nobody on board . . . man," he said, "that's going to make some people wonder."

"People need to wonder now and then," Charlie Badwater said. "It's good for their circulation."

He grinned at Thomas Cornstalk. "Come on," he said. "Let's peel this old fool off the deck and go home."

Counting Coup

Jack Dann

I t might have all been bullshit, something psychological in his
head, but John was right. Charlie couldn't deny that. It did get
worse as they drove south. Charlie became increasingly nervous,
as if some malevolent shaman was sitting right there in the back of the
car weaving spells and casting the evil eye. Charlie's mother had believed in the evil eye, but Charlie had always thought it was all nonsense. He still thought it was all nonsense, but he was nervous just the
same. He leaned over toward John, and pulled the bottle of scotch
away from him.

From there on it was numbness and nausea and easy breathing
and the plashing of tires along the highway, until Charlie missed his
exit for 95 and found himself on secondary roads, passing by pig
farms and rundown gas stations selling cheap cigarettes and fire-
works. Frustrated, he turned the car around and backtracked until he
found the exit. Once on 95, he drove like hell, as if troopers were after
him—and he might actually have a chance to outrace them in this car,
which they'd just jacked. The damn thing could certainly move, even
though it was the silliest goddamn piece of engineering he had ever
seen. Although the windows had to be manually raised and lowered,
the sideview mirrors were electric.

Charlie was all right through Richmond, and John was awake
enough to give him money for tolls. It was getting dark, and the traffic
was quite heavy, three lanes' worth of it, but then they were back on
open highway. It was as if they were moving backward through the
seasons. The trees were greener; autumn had not yet taken its full bite.
They drove through woods and rolling farmlands punctuated by gas
stations with signs on high poles and eateries that seemed to repeat
themselves. And Charlie felt alone. He had to keep drinking to keep
himself from suddenly turning around to see whatever it was that was
watching him. He wasn't going to be able to keep this up, he thought.
Not for long. But the booze did help.

"You want to stop for a while?" John asked. He'd been awake for a time, but hadn't spoken.

Charlie was weaving all over the road. It was just past dusk when what light was left seemed refracted into the blue. It seemed dusty, as if they were driving through a mist, or a dream—he wished it was a dream. "No, I'm doing just fine."

"Doesn't seem that way to me."

"Maybe we should get some coffee," Charlie said.

"I'm in the mood for pizza."

Just the thought of pizza brought a bitter, metallic taste to Charlie's mouth, but he stopped when they found a Pizza Hut. A waitress in a brown uniform gave them menus and asked if they wanted coffee. She appeared to be in her late thirties, and she was pretty, but it was a tired, faded beauty. Her long blond hair was pulled back into a ponytail, and although she was very tall, she wasn't a bit awkward. She had a smooth, experienced way about her.

John seemed to come to life as soon as he saw her. He was smiling and looking all over this woman. Immediately and unabashedly, he let it drop that he was a medicine man. Charlie could feel something quick pass between John and the waitress, and that made him jealous and insecure. Goddamn if she wasn't flirting back at John.

"I'll be right back with your coffees," she said to John. She spoke with a slight but noticeable southern drawl.

"We should take her along with us," John said as he watched her walk away. He smiled. "Make this trip more interesting."

"Maybe I should order some orange juice, the booze makes me thirsty," Charlie said, looking at the fold-out menu. Fuck John and fuck the waitress, he told himself. I don't need this shit. My place is with Joline and the kids. His family was his only salvation. Sonovabitch if *that* hadn't come to him as a shock after all these years.

"You're crazy," John said. "You drink orange juice and you'll be barfing all over."

When the waitress returned with their coffee and silverware, John said, "You know we been drinking ourselves numb, and doing some pretty mysterious things, and my partner here wants to order orange juice. Can you believe that?"

"I don't know about the mysterious things," the waitress said, "but if you've been drinking, I'd advise you to stick with the coffee. Juice might make you sick."

But Charlie insisted, as if he had to save face.

After she brought Charlie his orange juice and went back for John's pan pizza, John coaxed her to sit down. "The place is empty anyway," he said; and then he began his routine, working her, as if he were reeling in a sunfish from the ocean. He asked her name ("Kim") and where she was from ("Right here"), and they talked about the loud music and the high school kids who were trying to look like punks. John talked to her about medicine and vision quests, and she seemed interested in everything he had to say. Then he started talking dangerously.

"Now you should have seen Charlie, he's a regular hero," John said. "He stole a goddamn patrol car right out from a trooper. That trooper got himself so bent, he started shooting at us."

"Jesus H. Christ," Charlie said. "Shut the hell up! What are you trying to do, anyway?"

"She's okay," John said. "Trust me, I wasn't a medicine man for all those years for nothing." And he continued talking. He had her. She was laughing with him as if she'd been through it all with them. He told her about their adventures in detail, how they were stealing cars and staying drunk and going cross-country to show the whole fucking world that they were damn well alive, even if they were a shade over sixty.

"Is this for real?" she asked.

"If I really try to convince you, you're still not going to believe me," John said. "So what's the point? But even if you don't believe it, you gotta admit it's a helluva story."

"That it is," she said. "Are you really a medicine man?"

"If you're not going to believe the story, why would you believe I was a medicine man?"

"Good point," she said, smiling at him. "You know, I did some traveling once upon a time. I hitchhiked out west, got pregnant, and rode back home on a Harley." She laughed at that. "I just never could get comfortable out there. All the rocks seemed to be shaped funny, you know? I have a sixteen-year-old boy . . . he's taller than me, if that's possible. Don't you guys have any family?"

Charlie averted his eyes from her gaze, but he noticed that she had a faint tattoo: three dots on the knuckles of her right hand. An old boyfriend must have done that. Or who knows, maybe it was her husband's work, Charlie thought.

"Well, *he's* got a family," she said, meaning Charlie. "Why're you doing this, drinking and stealing cars and all that?"

"Why'd you go cross-country on a cycle and get knocked up?" John asked.

"I was a kid. Eighteen years old."

"Just like us," John said. Even Charlie smiled at that. But Charlie was nervous. He wanted to get out of here. He wanted to get John out of here—alone.

"That's not good enough," she said. She was suddenly serious, earnest.

"Okay, so we're two old fucks having a midlife crisis," John said, grinning. "You married?"

She looked surprised. "No."

"Then why don't you come along with us? Your son would be okay for a while by himself, wouldn't he?"

"We gotta *go*," Charlie said, and he stood up.

"Why don't you guys stay here for a while?" Kim asked.

John seemed to be considering that. Charlie touched his arm and said, "Come on. We got enough problems as it is. You can't bring anybody else into it."

"We're supposed to be having a party," John said, and his eyes looked hard, as if he could go crazy—*heyoka*—right here in a snap. He could go either way. But he said, "Okay, Charlie, you're right. We could have showed you some time, though," he said to Kim.

"I'll bet you could."

"Can we have the check?" Charlie asked, changing the mood.

"Wait one sec."

Kim went into the kitchen. When she came out, she had a large soda container capped with a white plastic top. "This is for the road, and don't shake it or open it here."

"What about the check?" John asked.

"On the house." And she turned and walked away to wait on the high school kids.

It had started to rain while they were in the restaurant. It was drizzling now, and the air was heavy with mist. The parking lot was dappled with puddles.

John insisted on driving.

When they got inside the car, he started the engine and turned on the heater—it was cold tonight. Then he shook the soda container. "This sure as hell isn't filled with water." He opened it and started to laugh. "Well, bless her heart."

"What is it?" Charlie asked.

"Good old home-grown. And she even dropped in a pack of Zig-Zag."

Charlie reached over and took the container from John. It looked like it was filled with tobacco. He smelled it. "I know what this is. I'm not smoking that crap, and neither should you."

"That a fact," John said, taking back the container. He expertly rolled four joints, licked them, and twisted the ends. "We need all the help we can get." He lit one joint and put the others in his shirt pocket. After taking a drag and holding it deep in his lungs, he passed the marijuana cigarette to Charlie. Charlie refused it. "Indian people been smoking this stuff for hundreds of years," John said, exhaling smoke.

There he goes again, Charlie thought. Now he's got Indians inventing pot. The pungent odor of the marijuana made him feel queasy—or maybe it was that orange juice. "You can't drive on that stuff."

John laughed and said, "Hell if I can't!" He threw the car into gear and drove like a wild man, puffing and coughing, trying to find the interchange. Charlie had to tell him to turn on the windshield wipers. John must have taken a wrong turn, for they passed what seemed to be miles of broken five-rail fences and dilapidated farm houses.

"I *told* you, you can't drive on that stuff," Charlie said, and they both started laughing uncontrollably. Charlie began to choke, and he opened up his window. He felt slightly numbed. Probably all that pot smoke, he thought; but he got the giggles, just as if he had been smoking the pipe with John. And that old pipe was still hanging from the rearview mirror, sliding back and forth on the dash as John rounded one turn and then another.

John lit a new marijuana cigarette and passed it to Charlie. "This'll open up your lungs. And you can't just turn down a present. This is holy shit."

So Charlie tried it, just to show John that he was in control. He gagged trying to hold the burning, sickly sweet smoke in his lungs. It didn't have much effect on him, he thought, except to make him a bit sleepy. But he didn't get sick—orange juice or not. It was a question of mind over matter. He could be in control, no matter how fucked up he got.

John found the interchange and got back on 95. Charlie slept some, although his thoughts seemed to be going every which way. He dreamed that he was taking part in one of John's sweat-lodge ceremonies and the steam was so hot that it felt like shards of ice lacerating his flesh. . . . He dreamed that the rocks and stones in the pit had turned into eyes, unblinking coal-red eyes, watching him.

He awakened with a jolt.

John was watching him.

"Keep your eyes on the road," Charlie said, and then he started laughing.

"What's funny?" John asked.

Charlie could feel the marijuana working through him like Novocain, and he started laughing again. "All that booze and dope turned *you* stone-cold sober."

"Certainly didn't do the same for you," John said. "But it's good to turn things into laughter. It's power. A good medicine man can usually laugh his ass off, no matter what, no matter how bad his situation might be. He could be dying and still laugh his ass off. You wanna be a medicine man?"

"I'll leave all that to you," Charlie said. Then, after a beat, "Let me drive for a little while now. . . ."

"You're too drunk to drive, honky," John said. He gently pressed the accelerator to the floor, and they passed the neon carnival that all the signs had pointed to: South of the Border. It glowed in the darkness like an image in a junkie's dream.

They pulled into the wide driveway of an old farmhouse outside of Hancock at four o'clock in the morning. They were just a few miles over the Maryland border. John had fallen asleep at the wheel several times, but Charlie kept waking him. Charlie was too wired to sleep. He was bone-tired . . . overtired.

It was cold out, and a dog started barking from somewhere in the vicinity of the house. The driveway was lined with cars, as if some sort of convention was going on there. Most of the cars were old beaters, except for a white sports car parked between two rusted-out pick-ups. A full moon, which looked hazy behind the slowly moving clouds, lent the sky some gray, and it *felt* like morning, although it could easily have been ten o'clock at night. An outside light over the doorway cast a harsh light into the driveway and part of the yard, giving the place a desolate appearance. The house looked white in the half-light, and it was long; most likely, a previous owner had made an addition.

"I'm going to stay in the car," Charlie said. "It's four o'clock in the morning, for Chrissakes!"

"*Some*body's up, there's lights on," John said. "Not to worry. These people are my friends."

"I don't care," Charlie said, but just then a door opened, more lights came on, and someone called, "Who's there?" It was a woman's voice.

John opened his door and stumbled out of the car, almost falling in the driveway. He looked toward the road, hands on his hips, his back to the house, and shouted, "It's John Stone, and he's drunk, and horny as a dog in the rut. And the stupid bastard's backwards and upside down again."

It was like a goddamn act, Charlie thought. He just turns it on like water from a faucet. But then Charlie remembered that look on John's face when he went for that black clerk in the liquor store.

A stocky woman walked down the driveway toward them. She was wearing some sort of sacky dress, and she didn't look like she had a curve on her. "John Stone, you're welcome here, even if you're sick again. But mind you, leave the young girls alone!" She was smiling and obviously teasing him.

John began to laugh. He turned around and let out a whoop. "So you got some college girls for Uncle John. . . ."

The woman looked inside the car at Charlie, but didn't say anything to him or acknowledge his presence, if she could even see him. "There's some hot coffee on the stove," she said to John. "And I can make up a fresh pot. There's also bread . . . and *wasna* and *wojapi*. I seem to remember that you like that kind of food. Well, are you going to kiss me?"

John said, "No," and then kissed her.

"God, do you stink!" the woman said. "You'd make a goat smell good."

"Thank you," John said cheerfully.

She stepped away from him. "You're welcome in my house, as always. Your friend, too. But I don't want you drinking. Not here."

"We've mostly run out of booze," John said. "Nothing left to drink, so you're safe." He leaned against the car. "What're all these cars doing here?" he asked, motioning with his arm. "You all going to sun dance?"

"Jesus, you are drunk," the woman said. "This is the wrong season for sun dance. And *you've* already been there."

"Then what's going on?"

"Friend of yours is here. In some trouble. Just like you, except you're too dumb and drunk to know it."

"Who?" John asked. Then his legs seemed to give way, and he slid down the car to the ground. He made himself comfortable and rested his back against the rear wheel. "Goddamn if everything isn't going around and around ever so slowly."

"Are you sober enough to help your friend?" the woman asked Charlie in a loud, raspy voice. Charlie didn't think he was going to like this fat, bossy woman—from what he could see, she was probably fat. But he got out of the car, feeling a touch of nausea and dizziness as soon as he stood up.

"Come on, John," Charlie said. "We're making an imposition on these people. Let's get the hell on our way and leave them alone."

"John's family," the woman said. "And so's anybody traveling with him."

"Goddamn right!" John said, but he wouldn't let Charlie help him to his feet. He pulled his knees against his chest and sat back against the tire. "Now tell me what friend of mine is here?"

"Joe Whiteshirt's wife—Janet. She left him. She told him he was acting like a witch. We just did a *yuwipi* for her. She had questions for the spirits, she needed help, like I expect you do, since you're here."

"It was on our way," John said. Then he asked, "Who did the *yuwipi?* And who brought her down here? She doesn't drive."

"Sam."

"What!"

"Sam's a good *yuwipi* man," the woman said. "You ought to know, you taught him most everything he knows."

"But it was *wrong* for him to be bringing her down here," John said. "Her marriage would've been fine if she hadn't been acting like a whore and fooling around with Sam. And Sam's supposed to be vision-questing! What the *hell* is he doing here?"

"Probably same thing you are."

"He was supposed to vision-quest, not steal another man's wife."

"You have a dirty mind, John Stone," the woman said. "They brought people along with them. They haven't been alone for a moment. What happened between them is over. It was a mistake. They both realize that."

"Tell that to her husband. I wouldn't be surprised if he showed up here with a gun looking for them. And in a way, I wouldn't blame him!"

"I don't think you know the whole story," the woman said. "Joe Whiteshirt's practically been living with Violet, the red-headed woman who used to always be hanging out at his camp. Remember her? Things haven't been so good between him and Janet."

"I already know the story . . . Sam told me. But you can't blame everything on the woman—Violet. There's too much passing the buck going on, and everybody's blaming every human thing on bad medicine. It's not good, not good at all."

"Well, you're the medicine man. Maybe you can help."

"I'm no medicine man anymore," John said.

"Well, if that isn't the biggest piece of bullshit I ever heard," the woman said. "And there's *something* going on. You can call it whatever you like, but it all comes down to the same thing, as far as I'm concerned. I think that woman Violet is a witch."

Charlie felt awkward standing there, privy to the conversation. "Let's go," he said to John. "I don't need to hear about all this bad medicine and voodoo crap. Excuse me, ma'am, I didn't mean any disrespect," he said to the woman.

"Don't pay Charlie any mind," John said. "He says he doesn't believe in medicine, but he's been shitting his pants ever since he was in a sweat lodge." After a pause he said, "Lorena, I'd like you to meet my good friend Charlie. Charlie, Lorena. Everybody seems to go to

Lorena's when they need some taking care of." He looked up at Lorena, beaming at her, and said, "You might as well become an Indian, for all the trouble you go to for us."

"We talked about that," Lorena said.

"Yeah, Joe Whiteshirt, that stupid bastard, wanted to give her a pipe to carry. It's not time for white people to carry pipes," he said to Lorena. "Even people as good and kindhearted as you. It would have been wrong."

"I still don't understand it," Lorena said, "but I've always trusted what you've told me. Still . . . *you* taught Joe Whiteshirt. . . ."

"And I taught Sam, too," John said in a disgusted tone. "And look how that turned out—Joe's probably going to kill him. Maybe you *should* carry a pipe, who the hell knows. Maybe all Indians should go to church and stop sweating and vision-questing and—"

"Stop it, John," Lorena said, looking upset. "You're a crazy-ass drunk, and you're going to say things you'll regret. We have enough trouble already."

"Her husband's a engineer," John said to Charlie. "That's how they can afford to live like Indians." John started laughing, his *heyoka* laugh, and Charlie felt embarrassed for the woman.

"I'll bring you two out some towels and soap," Lorena said, almost in a whisper. "In the meantime, you can go up to the creek and start getting undressed."

"For what?" John asked.

"You know goddamn well for what, John Stone. You're filthy and you stink. You need some cleaning up and sobering up . . . both of you, I think."

"It's too cold to wash," John said.

"That never bothered you before," Lorena said. "You used to brag that you were part Eskimo, remember? And neither one of you are coming into *my* house with all that dirt and stink and vomit. You two are a mess! You should be ashamed of yourselves. Now you *are* going to get washed up and clean." With that, Lorena walked away toward the house.

"I'll be damned if I'm going to jump into your goddamn creek," John shouted. "I'm an *Indian.* It's white folks who need to get themselves cleaned up."

"You're a real sonovabitch," Charlie said to John.

"Lorena's a good woman," John said, as if he had missed Charlie's point. "And she's done a lot for Indian people. But she's trying to *be* an Indian, and she's not. But she'd do anything in the world for anybody. I like her—I'm crazy about her—but I can't stand some of the people she takes in, all those nice middle-class kids looking for gurus, and the weekend Indians trying to *be* gurus. There's always groupies hanging around. Wanna-bes. You'll see."

"You use people," Charlie said.

"You're right, I did wrong. Lorena," John called. "I'm sorry. I'll be a good boy. We'll take our baths."

Charlie helped John to his feet—although Charlie wasn't in any better shape than John—and they stumbled up the grassy stone and dirt driveway. John led the way past the well-lit house and into the backyard, which looked like it was part of a natural clearing in the woods. Charlie could hear the soft gurgling and splashing of the stream, but he couldn't see it. He breathed in a wonderfully damp, woody aroma: the smells of moss and soil and trees. Widely spaced birch and pine trees looked silvery in the moonlight.

Suddenly John broke away from Charlie and started singing and dancing and throwing his clothes all over the ground. Buck naked, he ran toward a grove of hemlocks and jumped down the bank and into the stream below. Charlie heard him belly-flop into the water. "Come on," John shouted.

Charlie followed. The stream was about six feet wide and curved into the woods; it looked dark and cold and misty. Charlie remained on the bank, and John stood in the fast-moving water, his hands on his hips, legs apart, as the moonlight turned him to pale stone and shadow. "We're gonna need soap if we're gonna smell good," he shouted loudly enough to be heard at the house. "Now get your god-damn ass in here, Charlie," he commanded. "It's not so bad once you're in."

That was a lie. The water was icy cold, exhilarating, and sobering. Charlie stepped in cautiously, gasped, and for a few luminous seconds he was overwhelmed with sensation: the sharp bite of cold water, the shivering night-shadows, the shattered mirror surface of the stream reflecting silvery gray moonlight, John's face slipping in and out of darkness, changing each time, as if caught by a strobe light . . . and for those few seconds, Charlie was *heyoka*. He experienced only the moment. The past had sloughed away like old skin. The future was . . . nothing and . . .

Charlie was simultaneously an eagle, wings outstretched. A fish. A bull. The light on the water. The chill in the air. The splashing. He was all that until a callow-looking boy of about nineteen appeared with two bars of soap, which he threw to John and Charlie.

After he left, John said, "See what I mean about groupies? He should be in college smoking pot or something, instead of doing errands for Lorena." John rubbed the large, coarse bar of soap all over himself.

After much splashing and shouting and sobering up, John said, "Damn, that kid didn't leave us any towels." Then, in a loud voice: "If Lorena doesn't come right along with some towels, I'm going to walk into the house *naked.*"

"Oh, no, you're not," Lorena said.

"Why, you sly old fox," John said. "I think you've been standing around here all this time watching us. I'm going to tell your old man you're a peeping Tom."

"You can tell him whatever you like," Lorena said. "I'm leaving these clean clothes and towels for both of you. When you're ready, there's fresh, hot coffee inside. . . ."

It was warm and bright and cozy inside the huge kitchen, which had a wood-burning stove side by side with a gas stove. There was an old oak dining table on the far side of the room and a doorway that opened into a living room. In the middle of the living room was a swing for the children; it hung from the high-ceilinged rafters.

Three young people were sitting at the table—two women and the boy who had brought the towels to John and Charlie. They were drinking Lorena's strong, bitter coffee and eating the remains of a large chocolate cake. They looked wired, as if they were too excited to sleep. Although they were all wearing flannel shirts and faded dungarees, Charlie was certain that the women came from wealthy families. Both of them had almost perfect, even teeth, which Charlie perceived as a sure sign of money. The boy, on the other hand, had wide spaces between his teeth. His parents probably worked for a living, Charlie surmised.

Lorena made the introductions: The boy's name was Carl; the tall, lanky, chestnut-haired woman was Sharry; and the intense, nervous-looking woman was Heather. She had short-cropped black hair, and her name, which made Charlie think of freedom and wildness and open country, didn't fit her at all. Then Lorena ordered John and Charlie to sit down, and she served them coffee and cut them some cake. The coffee was just what Charlie needed, but the thought of swallowing that cake made him gag—he wasn't ready for that yet.

John made small talk, and the kids seemed to hang on every word he said. Carl and Sharry kept trying to swing the conversation around to religion. They especially wanted John to talk about *yuwipi*s and about how it was in "the old days." They wanted to hear about vision quests where medicine men would either hang from the sides of cliffs for days on end, or would be buried alive. John usually persisted, though, in sliding back into small talk, into that smooth and easy, chiding tone of voice that Charlie had heard him use with women before. But John was more animated tonight. He was after something. . . .

Although Charlie still felt chilled from the stream, he was sober and comfortable. He was a bit shaky and had that tickle in his throat, but he could breathe and he wasn't nauseated. He was tired, dragged-out exhausted, and he knew he was going to suffer for the beating he was giving his body—he would pay dues for this eventually! I should go to *bed,* Charlie told himself, but he was wide awake and so nerved up that everything looked dark and shadowy to him. If he went to bed, he would just lie awake and stare at the ceiling—but if he didn't get some sleep, he would get the shakes so bad he wouldn't be able to hold a spoon.

As he sat at the table, finished now with his coffee (and he had even taken a mouthful of cake), he found himself watching Sharry. Charlie began to think that she was pretty in her way, even sexy. She wore a cloth headband, as did Carl, who was sitting beside her—maybe he was her boyfriend. She had such a young, delicate face, and her eyes had a way of narrowing and looking crinkly. Charlie liked that, and he liked the way her mouth would purse. For such a thin girl, she had unusually full, sensual lips. Charlie thought of her as a flower in bloom. She looked so fresh and new. His wife, Joline, had had that kind of freshness about her, too, but she'd lost it . . . and just now Charlie realized how precious it had been.

"You know," John said, looking intently at Sharry, "when a man's *heyoka,* he can do anything he wants. He can be perverted and filthy and just plain bad, and yet he's holy all the time."

Sharry looked at Carl and then turned back to John, giving him her full attention. Carl moved slightly closer to her.

"And you never can believe *anything* a *heyoka* says," John continued, "because they lie about everything. Isn't that right, Lorena?"

"I think all of you would be better off going to bed and not listening to this broken-down old drunk of a medicine man," Lorena said, carrying a large bowl of berry soup to the table. "You want some of this?" she asked John.

"I want some dog first," John said.

"You want *what?*" Charlie asked.

"It's probably going to make you sick," Lorena said.

"That's what I want, is there any left?"

"I'll get you a piece from the pot, but . . ."

"Did you eat a piece of dog?" John asked Sharry.

"Yeah, she ate it," said Carl. "We all did . . . one of the harder things we had to swallow."

"Dog meat's not hard," Charlie said, laughing, mocking.

"Well, we did it for the ceremony," Heather said. She was chain-smoking cigarettes, which she kept in a beadwork pouch. Charlie smoked one of her cigarettes and started coughing again. He embarrassed himself by having to spit up in the sink. No one said a word while he was coughing and spitting, which made it even worse. When Charlie finished and sat back down, Heather said, "Sam didn't tell us at the time that we could have made an offering of the meat to the spirits and wouldn't't've had to eat it at all."

John laughed at that and said, "Dog soup is good for you, part of the ceremony."

Charlie couldn't help but stare at Sharry. She wasn't wearing a bra, and he could see the outlines of her small breasts right through her shirt. Charlie usually preferred women with large breasts, but he felt a sudden flush of desire for her, for her youth and innocence. It was overpowering. It was like being sixteen again, when his urges were so strong that he had to masturbate several times a day. Uncomfortable, he pressed his legs together. He thought about Stephie, his oldest daughter. Sharry's probably the same age as Stephie, Charlie told himself. It would be like fucking my own daughter, for Chrissakes. She's a baby. . . . Those thoughts brought on the guilt again, and more embarrassment, as if everyone in the room could see just what he was thinking.

But Sharry wasn't even looking at Charlie. She was too taken up with John. She had a look that said if he would've asked her to eat shit, she would have happily done it. Sonovabitch . . .

Just then Janet made her appearance. She walked into the room with a piece of grayish meat in a soup bowl. The meat was in a dirty-looking broth. There was skin on that meat and even some hair, and it made Charlie sick to look at it. He had met Janet before and was glad to see her, but Jesus, he thought, not *dog,* for Chrissakes. "You're not going to eat that in front of me," Charlie told John.

"I sure as hell am," John said. "It's part of my religion. Don't you have any respect for a man's religion?" Then he looked at Janet and said, "Isn't that right, hon?"

"I knew you'd be coming around," Janet said. She looked as if she'd just awakened from a deep sleep, but her high cheekbones and deep-set eyes could easily give that impression. She had the kind of strong, implacable face that could look mean, yet could also radiate serenity. Charlie liked this woman, had liked her from the first time they met outside of John's sweat lodge. He had been coughing, and she gave him sage. She had a darkness in her, a certain wildness that was at odds with her domesticity, and that attracted him. He felt as if she were family . . . a dark sister. He sensed that the darkness inside her was the same as the stuff inside him, the stuff that made him so angry and depressed that he'd chew up his own family and spit them out screaming.

". . . I sort of expected you to make the *yuwipi*," Janet said to John. "I kept looking for you, figuring you'd show up. I been waiting for you all night—in between cat naps. How's that for faith?"

"You have no business being here," John said.

"I knew you'd say that," Janet replied. "But it's not what you think."

"Don't matter," John said, as he started to eat the meat off the bone, pulling it away with his teeth. "You belong with your husband."

"I can't watch this," Charlie said, getting up. He felt queasy. It disturbed him—the notion that John was almost a cannibal. "You shouldn't be eating something like that," he continued. "It's wrong. I don't care *what* your religion says, it's just not right. I can abide a lot of things, but not that. Eating a dog is like eating something that's human."

"Charlie," Janet said, walking over to him and taking his arm. She pulled him back down into his seat and then rested her hands on his shoulders, calming him. "Give us a few minutes, and I'll tell you about the dog. I love dogs almost more than people, sometimes." Then she said to John, "You are a real bastard, aren't you? Couldn't you tell him what's going on? I thought he's supposed to be your friend?"

"He is," John said. "But fuck him."

"I should've expected as much from you," Janet said. She poured herself a cup of coffee and sat down, pulling a chair between John and Sharry. "I couldn't stay with Joe. He's going crazy, and he scares me. I'm sorry, but I can't help it. I care about him, and I'd do anything for him, but he's into something bad, something dangerous. I'm sure he's been doing medicine. Maybe it's the woman he's living with now, I don't know. But they're doing *something*. What happened between Sam and me was my fault. Or maybe it was Violet's medicine, I don't know. But Sam was just trying to help me. I got weak. I was scared. . . ." She looked exhausted.

"Dog tastes good," John said. "Charlie, you want a piece?"

"Stop acting like an asshole," Janet said.

"Who was your *yuwipi* man?" John asked, pushing away his bowl of dog and dunking a piece of bread into the sweet berry soup. "I don't know of any around here, except maybe Joe and that skinny Crow guy who dresses up like a goddamn stockbroker."

"Sam did it," Janet said.

"Why didn't you just have Joe do it, or maybe Lorena could've done it. What the hell, maybe women's lib should take its shot at traditional Indian religion." Then after a pause he said, "You're fucking *wrong* to do that!" There was hate in his face suddenly, burning, just as it had been when he'd paced around in his furnished room.

Charlie could in that instant see his strength, could see him as a leader, as a medicine man, but Jesus Lord the bastard was crazy. "Sam should have been taking care of his vision quest, not baby-sitting you and the rest of the honky Indians," John continued. "He had no business doing a *yuwipi* tonight. It's a wonder that the spirits didn't kill him dead . . . and the rest of you, too."

"Sam did get hurt," Janet said. "His chest and legs are all black and blue."

John started laughing. "So the spirits did kick the shit out of him."

"The spirits were there," Sharry said, tentatively, as if she knew she shouldn't be speaking, that she shouldn't even be there at all. But she went on. "Everybody could feel them . . . and see them as lights."

"I felt something move behind me," Carl said, "and I felt something against my skin. And then I realized that I was sitting against the wall, and there couldn't be anything behind me but spirits. . . ."

"What'd they tell you?" John asked Janet.

"They were just angry, that's all."

Then John started laughing, and he said, "None of them *really* saw or felt anything, did they, Charlie? It's all bullshit, isn't it, Charlie?"

"Is there a place I can sleep?" Charlie asked Lorena. He ignored John.

"Charlie, somebody should've told you what's going on," Janet said. "The *yuwipi* is a ceremony we do when someone's in trouble. We seek help from the spirits. It's a ceremony given to Indian people by God, and to have this ceremony, to bring the spirits down to us, into our hearts, a dog gives up its life. It knows it's going to die, and I've never seen a dog fight . . . it just knows. And we love our dogs, that's what makes this ceremony so hard for us. We give a life—the dog gives its life—so that we may live. It's a gift."

Charlie couldn't say anything. He didn't know what to say. What the hell am I doing here? he asked himself. Next, they'll be boiling up people!

"Don't be angry with Sam," Janet said to John. "He came down here to try and make things right."

"Doesn't matter to me," John said softly.

"Why, because you're drunk?" Janet asked. "Because you're pretending to be *heyoka* like you do every time life becomes too much for you?"

"That's right. And I'm not carrying the pipe, either. I'm done."

"You have people that need you," Janet said. "That depend on you."

"Well, fuck them!" John said. "No, I take it all back. I'll help whoever needs to be helped . . . for a drink. Right, Charlie?"

"I'm going to go to sleep," Charlie said. "I don't want to drink, I just want to sleep," and he looked at Sharry and realized that he had a hard-on, and there he was standing up like a dirty old man.

"I'll show you where you can sleep," Lorena said. Charlie followed her out of the kitchen, through the living room and upstairs to a large bedroom off the paneled hallway. The starkly furnished room contained a cot and a bed, several cane chairs, an old worn couch, and a table situated against the wall near the door. On the table were some neatly folded towels and a porcelain basin. "We have no water, except in the bathroom, and you have to pump that—it's a dry toilet, might take a bit of getting used to the smell. You can take the bed here; it's more comfortable than the cot. John's used to sleeping on floors and anything he can get, anyway."

"He can have his choice," Charlie said, but just the same he lay down on the bed. Even though the mattress was too soft and lumpy, he was asleep before Lorena had left the room.

It was after dawn when John brought Heather and Sharry into the room. Charlie heard them snickering and laughing and giggling and making "shushing" noises as they talked among themselves. John sounded drunk, but he might have just been *heyoka*. He'd certainly worked his charm on these two kids because they were as happy as babies with new diapers. Charlie lay facing the wall and listened, not letting on that he was awake. His heart was beating fast. Surely *something* was going to happen.

"So the selfish sonovabitch has taken the bed," John said. There was a puffing noise as he sat down on the couch, and then the clattering of his boots as he took them off and let them drop to the floor. Charlie listened to the rustling noises and the whispers and felt as if he were a kid again, all pimply faced and ugly and left out—always third man out. He wanted to cough, but he held it back. He tried to breathe evenly, feigning sleep. Although he didn't feel sick, he was shaking. Adrenaline was burning through him, and it was as hot and fast as hard liquor.

"Well, go on over," John whispered. "I told you, you'll be doing a good thing . . . something he'll remember forever."

Charlie heard someone get up and say, "I'm sorry, John, but I just can't do it." Then the clatter-clack of shoes on the hardwood floor. The door opened and closed, and John whispered something that sounded like swearing. "Well, the hell with it," he said. "He's asleep, anyway."

Charlie discovered that he was holding his breath. He exhaled slowly, carefully, afraid they would be able to tell he was awake. He wondered who had left the room. Was it Sharry or Heather? Probably Heather. She was more shy and nervous . . . a good girl.

But an image of Sharry seemed to hang before Charlie, and he could feel his borrowed dungarees become tight. Goddamn, it was wrong, but he wanted young flesh, as young as his daughter's. He thought of Stephanie and felt himself flush with guilt. He had been faithful to his wife, Joline, for over twenty years; that should count for something. She was a good woman, and had a good body, even if her teeth were bad and her breath had that metal smell. But every day of all those years Charlie had dreamed of other women, women he'd see on the street, or in the apartments when he was doing repair work for the Isaacs, or, worst of all, women he'd had before he met Joline— especially that blue-eyed Mexican whore who had taken care of him for a month after he lost his gas stations, who always used to leave a little money and a bottle of tequila on the tiny bedstand for him when he awakened. . . .

Now there was this Sharry, and she was probably going to screw John. She was young enough to be John's granddaughter, for Chrissakes, Charlie told himself. And John was in and Charlie was out, and no matter how good Charlie had been with the women when he was young, no matter how many adventures he tried to convince himself he'd had, he was still in bed alone, odd man out.

More whispering, and then John said, "You're sure you don't mind? I'll go and find Heather, and everything will be all right. I'll talk to her." Charlie heard the rustle of clothes, then heard them kiss. "I'll see *you* later," John said loudly; perhaps he was trying to wake up Charlie. He put on his boots and left the room, closing the door behind him.

Goddamn if Charlie wasn't scared.

He couldn't sleep, of course, and it would be too awkward to say anything. Let it lie, he told himself. The girl would fall asleep, and so would Charlie, eventually, and then it would be all over—right now that's what he wanted, just to have it all over. But the woman called to him . . . it *was* Sharry.

"Charlie, you asleep?" Her voice had a twang to it.

Charlie didn't answer. He had to go to the bathroom, and he felt nauseated again. He couldn't help it, but he started coughing. Sharry came over to the bed and said, "Charlie? Here, take these," and she put some toilet paper in his hand. "I always carry some . . . you know?"

He coughed into the paper, sat up in the bed, and lowered his head toward his knees, which always made him feel a little better. He was shaking, and it wasn't from the booze; he knew that much. He was piss-ass scared of a little twenty-year-old girl. She looked pale in the wan morning light, a child, except for the red slash of lipstick painted on her generous lips. She was as skinny as a rail, not Charlie's type at all, yet he wanted her, as if she could pass her youth over to him like currency or food. He could smell her natural odor; she didn't wear perfume. She probably doesn't shave her legs either, he thought sourly. "What's going on?" he asked. "What are you doing in *here,* and where's John? I thought I heard him come in with you."

It looked gray outside, and the room seemed smoky and muddled and cold, although it wasn't really cold, just cool.

"It was John's idea that we'd all get silly and fool around," Sharry said, "but when we got in here, Heather got scared or something and left. John went after her to calm her down."

"What do you mean, fool around?" Charlie asked.

"You know. . . ."

"Jesus, woman, I have a daughter almost as old as you," Charlie said. He fought the urge to touch her hair, which looked clean and soft and thick.

"That doesn't mean anything . . . I have a father almost as old as *you.* So what?"

"So what do you want to be fooling around with old men for?" Charlie asked, and then he asked for a cigarette.

"I think older men are . . . beautiful."

"Cut the crap," Charlie snapped. He must have frightened Sharry because she jerked backward.

"Okay, I didn't mean to get you upset," Sharry said. "John explained what you two are doing."

"What *are* we doing?" Charlie asked, pulling the strong tobacco smoke into his lungs, feeling its papery tickle at the back of his throat.

"You're taking your last shot, like you're proving that you're still warriors. It's like a holy thing."

"That's just plain bullshit," Charlie said, angry at John for whatever he had told these young girls. John didn't care about anyone but himself, Charlie thought. He's a user, just like I used to be. But I paid for the way I used people. I'm *still* paying for it. And Charlie thought about his two sons from a previous marriage who didn't even acknowledge he was alive.

"John said you and he were counting coup," Sharry said.

"What the hell is *that* supposed to mean?"

"When Indian people fought, in the old days, they would touch the enemy with a coup stick, and that was like killing him, even though you didn't. It was a test of courage, sort of, because it took more courage to get close enough to touch him with a coup stick than to shoot him dead with an arrow . . . you know? And even if the enemy was dead, you could still count coup on him by touching him with a stick, although the first coup was the most important. That's what they did to Custer."

"It's all bullshit," Charlie said. "It's just John's way of making a bender sound holy, and to get little girls like you into bed with him."

"You don't have *any* respect for women, do you?" Sharry said.

"I'm sorry, I didn't mean to hurt your feelings, but, shit, you know better than this. Your girlfriend did, that's why she got out of the room quick."

Sharry didn't answer. She just took a long drag on her cigarette and caught Charlie watching her breasts.

"How'd you get into this, anyway?" Charlie asked.

"Into what?"

"This whole Indian thing."

"How did *you?*"

"I asked you first," Charlie said. Sharry grinned.

"I'm looking for something," Sharry said. "I don't know what, yet, but I've found some of it here."

Charlie was going to tell her that she was young, that this Indian business would wear off, that she looked like a nice, middle-class preppy girl and would probably end up marrying a doctor, but he didn't. Maybe nothing would make any difference. Maybe that's why John was so free and easy about seducing white girls who hung around Indians. But that was John's way, not Charlie's. Charlie had paid enough dues, but it was too late, or too early, and he was too tired to try to explain himself to this girl. In fact, he wasn't even horny anymore. Maybe he'd really gotten somewhere. He felt better, but tired. He had to sleep. Right now.

"Do you mind if I stay here?" Sharry asked. "Just to sleep."

Charlie lay on his back and stared up at the raftered ceiling. "Sure," he said, and then immediately realized that he should have said "no."

Sharry got up and closed the thin white curtains over the window, then came to bed. She didn't take her clothes off, and Charlie let her snuggle against him under the covers, and he felt a thrill run through him, just to have someone this close, someone who wanted him who was not Joline. He felt himself getting an erection again, and he remembered how Sharry had looked downstairs when he was staring at her across the table. She was *supposed* to be with John, but this was the way it had worked out. Chance of a lifetime, but he owed Joline something, didn't he? He'd been faithful for all these years, and he could *still* go back because even though he'd made a mess of everything, it didn't matter as long as he was faithful. . . . Joline was like that.

But Sharry was snuggling against him, and he had his arm around her. He let his hand rest naturally against her arm, but he knew that he was also touching her breast—the little brat wasn't wearing a brassiere. Counting coup, he thought, as he started to fall asleep, feeling secure, even if his hard-on was hurting against the stiffness of his jeans. Goddamn, he was tired. And she pushed against him, and suddenly the decision was made. He didn't seem to have anything to do with it. He just did it. He had wronged Joline before he'd begun, and it didn't matter now because he had already jumped into hell with John, and he was never coming out right again. But it *did* matter, and Charlie desperately wanted Joline. He wanted her here right now instead of the little girl beside him. He wanted the perfumed security of Joline. He wanted his life back. But he had lost it. God, he really felt that way right now, and he needed comforting for that thought, more than he'd needed since *he* was Sharry's age.

Then he was massaging her breast, sliding his hand under the rough material of her shirt, and he felt himself descending into a kind of sweet, warm death, as everything he had tried to keep hold of in life slid away from him—his family, Joline, his word as a man.

Now *he* was sliding, falling deliciously, and Sharry wriggled around so he could unbutton her blouse, and she was moaning and kissing him open-mouthed and biting his cheek; and he was grinding against her, pulling at her jeans while she unzipped him. He moaned, feeling as if he were about to come, as if her long fingers were numbing icicles touching him. Sharry's strong, natural smells were like those of the woods. The pale morning light was a mist in the room, and Sharry's skin was as damp and cool as wet leaves. Charlie lay back as she pushed down against him. She was smooth and tight and young, and she took his penis in her mouth, and he thought of Stephanie and Joline, and then he remembered various women he had desired over the years. How young and strange this woman was with her warm mouth and even teeth against his penis. It was a fantasy . . . a dream. But it was also a nightmare, for he just could not dismiss the nagging apprehension that tonight he had lost everything forever.

He started to cough. Sharry stopped, pulled back, held him as if he were a child. Angry with himself, Charlie pulled her back down into the bed, kissing her, sucking on her neck and tiny erect breasts; he entered her, feeling that cleanliness he always felt when making love, as if he were in clear warm water. Then followed the terrible wheezing and breathing and hurting to orgasm. Through the cries and hoarse moans, through the tiny, controlled screams and wheezings, he felt the wrongness of what he was doing; and his guilt was as wet and warm as her slippery cunt.

He was raping her, taking her, as if she were Stephanie, as if to punish Joline—and himself, too—by sinning with cock and with his filthy-dirty thoughts.

He opened his eyes, as if he knew that he had to remember this, take it with him wherever he went, and he saw this young girl, this baby, with her beautifully thick brown hair spread across the sheets, the gray morning light touching her features, making them gentler than they were, flattening out her facial lines, which would deepen with age; and she was for this instant as perfect and unblemished as the picture of the Madonna that Joline had insisted be hung above their bed at home. Sharry was turning her head back and forth, as if she was in great pain, and Charlie held himself up on his hands, as if he was floating above her in clear, cool water, and he lunged inside her. She screamed, as if she no longer cared that she was in someone else's house, that she wasn't supposed to be in this room with this old man, and perhaps her thoughts were of her father, perhaps they were just of Charlie, but she shuddered and pulled Charlie down against her and came. She felt suddenly fragile to Charlie, and the guilt returned, intensified by that same frailty. But such an encounter could only happen to Charlie once. He had sinned against Joline for the first time; and after a while he felt himself stiffen again, inside Sharry, and he took her, as if she could give him back what he'd lost, as if he *was* a bull, as if he hadn't lived his life already.

Then he fell asleep, sweaty and sticky and cold, but he kept jolting out of his dreams, not quite awakening, but caught, drowning and coughing.

Through it all, he felt that someone, or something, was watching him, an eye that was like a hot coal burning malevolently through his dreams.

When he finally awoke, the room was empty and bright.

Hard Currents

Snake Medicine

Caroline Rhodes

Dianne Kittridge pulled up to the Northern Navajo Medical Center at Yellow Rock and got out of the car. She studied the building as she stretched a day's worth of inactivity out of her muscles. From the outside, it looked as big and modern as any hospital in Phoenix. She snapped the belt pouch around her waist, grabbed a notepad, and locked the car. She clipped her Health Department badge to her collar as she made her way through the front entrance. A Navajo woman at the information booth gave her directions to the intensive care unit, and paged Dr. Williams to meet her there. As she passed X-ray and the lab, Dianne hoped this wouldn't be one of those arrogant doctors who thought a chemist couldn't understand what was going on because she wasn't a physician. She'd interviewed more than enough of that type, and she wasn't in the mood to straighten one out today.

As she arrived at the nurses' station, a doctor came up to her and stuck out his hand.

"You must be Dianne. I'm Dr. Williams. Did you come up from Phoenix this morning?"

"Every mile of it. How are the patients?"

A frown creased his forehead and he pushed his brown hair back. "We're still getting new cases and don't have anyone who's pulled out of it yet. Mild lung involvement, mild fever, white count elevated, everything else is normal. We're administering antibiotics, including ciprofloxacin which covers gram positive and negative bacteria. Even with the supportive therapy in ICU, we're not getting a response—four people who've been admitted with it in the past week have died."

She looked through the chart he handed her.

"All of them here? Have you checked with other hospitals?" she asked, glancing up from the chart.

"Two of the patients were transfers from smaller hospitals on the reservation—one from Shiprock and one from Kayenta. I've checked others, but no one I talked to has seen any cases like this," he said.

"I called around and didn't find anything either." She continued leafing through the chart. "The blood culture was negative and the urine was normal, blood chemistry okay—were all the tests this normal?"

"Yes. We just can't get a handle on anything. The first two cases I was fairly certain we lost because they waited so long to come in, and then by the time they were transferred from the other hospitals, well, there isn't always time to get treatment started before the disease has progressed too far . . ."

He was looking for understanding, so she nodded. When test results were normal and the patient's illness nonspecific, there was little they could do but wait for the test results to change, more symptoms to develop, or scattershot antibiotics to take effect.

"Do you feel the last two patients were very ill when they came in?"

"No, they seemed to be okay. They were both ambulatory. Lung sounds were about what you'd expect, but they changed within a few days, like the lungs were undergoing some heavy scarring."

"What did the autopsies show?"

He spread his hands, palms up in a gesture of helplessness. "Hard to get Navajo families to agree to one."

"None?" He shook his head. "Any of these people know each other?"

"They all live around the Chuska Mountains."

"How many cases now?" she asked, closing the folder.

"Five more. Two are just kids. Come on," the doctor said, and led her to a nearby room where a bed engulfed the small brown body of a Navajo boy. His mother stood holding his little hand, watching his IV drip. Her jeans and knit shirt looked like she'd been in them for days. Her shoulder-length hair was mussed and the skin beneath her eyes was darker than the rest of her tanned skin. The woman's gaze searched Dianne's face for an answer. Dianne looked away. She had no answers for this woman—yet. Judging by the boy's stillness, she wouldn't have any answers in time. The boy's sister sat nearby, quietly reading. Dianne put the boy's age around five and his sister at nine. The girl looked up from the cot she sat on and gave Dianne a shy, sad smile. Mother and daughter had spent their nights by the boy's side. Dianne turned away.

Outside the room, she took a deep breath and ran her hand through her short brown hair. "How long's he got?"

"He came in two days ago. If he's lucky he'll last through tomorrow."

She nodded, wishing there would be an easy answer, something just waiting for someone to pluck it out of the high desert air. Sometimes it happened that way, but she had the feeling it wouldn't be like that this time. "I'll need a list of the deceased, the patients and their addresses and phone numbers."

"Not much phone service up here. I've already made a list for you, I figured you'd need it. Also copied the patients' charts. Where are you staying?" he asked, handing her a packet of rubber-banded folders off the counter.

"One of the hotels in Chinle. I'm meeting with a tribal representative . . ."

"Ray Blacksnake, right?"

"Right. How'd you know?"

"He's been up here quite a few times since this started. Talking to the families, checking things out."

"Right. Give me a call if you get any new lab results. Did you ever get a sputum culture?"

"The first two were too sick, the second two were noncooperative. The kids don't understand what I want. The other three adults we cultured two days ago and they were all normal flora, nothing unusual."

"Okay. Why don't you run everything again? That way I can report they were done twice, and we can be sure nothing's there. If that's a problem, I can send it to our lab in Phoenix, but if your lab is good here it'll save us some time. Let me know if you get any new cases or if you lose anybody."

"Sure. Nice thing about the reservation, people are real good about helping you get a message to someone."

"Thanks. Talk to you later." She left the hospital and turned her car towards Chinle.

Dianne lay on the hotel room bed thinking that she'd already put in more than her day's work just getting here and would gladly sleep until morning, starting immediately. But she kept seeing the Indian girl sadly smiling and reading in a room where her brother lay dying; the mother's expression of hope.

At least she could try to find her Indian contact. Before she got up, there was a knock at the door.

She opened it to find an Indian man in his early thirties, dressed in jeans and a copper T-shirt with a black leather vest and black felt hat and cowboy boots. His tanned face was gentle yet strong—peaceful, she thought. Not untroubled, but accepting. His long black hair was drawn back into a neat ponytail. Against the brown skin of his right cheek, a darker scar stood out; it looked like two snakes wrapped ca duceus

around a long, thin triangle with a notch out of one end—a crude caduceus, a doctor's symbol, she realized with a start. A series of rough
squares and rectangles were etched into his forearm, starting at a narrow taper just above his wrist, becoming a pattern that wound around
his arm, before the blackness disappeared beneath the sleeves. At the
open neck of the shirt, she could see an edge of black that refused to
complete the pattern for her.

"Hi. Ray Blacksnake."

"Dianne Kittridge, Health Department," she said, sticking her
hand out. His handshake was firm, usually a sign that she was being
taken seriously. She smiled. "Come on in, I was just thinking about
looking you up."

He sat in a chair while she closed the door. "I'd been keeping an
eye open. Saw the Health Department seal on the car and knew it had
to be you. So what have you found out?"

"You've probably already heard it all. Dr. Williams said you'd
spent a lot of time up at the hospital."

Ray shrugged. "I spend a lot of time wherever I think will solve
this. Did he have anything new?"

She summarized the information for him, and he didn't seem surprised by any of it. So he'd heard this already. What else did he know?
"Have you got any ideas?"

"There's a big waste dump about thirty minutes north of Little
Horse Springs. I'm not sure what's out there, but it's a popular party
place, especially with the kids. I looked around and there seemed to be
a lot of leaking drums so I called that in. Haven't heard of anyone
checking it yet. There's uranium mining west of here. My bet is that
it's not either one of those but something else. It's not bacterial, so we
can rule that out."

"We can't rule anything out until the tests are done," she said,
making notes.

"They've already done the tests and they're negative. Nothing's
shown any indication that it's bacterial. No family members are getting it. Let's move on to something that needs investigating," he said,
his voice sharp-edged.

"It all needs investigating, that's how we find out what's making
people sick. Once the test results are in, then I can start ruling things
out. Anything before then would be a guess, and the Health Department isn't in the business of guessing. Nothing will be included or ex-
cluded until everything's been fully explored."

He put his hands back behind his head, leaning back into a position for thought or perhaps intimidation. "I was hoping they'd send
someone who could still think," he said softly.

Her eyebrows rose, then her eyes narrowed and her back stiffened. "What do you mean by that?" she said distinctly.

"How long will it take you to run all your tests and come to a conclusion? Two weeks? Three weeks? More? Four people have died in the past seven days. How many more are you willing to have die just so you can be positive you've got all the possibilities pinned down?"

"I can't just jump to a conclusion. These things have to be carefully, logically tracked down and eliminated."

He leaned forward, resting elbows on his knees.

"Even after all your careful, logical work, you still might not be sure. You might never know. What will you do then?"

She didn't want to think about it. There was a darkness within her that one day she'd be unable to solve an epidemic, that people would just keep dying while she ran tests and tried to put the pieces together. It hadn't happened yet, and that fear drove her to earn the reputation as being the department's best troubleshooter.

"Look, you just don't understand how complicated these investigations are. I know it may look simple, but it takes time to rule things out, time to find the problem. I appreciate your assistance in translating and I'm sure you'll be a big help there, but please don't make my job more difficult than it already is. Stay out of things you don't understand."

He dropped his head down; a few stray pieces of hair had escaped his ponytail and fell alongside his face. Across the delicate curve of his neck was more tattoo blackwork, disappearing into the darkness of his shirt.

Finally he lifted his head. "You remind me of a woman I met at the university in a biochemistry classroom, who asked me to mop up a spill in the hall." He smiled, still watching.

She thought on it, tried to fit the pieces together. "You were a student?" she guessed.

His smile broadened. "The instructor."

She could feel the flush creeping into her face. Of course, and she had just made a similar mistake. She studied his face again, suddenly seeing things that should have been obvious but weren't. The instructor. Of course he was asking questions, making suggestions. "I'm sorry. No one bothered to tell me, but I should have figured it out."

He studied her with goldish brown eyes. "I'm sorry too. I do want this solved as quickly as possible. It's difficult to watch my people die while I keep calling for help and am brushed off. If I were white, my education would actually have meant something."

"Well, it means something to me, I just didn't know you had any.

Didn't expect you to have any, I guess, and that was stupidity on my part."

She watched him for some time, aware of his keen stare. Finally he nodded. "All right," he said.

"We need to talk to the patients' contacts, especially the ones who were around when they got sick. I've already requested that the hospital repeat all the tests, that includes more cultures. They'll rule out drugs, toxins, and other chemicals. We should have something back on that soon." She paused, chewing on the end of the pen, then looked up from her notes. "Can we still talk to some people this afternoon, or is it too late?"

"Sure, we can stop by two or three places. After you've been out here long enough, you can see in the dark." He smiled.

Dianne was up by six the following morning, organizing her notes from the previous day's interviews and reading the charts the doctor had given her. Nothing surprising so far. By the time Ray knocked on her door at seven, she had called the lab and requested an investigation of the waste dump and washed a breakfast bar down with instant coffee.

She grabbed her notepad and files and climbed into Ray's blue truck. "Nice car," she said.

He glanced at her, smiling. "Pick-'em-up truck. Thanks. Did some work down in Phoenix after I finished my Ph.D. Worked at a microchip manufacturer. Profitable but very messy. Came back here."

"What do you do with a Ph.D. in chemistry up here?"

He glanced her way again, easing the truck onto a rutted turnoff. The unpaved road they were following led into the mountains.

"I purify the land."

Some sort of environmental clean-up effort, she guessed. She was about to ask more when the road turned and Ray suddenly stopped. She followed him out of the truck and stood staring at the high desert mountains and rock formations that shot out of nowhere.

"Take a deep breath," he said. She inhaled, smelling the cleanness of the air, watching visibility that went on forever, feeling the wind blowing through her hair. She felt very close to the earth here, something that never happened in a crowded city like Phoenix, air so stagnant you didn't want to breathe, where the sun burned away any life. A greenish rock caught her eye a few feet away. She walked over to it and knelt down.

The rock was run through with veins of coppery green, and speckled with a lapis-like bright blue and flecks of gold. The rock seemed to be calling to her; it promised to answer all her problems, explain her worries, calm her fears, solve the epidemic. A wry smile twisted her face. A rock. Right. The blue was even stronger on the other side, covering nearly half the surface. It was comforting to hold, and she stood back up with it still in her hand.

"I think I can see why you came back," she said.

He smiled, studying her face. "Good. The land is a part of us, a part of our lives."

As Dianne climbed back into the truck, she slipped the rock into her pocket.

"By the way," he said, "traditional Navajos don't speak the name of their dead—afraid it calls the ghost to them. And don't use the name yourself."

"So what do I call them?"

"Say 'that man,' just to be sure. Not everybody minds, but some do, and you'll never talk to them after that if you foul it up."

The entire day was spent interviewing victims' families. Dianne was frustrated trying to follow the translation of a conversation that included two or three Navajos trying to tell their part of the story simultaneously. By the end of the day she felt as if she'd spent the afternoon in a foreign film festival where someone had swapped the subtitles. There was always a comment that she wanted to pursue, but people insisted on leading Ray in another direction. Even with Ray, people seemed reluctant to talk.

Late in the afternoon, Ray offered an explanation. "I think it's the notepad that keeps them from talking. They don't think you're listening, buried in all that paper," Ray said, turning the pickup into another sandy yard. The house was a single wide mobile home, with a half-rusted hulk of a car nearby. A filthy couch rested underneath an aluminum porch awning. Dianne left her pad in the car and they walked to the door.

By the time they reached the porch, an old woman waited there. She greeted Ray in Navajo and left the door open enough for them to enter. They followed her into the living room, where a black-and-white TV carried afternoon talk shows. While Ray explained to the old woman what they were doing there, and the need to answer the questions, Dianne studied the room. The couch and chairs were covered with faded greenish fabric. Drapes of shredded, sun-aged gold hung in tatters over the window, and a layer of dust covered everything. Finally, Ray finished.

"Her grandson was playing with their dog three days ago when he collapsed." Ray said.

Dianne thought of the two Indian boys in the hospital, wondering which one this was. She hadn't had a call from the doctor, so assumed the child was still alive. At least as of this morning. "Ask her where her grandson had been for the last week," Dianne said, wishing for her pad. She clasped her hands tightly in her lap while Ray translated the question, then listened to the woman's reply.

"He had been in school every day last week and was out to play in the afternoons. On Saturday he played in the morning and went to a party in the afternoon."

"Ask her where he played and where the party was."

A moment later, Ray turned back to her. "She says he plays everywhere. The party was at his cousin's. We can go there if you want."

"She has no idea where he plays?"

"There's a lot of reservation and not a big need to keep track of children—they're safe up here."

"Okay. Ask her—" She was interrupted by a car door slamming. A woman's voice called out, high, sounding panicked even though Dianne couldn't understand the words. The grandmother answered, started to rise from her chair, half-frozen.

The woman appeared in the living room, her dark hair wild, her eyes red and swollen in her fleshy face. A cry from her throat sounded like a wounded animal, and Dianne recognized her as the mother by her son's bed in the hospital. Then Dianne saw the look on the old woman's face as she shook her head as though to dismiss her daughter's words. Something new, and it wasn't good. Dianne looked at Ray, whose expression was guarded.

"Ray," she said softly, trying not to intrude, "what's going on?"

"This is the mother of the boy who's sick. Her daughter has collapsed at the hospital."

An eerie feeling crept up Diane's spine like a gust of hot desert wind. She had never known a patient before an illness like this struck them down. An image of the girl's shy smile filled her mind. How would this woman stand losing two so close together?

"Ask her if they're still alive," Dianne said, trying to collect her thoughts.

The mother let go of the grandmother and turned to look at her, face still wet with tears.

"That boy has died. My daughter is still alive, for now," the mother said.

Dianne was confused at first at the woman's statement, then remembered Ray's explanation. No naming of the dead. So it *was* her son. Dianne tried to hide her shock. "I'm sorry, I didn't know you spoke English."

"Who the hell are you?" the woman asked.

"I'm Dianne Kittridge, from the Health Department. When did your daughter fall ill?"

The woman's face crumpled, an expression that was either a prelude to anger or more tears. She smoothed a wet tissue out flat and collected herself. "Not long after that boy died. She was crying, then fell over. I thought she'd just fainted, but when she didn't get up I called the nurse."

"Was she around that boy at all when he got sick?"

"All the time, they were inseparable. Do you know what it is yet?" she asked, her expression desperate.

Dianne looked down at her hands, wishing she had something to offer. People had a tendency to panic, and her detachment usually provided a wall to hide behind. She tried to regain that distance. "I'll call the hospital, see what's going on. It could be something else."

"But don't you know what it is yet? Can't you help? You must have some idea—anything. Anything that would let them treat her rather than just watching her die like they did with that boy. Please."

Dianne watched the tears gathering in the woman's eyes again. "I don't know anything yet. The test results should be back—"

"Here," the woman said, thumping her chest with a fist. "Don't you know here what the problem is?"

"That's not how it works," Dianne said. "Did that boy and your daughter go anyplace unusual in the last week? Do you know where they played?"

"They went to the party, but they're at their cousin's a couple times a month. Nothing besides that. And they play everywhere . . . at least they used to . . ." The woman's voice broke, and tears rolled down her cheeks.

Dianne stood up to leave, giving the woman's shoulder a small pat. To hell with distance, it was the only comfort she could give the woman.

She and Ray climbed in the truck and headed back to the hotel in silence.

She wished she had an answer now. That she could somehow figure it all out without having to wait for the test results. That she had something to offer the woman that would save her from losing a second child this week. Maybe there would be something new when she called. She had investigated epidemics before, but never one in which such a short time elapsed between first symptoms and death, or one with such a high mortality rate. An epidemic that took healthy adults and children was frightening; too easy to imagine everyone would die.

She felt as if the world were spinning around her. "I need some food. And a little time to think."

Ray looked at her. "You look pale. I guess that apple isn't going to hold you until dinner."

She glanced at her watch. "It *is* dinner. Can we stop by the hotel so I can call the hospital?"

"Sure."

She caught Dr. Williams just before he left for the evening. He sounded tired. "We've been interviewing all day. What's happened?" she asked.

"I left a message for you with the hotel clerk. That little boy died, and now his sister's sick with it. I've put her into a hyperbaric chamber."

"I ran into their mother today. She was upset." She'll have another child to bury soon, unless we can solve this, Dianne thought.

"I sent her home for a little rest. A young male probably won't make it through the night, and we've got two new cases."

"From the same area?"

"Yes."

"How do the tests look?"

"Nothing. All the cultures were negative after twenty-four hours. We'll check them again tomorrow, but any bacteria should have shown up by now. No changes in the blood. How about you? Any clues?"

"Well, the only family ties are between that brother and sister. Everyone else's relatives are healthy. That's about it so far. Leave another message if there's anything else."

She hung up and went back out to the truck. "What did the doc say?" Ray asked.

"Nothing we didn't already know," she said. She summarized the conversation, then they rode in silence to a weather-beaten diner. After the waitress took their orders and Ray departed for the restroom, Dianne pulled the rock out of her pocket and studied it. Tiny golden flecks were sprinkled through the blue and green streaks like hidden answers. It seemed an eternity since she'd started asking questions about people's whereabouts and activities. All the information swirled around her like a desert sandstorm, but she couldn't get it to coalesce into an answer. Easier to get those gold flecks out of the rock.

As Ray slipped back into the booth across from her, she palmed the rock. "With nothing on the cultures, that seems to rule anything bacterial out. Since we're not seeing a pattern of primary and secondary contacts, if it's a virus, it isn't passing from person to person. There's no consistency of location, so it's probably not something everybody was exposed to at a common spot. It could be something carried by mice or an insect."

"Vector-borne, right?" he said.

"Yeah. Or it could even be an object. Part of the problem is people are dying before we get a chance to interview them about their contacts. Maybe relatives don't know everybody the patients saw. They didn't seem to all be in one place, but maybe they all saw the same guy."

"If that's true, that argues for something contagious."

"Unless he had something with him at all those places, something everyone was exposed to. Some sort of chemical agent, maybe?" she suggested.

"Something used as part of a ceremony, a healing." Ray's voice was flat and he sat very still.

"Sounds like we should start asking some questions along those lines. Maybe he takes it to each healing, so people were exposed at different times and places. Is that possible?" she asked.

Ray nodded, finally looking up at her. "Very possible. Somebody who's a healer, or thinks he is."

"We'll start asking when we're interviewing tomorrow." She was silent, remembering the girl reading on the cot. Her dark hair and eyes and that shy smile. Sad, but not without hope. Now there was no hope left for her. As she had watched her brother grow sicker, so would her mother now watch her. Both children would be gone from something she could fix, if only she could find the answer soon enough. At least there was still a chance for the daughter. "Damn! I just wish there were a way to solve this without having to wait for test results or more symptoms. Or for more people to get sick. There's nothing to tie the patients together, at least nothing we're hearing about in the interviews."

He reached out and wrapped her hand within his. She looked up, startled. His eyes mesmerized her, and the warmth of his hand was comforting. He turned her hand over and she opened it, revealing the rock within like a pearl. He pulled her hand toward him, gently, and studied the rock, turning it with one fingertip.

"What if there were a way to solve this? Now, tonight?" he asked, folding her fingers back over the rock.

"I don't know. I'd love to be able to act now, but I haven't a clue."

Ray took a deep breath and released her hand. "There's someone we need to go talk to. A wise woman. She interprets the earth around us. Your rock, don't you feel like it's trying to tell you something?"

She opened her hand and looked again at the golden-flecked

secrets within the blue-green matrix. A rock, telling her how to solve this epidemic? She'd been working too hard. "No," she said firmly.

His dark eyebrows shot up. "No?"

"Well, I feel sort of drawn to it, but that's probably just the color or something."

"She can tell you about its color too. Besides, we have to interview her anyway. We can head over there after dinner," he said as the waitress set their plates on the table.

After a few bites, Dianne had a question. "Some of those people didn't want to talk to us today. What did I do to make them so reluctant? Is my reputation preceding me again?" Dianne asked.

His black hair was loose from the ponytail and fell around his shoulders in an ebony cascade, nearly hiding the twisted coil on his cheek, the double helix stabbed clean through by the triangle. His lashes were dark and full, and her heart rate increased as he looked up, his golden brown eyes watching her. For a long moment he held her gaze, then turned back to his dinner.

"It wasn't you. It was me. People are not always pleased that I went to the university. I'm something of an outcast here."

"Why do you stay?"

He passed his hand over his forehead. "I stay to help my people. They don't always understand that, but it's why I'm here." He smiled, the irony twisting his lips.

"You said you do something environmental. I didn't quite get that. What exactly do you do?"

He set down his fork and turned his palms toward her. They were crisscrossed with hundreds of thin white scars. "I purify the earth," he said, then returned to eating.

Dianne was at a loss for a response. He obviously wasn't going to volunteer more, and she wouldn't push for an answer. They finished their meal in silence and then drove to the wise woman's hogan.

Ray spoke to the woman in Navajo for several minutes before she let them in. Dianne's eyes adjusted to the lantern-lit interior, crowded with all manner of things: jars of herbs, roots in a cardboard box on a small shelf, seashells and candles that huddled on small tables. Three comfortable chairs dominated the low-ceilinged living room. A bed and a woodstove were visible in the shadows, lighted by the glow from the stove.

Dianne sat and glanced nervously at the old woman as she lighted candles in the crowded sitting area. When they were all seated, Ray spoke to the old woman, and Dianne noticed that there was something in the woman's response, a hint of coldness in her wrinkled face, a sharp edge to her voice as she responded to him.

"Show her your rock," Ray said.

Dianne tried to nod respectfully, then dug the rock out of her pocket and handed it to the old woman. She studied it, her brown eyes tinged with blue, then she added a pinch of herbs to the candle at her side, closed her eyes, and began chanting.

Ray translated, his voice soft. "The blue of the rock is the blue of the oceans. The waters of creation that serve the Truth. The blue of intuition and feelings and emotions."

Dianne watched the candlelight play the shadows across his face, illuminating, then hiding the scar on his cheek. The tattoos on his arms seemed to come alive, stirring in the shadows. She wanted to reach out and feel the blackness, see if it was really moving, see what was stirring.

"The green of the rock is the green of Mother Earth and all her plants, the life of the Truth. The green of concern for all things living, and the dependence of all things living."

A wind seemed to disturb the candle flames, the shadows danced even more wildly, and the blackness on his arms was writhing, and the gold of his eyes seemed even more vivid now. She reached a hand out and touched his arm. The warmth of it blazed through her. The blackness was still, but when she removed her hand, it seemed to move again.

The old woman opened her eyes and spoke in a normal voice.

"You must go to the place where you got this rock and cut off a lock of your hair and offer it up. Then the meditation will put you in touch with the answers you seek."

A chill ran along Dianne's spine, listening to the woman's words in Ray's voice, still fascinated by the blackness that writhed along his arms. Suddenly she felt something at her leg. She jumped, looked down, and saw a cat. As she reached out to it, it ran off into the darkness toward the bed, leaving behind a small mass. She couldn't quite identify it in the shadows, and was afraid to touch it. The old woman leaned over with a candle; it was a mouse, dead. Her eyes met Dianne's, her wrinkled mouth pursed up. Her voice was now harsh as she sat back down.

Ray was silent. "What did she say?" Dianne asked, her voice not quite steady.

"She says that your mouse magic is dead."

She gazed into his eyes, seeking an answer in the amber depths.

"Your intuition . . . it's gone. You look at every tiny bit of information, but are unable to see the whole."

She stared into the candle's flame, thinking of all the years of college, every class that had snuffed out a bit more of her intuition, her ability to consider an incomplete picture and form a conclusion. She had to have it all there, every piece. Science didn't train you to guess, it trained you to avoid making decisions until every possible piece of data was in. It trained them all, the doctors and the scientists, trained them to run test after test, but not to use intuition to choose which road to go down. Not until all the pieces were there. Not until it was too late, sometimes.

The old woman started talking again, her voice rough. Dianne watched Ray, waiting for a translation but not getting one. He watched the floor. The old woman walked over next to him and started pulling on his shirt, tearing the top two buttons off, revealing the smooth chest beneath. Dianne felt a flush creep into her cheeks at the same time that she was fascinated by the blackwork revealed on his skin: the spirals that flowed down his arms were now clearly the ends of two snakes that wound over his shoulders, their heads resting on his collarbones; in the middle of his chest was a much more primitive version of the stylized scar on his cheek. The caduceus again—a healer's symbol. She shivered, then looked into his golden eyes, nearly reptilian in the shadows. The woman's voice was shouting now, and she was slapping Ray's shoulder, spittle flying onto his cheek.

Finally, Ray began translating. "I am the snake," he said, voice level and emotionless. "I was to be the purifier of the land. I deserted the old ways, and my people. I was given the marks to strengthen the magic within me, but I denied the power by going to the university, thinking I needed more than the magic I was given. I have brought the illness to the land by my disrespect for the old ways, by ignoring my place in the Truth. I devour all spirits, especially that of mouse. You are warned. Especially that of mouse." The old woman stood by her chair, glaring at Ray. He wiped the spittle from his face and stood up, bowed to the woman, and left. Dianne grabbed her rock and followed him out into the cool night air.

Ray guided the truck down the dirt road. "So I am the mouse and you are the snake?" She shivered and rolled up her window.

"Yes. But the mouse has many enemies, and the snake isn't always hungry."

They rode the rest of the way in silence. She glanced occasionally back at his chest, wishing for another glimpse of the snakes woven through his skin, but the shadows prevented her from seeing them.

Ray knocked on her door twenty minutes past their arranged time. His hair was pulled back severely, as though he had intended to capture every strand, keeping it all under control.

"How are you this morning?" she asked, wanting to help, yet not wanting to invade his privacy.

"Fine." The muscle at the top of his cheekbone clenched and released, like a captive animal pacing, seeking escape.

"I tried to meditate with the rock this morning. Nothing really happened, except I fell asleep a few times. I might have been doing it wrong." She carefully studied the table leg, embarrassed to have to admit she'd tried something that was not purely scientific. As his silence grew, she risked a glance at him.

"I was thinking about that. Academia really does help one to lose touch with the intuitive spirit. There was something that helped me when I returned. If you would be willing to try it, I think it might help you also. First we'll go back to where you found your rock, and you can give some sort of donation to the spirits—a lock of your hair, maybe—then we'll see how it goes. If nothing comes to you, then we'll resort to something stronger."

"Such as?"

"I know it sounds totally contrary to everything you learned, but I think you should use some peyote to try to reach your intuitive self."

"Peyote? Isn't that dangerous?"

"Not if you're healthy and you only take a small dose. And I'll be with you. I'll take care of you while you're in trance."

Warmth suffused her limbs, and a flush crept up her face.

"Have you done it before?"

"Of course. I use it routinely in my purification ceremonies. It's really quite safe, especially if you have someone making sure you don't throw yourself off a cliff or something."

She sighed, thinking it over. "I wish I had some idea of which way to go. I just wish I had an answer." She chewed her fingernail.

"You need intuition to put this all together. Maybe the peyote won't help—but at least it's worth a try. The intuition could help you solve this epidemic weeks or months ahead of the test results. It's not that bad," he said softly.

She spit out a gnawed fragment of nail. "If it's not that bad and if you do it routinely, why don't you do it this time?"

"I've tried. I'm afraid my talents lie more in the area of seeking out chemical contamination and neutralizing it than in finding sources of disease."

"That's why you were fairly certain the waste dump wasn't the source of the problem, isn't it?"

He smiled and shrugged. "My method works for small amounts and takes a long time. It would be years before I could purify that dump, and in the meantime it needed to be cleaned up. You've got to get people's attention while they're already looking."

"Right. I'll think about it while we interview the people in the hospital and their families. I'll drive—I actually know where we're going for a change."

Only two of the patients were coherent enough to answer questions. When asked if they had used a healer lately, patients and family members all dropped their gaze to the floor and mumbled that they hadn't.

Back at the nurses' station, Dianne stopped. "What was going on in there? Were they lying to us?"

"They probably didn't want to admit having gone to a healer if there was a chance the doctor would get angry. I think they don't understand that you're not a doctor."

"Why don't you go back and see if you can get an answer? I'm going to find Dr. Williams. I'll meet you back here in a while." Dianne had the doctor paged, and went to see the girl while she waited. The hyperbaric chamber was like a glass coffin. Which it essentially was, Dianne thought, unless they found an answer. The girl's skin was so dark against the sheets, and even then she looked paler than she had the other day. Her face was gaunt, as though she'd been sick for weeks. She opened her eyes then, and looked at Dianne for a long while before closing them again, without a smile.

Tears of frustration filled Dianne's eyes. It would take weeks at the rate they were going. Weeks this girl didn't have. Maybe Ray and the wise woman were right, maybe she needed her intuition. A nice, clean investigation pinned down every detail. If she was to save the girl, she didn't have that luxury this time. No telling how intuition would help; likely nothing would come of it, but it was her only wild card, and the time had come to play it.

Ray came up beside her, startled to find tears on her face. As she pulled a tissue out of her pocket, he put an arm around her shoulders.

"When can we try to find my intuition?"

He released her, turned so he could see her face. "Tonight. You should eat a big lunch, then fast. It works better that way."

She nodded, then noticed Dr. Williams entering the room. "Anything new?" she asked.

The doctor's expression was solemn as he glanced at the girl. "She's got meningitis."

"Meningitis?" Her eyebrows rose, and she paused while the doctor nodded. "Run an HIV test on her."

"Chances of that are really small . . . " the doctor said.

"I know, damn it. Just run the test. She's the only one who's showed with anything like that."

"Which means it's probably coincidental."

"She's also the only one in a hyperbaric chamber, and therefore the only one who's survived long enough to start showing something new."

"Right. I'll get a spinal tap and we'll culture that too."

He left to order the tests.

Dianne and Ray had lunch at the hospital cafeteria, then drove back to interview healers. They had learned nothing significant, and Ray had dropped her off at the hotel while he collected the things they needed for tonight. Dr. Williams called while she waited. The HIV test was negative, but blood work showed her immune system was suppressed. The spinal fluid culture wasn't back yet.

After she hung up, she considered the test results. From the secondary meningitis it wasn't tough to guess that the immune system was having troubles, but if it wasn't AIDS, what was it? She played with the rock, wondering if she'd learn any secrets tonight from this piece of insight that she couldn't quite understand.

She heard Ray out front, grabbed a jacket for the chill night air, and climbed into the truck. They rode in silence. She tried to think herself into a receptive mood. It wasn't difficult; she was ready for a miracle.

She got out of the truck at the site where she'd found the rock, cut off a lock of hair, and placed it on the ground and sat waiting for an answer. After a quarter of an hour she felt nothing, but Ray encouraged her to try for a while longer. Still nothing.

"Are you sure you want to do this?" Ray asked, holding a plastic sandwich bag containing objects that looked like buttons off a wool cardigan.

She thought of being able to know right now what path they should go down, what would keep people from dying, people who were already in the hospital, who would be dead by the time they figured this thing out: the book-reading girl with the shy smile who would die while the wheels of science and medicine ground slowly, slowly, plodding through every possible test, even the ones that weren't relevant. If she were able to cut through all that and have some direction, some intuition to find the pattern, she might save the girl.

"Yes. I'm sure."

As his gaze met hers, she felt warmth, safety, as though the snakes would protect mouse against her other predators.

He handed her a small button, about the size of a dime, and she chewed it, making a face at its bitter taste.

"You know that this is going to make you vomit, that's a normal side effect," he said calmly. His matter-of-fact scientific attitude toward it, coupled with his background and experience, was making it much easier for her.

As they sat and talked, the sun sank lower, and soon the sky was shot with pink and violet. It was beautiful. She briefly wondered if it was an omen that night was coming as the drug gripped her body. Suddenly nauseated, she stood up and walked over to a mesquite bush and dry-heaved. After a few minutes the feeling passed, and she pulled her rock out and sat back down.

Her heart was beating faster now, and she was starting to sweat, although the night air was cool. Ray lighted the lantern and set it a few feet away. He knelt beside her and looked at her eyes, his own eyes warmly luminous, glowing as though lit from within. He placed his fingers on her wrist, checking her pulse, and their warmth felt as though it were spreading through her blood and throughout her body. Suddenly she wanted to see the snakes on his chest, wanted to watch them move again.

She reached for his shirt and unbuttoned it, pulling it away to reveal the snakes. They were quiet tonight, moving languidly, as though slowing down as the air cooled. They were content, guarding their mouse, keeping it safe. She reached out to touch them and heard Ray's indrawn breath. His skin was warm and smooth, and she traced her hand along the snakes, from head to tail, spiraling from near his collar bone down to his navel, then along the matching image, mirrored on the other side of the sword. Like the caduceus; the healer of the land.

She reached for his hand, turned it palm up to feel the latticework of scars. "You heal the land with your blood," she said. Her voice was dreamy and disconnected and seemed to float off on the night air, spinning away before it could reach her ears.

She began to trace the snakes again, fascinated that they would hold still for her to stroke. Ray gently captured her hand, still looking into her eyes. He turned her head toward the lantern, and she felt the light searing into her brain. He stood and moved the lantern farther away, and that made her more comfortable. He removed his shirt and some part of her that had been sleeping for many years suddenly woke; a part that hadn't been free to act before was now given permission. Her limbs were heavy, entirely unable to carry out the wishes of her body, or her mind, she was unsure which at this point, only that she wished she could have the feeling and the freedom to act on it at the same time. Now, she felt trapped.

Ray sat down behind her, and as she tried to turn her head to follow him, the world dissolved into a smear of colors and shapes half-hidden in the darkness. Panic gripped her as she imagined hearing the engine of the truck starting, being abandoned in the darkness of this alien landscape with only a lantern that certainly wouldn't burn all night.

Instead, she felt warmth behind her as she was pulled back and cradled against Ray's chest, his arms enclosing her. Suddenly she was afraid. She was defenseless, vulnerable. Yet as the minutes passed, she began to feel safe and protected. Snake was protecting mouse, how strange; yet it seemed right.

She didn't know how long they had sat there, his warmth soaking into her back, when she saw the movement out of the corner of her eye. She turned and the entire darkness shifted with her. She could feel the warmth of his hand brushing across her ear, brushing hair back from her face. It tickled, and she lifted her hand, which was trembling as though dancing. There was a noise, and she jerked, trying to determine what sort of noise it was. His voice. Her name. He was calling her name. The shadows were moving again, out in the desert, moving and flowing as though running, seeking her, closing in. She started to whimper, trying to move her hands, trying to find safety.

He turned her within his arms, moving so that she was sideways and could hide her head against his chest. One leg was behind her back, the other under her knees, and his arms wrapped around her shoulders.

"It's okay, Dianne. You're all right," he murmured.

She wrapped her arms around his waist, her cheek against his chest. His hair hung down over her face like dark snakes, like the warmth of the snakes beneath her cheek. She studied them, able to see only that they were moving more now, as though restless. Suddenly they asked her if she was ready to leave. Her mouse body climbed on top of one of the snakes, and they started off over the desert. It seemed that the cool breeze created by their rapid passage over the desert floor ruffled her fur, her whiskers and nose tested the night air. They traveled for an endless time, passing under creosote bushes that towered above them, around cacti and rocks, past all the night creatures of the high desert, never stopping.

Finally she caught the hint of something on the clean air, and guided the snake toward a grouping of rocks, looming in the night like a mountain. The snake paused at the bottom, questioning. She twitched her whiskers. Yes, this was it. They traveled up through the sandstone, twisting through passages and around rocks until they suddenly came to a gaping slash in the rock. They went down through it into a huge cave. At the back was the opening of a small chamber. She could see a hand pick in the corner, and could smell the newly broken rock, as well as something darker, something more foul. Her whiskers twitched, and she urged the snake forward into the inner chamber. A skeleton lay within, accompanied by two molded bags of herbs. She jumped from the snake's back into the dirt, and brushed her whiskers against the skeleton. Buried here many years ago. Only disturbed recently. White fungus covering everything like thin mist. A large circle bare of fungus. The earth's darkness burning up through the whiteness. Something had been taken from here. Covered with fungus. Mistaken for dust. Wrong.

She returned to the snake's back and they journeyed across the desert. Before they had left the rocks behind, she turned, trying to etch the image in her mind.

Suddenly she was back in the warmth of Ray's arms, the drug fading from her body, leaving her still sluggish. She lifted her head from his chest and tried to focus on his eyes.

"I know," she said, her voice rough and thick. She felt her weight shift as he picked her up and put her in the truck. She slept as he drove back to the hotel, waking as he carried her in and laid her on the bed.

Before he could move away, she carefully reached up and turned his right cheek toward her. The scar was barely visible in the darkness as she brushed it with her fingertips. It looked as though it had been burned in.

"And the wise woman thought you deserted your people." She moved her hand back, brushing the curve of his ear, and settling at last in the fine, soft hair at the nape of his neck. Reluctantly she turned away, reaching for the phone.

By the time she called the hospital and asked for Dr. Williams, her head was much clearer.

"I know this sounds crazy, but I think it's a fungal infection," she said.

There was silence on the other end of the line. "What makes you think that?"

"Uhm . . . intuition."

"You want me to start them on amphotericin B with no more reason than intuition?" he asked.

"I'll be bringing you proof tomorrow. Do you still have those plates incubating?"

"I assume so. Why?"

"Take a look at them. If I'm right, the older ones should have fungus growing on them."

He paused. "Hang on."

Five minutes later he was back on the line, his voice sounding ten years younger.

"You're right, they're covered with fungus. How the hell did you find out?"

"Intuition. I told you. Hey, I'll see you tomorrow." She hung up and turned back to Ray.

The next morning they drove to the hospital at Yellow Rock and collected a set of disposable lab suits and masks. Dianne was relieved to find the girl still in the chamber, looking no worse. She glanced down at the chart. Tanya. Her name was Tanya. When the girl's dark eyes opened, Dianne pressed her hand to the glass. A tired smile appeared on Tanya's face. The girl closed her eyes almost immediately, and Dianne left her to rest. Dr. Williams had finally gone home after starting the patients on their new therapy, so Dianne and Ray headed back for the Chuska Mountains to find the source of the epidemic.

They threaded their way through the land, looking at rock formations, backtracking when necessary, trying every rutted road to get a new perspective.

Down one dusty trail, Dianne suddenly recognized the rock formations ahead. "That's it," she shouted.

"There'll be a turnoff up here," Ray said.

A few minutes later he pulled the truck down a narrow track mostly overgrown with dead grass. He stopped at the base of the rocks. They suited up in the disposable gear from the hospital, carefully fitting the filter masks over nose and mouth, taking no chances with the fungi.

"We look like lab techs on Mars," she said.

Ray laughed. "Bad movie."

The gently curving sandstone base gave way to huge boulders that they had to scramble over. It was awkward trying to keep the fragile outfits intact. Dianne came over one rock and stared down into a crevice, suddenly recognizing it.

"This is it. There's an outer cave, and then the inner burial chamber was walled up until it was disturbed."

Ray turned on the flashlight and squeezed himself down through the opening.

"This looks like the place. It's a long drop, I'll help you down," he called up to her.

Dianne lowered herself through the narrow, twisting opening, and felt Ray's hands helping her down. They were in the outer cave, but it seemed smaller than she remembered. Dianne was shaking as she knelt down, staring in awe at the burial chamber illuminated by the flashlight. It was just like she had seen, but now it looked incredibly tiny. So small that she was confused, then remembered her own size the last time she'd been here. Of course it seemed small by comparison; she'd been mouse-sized last time.

"Medicine man," Ray said beside her, his voice muffled by the filter mask. "His medicine bundle is missing. Those were his herb bags," he said, pointing. Dianne pulled the vials out of her pocket and scraped fungus samples into them. After they were full, she held them up and peered at them. "Will you look at this. There's two different colors of fungi in here. One's off-white, but the other has a pinkish tinge. I wonder if that's what caused all the trouble—both of them together."

"We'll see."

"I wanted to ask you something. If Navajos are so afraid of death, and so serious about their medicine men, why would anyone break in here and steal a medicine bundle?"

"Do all your people believe in the old ways?" he asked.

"No."

"Don't expect mine to, either. Ready to go?" She nodded. "There's something I want to do first," he said, and reached for the stones that had been torn loose. He stacked them up, working them back into the wall until the chamber was sealed again. "Okay. Now we're ready."

He boosted her up until she was able to grab the rock and pull herself out. He followed behind her, and they walked back to the truck in silence. He kicked away the rock that secured a plastic trash bag, and they put their used protective gear inside it, then headed back to the hospital with the fungi samples.

Two days later, they met Dr. Williams at ICU, making notes on a chart. A smile broke out on his face when he saw them. "Hi. Talked to the guy at the university who identified our fungi. He said there were two present, *Coccidioides immitis* and *Tolypocladium inflatum Gams.*"

"Cocci! Anyone who's lived in Arizona has developed antibodies to valley fever," Dianne said.

"I agree, but listen. *Tolypocladium* produces cyclosporine, an—"

"Immunosuppressive," Dianne finished for him. "So the Cocci learned how to produce cyclosporine from growing next to the

Tolypocladium and the cyclosporine suppressed the immune response that normally would have taken care of the Cocci. I knew bacteria could do that, but it never occurred to me that fungi could."

"My only question is how did this spread?" Dr. Williams asked.

Ray cleared his throat. "We finally ran into a guy who wanted to talk," he said. "Apparently Leon had this medicine bag he'd found up in the rocks behind his house. He went around doing healings with it, until he got sick. Then Bill took it and did more healings. This guy said he was afraid because the bag was taken from a dead medicine man, so he didn't get anywhere near it, just heard about it. Anyway, he knew who'd had it and where it'd been. We finally found it in a box under Bill's bed."

"Huh. Well, we haven't had any new cases, so maybe that'll be the end of it," the doctor said.

"How's Tanya?" Dianne asked.

"Her lungs sound better, the meningitis is clearing, and the fever's gone down. We took her out of the hyperbaric chamber this morning. Would you like to see her?"

The girl lying in the bed looked much better than she had the last time Dianne saw her. The shy smile was back and most of the sadness gone. The mother sat in a chair nearby, looking as though she had gotten a little rest, but still too tired to stand by her daughter's bedside. She smiled at Dianne. "Thank you for finding an answer in time. You looked in the right place," she said, touching her heart. Dianne remembered the angry gesture from that day her daughter first fell ill. Now the gesture was strong and gentle.

"I should thank *you*. I learned a lot here." As they stood by Tanya's bed, Dr. Williams's curiosity got the best of him. "Tell me, how did you really solve this?" he asked.

"I told you, intuition." Dianne felt a hint of warmth in her face.

"The reservation is a good place for intuition," Ray said, grinning.

Mother Called It Daddy's Junkyard

Debra White Plume

The oily smell of burning kerosene hung thick in the small, almost airtight house. Now and then a moan escaped from the young woman lying on a narrow bed against the wall. In the yellow lamplight she lay twisting and turning, sometimes; motionless and breathing quietly, other times; but always with a glazed, wild look haunting her usually beautiful eyes.

She'd been in the little narrow bed for two days now, alone in the log house she shared with her parents and two brothers. The blizzard that had blasted snow against the house for the last two days had ceased around sundown, leaving the prairie in a stillness without wind or motion. Not even the animals had come out yet into the crisp, cold air. The night sky was glittering with bright stars and a new moon, glittering with a clarity that only exists in the middle of the prairie.

She lay on her side, absently stroking her hard, rounded stomach. She watched the eerie shadows playing on the far wall, cast by the flickering of the lamp burning on the chair at her bedside. Even though she was almost eighteen, she feared the dark and would not let the lamp go out. Her eyes scanned the room. She saw her parents' bed on the other side of the room, banked on each side by stacks of large, dark trunks that held their clothes and her mother's treasures.

Against the eastern wall stood more trunks and two quilt-covered roll-away beds that were folded down each night for her brothers, then folded back up each morning. The western wall held the ancient cupboard her grandfather had built, the table and chairs, and a stand that held a basin and pitcher of water. Above the stand was the house's only window, and under the stand were three cans full of water, and a slop bucket. In the center of the house was a huge iron stove that served to heat the house and cook the food.

Everything was in its assigned place, without clutter, as there never is when many people live together in a small space. The linoleum floor was mopped with clear pump water each morning. She never noticed the dinginess of it, or the worn-out spots in front of the door and the stove. She just noticed that it was clean and smelled like Pine-Sol and felt smooth and good against her bare feet.

She rose suddenly from beneath her many blankets and struggled to stand. Her face was contorted with pain, and sweat gleamed off her skin. Her thin shoulders were taut from strain, and her hands shook with the effort of swallowing unvoiced pain.

She did not take a blanket to cover herself, or stop to put on her shoes. She simply walked barefoot out of the house, leaving the old, heavy door open behind her. She knew where she was going. She walked through the ankle-deep snow to the gate that opened onto the blank plains and the unplanned arrangement of corrals and buildings that had sprung up over the past fifteen years. Her mother's sleeveless summer dress hung loose around her, but she did not feel the cold. Her blood fired through her with a fever that had begun the evening everyone left for town.

The gate abruptly snapped shut behind her, pulled fast by the spring that her father kept tightened without fail—he did not want his dogs out when he wanted them in.

She continued walking until she reached the area where her father kept his "personal stuff." Her mother called it his junkyard. Her mother said that all the junk her father had gathered over the years was placed in this pile. Her mother said that all the things her husband had started, and did not quite know how to finish, were gathered here in this junkyard.

She finally reached her father's personal trash haven and crept slowly over the rusted car and tractor parts, scrap metal and iron, rotting wood and mulch, long-forgotten nails and cans, as well as an array of foreign, unknown objects, whose shapes seemed black and edged in the dark. All these things he treasured, he kept. He refused to move them to the toolshed beyond the end of the yard. He said he needed the disheveled items, he would not part with them. These things were personal, important.

She found a little space between an old transmission and a battered, ice-filled cream can. She nestled herself down, down between these two objects and reached up to grip each one tightly. She lowered herself into a squat, and she pushed. There was not one single sound here on the prairie where she lived, far from the nearest highway, and farther still from any other living human being.

She pushed and breathed, pushed and breathed. She moaned, shivered. Finally, a ripping flow surged across her back, her stomach, her thighs, her insides. Pushing with all her strength, she felt the baby slip from inside her. The body made a dull thud as it landed in the snow at her feet. Steam rose to envelop her in its mist. She scrunched her eyes tightly shut, she did not want to look at it.

Sweat trickled down her face, making her hair cling to the hot skin of her face. She leaned against the cream can and rested for a while, then breathed deeply a few times, and pushed again. She felt a hotness slip out of her, and land. She felt lightheaded and weak, but she made herself stand up. She steadied herself, and stepped over the baby and the blood. Creeping slowly over the cluttered mess of her father's personal things.

She almost kept going, but turned and reached beneath her, groping in the moonlight for the baby's cord. She found the hot slipperiness of it. Stooping over it, she bit with all her strength, and she shook her head until she felt the cord break. She took a hair barrette from the end of her long braid, and attached it close against the baby's belly. She would give it that chance.

She raised herself once again into an upright position, and walked through the snow, across the short distance toward the fence.

She went through the gate and back into the cabin her father had built fifteen years ago, when he was still a young man, and the hills around the house rang with the happy laughter of a little girl.

Gator Bait

Jay Littlehawk

I n his tiny dressing room, at the rear of the building, even with the door closed and the radio on, Harry Gallager could hear the audience. His audience. Like the hum of some giant electrical generator, the noise echoed along the hallway and sent snippets of laughter and conversation into the four corners of the room.

There was a sharp knock at the door, and a voice said, "Five minutes till showtime."

Harry didn't reply, made no move to answer the door. Let them wait, he thought. He replaced the cap on the bottle of bronzing cream and continued to study his reflection in the mirror. The man who stared back at him from the depths of the smoky glass was short and wiry, with high cheekbones, a hook nose, dark skin, and coal-black hair. The hair, like his skin, was also artificially colored. Satisfied that his skin coloring was perfect, and that every hair was in place, Harry slipped on a pair of blue jeans, socks, cowboy boots, and a vest made of tanned alligator skin. He turned again to study his image in the mirror. And smiled.

No one who saw him ever guessed that he was a thirty-seven-year-old ex-salesman from New York City, of German and Irish descent. Instead, they all believed that he was a Native American, fresh off a Florida reservation. A child of the swamps. And that was exactly what he wanted people to believe. For Harry Gallager, who had never made much money as a salesman, was making a fortune as Indian Joe, the World's Greatest Alligator Wrestler.

He crossed the room, opened the door, and stepped out into the narrow hallway that led backstage. The hallway was empty, and greatly magnified the noise of the crowd. From the way it sounded, Harry was certain that the Cow Palace of Orlando, Florida, was again filled to capacity. Saturday nights were always good, but they were even better during tourist season. Most of the customers would be Europeans, in town to visit Disney World or one of the other theme parks, their accents as thick as the cigarette smoke floating above their tables.

A short flight of stairs led up to the stage. Harry took the steps two at a time. The stage was empty, except for a shallow wading pool off to one side. Inside the pool, with only his eyes and nose above the murky water, was Harry's co-star, George, an eight-foot Florida alligator. George's mouth had been taped shut with duct tape to keep him from biting the stagehands who would handle him before and after the show. Harry would remove the tape at the beginning of his act, but wasn't too worried about getting bitten himself. For one thing, old George was blind, and had been since birth. For another, prior to each show, Harry paid the stage crew to stick George in a walk-in cooler to lower his body temperature and make him sluggish. With the house lights dimmed and most of the audience drunk, nobody ever noticed that George never acted as spunky as a gator in the wild.

A sudden blast of music from out front informed Harry that he was about to go on. He took his place in the center of the stage. A few seconds later the announcer's voice came over the loudspeakers.

"Ladies and gentlemen, boys and girls. This is the moment you've all been waiting for. The Cow Palace of Orlando, Florida, is proud to present to you a show of death-defying courage and daring, as one man pits himself against the most dangerous creature alive. Direct from the Florida Everglades, I present to you Indian Joe—the World's Greatest Alligator Wrestler!"

The curtain parted to thunderous applause. Harry would have smiled, but that would ruin the illusion of the noble red man he was trying to create. Instead, he stood as rigid as a statue, his arms folded across his chest, staring out over a sea of expectant faces.

The house lights dimmed. A single spotlight sought him out, found him, illuminated him like some powerful deity. A hush fell over the audience. Harry allowed the silence to stretch for effect, then raised his hand in greeting.

"Welcome, my brothers and sisters," he said, speaking in his best Indian voice. A voice acquired from watching countless old westerns on television. Several people in the audience leaned forward, eager to hear what he had to say.

"My name is Indian Joe. I am a gator wrestler. I have wrestled alligators ever since I was twelve years old. My grandfather taught me, as he taught my father before me."

Harry paused to look around. "What I do here tonight is no trick. It is real. The alligator I am about to wrestle is not someone's pet. It was caught in the swamp only yesterday and is not very happy about being here." There were a few chuckles from the audience. "Alligator wrestling is not a sport, it is a way for a Native American to show courage and put his faith in the Great Spirit."

He turned and watched as six stagehands lifted George from the wading pool. Even though the alligator was blind, and his mouth had been taped, he could still put up quite a fight. Cautious of his powerful tail, the stagehands approached the gator from the side. Four of the men grabbed his legs, while the other two quickly moved in and secured his tail and head.

As the stagehands struggled with the hissing gator, Harry allowed his gaze to wander over the audience, savoring the atmosphere of excitement and fear. He was just about to turn away when something in the front row caught his attention and set off a warning bell in his head.

Harry looked again, staring past the spotlight that nearly blinded him. There, in the center of the front row, alone at a table, sat a man who stood out in sharp contrast from the others around him. He was tall and muscular, with a dark complexion and shoulder-length black hair. He wore blue jeans and boots and a yellow shirt that had a wide, multicolored patchwork stripe across the chest. A Seminole shirt.

Indian.

Harry frowned slightly. An Indian in the audience could mean trouble. They generally took a dim view of white people pretending to be Native American, especially those making money at it. He had heard that the American Indian Movement had a large enrollment in the state of Florida. So far he had been lucky and hadn't ended up on AIM's "hit list." Maybe they didn't know about him. But now . . .

He doubted if the Indian had come in just to see the show. He didn't look like the type that frequented tourist attractions. A fellow gator wrestler? Perhaps. He looked rugged enough. That thought made Harry a little nervous. The last thing he needed was for a real gator wrestler to watch his act. But it was too late to worry about it now; he had a show to do.

The stagehands set the thrashing alligator down in the middle of the stage and moved back. Harry approached it from the side, careful of its tail. He stepped in quickly, straddled the gator, and grabbed its head from behind. He held its mouth closed with one hand while he removed the tape with the other. With the tape removed, the alligator hissed and opened its mouth wide—much to the delight of the audience.

Careful to keep his fingers clear of its mouth, Harry went into his carefully rehearsed speech about the dangers of alligator wrestling. Halfway through the presentation, he glanced toward the first row of tables. The Indian was gone. Harry wondered where he had gone, but only for a moment. He had his hands full.

The show was a success, as were all his shows. He wowed the audience, who never suspected that George was blind, with a series of well-rehearsed moves. Once the gator's mouth was again taped, and he was safely back in his pen, Harry took time out to sign autographs and pose for a few pictures. He hung around and answered questions until the band started to play, and then, grabbing a beer from the bar, walked slowly back to his dressing room, happy in the knowledge that he had the following night off.

Harry didn't see the man until it was too late. He stood just inside the doorway of the dressing room, concealed in the darkness. As Harry entered the room, the man stepped forward. Harry started to yell, but a fist lashed out. Darkness followed.

His head and jaw throbbed with pain, and there was a vile taste in the back of his mouth. Blood. As he slowly regained consciousness, Harry Gallager became aware that he was moving. His body swayed slightly, and the sounds of an engine vibrated through him. He opened his eyes and looked around, trying to get his bearings. He lay in semidarkness; a metal roof curved overhead. A moment passed before he realized that he was lying in the back of a van. But whose van was it? He tried to move, but couldn't, and realized that his ankles and wrists were tied.

Kidnapped. I've been kidnapped!

A knot of fear settled deep in the pit of his stomach. He lifted his head and looked forward. The van had two seats, but only the driver's was occupied. A man was driving. In the faint glow of the instrument panel, Harry could see his muscular arms, his long hair and the yellow shirt that stretched across his broad shoulders.

The Indian.

"Where are you taking me?" Harry asked, his voice barely a whisper.

The Indian looked up and studied him in the rearview mirror, but didn't answer.

"Kidnapping is against the law," Harry said, feeling his face flush with anger.

"So is fraud," the Indian replied.

"What are you talking about?" Harry asked. He figured if he could get the man engaged in a conversation, he might be able to find out why he had been abducted and what was in store for him.

The Indian reached up and adjusted the mirror. Harry could see part of his face. His eyes glowed yellow from the dashboard lights. "You call yourself Indian Joe," he said. "but I doubt there is even one drop of Indian blood in you. Am I right?"

In his present predicament, Harry thought it best not to lie. He nodded.

The Indian smiled. His teeth were tiny and sharp-looking. "I thought so. What's your real name, white man? John? Fred?"

"Harry Gallager," he answered. "And yours?" Harry didn't expect the Indian to tell him, and was surprised when he did.

"Wowakan," the Indian said.

What a name.

"You claim to be the world's greatest alligator wrestler," Wowakan continued. "but that is not true, either. Is it? You may fool the tourists, but you didn't fool me. The gator you wrestled tonight was blind."

Harry was shocked. "How did you know that?"

"He told me," Wowakan replied.

"Who told you?"

"Why, the gator, of course."

Sweat broke out on Harry's forehead as he realized that he was dealing with a madman.

"Not much of a challenge in wrestling a blind gator, is there, Harry?"

"It's just a show," Harry said. "I'm an actor."

"Then you should tell people that you are an actor, instead of claiming to be something you're not. That alligator didn't move very fast, either. Why was that? Drugs?"

"We lowered his body temperature before the show," Harry answered.

"You did what?"

"We put him in a cooler and brought his body temperature down. It makes him easier to handle."

The Indian grew angry. "You make me sick," he spat. "You take a blind, helpless creature and kill it a little more each day so you can pretend to be something you're not. A real alligator wrestler would never do something so cruel. He respects the gator he wrestles. It is his brother. His equal. And in some cases, it is also his teacher.

"For a long time now we have heard of you and your little show. At first we chose to ignore you, hoping you would grow tired of playing Indian and go away. But you didn't go away; you stayed instead, insulting my people, making a mockery of something sacred—something you could never understand. Finally, we could stand it no longer. Something had to be done."

Harry didn't like Wowakan's tone of voice. He had a feeling the Indian had more in mind than just putting a good scare into him.

"What are you going to do?" he asked, trying to disguise the fear in his voice.

"Do?"

"Where are you taking me?"

Wowakan smiled. "Where? Why, Harry, I am going to give you a chance to prove yourself. Tonight you're going to give an encore performance for my people. I can see it now: Indian Joe, the World's Greatest Alligator Wrestler, will amaze the world as he wrestles the world's greatest alligator."

Harry felt his mouth go dry. He struggled at his bonds, but to no avail. Finally, his shoulders and neck muscles fatigued, he laid his head back on the floor. As he stared up at the ceiling, listening to the sound of the tires spinning below him, he whispered a short prayer for help. The last thing in the world he wanted was to wrestle a healthy alligator.

There was no way of telling how long they drove, but it seemed like forever when the van slowed and turned off the highway onto a bumpy side road. About half an hour later, Wowakan stopped the van and killed the engine.

Oh, God . . . this is it.

Harry's heart pounded in fear, and he found it difficult to breathe. He lay motionless as Wowakan opened his door and climbed out of the van. He heard him walk around the van, and then the side door slid open.

Fresh air entered the van, bringing with it the cries of crickets and the scent of night-blooming jasmine. Harry took deep, gasping breaths. He raised his head and looked out through the opening. Beyond the van, trees crowded close together. They were in the woods. But what woods? And where?

Wowakan stepped into view, his immense size nearly blocking the view. He pulled a knife from the sheath on his belt and ran his thumb along its edge. "End of the line, my friend."

Harry knew he was about to die. The crazy Indian was going to cut him into little pieces and bury him in the woods. But to his surprise, Wowakan used the knife to cut the rope binding Harry's ankles. He then helped him climb out of the van.

His body stiff from both the ride and being tied up, Harry had to lean against the van until the feeling returned to his legs. Beyond the narrow road where they stood, the ground sloped away to murky water from which grew gnarled trees, vines, and other plants. Harry had never been in a swamp before, but knew he was in the middle of one now.

Wowakan stepped in front of him. "As I have said, tonight you will have a chance to prove yourself. We will see what kind of alligator wrestler you really are—what kind of man you are."

He pointed out a narrow path of dry ground leading into the swamp. "That path leads through the middle of this swamp, through the very heart of my people's land. It is not an easy path to follow, for it is filled with many dangers. Men far greater than you, Harry, have tried to walk this path and failed. And now it is your turn. You are to follow the path until you reach its end, or until you meet your death. Whichever comes first."

"And if I refuse?" Harry asked.

Wowakan opened the van's passenger door, and took out a lever-action rifle. "If you refuse, then I will be forced to gut-shoot you and leave you to die." To emphasize the point, he cocked the rifle and aimed it at Harry.

"It doesn't look like I have much of a choice, then," Harry said.

Wowakan grinned, again displaying a set of teeth that must have been artificially sharpened. He stepped forward, turned Harry around, and cut the cords binding his wrists. Harry rubbed his wrists, feeling the circulation slowly return to his hands.

"Another thing," Wowakan said as he stepped back. "If you should attempt to turn around and come back to this road, my people will kill you."

His people? Are there other Indians out here?

"Your destiny awaits you, Harry Gallager. Go now."

Harry started to argue, but didn't. He thought about trying to take the gun away from Wowakan, but figured he'd only get himself killed. Heroics against bigger opponents only worked in the movies. Like it or not, he had no choice but to do what he was told. So, without another word, he turned and started down the path.

The path was narrow, the ground spongy. Branches of trees arched overhead and created the illusion that he walked through a long, dark tunnel. Spanish moss shimmered like silky spiderwebs in the moonlight, while tree roots stretched twisted fingers along the ground. The air was heavy with the smell of decaying vegetation, and the night echoed with the cries of frogs.

About thirty feet down the path, Harry stopped and turned around. The foliage was so thick he could no longer see the road or the van. He thought about going back, but quickly dismissed the idea. Wowakan would be waiting for him. Harry had no doubts that the

Indian's threats were real. The man was insane. No, his best bet was to continue on and hope for the best.

Fifty or sixty yards farther on, the path took a sharp turn to the right. At the bend of the path, a log had fallen across the trail. Harry was about to step over the log when it moved.

"Jesus Christ!" Harry exclaimed as he jumped back.

The alligator hissed and twisted, lashing out with its tail. Harry tried to get out of the way, but the tail slashed painfully across his left calf.

Harry's foot slipped and he almost went down. If most of his weight hadn't been on his right leg, the gator would have taken his legs out from under him. He stumbled back out of the way as the alligator turned toward him, its mouth open wide. The alligator lunged, but Harry had recovered his balance and jumped out of the way. He landed to the side of the gator, leaped over its tail, and fled down the path. Only after he was a safe distance away did he stop and look back.

He expected the alligator to chase after him, like some reptilian guard dog, but it didn't. Instead, it gave a final hiss and a flip of its tail, and then slipped slowly from the path into the stagnant water, perhaps to sulk. Once in the water, the gator was all but invisible. Only its eyes could be seen. He heard it grunt as it swam away. The grunt was answered by a deeper grunt from off to the right. Harry turned and spotted a second pair of eyes in the water gliding toward him.

"Oh, no. Not another one."

From farther away, several other grunts sounded, as well as from behind him. The sounds drew nearer, closing in on him. Harry broke out in a cold sweat as he realized he was surrounded by alligators. And as he listened to their deep-throated cries, he got the feeling that they were deliberately setting a trap for him. But that was ridiculous. Alligators weren't intelligent. They were dumb, cold-blooded reptiles. Or were they? Suddenly, some of the things Wowakan had said seemed to make sense.

But Harry's sudden insight about alligators didn't lessen the danger he was in. If anything, the knowledge only made things seem even more desperate. His only hope for safety lay in getting out of the swamp, and back to civilization, as quickly as possible. If he remained where he was, he was certain to end up as gator bait.

After what seemed like hours, Harry breathed a sigh of relief as he came upon an island of dry ground approximately twenty feet in diameter. The island was apparently maintained by someone, for all but one of the trees had been cut down and the vegetation cleared away. Though he was still surrounded by swamp, the tiny clearing offered a temporary reprieve from the narrow path he had been forced to walk for most of the night. Harry saw that the path continued beyond the island, but he had no desire to set foot upon it. Not yet, anyway. Instead he sank wearily to the ground, resting his back against the trunk of the one remaining tree.

It felt good to rest for a moment, to allow his heartbeat and breathing to return to normal. He leaned his head against the tree and looked up at the night sky. There was no moon, and he wondered if it had already set for the evening. If so, then morning wouldn't be too far off. Things would be better in the daylight. The dangers lessened. He contemplated remaining where he was until then, but knew that the Indian would come looking for him. At least he could stay for a little while.

He must have dozed off, for the next thing he knew, the sky was noticeably lighter. And there was a crick in his neck. Harry blinked several times, wiped a hand slowly across his face, and lowered his head to look around—

And got the shock of his life.

There, no more than five feet from him, was the biggest damn alligator he had ever seen. The gator, which must have crept up on him while he dozed, was at least ten feet long, and probably weighed around five hundred pounds. There was no way to get around it, for the gator was directly in front of him, close enough to be upon him in a single lunge. To make matters even worse, the tree, which had offered comfort earlier, prevented Harry from backing away.

He was in a trap with only one way out—straight ahead. But that meant taking on a bull alligator much bigger than he was. And this one wasn't blind or half-frozen. Harry watched in horror as the alligator hissed angrily and moved toward him.

Slowly, carefully, Harry shifted his weight forward, moving from a sitting position into a squat. He fought to maintain his balance as the muscles in his legs trembled from both fear and sitting so long. He held his breath as he stood up. The gator hissed again and opened its mouth.

Harry stared into the gaping jaws of the alligator, mesmerized by the soft whiteness of the creature's throat, and terror-stricken by the cruel sharpness of its teeth—teeth that looked like rows of nails set into the lid of a coffin. His coffin.

His heart about to burst, Harry fought to control his fear. He could not afford to be afraid at a time when one false move could spell death. He took a deep breath, swallowed, and then inched forward. With its mouth open, the alligator could no longer see straight ahead, so Harry approached from the front.

Easy, Harry. Easy. Not too fast. Relax. This is no different from your act.

But there was a difference. A big difference. This time it was for real.

Damn that Indian.

No more than a foot away from the gator, he slowly reached his right hand out, palm up, arm low to the ground. His fingertips touched beneath the gator's lower jaw, glided back along the rough skin, seeking a handhold.

Whump!

The gator's mouth slammed shut. Harry wet his pants. He jerked his arm back and almost lost his balance. As he watched, the alligator's mouth again opened.

Come on, Harry. Come on. One more time. One more time and you're home free. You can do it.

But Harry wasn't so sure. He had never wrestled a gator that could hurt him.

A minute passed. Two. Harry regained his composure and tried again. He reached out slowly, his fingertips again coming in contact with the underside of the alligator's lower jaw. This time, however, the mouth stayed open. Carefully, Harry slid his fingers back until his whole hand was under the jaw. He lifted upward. There was a little resistance, but not much.

Easy. Gentle. Not too fast.

He continued to lift until the alligator's mouth was closed and its head tilted backward.

Now, Harry now. Before it can back up.

Quick as a snake, he jumped forward and slapped his left hand down on top of the alligator's nose, preventing it from opening its mouth again. The gator tried to pull back. Harry held tight. If he let go now, he would lose his arm.

The gator twisted its head and lashed its tail. Harry gripped tighter, holding the alligator's mouth closed. He stepped to the side, careful of the tail, and climbed onto its back. The alligator twisted and shook, whipping its tail from side to side. Harry pulled the gator's head back, riding the struggling reptile like a cowboy atop a bucking bronco. As long as he kept its mouth closed, and stayed on its back, he was safe. But he couldn't hold on forever. He would have to find something to tie its jaws shut.

My belt.

Good idea. But how could he get his belt off without releasing the alligator? There was only one way Harry knew of—a trick he'd seen a Seminole Indian do. He had never tried the trick himself, for even with a blind alligator it was very dangerous.

Harry bent the alligator's head back even farther and placed the tips of its jaws beneath his chin. He lowered his head, trapped the gator's jaws between his chin and chest, and let go with his hands. With only the strength of his neck muscles holding the alligator, he unbuckled his belt and slipped it free of his trouser loops. Sweat poured down his face, and he felt his strength giving out, as he hurried to fasten the belt around the gator's mouth. Once it was tied, he stepped clear as the alligator struggled and thrashed about, unable to get the belt loose.

He'd done it! He'd actually wrestled a real gator—a bloody big damn gator—and won. Elation washed through him as his body trembled with fatigue.

"Hah!" Harry yelled. He put his hands on his hips and struck a pose of defiance. "That's what you get for messing with Indian Joe—the World's Greatest Alligator Wrestler,"

"Ah, but that still remains to be seen."

Startled, Harry spun around. Wowakan stood at the edge of the clearing, watching him. Harry clenched his fists in anger. He took a step forward, then spotted the rifle and stopped.

"I'm impressed," Wowakan said, nodding toward the alligator. "He's quite old, but at least he can see."

"Look," Harry said. "I've proven myself. I've wrestled a gator for you. Now I demand that you get me out of this swamp."

The Indian shook his head. "You still don't understand what this is all about, do you? You've wrestled a gator—you've even beaten it—but you didn't show any respect for it. An Indian always respects the alligator he wrestles. It is his brother—"

"I'm not an Indian," Harry interrupted.

"True," Wowakan nodded sadly. "And there is no respect in your heart. That is why my people are angry at you."

He emptied the bullets from the rifle and leaned it against the tree. He then took off his shirt, folded it, and laid it on the ground beside the rifle. Wowakan flexed his muscles for a moment, and then removed his boots and socks.

Suspecting some new danger, Harry tried to get on Wowakan's good side. "Wait a minute. I'm a new man. Honest. You Seminoles have proven your point. I have nothing but respect for alligators."

Wowakan cocked an eyebrow. "Who said I was a Seminole?" He removed his pants and underwear, and stood naked before Harry.

"You did. I mean, that's why I'm here, isn't it? You and the other Seminole gator wrestlers were offended by my act." Harry grew suddenly suspicious. "Hold on. If you're not a Seminole, then what's all this 'my people' crap you've been laying on me?"

The Indian shook his head. "You seem to have misunderstood me,

Harry. Perhaps I didn't make myself clear. What I said about Seminole gator wrestlers is true. They do have a deep respect for the alligators they wrestle. Just as the gators have a deep respect for them."

As Wowakan spoke, the muscles in his chest and arms began to ripple, like waves upon the ocean.

What the hell?

"No, Harry, I'm not a Seminole. Nor am I an Indian. My people were here long before those who call themselves native to this land. I apologize if my appearance has fooled you. I sometimes find it necessary to travel in the shape of my brothers, as was the case tonight." He smiled. "You might say that I too am an actor."

Harry watched, spellbound, as Wowakan changed before his very eyes. The bones in his back cracked like rifle shots as they twisted and realigned. He grew taller, thicker, more muscular. His skin stretched taut, came close to splitting apart, and then wrinkled, darkened in color, and took on the texture of old leather. Wowakan's hair disappeared back into his head like worms into the ground, exposing a scaly scalp. The scales spread. Like a waterfall, they cascaded over his shoulders and down his back.

His arms shortened, and his thumbs disappeared. A thick yellow nail sprouted from the tip of each remaining finger. There was a wet, sucking sound as his penis withdrew into his body. The sight sickened Harry.

"My people have a great respect for the Indians, Harry Gallager, for they have a great respect for us. You, on the other hand, have no respect for anything but money. That is why you were brought here tonight. To learn respect. It is a pity that death has to be your teacher."

Another series of cracking sounds rang out as a tail sprouted from Wowakan's backside. The tail grew in length until it reached the ground. His legs also shortened. No longer able to stand upright, he fell to the ground at Harry's feet.

Terrified nearly out of his mind, Harry stared in disbelief as Wowakan's face changed. Muscles twisted and moved beneath the surface of his skin like a nest of rippling snakes. His ears vanished, first the right, then the left. His jaws widened and extended forward. Teeth appeared.

And, as the last of the transformation took place, Wowakan—who was no longer an Indian, but something else entirely—looked up at Harry and said in a voice that was less than human:

"Don't you find it fitting that the world's greatest alligator wrestler will learn respect by wrestling me, Wowakan, the world's greatest alligator?"

Harry screamed and staggered back. The gator attacked.

Muuki, a Children's Story

George Guthridge and
Meredith Raymond

Muuki sat on a patch of frozen tundra grass amid Aghaayaq Mountain's boulders and, using binoculars, watched his father and the other island warriors thread the *angyat* between the ice floes, the boat laden to the gunnels with old army blankets. A gift for the Siberians, the blankets were infected with sleep.

The men did not like giving the tainted peace offering. Better to fight—and die, if necessary—in the clear cold air with a clear soul. They had argued long and loud in their silent way before dancing the dance that brought the infection.

There was no other way, the men knew. It was a matter of survival. Few walrus and seal remained, and their diminishing numbers could not sustain the island population *and* that of the Siberians. The blankets would make the Siberians nod off into uncaring slumber, and they would not hunt.

If the dancing had been correctly performed. There was no way of knowing. No one had danced a sleep-instilling dance before. There had never been a sleep-instilling dance before.

Muuki sighed and, letting the binoculars dangle, worked his way to the mountain's flat top. Three, where the sun made the snow sparkle and dance, the villagers had danced, the men in gloves or beating the walrus-skin drums, the women in colorful *qaaphags*. Their footprints still lay in the snow, and the chanting still hung in his ears.

He too had danced, though, try as he might, his motions had not spoken his heart. He longed to sail west with the others, out where the Siberian mountains lifted into the light. There, if the blanket trick failed, the vastly outnumbered St. Lawrence Islanders would make their stand on the frozen beach, yielding not an inch except in death. That way, even if they lost their lives and hunting heritage, they would not lose their dignity.

But Muuki, though he was eleven and thus old enough to help with the rowing, had to stay behind with the women and children. The radiation poisoning that had killed his grandfather had entered his lungs. He had the desire but not the strength to pull the oars.

Out on the ice-clogged Bering Sea, even with binoculars the boat was but a speck.

He edged down the mountain's rocky slope, to where his grandfather's coffin lay partially covered with rocks. On the lid, propped up against some tools, sat Muuki's sealskin teddy bear, outfitted in tiny pieces of whalebone and baleen—the tongue of the whale—tied together with sinew. It was the model of the real Eskimo armor he was making for his father. If his father returned.

He set to cutting sinew into strips with his *ulaaq*. He had already shaped the baleen shoulder harness and the whalebone breastplate. There was still much to do, and the work was hard. It gave him calluses and sometimes made blood seep from beneath his nails, but the discomfort mattered little; only work could help him forget the pain in his heart.

He remembered his grandfather's words, the day Muuki had first realized he lacked the lung power to keep up with the other boys his age. "You must learn to be a man in ways they have not thought of," the old man said. "You must be stronger than they are, Muuki."

Even then Muuki had believed the words only a moment. Now he believed them not at all. His only hope lay in the armor, that it might someday stop a Siberian spear.

He worked until the setting sun turned the sea ice into a golden blaze. Then, after momentarily placing his hand on the coffin, he went down into the village.

Aproned with snow, the prefab houses were deserted. The villagers used them for storage, now that the oil supplies were gone. The villagers who had survived the Deathtime had returned to the *ningluks* of their forefathers.

He crawled through the subterranean entryway of his house and stood up in the main room, blinking against the smoke of the seal-oil lamp. His mother sat in the corner, on the tamped-earth floor, using what remained of her dental-floss supply to sew a parka. Strips of dog fur lay nearby; the eastern winds that had brought the radiation had driven the polar bears and wolverines into extinction.

"Father will like it," he commented.

She did not look up. Her lips compressed into a tight, bitter line. "Or you."

"He'll be back. They'll all be back."

"Time will tell, Muuki."

He watched her, not speaking, for a long time. Then he crawled up onto the family's sleeping platform and lay looking at the guttering seal-lamp flame and the teddy bear beside it, so ready for battle. He dozed off.

When he awakened, his father was in the corner, his face sharded by shadow. He stared straight ahead into the darkened entryway and spoke in a hushed, clipped, angry tone. Muuki's mother squatted beside her husband, her face a study of concern, her hand on his upper arm.

"The Siberians just stood there . . . they and their AK-47s. Saying nothing. Their eyes mocking us. Like we were some kind of sea animals washed up on the beach. I thought we were beyond that . . . using the white man's weapons, I mean. I thought . . ."

He shook his head sadly. Then, glancing up, he eyed the teddy bear with anger, seized it, and hurled it across the room. It bounced off a whale-rib rafter and fell, its armor clattering, onto the plank where the coffee pot sat.

"Please . . ." Muuki's mother said. "The boy . . ."

"More white man's crap!" Muuki's father looked toward the sleeping platform, where the boy pretended sleep. The man's eyes, though hard and dark, briefly hinted of self-reproach. Then anger displaced the look and, pulling forward the hood of his parka, he ducked into the entryway.

The bear's Eskimo-bead eyes reflected the light. A feeling of hurt pulsed in Muuki's throat as he lay squinting toward the bear. How silly he had been, how much a child! His grandfather had had the teddy bear, won at a California carnival, well into manhood. "Only one of two inventions of American white people worth bragging about," he had liked to say. "Only thing someone would *want* to put in one of those time capsules. This and Mickey Mouse."

That was before the war.

Muuki turned away. He stared at the oil-blackened wall until an angry mindlessness took him and he entered a world where time and sleep and waking did not exist.

"Muuki, you awake?" Someone shook him. "Muuki?"

Muuki rolled over and looked up at his mother.

"Breakfast," she said, nodding toward the dried Dolly Varden fillet she had laid out. She smiled and, sitting, went back to her sewing.

He climbed down, picked up an *ulaaq,* and, after a moment's hesitation, lifted the teddy bear from the lamp shelf, where his mother had again placed it. He put the bear on the ground and his knee on its chest, as if it were alive and squirming, then brought the knife's crescent-shaped edge to the bear's throat.

"Muuki." There was neither horror nor remonstration in his mother's voice, only a note of sadness.

"White man's—"

"I think you better ask your grandfather about that, Muuki."

He looked at her, puzzled, then set the *ulaaq* aside and, wordless, pulled on his parka and went out.

He walked through the village, on his way to the mountain.

Someone had burrowed into the snow mound that covered the National Guard armory, exposing the door. Muuki went inside.

The village men were sitting on the ice-frosted floor, a seal-oil lamp in the middle. Their eyes looked old and tired in the weak light. Muuki's father was speaking.

"For four thousand years we have fought our ancestors, the Siberians," he said. "They would come to the island and raid for our women and our food, and we would drive them off. Later they came for Eskimo games, and we would beat them at that, too, though our population was much smaller.

"Then the American whites became enemies with the Soviets, and the interaction between us and the Siberians stopped. The whites did not realize that, to us, it was only an interlude in a war almost as old as time itself.

"Then the border between America and Russia was reopened, only to be closed when what used to be the Soviet Union began fighting among itself. Then the bombing began. So now the whites are gone, at least from here. They relied on weapons they could not control. We Eskimos have gone back to fighting as we have always fought. At least, so we believed.

"The Siberians met us with automatic rifles this time. I thought it was agreed, though nothing formal was ever said, that such things would never be used. Who knows what else we might face, should we again sail to Siberia. Perhaps the Siberians possess weapons they too cannot control."

He paused and looked from friend to friend. "I say we unlock the M-16s and do what we must against the Siberians, or at least what we can against them . . . now."

Assent was slow, but eventually all the other men agreed, nodding sadly, one after the other.

Muuki left quietly, climbed the mountain, and sat beside his grandfather's coffin. He sought to commune with the old man, but the words did not come through his lips or in his mind.

He felt exhausted, though he had been awake only an hour. Putting his head down on the teddy bear, he closed his eyes.

His grandfather stirred in Muuki's soul.

Muuki saw his grandfather lying within the casket, dressed in his snowshirt and the white *kemek* boots with their polar bear trim. Across his chest was the great ivory butterfly Muuki's father had carved in tribute. Beside him lay his favorite lance, its haft wrapped in sinew worn smooth by the many times he had gripped it.

Under his head was a teddy bear.

Muuki blinked open his eyes, his heart pounding. Grabbing his bear he hurried toward the top of the mountain, his chest heaving from the effort.

He set the bear down where the sun was about to reach, and began to dance.

He knew not what words to sing or what motions to follow, for he sensed this must be a new song, a new celebration. He felt foolish and clumsy, but he kept moving.

The light touched the bear. Its eyes sparkled darkly, and Muuki thought of his grandfather, alone with his bear and his memories. A feeling of power and certainty entered Muuki, and he began to sing.

Apaka aagna samegaga . . . apaka aagna samegaga . . .

His feet lifted and crunched against the snow. His pulse pounded. He squinted into the sunlight, and his arms began to pull the oars. The boat he saw in his mind shot forward between the floes, heading for Siberia. His lungs were aflame but still he rowed, still he danced and sang. Within his parka, his body became drenched with sweat. The words lifted and rolled from his mouth. Muuki danced. His grandfather danced. Sitting in the sunlight, the bear watched . . . and waited.

No one paid attention to the tarp in the front of the *angyat.* Later, some of the men would say they thought that someone had left rope or a spotted-seal float under there.

No one noticed Muuki until the boat nosed the Siberian shore.

He jumped out onto the pressure ridge, stumbled among the jumbled ice, and leaped the jagged break that demarcated sea and shore. Up the slope, their parkas covered with white cloth, the Siberians waited, rifles ready, in trenches dug in the snow.

To the left, down the beach, sat a pile of blankets, the Siberians apparently not having touched what the St. Lawrence Islanders had left.

"Muuki!"

Father raced after son. Muuki sprinted toward the Siberians. He could hear rifle bolts ramming home as rounds were chambered.

His father tossed his rifle aside and came onward, waving his arms. A Siberian, binoculars in one hand and a pistol in the other, crawled from the trench.

Muuki dived close to the man.

"Are you crazy!" Muuki's father shouted, grabbing his son by the leg and trying to pull him back to safety.

The Siberian cocked the weapon as Muuki reached beneath his parka . . . then lowered the pistol as Muuki lifted out the teddy bear.

"You *are* crazy!" Muuki's father kept dragging the boy backward, heedless of the pistol.

"Wait!" Muuki cried. "Let me tell them about the bear!"

The Siberian raised the pistol toward Muuki's father. "Let the boy speak," he said. His voice was calm, that of a leader.

When Muuki's father let go of the boy's leg, Muuki turned over, gazing up at his father's face. It was dark with wrath.

Then he swallowed thickly and, pulling back his parka hood, climbed to his knees and began to speak.

"Yesterday my people brought you a gift. It was . . ." He started to look back at his father, but he knew if he saw his father's eyes again, he would stop talking. Instead he glanced down the beach, at the blankets. "Not a very good gift," he managed to say.

"Not a gift at all," the Siberian said. He eyed Muuki's father angrily.

"So today I . . . my grandfather and I . . . wanted to give you a better gift." He gazed down at the ice, then handed the bear forward. "For you."

Startled, the Siberian took the bear and, looking at it suspiciously, checked it carefully. Then he snorted in contempt and thrust the bear back into Muuki's arms. He tilted his head back and, hands on hips, began to laugh in disgust. "The little islander brings a sealskin bear!" he roared, turning toward the other men. They too began laughing.

Then, to Muuki's father, he said, "Go back to your boat. Or did you bring the boy to do your fighting as well?"

He turned and strode toward the trench.

Muuki sprinted after him, the Siberians again snapping their rifle stocks to their shoulders, and clutched the elbow of the man's parka. "Please. Hear me," he said desperately. "It's not just any bear. It's a magic bear."

The Siberian did not turn, but Muuki could see the man's face harden as the leader fought to control his indignation.

"It's what the bear stands for that's important," Muuki went on. "That's its magic." He held up the bear toward the man's back. "It was named for President Theodore Roosevelt, one of the first great conservationists. That's what it has to tell us about . . . about there not being many sea mammals anymore." He glanced around anxiously, as if half expecting a bearded seal to come sliding up from between the ice floes and onto the beach to emphasize his point. "We need to conserve."

"So we're supposed to stop eating seals and walrus. That would solve everything," the Siberian said contemptuously.

"Conserving doesn't mean only to stop something; it also means to *start*," Muuki replied. "To do anything that will replenish a resource. We could farm the sea just as some people do the land. Raise and release seal and walrus pups, just as people used to with salmon."

The Siberian turned and blinked, and his face appeared to soften.

"It's worth a *try*," the boy said.

A thoughtful look entered the Siberian's eyes. He gazed at Muuki's father as if seeing his distant relative for the first time. "The island and the mainland have been apart for many years," he said. "Perhaps someone should change that."

"Perhaps," Muuki's father said, and, as the boy held the bear close, put his arm across his son's shoulders.

Nuniva

Merle Apassingok

H igh cut deals," Ulaaq said.
Ulaaq had come over for tea . . . cards . . . talk . . . endless
talk.

Outside, snow flurried against the house. The damper on the stovepipe flapped. Nuniva felt nervous and tense. The walls seemed to be closing in. He wished he could be out, alone, on the tundra's broad expanse. He daydreamed about when he'd been a boy, camping with his uncle.

"I said, 'High card—" Ulaaq began.

Nuniva's daydream broke. Rage and an urge to hit something filled him with fire. He swore to himself. The room seemed to blur. He lashed out. . . .

The weather was cold but clear. Nuniva's short beard was frosty. He turned over the frozen carcass of the seal amid the three fox traps. He picked up the fox he'd taken in the fourth trap, then dug up the trap's anchor. This would be his last trapping expedition, he knew, and three traps would be more than enough for his nephew. He walked to the sled.

A snowmobile appeared on the horizon, its engine disturbing the Arctic stillness. Nuniva continued with his work as the machine drew closer. The trooper climbed off the Yamaha, rifle in hand.

"You know why I'm here," the trooper said.

"Just let me fasten the fox onto my sled."

Metal doors slammed up and down the corridor. Outside the cell, prisoners traded shouts, catcalls, insults. Nuniva sat on the top bunk, his legs over the side, his head bowed because of the low ceiling. He wondered how his nephew was handling the trapline. *Should have beaten up the trooper and fled, instead of giving in!* The walls were closing in again. Except it was worse here. Nothing outside except . . . nothing. Between the prison space station and the white freedom of the Arctic were six hundred kilometers of emptiness.

He jumped off the bunk.

"Hey, watch it!" Joe, on the lower bunk, threw down his crumpled magazine and stood up. "Watch your damn heels! This isn't some igloo."

Anger flared within Nuniva. He was bulkier than Joe, and could handle him easily. He squinted in rage. He couldn't help focusing on Joe's face; it was as if the walls, drawing in, were framing it. It was the same feeling he'd had when he'd hit Ulaaq so hard that his friend had died. The fire inside him kept building. . . .

He stormed past Joe and grabbed the cell bars. "Guard! Help me—before I kill someone else!"

"Every time I'm around people, they seem to disturb me," Nuniva told the psychiatrist. "Sometimes I can't hold back my temper."

"It's always uncontrolled?" Tall and thin, the psychiatrist walked around the prisoner in the easy chair.

"Not when I'm outside. It only happens when I've been closed in too long. Like with Ulaaq, there'd been a blizzard for a week. And here in Maxintern, I'm confined to my cell up to eighteen hours a day."

"So it isn't Joe you're angry at. Nor"—he glanced at his folder—"was it Ulaaq."

Nuniva shook his head sadly.

"Territorial imperative," the psychiatrist said quietly.

Nuniva looked up. "What?"

"Studies using galvanic skin-resistence electrodes have shown that people who tend to be violent need more room than do nonviolent people."

"So?"

"So there's an experimental exile program for people like you. Interested?" The psychiatrist flipped a switch on his desk's control panel; the far wall slid open, exposing an alcove. He turned a knob; the alcove glowed with colorful lights, then focused to a three-dimensional image showing kangaroos bounding among thorn bushes. "This is region E-8, one of the first areas back on Earth designated for possible prison exiles. We have two dozen places to choose from—for the right individuals."

Nuniva remained silent.

"After reviewing your file, my personal feeling is that maximum security might not be necessary in your case," the psychiatrist said after a moment. "You showed a lot of heart, coming to us, rather than . . ."

Nuniva felt the walls within him begin to crumble. He scooted his chair closer toward the holo and stared into the outback. "Have anything near the Arctic?"

The other man flipped the knob again. A wolf appeared, running across the frozen tundra. "Region C-4, near Frobisher Bay."

"When do I leave?"

"We'll arrange your transfer."

Nuniva lay in his bunk, drumming his fingers against the wall. How long before that shrink busted him out!

A guard opened the door. "Someone here for Nuniva."

Nuniva climbed off the bunk. The psychiatrist entered, his face drawn. He looked at Nuniva for a moment, then said, "Your transfer has been denied. The public's worried about Region security, so Congress has put a hold on our request to increase the exile population."

"For how long?" Nuniva asked desperately.

The psychiatrist stared toward the floor.

"They can't do this to me!" Nuniva slapped the cell wall and stood glaring, hands on hips. Joe turned away, a frightened look on his face. The guard reached for his billy club as the psychiatrist backed from the cell.

Then Nuniva remembered being out camping with his uncle, learning about life, and he lifted his hands, palms out. "It's all right. I won't try anything stupid." But the Frobisher thing . . . he couldn't lose that! "Let me think," he said.

Clouds rolled, pushed by the wind. A white fox trotted across the frozen lake. To the east, pack ice was jumbled against the shore.

Nuniva set the jaws of the trap, then hid behind a snowbank. The animal ambled across the trap and down the bank, passing through Nuniva.

Back in Maxintern, Nuniva smiled as the fox walked away. He turned off the holo, and the wintry tundra vanished. He was living a two-way existence, the holo having been hooked up to computer simulations. For two hours a day he could project his image down into the Arctic. Not the same as being there, but it was all he had. It was enough, for now—until his sentence was served.

Patterns

Esther M. Friesner

Benjamin Cates got off the bus in Flagstaff and looked around for the beat-up blue pickup truck Joe had described to him in such loving detail. The Arizona sun beat down on his un-shielded, balding head, but he made no attempt to cover up or take shelter.

Almost like I'd welcome death by sunstroke, he thought, scratching the one itchy place on his dome. *But that's not true. Right now I'd welcome death by anything.*

He scanned the street near the bus stop. There were about four trucks parked there that matched Joe's description—five, if you counted the faded sea-green paint job on one specimen as a shade of blue. *All of them blue. But* powder *blue, Joe said,* Benjamin thought. *His wife's idea when it came time to repaint the clunker. What else did he call that shade? Oh yeah . . . Alice blue, like his girl's name. Whatever the hell kind of blue that is.*

He sighed and leaned against the depot wall. *Blue's blue to me. Marjorie would've known what he meant. She was always spouting stuff like that when she was decorating the house, stuff I never could understand. What's siena, anyway? What the hell's a valance? The army should've drafted women and put them into the Code Talkers with Joe and his tribe. The Japs'd go nuts before they understood anything a woman had to say!* He chuckled over that, then felt the stab, sharp as always: *But Marjorie's dead.* The echo of the police phone call played itself out in his mind all over again, breaking his heart anew: *. . . lost control of the car on Hill Road.* Hill Road, where the cemetery was. She'd been visiting Kevin's grave, even in that blinding rain that turned the roads to sheets of crystal too slick for any tires to hold. Was it only three months ago? It seemed like forever. It seemed like yesterday.

A horn honked stridently from the street. Benjamin wiped sweat from his eyes and shaded them against the midday glare. A beat-up

blue pickup truck with New Mexico plates was idling, obviously waiting for him to get the lead out. The shadowy figure in the driver's seat
looked too small to be Joe. Benjamin muttered a curse—old army, full
strength—that he hadn't used since he'd been mustered out and Marjorie'd got the noose of civilization around his neck, made him behave.

Not the wife, he prayed under his breath. *Jesus Christ, don't let it be
the wife!*

It wasn't Joe's wife at the wheel; the woman driver was too young,
too tall to be the tiny Jap doll Joe'd brought home with him. Benjamin
had never set eyes on that slant-eyed female in the flesh, but he still
remembered how he'd felt when he opened the letter from Joe announcing his marriage: betrayed.

Benjamin let his breath out slowly, relieved, as he climbed into the
cab. The daughter he could handle. Hadn't he and Marjorie spent
enough late nights deciding just how they were going to handle the
daughter? *It's what Kevin wants,* Marjorie's ghost whispered in his ear
once more. *We have to try to make the best of it, for his sake.* All right.
For Kevin's sake, then, and Marjorie's. For the sake of all of Benjamin Cates's ghosts.

Inside the cab, cool black eyes regarded him from a face as beautiful as marble, as impassive as a gravestone.

"You must be Alice," he said, offering his hand to the girl who by
now would have been his daughter-in-law, if only—

"Welcome, Mr. Cates," she said. She ignored the outstretched
hand, made no attempt to help him shift his suitcase. He had to wrestle it aboard himself—he refused to entrust it to the flat, open back of
the truck—and stow it behind the seats in the cab as best he could. It
wasn't hard work, but it was awkward. He found himself breathing
heavily when he was through.

Getting too old to do stuff like this alone, he thought. And then:
Better get used to it. He settled into his seat and said, "Okay, let's go."

The sun assaulted his eyes when he looked out of the cab, trying to
avoid looking at Joe's girl too much. Squinting until his temples
ached, he finally gave up and turned his gaze back to Alice. It hurt him
to look at her, too, but in a way his eyes could bear, even if his heart
could not. He watched her drive, calm and efficient at the wheel. She
had a wide mouth, full lips. Benjamin found himself wondering what
they'd look like if she'd smile. More welcoming than her words, that
was sure. He tried to imagine Kevin seeing her on the university campus for the first time, smiling at her exotic beauty, her seeing him, hesi-
tating, smiling back, warmth creeping over that cold, lovely mask, and
then—

What did my boy see in you? he wondered. *It had to be more than just how pretty you are. It'd have to be, for him to tell Marj and me that he was going to marry you. He knew the part about you being half-Indian didn't matter so much, but he knew how we felt about Japs, and you're half-Jap, too; I don't care if I owe your daddy my life once or a thousand times.*

As they drove on, he tried to settle himself more comfortably into the seat beside her. A carefully folded Indian blanket was laid across the vinyl, an abstract pattern in reds and browns. He fingered the one spot where the weaver had made her deliberate flaw—a jag in the outline of an otherwise perfect diamond shape—and winced when he felt the pinch of a sprung coil poking through.

So they do make them that way, he thought. *The books were right. How about that?*

His bus-weary bones protested any further mishandling, but he knew there was no help for it, no relief for them. Joe didn't live anywhere near the Flagstaff depot. There were miles of open road to travel until they reached his place, on the fringes of the reservation lands. Benjamin only hoped the truck had working shocks. Even as he said his old-man's-bones prayer, he got a jolt strong enough to let him know that it was going to go unanswered.

He got a certain grim satisfaction out of it when the rest of the journey proved him right again and again. The powder-blue pickup wasn't the smoothest ride on paved highway, and it lurched and bounced something awful when the girl turned off the government roads and hit the dirt tracks.

Dust flew up on both sides of the truck, barging its way into the cab, where the windows remained down on account of the heat. Joe's daughter stopped the vehicle only once, to pull a blue cotton bandanna up over her nose and mouth and to offer one to Benjamin. He took it as solemnly and silently as it was offered, and tied it behind his head. It gave him a brief, strangely young feeling, making him want to laugh and aim a finger at the girl. *Bang, bang, Injun, you're dead.*

His eyes met hers over the top of the bandannas. Did she get the joke too, appreciate how ridiculous they both looked? Two little kids playing desperadoes, riding their battered steed out across the desert to intercept the gold train—

Nothing. Her eyes stayed as cold as a snake's. *Takes after her mother,* Benjamin thought, and he remembered other eyes like that staring at him as he filed past, across the compound in the jungle, behind the other prisoners of war.

Canyon walls rose up around them, red sandstone walls dwarfing the little truck and the people in it, stealing the breath from Benjamin's body as he gazed up and up and up, seeking the sky in vain. He pulled the bandanna down off his nose and mouth and craned his head out the pickup window, gaping like a rube in the big city.

And then, without warning, they stopped. The pickup lurched to a sudden halt and Alice swung her door wide, springing out of the cab and loping across the red earth without a backward glance at her passenger. By the time Benjamin climbed down out of the cab, she was a blur of churning ankle-length skirts and flying black hair that vanished around the side of the battered earth hogan.

Benjamin didn't know whether to find Joe first and get some help with his bag, or haul it out himself. In the old days there never would have been any question, but now he felt as though he were a stranger living in his own body. *Something leaves you when you get old,* he thought. *Maybe it's God's way of reminding you you're not going to live forever, no matter what you thought when you were young. Little by little, you lose the pieces of your life you thought were always going to be there. The patterns you laid down fray and come apart. Okay, I got the message long ago. Only . . . why did I have to lose so much?*

He ached too much to bother with the suitcase just yet. Instead he walked toward the hogan. The cone-shaped mound of earth, its doorway open to the east, was familiar to him even though he'd never laid eyes on it until now. After the war, he and Joe had written letters back and forth so regularly—enclosing photos when they could—that Marjorie often teased him about his unmasculine devotion to the pen.

"See? That's why I'm never going to take you west to meet Joe," he'd teased her right back. "You'd probably ride him about how it's un-Indian to write so many letters."

"I never would!" Marjorie had pretended to take offense. "He'd probably whip out his tomahawk and scalp me if I said 'boo.' "

"Joe's Navajo." Benjamin had spoken slowly, as if he were explaining something to a child. "The Navajo don't scalp people with tomahawks."

Marjorie had laughed. "That's how much you know about the Navajo!"

And it was then that Benjamin had realized he knew nothing about his friend's people at all.

"Ben! Hey, Ben!" Joe's voice was hoarser than Benjamin remembered it, but it still carried through the hot, dry air. The shadows of the hogan gave up a man who was only a year older than Benjamin, but whose face was crimped and creased with wrinkles like the cracks in a drought-dry arroyo bed. His chin-length black hair had lost the luster his daughter's still possessed, though there were only a few threads of gray running through it, lightning against a midnight sky.

He wore it bound back from his face with a bright band, patterned blue and yellow. Heavy silver bracelets bulked at each wrist, and a belt buckle of the same bright metal, thick with inlaid turquoise and coral, made his worn dungarees look even shabbier. Strands of turquoise beads covered the open neckline of his plain red rancher's shirt.

All that jewelry, Benjamin thought. *I couldn't get away with wearing stuff like that—wouldn't want to—but on him it's all right.* He hurried forward to meet his old friend.

"You came," Joe said, clasping Benjamin's arms and looking at him as if he'd never seen the white man's face before.

"Nothing to stop me from coming," Benjamin replied. "Marj—" He saw Joe flinch and stopped himself from saying more. Marjorie was dead; they both knew it. *That's how much you know about the Navajo!* she'd said, teasing him. Well, now he knew. Over the years he'd made it his business to know, to learn as much as he could. Retirement had given him extra time, making his quest to learn easier. Now he knew enough to keep his lips from forming the names of the dead.

"I am sorry I never had the chance to meet the woman you married," Joe said, his hands clasping Benjamin's shoulders. This way was all right, this roundabout way of speaking about Marjorie. To name the names would be to attract the angry ghosts. You were even supposed to destroy the hogan where someone had died, build a new dwelling elsewhere. After death, all that was good and benevolent about a person was gone; only the evil remained. It didn't pay to draw the attention of evil.

"Yeah, well—" Benjamin shrugged. He felt awkward, worse than the way he'd felt in the truck with Alice. *What am I going to call Kevin, when we speak about him?* he thought, aching. *Is it safe to call him "son"? Or does he have to be called—I don't know what—the boy I fathered on a woman without a name? Are ghosts so easily deceived? I don't think so. It's more than names; they come when they're called by the heart.*

"I can't tell you how happy I am to see you again, after all these years," Joe said. His eyes glittered with tears. "I hoped—"

Oh God, here it comes! Benjamin thought in anguish. He knew Joe's hopes—so like his own, once: to see their families united in Alice and Kevin. That hope was gone now; so much else was gone. "Is Alice all right?" he asked quickly.

Joe shrugged. "She keeps busy, doesn't say much. She dropped out of college, you know. I guess the shocks, one after the other, they were too much for her. She takes after me too much, loves too deep."

"I never thought that was a bad thing," Benjamin said softly.

Joe's keen eyes fixed on his. "It is when it makes you forget." His voice sounded harsh and hollow, like an echo heard in dry underground caverns, with no one there to have made the original sound but spirits.

Benjamin took a deep breath and let it out slowly. "I could talk to her now, if you like."

"That's a good idea," Joe replied. "Glad you thought of it. A fine idea—if you don't mind doing it so soon after you got here," he added hastily. "Look, let me get you something to drink first, and then— great idea, great idea." He tried to hustle Benjamin toward the hogan.

Benjamin dug in his heels and wouldn't budge. Part of his reaction was fear—Joe's wife had to be in the hogan, and he still wasn't sure how he'd react when he saw her in the flesh—and part of it was just plain confusion. "What do you mean, you're glad I thought of it? Hell, it was *your* idea."

Joe froze. "Mine?"

"That's what you wrote me, anyhow. 'Come out here for a visit and see if maybe you can talk to Alice about—' " Again Benjamin stopped himself. In the letter Joe had written: *about the one who died.* It was left to Benjamin to understand that the Navajo meant Kevin, even though Kevin's was far from the only death.

"Oh." Joe's face was unreadable. "Yeah, I guess I did." The queer expression melted into a smile. "You can't fault a man for being proud of his own ideas, can you? Come on, I'll get you something inside." Again he tried to pull Benjamin toward the hogan.

Benjamin wriggled his arm free of Joe's grasp. "I'm okay," he said. "Really. Look, I think maybe it'd be better if I went to see Alice now. I couldn't talk with her in the truck coming here—too tired. Now I've got my second wind, I should try. She might think I don't want to talk to her at all if I leave it go much longer."

"I'll take you to her, then," Joe said. "She's probably back at her loom, working on that big blanket." His grin spoke of honest fatherly pride. "I thought I was the one with all the weaving talent in the family, but she outdoes me without even trying hard."

"You weave?" Benjamin's imagination tried to put a shuttle in Joe's hands and failed.

Joe chuckled. "Yeah. It's not what you expected, is it? Women's work, mostly. Silversmithing's for men, but I'm one of five sons, no sisters. No one cared when I took an interest in the loom, and now Alice loves it too. Hey, my family's always been different. See this headband? She made it for me when she was just a little girl." Proudly, Joe showed off his daughter's handiwork, even pointing out the obligatory "mistake" that every wise weaver always left in to let the creator's soul escape from the thing so wholeheartedly created. His grin lit up the seams of his face.

The two men started off in the direction Alice had run, but before they left the hogan too far behind them, a voice came from the conical earth house, calling, "Joe? Joe?" The fluting query sounded more like a command. Joe halted in his tracks. Benjamin could have sworn that his old army buddy's skin stiffened along with his bones.

"Yes, Kohana," he told the empty air in front of him.

"Who is that there with you, Joe?" the voice from inside the hogan asked. It was high and sweet, as tremulous as a dewdrop on the petal of a rose.

"It's Benjamin," Joe replied, still without turning, almost without moving. "Benjamin Cates. I told you how he wired he was coming out to visit us. You said he—"

The voice laughed, a sound that put Benjamin in mind of cheap glass wind chimes tinkling. "Ah so, yes. I remember. The American." And then: "Kevin's father."

Benjamin saw Joe flinch at the naming of the dead. As for himself, he half hoped that Joe's beliefs were true, that naming Kevin would bring him back, even if the only part of him left behind to harken to the summons was evil. Benjamin couldn't begin to tell how easily, how gladly he'd open himself to any risk if it meant the chance to somehow—anyhow, at any price!—touch his son again.

"We're just going to have a look at Alice's loom," Joe said, voice and body still taut and strained. "We'll be back in time to eat."

"You come here now, Joe. You know what Alice's web looks like. I want you here, with me. Let the American go his own way. I will see him later."

Benjamin gave Joe a quizzing look. The Navajo shrugged and forced a smile. "Women. What can you do? I bet she wants me to help her with the meal. It's not easy for Kohana—remember how I wrote you she was so sick?"

Benjamin nodded. "A little over three months ago," he said, remembering. The letter had been painful to read. Joe was no great writer, but the straightforward anguish in his words when he told about how ill his wife was said what he didn't dare say: how afraid he was of losing her.

Three months . . . Benjamin did remember. It was winter; Kevin was home from college on vacation. If the boy had had his way, he'd have spent the time with his beloved Alice, but Marjorie had insisted he come home for a while before she lost him altogether to the "other woman." Benjamin recalled looking up from that letter to meet the eyes of Kevin and Marjorie. He remembered how Joe's unspoken fear of losing one he loved so much had touched him to the point where he'd embraced wife and son in a hug he imagined—fool that he was— was a fortress strong enough to shield them both forever.

And now three months had passed, and there was Joe's Jap wife still alive while Kevin and Marjorie were dead.

"Look, I've got to stay here," Joe was saying. "Kohana's right; you can find Alice's loom easy. See, just follow this path and you can't miss it. It winds around the face of the bluff. I don't know why the girl has to set herself up so far away from the hogan, but like I said— women." He turned swiftly on his heel and was gone before Benjamin could utter another word.

Alice's loom was as simple to find as Joe promised. Even tired as he was from the trip, Benjamin found the path easy going. It dipped down and around the bluff that sheltered Joe's homestead, passing a small garden where flowers and vegetables grew in neatly kept rows, a cornfield where golden tassels brushed the sky.

He found Alice kneeling on a pile of fleecy sheepskins before a towering loom. A short distance away stood a second loom, but this one had no comfortable pile of sheepskins before it. From where he stood, Benjamin could see that both looms held weavings that were near completion. His eyes weren't keen enough for him to be sure, but he'd almost swear that the amount of weaving done on each loom was the same.

Exactly the same. The conviction struck him from nowhere logical. It was simply something he *knew.* Strange, but not half so strange as the fact that Joe's daughter Alice knelt before her handiwork silent and unmoving. The weaver did not weave, the basket of colored yarns rested untouched beside her.

Benjamin kept his distance. He had the peculiar sensation that he had stumbled into a cathedral built of red rock and silence. The sunlight played with glossy blue shadows over Alice's hair. Without speaking, he studied the web held taut in the framework of her loom.

He recognized them at once, the Holy People, even though his readings in Navajo lore hadn't gone deep enough to let him tell one from the other. They were the supernatural beings who had given the Navajo all the skills, all the knowledge that *Diné,* the People, needed to survive in this world. They were the ones invoked during the many complex ceremonial Ways—the Mountainway, the Featherway, the Blessingway, so many more—that could do so much to protect and preserve, to heal and restore lost harmony. Theirs were the images painted in carefully sprinkled sand on the floor of the hogan that housed a sufferer, and theirs were also the figures captured in symmetry and beauty in Alice's web.

They were drawn in abstract forms long set by tradition: Bodies unnaturally elongated, shaped like towering, thin rectangles, heads square or reminiscent of the blunt noses of bullets, slits for eyes and mouths, short legs, dwarfed arms that could still hold so much power. Two to the left, two to the right, they flanked a stylized representation of a hogan while one arched above it like the rainbow. Besides these, there were four creatures set to what would be the four points of the compass in this map of a madness Benjamin did not understand. He leaned nearer to peer at one of them.

"They're gila monsters," Alice said, without turning around.

"Oh," he responded, unsure. "Yyyyyes. Yes, I see now."

"You don't see. Not yet. To you they look like roadkill; you can admit it, I won't mind. They're Guardians, the gila monsters." She pointed to each of the four as she named it: "Black to the east, blue to the south, yellow to the west, white to the north." She sighed. "Maybe if I were a man, trained in the Ways, I could have used them better. I know I have no right at all to invoke them like this, but I couldn't stand by and do nothing."

Benjamin came up behind her, lifted his hand, and brought it close to the yellow gila monster. Alice was right—to him, all the Navajo representations of animals looked like a bird's-eye view of roadkill— but he was a man who could open his eyes wider, go beyond what he merely saw. His palm throbbed the longer he held it near the yellow gila monster. He could swear he felt heat pulsing from the web.

"I feel—" he began, then changed his mind. "Which Way is this?" he asked instead.

"None." Alice held her own hand up to the web, over the hogan. "It's my own creation—my own damnation, maybe, but I don't care. I've done what I could, what I had to do. I told you, I'm not trained. But I can't go after one who is. I have to account for my comings and goings, even though I don't dare take too many of those. I've had to make do, but if I had the power—"

Another sigh, this one shuddering her whole body. "We need an Evil-Chasing Way here, Mr. Cates. We need to be free of our ghosts." All this she said without taking her gaze from the loom.

As stealthily as he could, Benjamin pulled back from Alice's handiwork. With a sidling step he tried to sneak toward the second loom, in order to see the pattern on that.

"You won't see anything, Mr. Cates." Alice's voice, quiet yet commanding, stopped him before he had taken three steps. He turned and saw her staring at him. "You won't see a thing," she repeated. "Not unless she wants you to. You'd better hope she doesn't."

Alice's eyes made Benjamin feel sick at the pit of his stomach. Had grief for Kevin's death done this to her, made her sound as though she wasn't quite sane?

Maybe she blames herself, he thought. *After all, Kevin did die here, while visiting her. No one ever told us how he . . . just that his heart failed. A young man like that, strong, and his heart gives out. Not right. What happened? Maybe they were—?* He shook his head slowly.

Alice saw and smiled. "You think I'm crazy," she said confidently. Her laugh was drier than the desert air.

"Look, I never—" This was going badly, worse than in the truck. Benjamin felt as if he were floundering in deep water, no hope of rescue in sight.

Then Alice said, "I wrote the letter, Mr. Cates."

He tried to say something, but he was too surprised to do more than repeat, like an idiot, "Letter?"

"The letter that brought you here," the young woman went on doggedly. "I would have done it sooner, but it took me this long to learn how to forge my father's handwriting well enough to pass muster, longer to get the chance to send it without her stopping me. And then there was the weaving to do." She made a flat-handed gesture at the pattern on the loom.

"It's beautiful," Benjamin said, clinging to the fact of the weaving's beauty the way he'd clung to the shelter of a palm tree when his unit took yet another coral dot in the Pacific. He'd clung to that tree, knowing fear as snipers' bullets zinged past him and mortar fire from entrenched Japanese troops chewed up huge stretches of the jungle, chewed up men and spat them out as blood and bone. And because even with the fear in him he had left the shelter of the tree, gone forward with his men in spite of it all, he now asked, "What's wrong here, Alice? The weaving—what's it got to do with—"

"She killed him, Mr. Cates. She killed your son."

"What?" A band of metal tightened around his heart. "Who?" But he knew. Kevin had died here, in the middle of nowhere. There was only one other female here, besides Alice. "Your . . . mother?"

Alice stood up and kicked away the sheepskins. Beneath them lay an oblong pattern of stones marking the dimensions of a grave. "My mother is here."

Benjamin shook his head again, violently this time. He refused to believe what he was seeing. Knowing all he did about Joe's people, he had no choice except disbelief. "That's impossible! I heard her voice coming from inside the hogan. I heard your father call her by name. Dammit, that hogan's the same one in the photo Joe sent us when he and your mother first came back here. If anyone had died in there, it wouldn't still be standing!"

"You do know." Alice spoke like a teacher, satisfied with a pupil's response. "My father said you were pretty well versed in our traditions, but I wasn't—"

"Your traditions won't let you stay near the dead," Benjamin said, pointing an accusing finger at the grave beneath Alice's feet. "Why are you talking to me about your traditions when you're destroying them yourself?"

Alice reacted fiercely. "When my father went to fight your war, he and the other *Diné* had to adjust their ways. Try to fight a war and stay away from the dead! Were you so scandalized then?"

"Then I didn't know a damn thing about what your people believe," Benjamin countered. "Besides, like you say, it was war."

She lowered her eyes to the grave beneath her feet. "This is war too, Mr. Cates. These are my battlefields." Her hands spread to encompass the grave and the web. "And that." She lifted her head toward the second loom.

She took his hand without asking leave. He let it happen, a man bewitched, and made no effort to prevent her from leading him where she would. As they walked across the hard ground, the distance between the two weavings seemed to stretch like taffy in the sun. Every step of the way, Alice kept on talking in her quiet, impossible-to-ignore voice:

"Your son came here soon after my father wrote to you about how sick my mother was. He knew how much we loved her, and he wanted to be there with us, to help in any way he could, if the worst should come. If he had arrived sooner, it might have been all right. As it was, she'd been dead five days before he got here."

"No," Benjamin said, trying to pull back. Her fingers—soft with lanolin, callused from hard work with the carding combs—tightened slightly and refused to let him go. "No, that's not right. He wired us the day after he got here. He said your mother was well!"

"She was dead." Alice's voice betrayed no feeling. "She was dead and in her grave. My father dug the grave for her himself. He wouldn't burn the hogan with her body in it. He said that was our way, not hers." A bitter smile curved Alice's lips. "He wouldn't listen when I told him that in Japan they also burn the bodies of their dead. I know why he wouldn't listen: he wouldn't believe it. He refused to accept the fact that she was gone. None of the rituals, none of the taboos, nothing that admitted my mother was dead, none of that was permitted."

Alice stopped and looked Benjamin in the eye with a gaze so penetrating it made him tremble. "When we were in the truck, riding to pick up your son at the bus depot, I asked my father, 'When do you think we should tell him that she's gone?' You see what a good girl I was? I didn't even call her my mother anymore—just *she.*" She wet her lips. "He pulled the truck over to the side of the road and slapped me. He slapped me twice, then shouted in my face, 'Kohana's not gone, you hear me? Kohana's not gone!' Then he started up the truck again and drove on as if nothing had happened."

"Something did happen," Benjamin said, again prisoner in that awful sense of *knowing.*

Alice nodded. "My father did all the talking in the truck on the ride home. He wouldn't let me get a word in edgewise, wouldn't let your son say more than hello and how are you. He was trying to keep anyone from talking about my mother, mentioning her, asking questions. I guess he felt that he was entitled to these last few minutes of pretending nothing had happened and that she'd still be there, waiting for us, when we came home." Alice brought them right up to the second loom. "She was."

They were standing in front of the web. Unlike the strongly colored designs in Alice's weaving, this one was blank, the gray of dirty stormclouds blowing in low over a cold and hungry sea. As Benjamin stared at it, he thought he must be losing what little grip on reality he'd had since coming out here, hearing the fantastic tale Joe's girl told.

Alice glanced at him, could not help seeing the look on his face. "So she does want you to see," she said quietly, with pity.

And Benjamin saw. The gray web swam like a heat mirage, ripples and undulations passing over the face of the captive cloth, leaving trails of ghastly light behind them. The longer he stared, the more distinct and determined the ripples became, until, as he watched, a pattern emerged like the face of a drowned man slowly floating back out of the depths to meet the sun.

The web was a travesty of Alice's own weaving. The Holy People were no longer holy. The elongated bodies and square heads that had looked so right when formed by Alice's hand were now grotesque, the slit eyes and mouths narrow with viciousness. The gila monster Guardians of the four points were gone, replaced by snarling reptilian monsters, their claws drenched in blood.

And in the center, the hogan was a Pacific island where palm trees stood shorn in half by artillery fire. A younger Joe crouched in the underbrush over a radio. Like so many of his tribesmen, when war broke out he had volunteered to serve in the military of a nation that had almost destroyed his own less than a century before. He became a Code Talker, a radioman whose task was to relay information in a way that would protect it even if the enemy intercepted the transmission. Specially trained, he did not merely use the Navajo tongue to thwart the enemy, but used his language in encoded form—English words like *back* spelled out into bear-apple-corn-kick, transmitted as the Navajo words for each of these. Even if the Japs caught another Navajo warrior, it wouldn't help them understand the messages any better unless they caught an actual Code Talker. The odds were against it, the secrets safe.

Then the scene within the hogan changed. Joe had a rifle in his hands. He was more than a trick of military intelligence; he was a warrior too. The men around him crashed through the jungle, erupted into the clearing where a POW enclosure stood. Unable to breathe, Benjamin Cates stood witness to his own rescue as Joe and the others met the Japanese resistance with hot, sharp, final replies. A young officer panicked, seizing Benjamin and trying to use his body as a shield between himself and the invading Americans. Joe's swift single shot taught the officer the futility of his gamble once and for all.

That was some shooting, Benjamin heard his then-self say, managing a shaky grin.

Yeah, well, we get pretty good eyes out where I come from, the vision-Joe replied.

The picture changed again. Instead of Joe's face as it had been, Benjamin saw it as it was. His friend, his rescuer, sat in the shadows of the hogan. His eyes were empty of all hope, but his mouth formed the words *I love you, Kohana.*

"Say my name again." The female voice, delicate and meek, seeped from the center of the web.

To his horror, Benjamin heard Joe's voice emanating from the same place, saying "Kohana."

The female voice giggled, high and shrill. "Again!" it directed. "Call me back again!"

"Kohana . . ." This time there was a terrible pleading note in Joe's voice, though the web showed no change in his expression. "Kohana, please don't—don't hurt Kevin!"

"But you know what he is." The female voice purred, sticky-sweet, insinuating. "Blood of the ones that spilled my blood, yours."

"Kohana, he's only a boy!"

"He will grow, mix his blood with ours if we allow it." The female voice now had a hard, glittering edge to it. Abruptly it dropped back to its former wheedling tone. "I can fix that, Joe. I can make his blood ours, worthy."

"How?"

More giggles, almost like the sound of madhouse laughter. "Did you ask for *how* when you found me waiting here for you, my darling? Will you still ask for *how* if it means that I will tell you, then vanish again, forever?"

"No . . ." The word choked itself out of Joe's throat. "Never."

"Ahhhh. That is good. Now I can begin—our blood and his. This is my own Way, my husband. You see? I have learned from so many years among your people, even if they never truly accepted me as one of them. I have made a Way of my own."

Joe's image filled the hogan. A long, brittle, hairy shadow fell across his right shoulder. Slowly the thing that cast the shadow came into view. It was the leg of an enormous spider, a creature whose globular, glowing eyes now peered over Joe's shoulder. Mandibles clacked and gnashed as the same sweet, persuasive female voice came from the monster's mouth in an awful parody of wifely devotion.

"Just a little blood," the creature breathed, and the spider-mask melted into the face of a pretty little Japanese woman. Her red lips parted in a smile that showed the piercing mouthparts of a spider.

Benjamin's cry of horror shook the vision from the loom, leaving only the grotesque pattern of desecrated Holy People behind. He staggered back, into Alice's arms.

"Is that—was that—that *thing* what killed my boy?" he gasped, pointing wildly at the loom. Alice's silence confirmed his words. "What's wrong with your father? Couldn't he see what she—his own wife—dear God . . ."

"You know a lot about us, Mr. Cates." Alice spoke as if trying to calm a panicky child. "My father told me so, and your son said the same thing. Your interest in the things of the People sparked his own. Do you know how funny I found it to hear a white boy talk so knowledgeably about tribal matters, our beliefs, our Ways? And with respect, always with respect. Other kids on campus used to buddy up to me so that they could take me around to their hippie friends and show me off like I was some chunk of turquoise jewelry they bought to make them look *tribal.* Your son never made me feel like I was a trophy he'd won for being liberal enough to talk to an honest-to-God Injun."

Benjamin's eyes shifted from her, remembering his stupid pantomime in the truck cab earlier that day. *Bang, bang, Injun, you're dead.*

"Meeting your son, knowing him, I realized how little I knew about myself, the part that wasn't *Diné,*" Alice went on. "So I started reading all I could about my mother's people. There's a story, in Japan, about a great warrior whose strength was drained night after night by the Earth Spider. He could have slain the monster, if he'd known it for what it was, but his eyes were tricked. He thought it was something else, something harmless, only a painting on the paper screen in his room. I remember being surprised by that story. For us, Spider Woman and Spider Man are benevolent beings. So maybe she's worked a spell to make my father see her as she was in life, Mr. Cates, or maybe he sees her as she is and can't believe she's anything evil." Alice's fists clenched. "Not even when she stole my lover's life."

Benjamin felt old, weary. He too wanted desperately to believe, with Joe, that there was nothing wrong here, nothing out of the ordinary. "And these?"he asked, indicating the twin looms.

"My Way is there." Alice nodded toward the weaving erected over her mother's grave. "Hers is here." Another nod at the fearsome alternate version. "I've lived with horror long enough; I wanted to do something—anything—to end it. I thought to undo her spells like this, but she found out. I must have been on the right track, because she felt threatened enough to build *this*." Her hand came near one of the accursed loom's uprights, but did not touch it. "Now when I weave the Way to set my father free, she weaves her Way to keep him captive. Figure for figure, line for line."

"Checkmate," Benjamin murmured. "Was that why you couldn't tell me anything about this in the truck?"

"If I had told you anything before you'd seen this, what would you have done?" Alice countered.

He saw her point. "Jumped out and run all the way back to Flagstaff," he admitted. "Even if I dropped dead in the middle of the road." He looked from loom to loom. "So this is why you brought me here. But I'm no medicine man. What can I do?"

"You have studied us, Mr. Cates. You know how much the weaver puts into her work."

"Never the same pattern twice," Benjamin replied. "Never the same portion of your spirit." There was something else, but he couldn't quite remember what it was. He was still trying to call it to mind as she led him back to her own loom.

"Into this web I've woven the part of my spirit that loved your son. I have woven it with my heart. But as long as her weaving keeps pace with mine, it's useless. Her powers cancel mine."

Alice glanced at the sun. It was beginning to set. Benjamin followed her gaze and wondered how long they'd stood here, held in an invisible web of words, more powerful than any *Diné* Way or Earth Spider's dark enchantment. Why hadn't Joe come after them? He shivered. Joe was trapped in a prison more terrible than any South Pacific island compound. What did it matter if he had spun the bars of his prison himself? Not even the Holy People could teach their children how to fight against the blinding strength of love.

"What can I do?" he repeated.

Alice relaxed. A halfhearted smile made her lovely. "I can't tell you that," she said. "She would hear. A ghost has ears on the wind. Today I will finish the pattern on my loom. She will come to finish hers too, figure for figure, line for line. All I want you to do is stand here, at my back, and watch."

"That's all?" Benjamin was taken aback. "Just watch? Hell of a thing to bring me all this way for. Look, doesn't your father have a gun on the place? His old army rifle? I'll get that, and when she shows up to finish that weaving—"

"No, Mr. Cates." There was a trace of wistfulness, a little pity in Alice's words. "You can't destroy a ghost with bullets. Besides, your days as a warrior are done. You are an elder now. I need to trust in your wisdom more than your courage."

He gave a sheepish laugh. "That's the first time anyone's accused me of being wise."

"I'm doing more than that," Alice said, her face grim again. "I am gambling with more than my life against your wisdom. I've told you all I dare. Now come. Sit. As soon as I pick up the shuttle, she will be here."

Benjamin settled his creaky bones on the sheepskin Alice spread for him between the looms. He took care to position it so that no part of it touched Kohana's grave. Alice reached for the shuttle, but paused with her hand hovering an inch away. She gave him one last, steady look. "What I put into my weaving, she puts into hers. It was Spider Woman who first taught us the secrets of the loom . . . and the dangers. Remember that." She picked up the shuttle as the sun dipped green below the horizon.

All at once the looms glowed with a sickly, unnatural light. Benjamin held his breath as he saw the blaze engulfing Alice's work deepen from ashy pale to the deep golden glow of sunrise. But the other loom remained bathed in corpselight. Shadows snickered and danced around the uprights, slithered over the heddles. The fragmented bits of darkness coalesced as he watched and a hulking spider, as big around the body as a plowhorse, sat hunched before the second loom. The monster had the face of a woman.

"Honored guest of my husband, I beg your forgiveness," it said, its voice the selfsame one Benjamin had heard coming from Joe's hogan and from the hogan woven into the creature's web. "I owe you hospitality. I would have given it to you on your arrival, had my husband persuaded you to enter our home willingly. The weak one, he could not! Be assured, when this game is done, I will give you the same welcome I gave your son."

Benjamin started up, but there was pain in his joints and Alice's hand rested gently but firmly on his forearm. He settled back, determined to ignore the monster's taunts.

The spider tittered. "You think that child will defeat me? She is like you, like all Americans. She steals little scraps of power, makes a patchwork life out of what she tears away from those who have the right to hold it. The *right!*" Her voice rose shrilly. "What right did you have to come against us? The Pacific was *ours*. What gave you the right to destroy my father, my brothers, my betrothed? I was left to scuttle in the ruins, forced to marry *that* one"—a spindly leg cut the air sharply, gesturing back in the direction of the hogan—"just so that I could live. He brought me here, far from my true home, and here I *died!*" The spider fell silent. Then, so softly Benjamin could barely hear it: "Now I am death."

Benjamin stared at the monster in horror, but it was a horror that went deeper than mere revulsion. *Is that what I'll leave behind?* he wondered, trembling. *When all that's good about me is stripped away, will I be such a living core of hate?* He recalled how he had despised Joe for taking an enemy wife. Enemy! Had Kohana held the knife to his throat? Would Kohana—the real Kohana, not this nightmare—be capable of raising a fine, brave young woman like Alice, and at the same time of destroying a boy like Kevin simply because of whose blood ran in his veins?

If there was enough hatred in Kohana's soul to create this monster, what must there be in mine?

Benjamin forced himself to stand. The earth rolled like the deck of a storm-tossed ship beneath his feet, but he clung to his sense of balance desperately. This time Alice made no move to restrain him. Her eyes were on the loom, her hand on the spindle of blood-red wool.

She began to weave.

A wind came sweeping across the desert, whetting itself to cruel keenness against the flanks of the canyons. Alice's hair whipped out behind her in the blast; the uprights of her loom creaked and bent as the weaving stretched between them bellied in the gale. The spider's weaving hung slack, secure in a zone of dead calm. The creature raised its body and gathered silk from its spinnerets, silk that transformed itself into as many colors as its mistress desired. Hairy black legs flew across the face of the weaving, following the pattern of Alice's creation line for line, changing the woven Way to a parody, from a thing of beauty to a thing of evil.

"Be with me," Alice said between clenched teeth. Benjamin had to cup an ear to hear her words against the roaring wind. "Father of the one I loved, I brought you here because of who you are and what you know. Use your wisdom now. Help me."

"How?" Benjamin whispered. And again, louder, into the wind: "How can I help you?"

"By using what you know!" Alice cried. Her words were snatched from her mouth by the blast. "What I do, she must do if her power is to counter mine. What I put into my weaving, she must. Everything that I put into it, do you understand? *Everything.*"

"Everything?" Benjamin hung on to the upright, lost. He did not understand what Alice wanted of him. What did he know? Her people's ways were as alien to him as the spider's exotic magic. He was a dabbler, a dilettante, a beggar who, as the spider had said, stole scraps of power from other worlds to decorate a life bare of enchantment.

What do I know? The words wailed through his skull. The wild wind seemed to blow all that he had read and gleaned and gathered of *Diné* ways clean out of his mind. He was no warrior, he had no magic, and he knew only a few words of the language that had so thoroughly frustrated and bewildered the Japanese. What could he do? He was old. He could make no more war.

And so he clutched the upright of the loom and watched helplessly as Alice wove the last lines into her pattern. Below the hogan a final figure was taking shape, a figure smaller than the rest, styled after the Holy People, but small, so small . . .

A child.

The baby was bound to a cradle board, swaddled tightly so that its limbs would grow strong and straight. The Guardian gila monsters flanking it seemed to twitch with life as the wind swelled the web its mother wove, swelled it to the contours of a fruitful womb. Benjamin's eyes were wide. He looked down at Alice's grim, drawn face with new understanding and saw the secret that her voluminous skirts would soon no longer hide so well.

Kevin's child.

A peal of cold laughter burst over his head like a thunderclap. He looked sharply toward the spider's loom and saw the child's image repeated to perfection, line for line. But here the round face of innocence was drained and hollow, angles sharp with the bones beneath, eyes no more than holes in the fragile skull. It was a baby as different as could be from the one of Alice's weaving, and yet Benjamin Cates knew that it was the soul of his unborn grandchild that the spider-ghost held hostage in her web.

Then he heard Alice's gentle sigh, and it was finished. The wind died—not fading away by natural degrees, blowing more and more weakly until it stole back into the rocks, but perishing suddenly, utterly, completely. The twin webs stood stiffly in their frames, the weavers rigid before them. Benjamin looked from web to web, from weaver to weaver. All was done; all was still.

"Alice?"

She did not move, did not answer. Her eyes were fixed and frozen on the image of the child. The spider too sat immobile, its female face a slab of ice. Benjamin touched Alice's shoulder; he touched wood.

"No . . ." He shook his head. This was wrong. Her magic had gone out to capture and hold her enemy; it should not hold her too. Holding her, it held the child. "No. *No!*" His shouted protest was flung back in his ears by echoes. Perfect silence mocked him.

Perfect . . .

You know how much the weaver puts into her work.

What I put into my weaving, she puts into hers.

The wind blew softly at Benjamin's ear, though there was no wind. A voice of love caressed him, whispering, *Remember what you told us once, Dad? When Mom asked you why Joe sent us that blanket for a Christmas present and there was a snag in the pattern? She was teasing you about it. She said he was some friend, sending you a factory second. Do you remember what you said? "The weaver puts her soul into her web. There must always be an imperfection in any weaving, or the creator's soul will be trapped in the perfect pattern forever."*

The breath of ghosts took wing on Marjorie's lost laughter, Kevin's hushed *Remember* . . . leaving him alone once more.

Desperately, Benjamin cast about for a sharp bit of rock. The thickening darkness made it a scrabbling search done by touch alone. He gasped as a tooth of stone from the border of Kohana's grave bit into his flesh. His own blood stained the weaving as he jabbed the earth-dagger in—only a tiny nick in the web, no more—not to destroy, but to free.

"Ahhhhhh." A body slumped against his legs. He knelt on the sheepskins to cradle Alice in his arms. She put her arms around his neck and wept. He found himself mumbling all the small, comforting, nonsense words he'd used when Kevin was a little boy and ran to have Daddy's magic heal him of scraped knees and bruised shins and the pain of stumbling out of childhood. "There, honey. Shhhh, hush, don't you cry. There."

"Ben? Hey, Ben!" Joe's voice hailed him. Still holding Alice tenderly, Benjamin turned at the sound. A dot of light was coming toward them, bobbing along the winding downslope path. Benjamin jerked his head the other way, trying to see the spider, captive in its own web. What would Joe say when—?

He saw nothing. There was only Alice's loom left standing.

"She is gone," Alice whispered against his chest. "Father will remember nothing of her return. As if she'd never been, except for—"

"Shhh." What the angry ghost had done was done. Kevin was gone.

He held his hand over her belly and made an inquiring sound. Alice nodded, smiling serenely. He rested his palm over the place where his grandchild dreamed.

"Here, Joe!" he called. "We're here!"

The dancing light picked up speed, hurrying toward them until Joe's shape emerged from the darkness. He gave a cry of fear when he saw Alice lying there until her smile reassured him that she would be all right. The two old men knelt on either side of her.

The sky overhead rumbled, and from its heart a lightning stroke scorched through the atmosphere. A roar shook the earth, throwing the three people together. From somewhere behind the curve of the path came the hungry roaring of fire.

"What the—?" Joe sprang up, dashed off, his racing footsteps crunching the dirt. More slowly, Benjamin and Alice followed.

They found him standing within sight of the hogan. The earthen mound was ablaze. "How—?" Joe could not even frame a way to question the physical impossibility of earth that burned as strongly, as brightly as the most carefully seasoned wood. There was a shuddering of the walls, and the hogan collapsed.

Benjamin felt Alice's hand steal into his own. "In beauty it is finished," she murmured. Still holding Benjamin's hand, she reached out and took Joe's.

"Father, there's something you need to know . . ." she began.

In beauty it is finished, Benjamin thought. His free hand closed around the hand of a child not yet born. *In beauty it is begun.*

The End of Childhood

James David Audlin

1

Little voices whispered in the room all day. Tiny syllables floated about like motes of dust in the patch of sunlight slowly shifting from high up the wall to the floor. These tiny words danced slowly, waiting for the girl to return home from school and come back to her friends. Then they would play their games together until it was time for supper.

"Elayne! Elayne!" she would hear them chorus every day as she came home from school. She would feel their mounting excitement as she climbed up the stairway to the apartment, threw her schoolbooks on the kitchen counter, and almost ran down the hallway to her room.

Dawn Wissler listened to her daughter climb the stairs, go down the hall, enter her room, and close the door, just as she would do every day when she came home from school. She said hello as the girl went by, but received no response. Perhaps this should bother her, but it did not. Dawn would think of her own deprived childhood on the rez, and feel glad that she could ensure it would be different for her own child.

For hours now, until suppertime at least, she knew Elayne would stay in there, just playing with her dolls. She wouldn't go outside, or play with friends. She never read books, or watched TV, or even played video games.

When Dawn had been a girl herself, on the Second Mesa, they had had no television. Instead they had learned the stories and the songs of her Hopi people. Even though they had been poor, even though Dawn would never go back to the dirt and the hunger and the hopelessness, that was one thing she felt they had done right: encouraging dolls and stories instead of television.

All the other mothers coming into the shop complained about their children showing no interest in anything but the television, and hoped that maybe a lovely new doll might distract them from it. Dawn wanted to brag to them that she had never had that problem with her own daughter.

It made the mother smile to know that, despite the divorce, she was providing Elayne with the ideal life for a little girl. She rejoiced to see her child living in a world of dolls, free to play in the fantasy worlds of her imagination. It would be wonderful if she could keep Elayne forever a little girl, and protect her from ever having to enter the hard, cold world of adults.

Some day, Dawn knew, she would have to let her child grow up, but, for as long as possible, she wanted to resist that, to let her girl *be* a child for as long as possible before she would have to enter the hard cold world of reality. It was for this reason more than even the need for income that she had set up Living Dolls.

Being a single parent was not an easy task, Dawn reminded herself often, but at least she had the doll store downstairs as a source of income. Her ex, Bill, had always been prompt about sending her the alimony checks, even if she had no doubt he could afford a lot more, given what he was making as an investment consultant. At least he took Elayne off her hands during school vacations, so she could go to doll collectors' conventions. Which reminded her.

"Oh, Elayne?" she called down the hall. "I just remembered something."

No answer.

Dawn put down the pen and the unpaid bills, trying to ignore the rising tide of frustration, and walked down the hall to the girl's room. Opening the door a bit, she poked her head in and smiled as warmly as she could. "Elayne, dear?" she tried again. "You're going to have to spend some time with your father over the weekend, okay? I have to go to Santa Fe to get some inventory."

Elayne looked up at her mother once, briefly. The look was as though her mother hardly existed, as though her mother's voice had no more immediate relevance than a voice on a radio, a minor annoyance that had interrupted her with the semblance of sentience.

Elayne looked down again at Eototo, listening to the bear's voice with such attentiveness that she didn't even hear her mother close the door again.

"You don't want to go see him, do you, Elayne?" Eototo the bear said, his painted eyes dancing with sorrow on his gaudy wooden face.

"No," she agreed, her tears beginning to flow, stroking Eototo's plush brown fur. "I hate him."

Knayaya piped up in her funny cow voice. "Can't moo stay here with us, Moolayne?"

"I want to. I want to. But Mommy's going away again!" By now the tears tracked uncontrollably down her face.

"Take us with you!" Knayaya suggested hopefully. Elayne picked up Knayaya and cradled the purple cow in her other arm.

"I can't. Remember what Daddy said."

Indeed, they all remembered very well. Her father had forbidden her to bring any dolls with her, saying it was high time she outgrew them, and grumbling about her mother encouraging this infantile behavior.

"You're afraid of him, aren't you?" another voice interposed on the sorrowful silence. It was Sikyatavo the bunny, who didn't speak very much.

To this Elayne didn't reply. There was no need to reply. Every one of the dolls knew what her father had done to her last time. For they had all been there, and they all had seen it. An unspoken agreement manifested itself not to discuss the subject further, but their playing was subdued.

2

In the morning her mother drove them the hundred and eighty-five miles to Santa Fe and stopped in front of her father's condominium. Elayne knew her mother was not going to see her to the door, so she got out of the back seat, taking her suitcase with her.

" 'Bye, sweetie. I love you!" her mother said, kissing her cheek through the car window. "If you need me, call me at Drexler's, okay?"

Elayne walked alone up the sidewalk to the door, not looking back, but only listening to the sound of the car leaving. She reached the door and rang the bell, already sure her father wasn't home. He was certainly still at work, she told herself. Even on Saturdays he was out there making lots of money.

When, after a while, there was no answer, she let herself in with the key hidden behind the bushes. She closed the door behind her and stared, as if expecting him to come out, even though it was obvious he was out.

The condominium was, as always, impeccably neat. Her mother didn't mind a little clutter. But her father hated disorder. In his place, nothing was out of its place. Everything looked just like it should, just like in the pictures in the magazines on fancy homes her father got. She glanced at them, in a neat pile on the mahogany coffee table, next to the equally orderly piles of computer magazines and investment reports.

Her father had only one real bed. She pulled the little cot out of the closet in his bedroom, and set it up in the dining room, next to the table, where it always went when she came to stay. This done, she hoisted her suitcase up onto the cot, unsnapped the latches, and threw back the lid. All her friends looked up at her with relief.

She smiled to see them. Her mother had asked her about fifty times if she had her nightgown and toothbrush and everything else she would need. All the necessary things were packed, but as much space as possible had been crammed with her dolls.

"There, is that better?" she asked, taking them out one by one. The dolls looked around, appearing somewhat disoriented at first.

"Are we there?" Sikyatavo's little nose was twitching with anticipatory fear. Elayne nodded.

Eototo had a suggestion. "Elayne, I think you ought to hide us, so your Daddy doesn't know we're here."

"That's a good idea." Without delay she took the dolls out of her suitcase, those most precious dolls she couldn't bear to be without, and knew she could rely on while she must stay with her father, and hid them in the drawer that was hers to use in the big dresser. The rest of the contents of her suitcase—the things her mother had been worried she'd forget—clothes, hairbrush, and toothbrush—she put as well in their proper places.

Once this was completed, she took out the bear again, and played with him until her father should return. They talked about many things, Elayne and Eototo, until the minutes became nearly two hours. Eototo told the girl again the story she loved most to hear, how he was the Chief of the Bear Clan among his spirit people. He explained again how the living people in the Fourth World would dance until his spirit people came, with him, Eototo himself, leading the procession into the underground church. He told her of their many adventures, until the girl laughed with delight.

When she heard the front door opening, she quickly put the doll away with a hurried good-bye, and left the bedroom.

"Hello, Elayne," her father said with the right inflection of friendliness, but somehow still tonelessly, carrying the insinuation of resentment that he must be saddled with this child for however brief a time.

"Hi, Daddy." Her voice carried no more warmth than his. They looked at each other; they were stuck with each other.

For a moment he looked as if he was going to say something to her, but then he turned away. Going to the liquor cabinet, he poured himself a drink. "I'm going out for dinner," he announced, without looking back at her. "Not going to be back until very late. I expect you in bed by eight o'clock."

She thought about protesting that Mommy always let her stay up until nine on weekend nights, but decided it wouldn't be wise. She nodded her acquiescence.

"All right. I'm going to take a shower. Have you eaten?" To her silent shaking of her head he replied, "There's stuff in the fridge. Why don't you find something while I get ready?"

But there wasn't much. While she ate a pastrami sandwich and drank some ginger ale, the hissing of the shower could be heard through the wall. The sound stopped. He'd be shaving and getting dressed now.

As she was finishing a slice of store-bought pound cake, her father came out, dressed for a night of dancing. He looked at her, and she stared back, her small face heavy with an adult frown.

Her father's blond hair swept back from his high forehead like an ocean wave, accentuating the relief of his profile. His shirt was open almost halfway down his chest, pointing the way to his skin-tight pants. "How do I look, honey?" he asked. She nodded because he wanted her to nod. "Well, good night, then. Remember, be in bed by eight." He was gone before the "yes" in her constricted throat managed to emerge.

The car roared down the driveway. Elayne listened until the whine of its engine subsided into the sounds of the gathering night.

3

"Is he gone?"

"Yes, Eototo. You can all come out now!" She gathered all of the dolls together, and they danced the Hoya Dance round and round the room in a joyous circle of celebration. They sang together the old songs Eototo had taught them. They played all their favorite games. It felt as if there could be no end to their happiness.

And then it ended. A voice from the doorway. "What is the meaning of this?" Elayne looked up and saw her father looking into the bedroom. She looked about wildly, but there was nothing she could do; her dolls were everywhere. They had all frozen the moment he appeared, afraid to move, caught in the motions of the dance. Eototo was flopping over on a chair. Tocha the hummingbird and Avachhoya, painted like Indian corn, were on the floor. Sikyatavo was on the bureau. Knayaya and the little-girl doll that didn't have a name yet were on the bed. Elayne sat in the middle of the rug, as motionless as the rest of them, staring at her father.

"Good thing I had to come back for my wallet," he growled. "I told you before. None of these god damned dolls! You're too old. Your damned mother has no sense! It's time we got rid of these things. It's time you learned to grow up."

He picked up the first doll to come within his reach. Sikyatavo.

"No!" she screamed, knowing what he was about to do. But before she could move, he had begun to tear the little bunny to pieces. She could hear the doll crying with the pain of death, helplessly watching the cotton batting float through the air like snowflakes. He threw down the torn cloth skin and reached for Knayaya. With one yank her swaying head was ripped off.

"No! No!" she kept pleading, striking out against her father's legs. "Don't kill them! Don't!" He only continued his methodical murdering of her dolls, now reducing the little-girl doll to fragments. Elayne felt the pain of each one of them as it died. She clutched her fists to the sides of her head, trying to block it out.

The sounds of tearing continued, and with the stilling of each little voice in turn it seemed to her as though the whole world were going silent. After he had dismembered all the cloth dolls, he began to do the same to the gaily painted cottonwood dolls her mother had made, decorated with feathers and beads.

Avachhoya was gored and shredded by the furious hands of her father, followed by Tocha. The pile of broken figures grew on the rug in front of her. She picked up a piece at random. It had come from Knayaya, a piece of fuzzy purple cloth. She wiped her eyes with it.

And she looked up and saw him now reaching for the last doll. Her favorite doll. The one that was so wise and good and loving and wonderful. "No, not Eototo! Anything but Eototo! Please!"

As her father was about to tear the limbs from his little wooden body, Elayne leaped up and wrested Eototo from her father's grasp. She threw herself to the floor, atop the pile of shredded dolls, protecting Eototo with her body. She could feel him moving slightly beneath her, and knew he was alive and safe for now. Her head sank down into the pile of ruined dolls, aching and numb and relieved and afraid and beyond tears.

An explosion of pain erupted on her back. With more surprise than distress, she looked up. Her father was standing over her, legs apart, raising his belt to strike her again. Uncomprehending fear took her over. He was, her child-mind reasoned, going to take her apart too, now, just like her dolls.

Her face pressed into the familiar smells and textures of her precious dolls, but all jumbled together, the lashes of agony pelted down on her like lightning. She had gone into a tiny safe place well inside, keeping away from the hurt of her body. She hardly heard her father say, "You're not a little girl any longer. You're a young woman. Time to learn that. When I come back . . ." Some small part of her that was paying attention to these words cringed. "When I come back, I will expect this nonsense to be forgotten."

And then he was gone. For a long time she continued to lie there unmoving, not yet wanting to come back to her body, knowing that when she did she would have to deal with the pain, and decide just what to do.

But she had to get up. The familiar scents of her dolls, pressed close against her face, were now like the smell of death. She couldn't bear to smell them any longer. She got up, struggling not to grimace with the pain.

"Elayne!" For a long time she didn't hear the voice of the doll, muted now for some reason. "Elayne! Elayne!"

"What is it, Eototo?" It occurred to her that perhaps the little bear needed consolation just as much as she did. She picked up the little shape again and cradled it in her arms.

"You couldn't have saved us, Elayne. You can only save yourself. You have to get away from here. You have to go to your mother and tell her what your father has done."

The girl's tears spilled over. "But I want my friends! He killed all my friends!"

"Listen to me, Elayne. There's nothing you can do now. The time for kachinas, the time for dolls, has come to an end. Your father is right. You're becoming different. You will soon be an adult, and forget about us."

"Never, Eototo! I could never forget you!"

"This has all happened before, little one. Remember my telling you about the living humans my spirit people live among? The Hopi people? They were conquered by men like your father. We remember their coming, and their talking about a different God from ours. The land and the people were both ripped to shreds and left to die."

Elayne didn't understand. She said nothing. Her stomach hurt.

"Elayne, your mother is a descendant of our people, though she doesn't know their wisdom. She makes kachinas using pictures, but she doesn't know who we really are. She thinks kachinas are nothing more than toys for children."

One of the dolls, still barely alive, moaned. Eototo continued to speak. "Like so many of her ancestors, she has chosen to forget us, to be like the Qochata, the white people. Soon that's all we will be, if the Hopi people forget who we really are."

"What should I do, Eototo?"

The sad-eyed bear told her to leave before her father should come back.

■ ■ ■

4

Taking nothing with her but Eototo, she left her father's apartment and began to walk downtown. On one side of her were homes, warm and bright in the gathering gloom of evening, and on the other the steady stream of smelly traffic, staring at her with pair after pair of headlights. The sidewalks were filthy with glass and cigarette butts and tufts of unpleasant-looking weeds. With every step she tried to pound down into the earth all the pain and fear she felt for what her Daddy had done to her dolls, and what she was afraid he was going to do to her.

Eventually human habitation gave way to businesses: gas stations, variety stores, video rental places. The buildings got taller and older. Elayne's feet hurt from walking, but she kept on. There was a growing number of pedestrians around her, whom she circled around as children do.

The lights of the shopping district glowed ahead of her. She kept on, carefully spelling out the name of each store. Within a few blocks she found the familiar blue-and-red letters of Drexler's Fantasy World. The flowing crowds of shoppers seemed to pull her in like an ocean tide.

She had never done this before, come looking for her mother, and she had no idea what to do, or where to try first. She wandered almost aimlessly at first, past the sports equipment, past the war toys, and through the huge display area for bicycles. At last she found, toward the back, the doll area. Surely she would find her mother back here.

There were several aisles of doll displays, and she walked past the end of every one of them, looking down each one in turn for her mother. But there was no sign of her. Telling herself she might as well just look, while waiting for Mommy to find her, she entered one aisle and began to look at the dolls.

It was hard at first to look at them, the pain of seeing her own precious friends torn into shreds still fresh in the theater of her mind, but how could she resist? There they were, displayed in attractive boxes from the floor nearly to the ceiling, maybe hundreds of kinds of dolls.

Did she miss Knayaya? There were countless varieties of cows here to choose from, even including purple ones. Did she want another bird doll? Here was one that looked surprisingly similar to Tocha. Bunnies were here too, and surely another Sikyatavo could be found. Or little-girl dolls? Unicorns? Princesses? Every aisle contained shelf after shelf of wonderful and amazing creatures.

She was lost in admiration and amazement. With Eototo cradled in her arms, looking out wonderingly, they saw box after box, each with a little face inside, staring out at them. Each one of them seemed to be pleading with her to take it in her arms and bring it to life with her love. It was just like once when her mother had taken her to the animal shelter, and all those little kittens and puppies had stared at her with aching, yearning expressions, begging her to take them home with her.

She found a section displaying her mother's own creations, with the "Living Dolls" logo in its familiar pink swirl lettering. There were several boxes of identical Eototos, Sikyatavos, and Avachhoyas. Elayne had always thought her dolls were special, but it appeared not to be so. Her mother didn't care about the dolls, she just cared about selling them.

Neither of her parents was really interested in her either, she thought to herself. They just wanted her to behave, which meant to bug them as little as possible. Young as she was, she knew, with the maturity that the divorce had brought early to her, that they didn't like each other and were playing tug-of-war with Elayne herself for the rope. But she, she vowed to these walls of dolls waiting to become alive, would never be such a mother.

"I will love you *all*," she promised them. "I will take care of *all* of you!"

All of them stared silently down at her as she spoke, their faces unmoving behind the plastic windows of their boxes, their eyes shining with unshed tears for being imprisoned in this place.

To her child's eye, remembering one of the movies her mother had rented, they looked like rows and rows of dead bodies displayed in some gigantic mausoleum. She would love nothing more than to free all these prisoners from their boxes, from the plastic manacles clipping them to the white cardboard inside, and fill them with life.

Immediately her hands started to suit action to thought. She grabbed a box and opened it, freeing the doll trapped within. She put the little Tocha down, and turned to another. Within minutes the floor was littered with empty boxes and freed dolls, still too weak to move.

"Elayne?" She whirled around. The dolls all around her held their breaths.

"Are you Elayne?" the man asked. At first she thought he was a police officer, but on second inspection she realized the man was some kind of store detective. It wasn't that he was a bad man; he obviously meant well, but he was smiling a false smile at her, like grownups do when they want something out of you.

"Hi, Elayne," he said, assuming her identity without her confirming it. "Your mother's going to be here soon. Your father is coming too." He kept smiling that smile, obviously trying to win her trust.

When he raised a transceiver and spoke into it, Elayne saw her chance and bolted. She scurried in a zigzag way along several aisles, racing through the video games, through the musical instruments, and into the bedroom furniture area.

She hid under one bed, furtively peeping out, on the lookout for pursuers. None appeared. Slowly her breathing subsided and her heart slowed down again. It was nice and dark and quiet under the bed. She was safe here.

She looked at her little friend, clutched in her arms. "Eototo? What should I do, Eototo?"

Eototo didn't answer.

"What am I going to do, Eototo? I can't stay here forever."

Legs swished by beyond the fringe of the bedspread, some in skirts, some in pants. A lot of them were children's legs, accompanied by their parents. "Am I going to become like them, Eototo? I don't want to be like them. I don't want to forget you, and all the others!"

She rolled over onto her back and looked Eototo in the face, holding him right before her eyes. "I want to play with you forever, Eototo, and always be happy." Tears trickled down into her ears, but she did not notice them. "I don't want to turn into a grownup. Not if it means I have to lose you."

Still Eototo was silent. "Aren't you going to talk to me any more? Don't you know I love you more than anything?" The painted face just looked at her. "Am I growing up now? Am I going to be like them? No more magic, no more love?"

Two pairs of legs stopped, a man's and a woman's. "Come on out now, Elayne," her mother's voice said. "We can hear your voice under there." There were other legs behind those of her parents, the legs of more security guards. "Come on out," she repeated. "You've caused enough trouble."

"It's time for you to grow up now," her father added. "Time for you to put away childish things. Big girls don't play with dolls."

Elayne spoke with the sorrow of despair, feeling within herself that her parents must be right, even though she did not want them to be. "My dolls are alive. They're kachinas. They're sacred to the Hopi people."

"You have to stop letting your imagination run away with you," her mother added. "The kachinas are just old legends. They're nothing more than dolls to play with."

There was nowhere else to go. Nothing else to do. She couldn't stay under the bed forever. Elayne came out from where she had hidden herself. She felt ashamed, as though everyone in the store were staring at her. She felt the tears hot on her cheeks.

Standing out there before the whole world in the hot, bright lights of the store, and her parents surrounded by security guards, she felt unprotected and scared. Her whole body tightened into a protective knot as she followed her parents, momentarily joined together in a common cause to locate their daughter, out of the store and into the night.

Elayne's tears soon dried on her face in the cool New Mexico night. The tears of the little bear left on the bed in the store took longer to fade away, but nobody noticed them.

Destinations
■ ■ ■ ■ ■ ■ ■ ■ ■ ■ ■ ■

■ ■

Paints Her Dreams
Gabriel Horn
(White Deer of Autumn)

I t was during Peace Time that I first saw the image of Paints Her
Dreams. Though the timing seems understandable to me now, it
wasn't until later on, when I had learned from her that War did
not exist back then, that it all began to make sense to me somehow.
That War was only a monster in a dream—a dream she had as a
young girl, back when there were no people called Indians living here,
only the Calusa, and there was no land called Florida, but only The
Land Where the Wind Is Born . . .

She was a hazy form shimmering in the sunlight of a warm December morning. The beach where she sat on bended knee watching my
children as they played along the water's edge was deserted except for
clusters of quiet gulls gathered among the dunes, and an occasional
line of brown pelicans that would sweep down just beyond the sand
bar where small waves broke with an incoming tide. I wondered if I
hadn't fallen asleep to the sounds of the waves and the playful laughter of the children and if upon my sudden awakening, my eyes were
not adjusting well to the slant of a solstitial sun and its reflection off
the gleaming green water of the Gulf. . . .

She was barely visible in the soft sunlight of that warm winter
morning, yet I could see that she was young and beautiful simply by
the way she sat so gracefully upon her knees and watched so lovingly
as the children played around her.

I wondered, Is this real, what I am seeing? And then I was aware
that I was sitting fully conscious in the bone-white sand, staring at her
waist-length hair. I thought that maybe she was an Indian who had
once lived in this place.

I questioned the meaning of her presence. Why did she want to be
near my children? Then I wondered if perhaps she had once had children of her own, and if the sounds of playful laughter and the joy of
native children had somehow brought her back from another world,
another time, in the way that those same sounds and feelings lured me

from my sleep. "The ghosts are of the land they love," Uncle Nip would say. Still I wondered if she had appeared for reasons I would never know.

I don't recall how long she remained there on the beach watching my children play, or exactly when she faded away. I know only that the hazy form that shimmered before my eyes that warm winter day was real enough to make me feel as though I wanted to know who she was. Maybe she was some connection to our past, or perhaps even to our future. I remembered Uncle Nip telling me about past and future ghosts—how a ghost will manifest for good or bad reasons, how it is powerless to act, how it can only observe and evoke feelings among the living, feelings that can cause things to happen. . . .

These were some of the thoughts that swirled through my mind then, even as Peace Day that year arrived.

My wife and I, along with our three children, who were all named for extinct peoples—Ihasha, six; Calusa, four; and Carises, two—were gathered with our elder uncles, Nippawanock and his brother Metacomet, and some close family friends on the red-brick-tiled living room floor of our home in a circle near the Peace Tree, playing "giveaway." The gust of an unusually warm tropical breeze would occasionally pass through the open jalousies of the front door.

"Your tree is lovely again this year," Nip commented to Simone and me, as he reached up to the tree behind him. He held one of the eagle feathers that hung from one of its synthetic branches in a strand of colorful beads.

"I strung the beads, Uncle," Calusa said. "Mommy helped me some."

"And a pretty strand it is, indeed, Calusa." Nip's fingers ran the length of the beads. "You have a way of stringing pretty colors together—just like your mother. Each one blends into the next."

Then he turned to face the circle we had formed on the floor. In the middle was a pile of presents, all painstakingly wrapped but without cards to identify their owners. That was the idea, and why it was called the "giveaway." Uncle instructed each of us to take a turn and pick out a present from the pile. The one who picked the present would open it and then decide who in the circle should have it or would like to have it most. If the one who picked the present wanted it and gave it away, then the person it was given to could give it back. It was a game to help keep us aware of the things that could make one another happy and to help teach us generosity and to guard us against selfishness. It was also a lot of fun—giving away.

Such a tradition was always practiced among the People. "It's what made our nation strong," Uncle would say. "It's the kind of tradition that gave them identity."

This particular giveaway, though, was one that only occurred during the time of the winter solstice. That was what made it so special, for it allowed our children something to fill the void that Christmas and Hannukah created for them. It brought back a native tradition that the missionaries had nearly stolen from the People's memory, a giving tradition to honor a special spirit that otherwise could have been forgotten. If a spirit no longer exists in the minds and hearts of the People, it can lose its power; it can even die. Uncle would explain that to keep this from happening we should honor the spirit of Nokomo this time of year. He said that we should invite Nokomo into our home, for Nokomo is the Spirit of Giving.

Peace Time was also an occasion that reminded us of our connection to cosmic events and to family ties of love and sharing, not only among people, but among our other relatives, the earth's other life forms. This time of peace also helped us recall our connection to Mother Earth. "It is a rare time, however brief," Nip would say, "when the world is at peace."

Nip also showed us how to use the winter solstice to teach the children their native history, and to tell them the stories of how our people found ways to live in peace, so that peace, not war, became a way of life.

And so we would start telling the children, before they even understood the meanings of the words, the stories about the native Peacemakers who walked the Americas before the white man came. We would tell them about the virgin birth of Deganawida, "a true prince of peace," and about his work with the great orator Hyonwatha in establishing the Law of Great Peace among the Iroquois. We would tell them how the Iroquois uprooted a great pine and, into the cavity it left, into the depths of the undercurrents far below the earth, cast all weapons of war forever. We would tell them how the great pine was replanted among the People of the Longhouse and from then on was called the Tree of Peace.

We would tell them the story about the White Buffalo Woman and how she brought the Buffalo Calf Pipe to the Sioux. How she instructed men and women to form a circle of love and peace when they smoked from the sacred pipe.

We would tell them stories about the People who lived across the waters of the Gulf. How, long ago, Quetzalcoatl descended from the sky as a feathered serpent. How he took the form of a fair-skinned man who discouraged human sacrifice and revitalized the People's arts. We explained to the children, in the way that Uncle Nip had explained to us, how Quetzalcoatl had shown the ancestors of the Aztecs and Mayans that, through creativity, their people could demonstrate their gratitude to the Giver of Life in ways other than human sacrifice.

Uncle Nip said that the Feathered Serpent's influence was so strong that Aztec and Mayan art and knowledge became something the world had never before seen or known. He said that the art that they created out of love and gratitude has never been surpassed.

"It's about peace and giving," I'd tell the children, and I'd feel those ties to the past that made us Indians grow stronger inside me.

As the children grew to understand the meanings of these words, we would also teach them about the sacred symbolism of those decorations that hung from the artificial pine that we called the Peace Tree. It was artificial, we explained, because we did not believe in killing a tree for a decoration, no matter how meaningful we might attempt to make it. We told our children that we didn't want a tree dying a slow death in our home. "After all," Simone would add, "look at all that the Tree nations have given to us. How could we kill one of our tree relatives for a decoration this week, then discard it like trash the next?"

Ihasha was a year old when Uncle Nip first stood by the Peace Tree, holding him in one arm while pointing with his free hand to each item hanging from the tree's metallic branches of soft nylon needles. "The feathers are for the winged nations of the earth," Nip said. "And the colorful balls are for the round things of the universe: the earth, the sun, the moon, the planets." Nip lifted a strand of popcorn and touched it to Ihasha's hand. "These strings of popped corn," he continued, "represent the foods of the earth." Then he held up the deer hooves. "These," he said, "represent the animals which have served our people unselfishly as teachers and providers." Then he looked up toward the top of the tree. The eyes of the child in his arms followed his. "And the silver star you see up there is placed above us to remind us of our ancestors and our special relationship to the stars."

The giveaway game just added to the fun and to the learning and to everything else on Peace Day, and when it had ended and the wrappings were all gathered up, I glanced over at Uncle Nip. He had retired to the soft rattan chair near the Peace Tree. He was perspiring. His face seemed flushed. "Are you okay, Uncle?" I asked.

He nodded and smiled. "Fine," he said. "I'm just fine."

I turned my gaze around the room at my wife and our friends and our children—all engaged in quiet conversation or play. It was at that moment, when I felt the warm gust of an unusual winter's day once again sweeping through the front door and around us all, that I remembered her, and I suddenly had an overwhelming sense of love and family. Such a moment made everything seem more special to me. "Why is this so, Nip? Why does it feel so special this time?" I asked.

"Because you're becoming aware that these times are not going to last forever, nephew. There won't be many more."

I reached into my pocket and pulled out a shard of old pottery. I rubbed it with my thumb as I clutched it in my palm. Then I handed it to Nip.

"What do you think?" I asked. "It was given to me the other day by one of the park rangers. He said it was like no other piece found in the area. He told me that its design and black color were so unusual that no one could figure out what tribe it came from." Nip held it up and studied it. "The ranger said I could keep it for as long as I needed, to see if I could learn anything about it, in a psychic kind of way. Is that crazy, Uncle? I mean I'm no psychic."

Nip held it some more and examined it for a long time. He rubbed it again and again.

"Did anything unusual happen . . . recently?" he asked. Another warm breeze swept through the front door. It lifted some of the decorative balls hanging from the tree, and rushed past me.

"I saw something on the beach the other day. I think maybe it was a ghost."

Nip handed the old pottery piece to me. "Was it in the morning . . . around nine?"

I told him that it was, but not how surprised I was when he mentioned the time. I told him that I was certain the ghost was that of a young maiden. He nodded slightly. His lips tightened, and he seemed for a moment to be looking within himself. "I know who it was," he said. "And someday I'll tell you. But not now. Now isn't the time."

I asked why he couldn't reveal her identity to me now. He just shook his head and said that if he died before that could happen, Uncle Met would tell me.

For the rest of that winter I felt uncomfortable and morose. I slept restlessly. The winter turned bitter by Florida standards, too. It took its toll on the weak and the old. A freeze nearly wiped out the orange groves. Cold air toward spring almost ruined the March strawberry harvest. And Uncle Nip had a heart attack. His surgery went well, but he said that he'd never go through it again.

Spring finally arrived. Cold waves from the north became warm ones on the Gulf. The children and I spent much of our days back on the beach, riding and playing among the white foamy crests of the Gulf's waves. That's when she returned. . . .

She appeared standing between two small dunes, among the tall stalks of golden sea oats. Her form was barely discernible, but I recognized it just the same. Her long hair shimmered as she blurred and soon faded away.

When we came home that afternoon, the children headed outside to play, and I went into the bedroom, where I fell onto the bed—thinking about her. The slight hum of the ceiling fan and the soft rattle of sabal fronds outside the open bedroom windows made the room feel warm and peaceful. It was very peaceful. . . .

I don't recall falling asleep. I don't recall lifting the mattress or taking out the pottery piece I had shared with Uncle Nip that winter. It's the voice I heard beckoning me that I remember. The voice and what I saw as I lifted free of my body and floated through . . .

Time is of the Mystery. It's not something artificially measured by a clock. It doesn't flow in a straight line beginning at one point and ending at another. Time moves in circles and cycles in which events interwine. I found myself traveling like a spirit over her village. Below, I could see the thatched homes where her people lived. They were built on rows of mounds, clustered among sabals and pines not far from the water's edge. I could see smoke rising from the fires that burned inside and outside the lodges. Myriad fish moved about in the clear emerald water. I could see the children playing. . . .

That's when I became aware of her voice. All along this spirit-journey she had been speaking to me. The language was hers, yet I could feel its meaning, and somehow understood things with my heart that my head could not explain. I know now that what I was seeing was the way things were before she had her dream, before the monsters of War and Disease came for her.

I lay gazing up at the ceiling fan. Moonlight filtered through the sabals outside the bedroom window, casting shadows on the wall that played with the spinning blades. How long had I been gone? How long would I feel the pain that comes when you lose someone close? How long would I feel lonely for a time that no longer exists?

Truth and the need to tell it could help manifest a ghost. There's no other way I can explain it. For five years I had struggled to hear the ghost's voice and tell her story. For five years I had felt haunted by the memories she gave to me. And so I wrote her story the way it came to me, only this time Uncle Nip would write the last line of the telling.

"The children grow like Florida weeds," he said on the last Peace Day he would see them playing on the shore. The sun was the color of an orange as we watched it set over the Gulf. Simone sat on one side of him and I on the other. Uncle Met was too ill to be there.

You know the feeling that comes when you're totally aware of the moment you're living in? When you're aware that our time on the earth is so short? Well, that feeling wrapped itself around me. I savored everything: the color of the sky, the thin layer of cirrus floating like white feathers across it, the emerald shade of the water, the laughter of the children. . . .

"There won't be many more like this, huh, Uncle?" I said, staring at the sun. I guess I needed the affirmation that I was, indeed, understanding something about life that my youth couldn't know so many Peace Times ago. Or maybe I was hoping he'd say, "No, just a few."

Nip watched the children on the shore as if he were etching into some soul-memory how they looked that lovely winter's day. "The water is always," he whispered softly to me.

"Yes, Uncle," I said. "The water is always."

Nippawanock died a week after that Peace Day in 1987. He never got to tell me who she was, nor did my Uncle Met, who died soon after. She called herself Paints Her Dreams in the story I wrote. And though Uncle Nip didn't reveal what he knew about her before he died, he did read the story. It was on Thanksgiving night, after he'd gotten into a quarrel over Christianity with Princess Red Wing, his adopted mother. Red Wing was also the direct descendant of the Massasoit Osamekun who befriended the Pilgrims, and of his son Metacomet, called King Phillip, who was forced to involve himself in the war that bears his name.

And though it was the unspoken rule that he and Red Wing did not argue over religion in Uncle's house, that night became the exception, perhaps because Nip understood that death was the shadow that had come to him that autumn, and there was too little time left to be tolerant of conflicting ideas and the people who would be so bold as to articulate them in his presence. It could have been that he and Red Wing argued over Christianity because he recalled with clarity those early days on Quapaw land when he became "the son of that half-breed," and the only women who would take care of him while his mother worked were the local prostitutes in the mining town of Pitcher.

Perhaps he argued with Princess Red Wing that night because he was remembering the time the Christians took scissors to his hair and forbade him to speak "the language of the devil." Or maybe he had simply learned and experienced enough of their pious words and inhuman behavior. Maybe it was one or none of these things that sparked and fueled the bitter argument that Thanksgiving night when he told Princess Red Wing that, after all the horror Christians had inflicted on our people, to support or believe in what they did was like dying. He said that their missionaries had taught us to think only of ourselves. He said they had taught us to reject our belief in the Great Holy Mystery. He said they had taught us that the earth was not our mother, that animals had no souls. He said that their religion had cleared the path for the monster of War. He said this after the television news had just reported the slaughter of an Indian village in Guatemala.

It was very late and stormy that night when Uncle Nip scribbled a notation on the back of the last page of the story, which was titled "A

Piece of Pottery." He said that reading it had made him cry, for he had discovered that Princess Red Wing and Paints Her Dreams had something in common. Even though he never told me outright what he knew about Paints Her Dreams, he did write the final line of her story. It haunts me still. . . .

"He cried for a beautiful maiden sacrificed."

AUTHOR'S NOTE:

"A Piece of Pottery" was sent to Sylvia Tankel of *Short Story International,* where it was published that same year, the year Uncle Nip died—1987. I never saw Paints Her Dreams again.

■ ■

Monuments to the Dead
Kristine Kathryn Rusch

THE CALIFORNIA PERSPECTIVE: REFLECTIONS ON MT. RUSHMORE
by L. Emilia Sunlake

The union of these four presidents carved on the face of the everlasting hills of South Dakota will contribute a distinctly national monument. It will be decidedly American in its conception, in its magnitude, in its meaning, and altogether worthy of our country.

—*Calvin Coolidge at the dedication of Mt. Rushmore, 1927*

Cars crawl along Highway 16. The hot summer sun reflects off shiny bumper stickers, most plastered with the mementos of tourist travel: Sitting Bull Crystal Cave, Wall Drug, and I ♥ anything from terriers to West Virginia. The windows are open, and children lean out, trying to see magic shimmering in the heat visions on the pavement. The locals say the traffic has never been like this, that even at the height of tourist season the cars can go at least thirty miles an hour. I have been sitting in this sticky heat for most of the afternoon with Kenny, my photographer, moving forward a foot at a time, sharing a Diet Coke, and hoping the story will be worth the aggravation.

I have never been to the Black Hills before. Until I started writing regularly for the slick magazines, I had never been out of California, and even then my outside assignments were rare. Usually I wrote about things close to home: the history of Simi Valley, for instance, or the relationships between the Watts riot and the Rodney King riot twenty-five years later. When *American Observer* sent me to South Dakota, they asked me to write from a California perspective. What they will get is a white, middle-class, female California perspective. Despite my articles on the cultural diversity of my home state, *American Observer*—published in New York—continues to think that all Californians share the same opinions, beliefs, and outlooks.

Of course, now, sitting in bumper-to-bumper traffic in the dense heat, I feel right at home.

Kenny has brought a lunch—tuna fish—which, in the oppressive air, has a rancid two-days-dead odor. He eats with apparent gusto, while I sip on soda and try to peer ahead. Kenny says nothing. He is a slender man with long black hair and wide dark eyes. I chose him because he is the best photographer I have ever met, a man who can capture the heart of a moment in a single image. He also rarely speaks, a trait I usually enjoy, but one I have found annoying on this long afternoon as we wait in the trail of cars.

He sees me lean out the window for the fifth time in the last minute. "Why don't you interview some of the tourists?"

I shake my head and he goes back to his sandwich. The tourists aren't the story. The story waits for us at the end of this road, at the end of time.

When I think of Mount Rushmore, I think of Cary Grant clutching the lip of a stone-faced Abraham Lincoln with Eva Marie Saint beside him, looking over her shoulder at the drop below. The movie memory has the soft fake tones of early color or perhaps early colorization— the pale blues that don't exist in the natural world, the red lipstick that is five shades too red. As a child, I wanted to go to the monument and hang off a president myself. As an adult, I disdained tourist traps, and had avoided all of them with amazing ease.

Later I tell my husband of this, and he corrects me: Cary Grant was hanging off George Washington's forehead. Kenny disagrees: he believes Grant crawled around Teddy Roosevelt's eyes. A viewing of *North by Northwest* would settle this disagreement, but I saw the movie later, as an adult, and found the special effects not so special, and the events contrived. If Cary Grant hadn't, stupidly, pulled the knife from a dead man's body, there would have been no movie. The dead man and the knife were an obvious setup, and Grant's character fell right into the trap.

Appropriate, I think, for a Californian to have a cinematic memory of Mount Rushmore. As I study the history, however, I find it much more compelling, and frighteningly complex.

The Black Hills are as old as any geological formation in North America. They rise out of the flatlands on the Wyoming-Dakota border, mysterious shadowy hills that are cut out of the dust. The dark pine trees made the hills look black from a distance. The Paha Sapa, or the Black Hills, were the center of the world for the surrounding tribes. They used the streams and lakes hidden by the trees; they hunted game in the wooded areas; and in the summer, the young men went to the sacred points on a four-day vision quest that would shape and focus the rest of their lives.

According to Lakota tribal legend, the hills were a reclining female figure from whose breasts flowed life. The Lakota went to the hills as a child went to its mother's arms.

In 1868 the United States government signed a treaty with the Indians, granting them "absolute and undisturbed use of the Great Sioux Reservation," which included the Black Hills. The terms of the treaty included the line "No white person or persons shall be permitted to settle upon or occupy any portion of the territory, or without the consent of the Indians to pass through the same."

White persons have been trespassing ever since.

Finally I can stand the smell of tuna no longer. I push open the door of the rental car and stand. My jeans and T-shirt cling to my body—I am not used to humid heat. I walk along the edge of the highway, peering into cars, seeing pale face after pale face. Most of the tourists ignore me, but a few watch hesitantly, fearing that I am going to pull a gun and leap into their car beside them.

Everyone knows of the troubles in the Black Hills, and most people have brought their families despite the dangers. Miracles only happen once in a lifetime.

I see no one I want to speak to until I pass a red pickup truck. Its paint is chipped, and the frame is pocked with rust. A Native American woman sits inside, a black braid running down her back. She is dressed as I am, except that sweat does not stain her white T-shirt, and she wears heavy turquoise rings on all of her fingers.

"Excuse me," I say. "Are you heading to Mount Rushmore?"

She looks at me, her eyes hooded and dark. Two little boys sleep in the cab, their bodies propped against each other like puppies. A full jug of bottled water sits at her feet, and on the boys' side of the cab, empty pop cans line up like soldiers. "Yes," she says. Her voice is soft.

I introduce myself and explain my assignment. She does not respond, staring at me as if I am speaking in foreign tongue. "May I talk with you for a little while?"

"No." Again she speaks softly, but with a finality that brooks no disagreement.

I thank her for her time, shove my hands in my pockets, and walk back to the car. Kenny is standing outside of it, the passenger door open. His camera is draped around his neck, reflecting sunlight, and he holds a plastic garbage bag in his hand. He is picking up litter from the roadside—smashed Pepsi cups and dirt-covered McDonald's bags.

"Lack of respect," he says, when he sees me watching him, "shows itself in little ways."

■ ■ ■

Lack of respect shows itself in larger ways too: in great stone faces carved on a mother's breast; in broken treaties; in broken bodies bleeding on the snow. The indignities continue into our lifetimes— children ripped from their parents and put into schools that force them to renounce old ways; mysterious killings and harassment arrests; and enforced poverty unheard of even in our inner cities. The stories are frightening and hard to comprehend, partly because they are true. I grasp them only through books—from Dee Brown to Peter Matthiessen, from Charles A. Eastman (Ohiyesa) to Vine Deloria, Jr.—and through films—both documentaries (usually produced by PC white men) such as *Incident at Ogala,* and fictional accounts (starring non-Natives, of course) from *Little Big Man* to *Thunderheart.*

Some so-called wise person once wrote that women have the capacity to understand all of American society: we have lived in a society dominated by white men, and so have had to understand their perspective to survive; we were abused and treated as property within our own homes, having no rights and no recourse under the law, so we understand blacks, Chicanos, and Native Americans. But I stand on this road, outside a luxury car that I rented with my gold MasterCard, and I do not understand what it is like to be a defeated people, living among the victors, watching them despoil all that I value and all that I believe in.

Instead of empathy, I have white liberal guilt. When I stared across the road into the darkness of that truck cab, I felt the Native American woman's eyes assessing me. My sons sleep in beds with Ninja Turtles decorating the sheets; they wear Nikes and tear holes in their shirts on purpose. They fight over the Nintendo and the remote controls. I buy dolphin-safe tuna, and pay attention to food boycotts, but I shop in a grocery store filled with light and choices. And while I understand that the fruits of my life were purchased with the lives of people I have never met, I tell myself there is nothing I can do to change that. What is past is past.

But the past determines who we are, and it has led to this startling future.

I remember the moment with the same clarity with which my parents remember the Kennedy assassination, the clarity my generation associates with the destruction of the space shuttle *Challenger.* I was waiting in my husband's Ford Bronco outside the recreation center. The early-June day was hot in a California-desert sort of way—the dry heat of an oven, heat that prickles but does not invade the skin. My youngest son pulled open the door and crawled in beside me, bringing with him dampness and filling the air with the scents of chlorine and institutional soap. He tossed his wet suit and towel on the floor, fastened his seatbelt, and said, "Didja hear? Mount Rushmore disappeared."

I smiled at him, thinking it amazing the way ten-year-old little boys' minds worked—I hadn't even realized he knew what Mount Rushmore was—and he frowned at my response.

"No, really," he said, voice squeaking with sincerity. "It did. Turn on the news."

Without waiting for me, he flicked on the radio and scanned to the all news channel.

". . . not an optical illusion," a female voice was saying. "The site now resembles those early photos, taken around the turn of the century, before the work on the monument began."

Through the hour-long drive home, we heard the story again and again. No evidence of a bomb, no sign of the remains of the great stone faces. No rubble, nothing. Hollywood experts spoke about the possibilities of an illusion this grand, but all agreed that the faces would be there, behind the illusion, at least available to the sense of touch.

My hands were shaking by the time we pulled into the driveway of our modified ranch home. My son, whose assessment had gone from "pretty neat" to "kinda scary" within the space of the drive (probably from my grim and silent reaction), got out of the car without taking his suit and disappeared into the backyard to consult with his older brother. I took the suit and went inside, cleaning up by rote as I made my way to the bedroom we used as a library.

The quote I wanted, the quote that had been running through my mind during the entire drive, was there on page ninety-three of the 1972 Simon and Schuster edition of Richard Erdos's *Lame Deer: Seeker of Visions:*

> One man's shrine is another man's cemetery, except that now a few white folks are also getting tired of having to look at this big paperweight curio. We can't get away from it. You could make a lovely mountain into a great paperweight, but can you make it into a wild, natural mountain again? I don't think you have the know-how for that.

Lame Deer went on to say that white men, who had the ability to fly to the moon, should have the know-how to take the faces off the mountain.

But no one had the ability to take the faces off overnight.
No one.

We finally reach the site at around 5:00 P.M. Kenny has snapped three rolls of film on our approach. He began shooting about sixty miles away, the place where, they tell me, the faces were first visible. I try to envision the shots as he sees them: the open mouths, the shocked expressions. I know Kenny will capture the moment, but I also know he will be unable to capture the thing that holds me.

The sound.

The rumble of low conversation over the soft roar of car engines. The shocked tones, rising and falling like a wave on the open sea.

I see nothing ahead of me except the broad expanse of a mountain outlined in the distance. I have not seen the faces up close and personal. I cannot tell the difference. But the others can. Pheromones fill the air, and I can almost taste the excitement. It grows as we pull into the overcrowded parking lot, as we walk to the visitors center that still shows its 1940s roots.

Kenny disappears into the crowd. I walk to the first view station and stare at a mountain, at a granite surface smooth as water-washed stone. A chill runs along my back. At the base, uniformed people with cameras and surveying equipment check the site. Other uniformed people move along the top of the mount; it appears that they have just pulled someone up on the equivalent of a window-washer's scaffold.

All the faces here are white, black, or Asian—non-Native. We passed the Native woman as we drove into the parking lot. Two men, wearing army fatigues and carrying rifles had stopped the truck. She was leaning out of the cab, speaking wearily to them, and Kenny made me slow as we passed. He eavesdropped in his intense way, and then nodded once.

"She will be all right," he said, and nothing more.

The hair on my arms has prickled. TV crews film from the edge of the parking lot. A middle-aged man, his stomach parting the buttons on his short-sleeved white shirt, aims a video camera at the site. I am not a nature lover. Within minutes I am bored with the changed mountain. Miracle, yes, but now that my eyes have confirmed it, I want to get on with the story.

Inside the visitors' center is an ancient diorama on the creation of Mount Rushmore. The huge sculpted busts of George Washington, Abraham Lincoln, Thomas Jefferson, and Theodore Roosevelt took fourteen years to complete. Gutzon Borglum (Bore-glum, how appropriate) designed the monument, which was established in 1925, during our great heedless prosperity, and finished in 1941, after the Crash and the Depression and at the eve of America's involvement in World War II. The diorama makes only passing mention—in a cheerful, aren't-they-cute 1950s way—to the importance of the mountain to the Native tribes. There is no acknowledgment that when the monument was being designed, the Lakota filed a court claim asking for financial compensation for the theft of the Black Hills. A year after the completion of the monument, the courts denied the claim. No acknowledgment, either, of the split between Native peoples that occurred when the case was revived in the 1950s—the split over financial compensation and return of the land itself.

Nor is there any mention of the bloody history of the surrounding area that continued into the 1970s with the American Indian Movement, the death of two FBI agents and an Indian on the Pine Ridge Reservation, the resulting trials, the violence that marked the decade, and the attempted takeover of the Black Hills themselves.

In the true tradition of a conquering force, of an occupying army, all mention of the ongoing war has been obliterated.

But not forgotten. The army, with its rifles, is out in force. Several young boys, their lean, muscled frames outlined in their camo T-shirts and fatigue pants, sit at the blond wood tables. Others sit outside, rifles leaning against their chairs. We were not stopped as we entered the parking lot—Kenny claims our trunk is too small to hold a human being—but several others were.

One of the soldiers is getting himself a drink from the overworked waitress behind the counter. I stop beside him. He is only a few years older than my oldest son, and the ferocity of the soldier's clothes makes him look even younger. His skin is pockmarked by acne, his teeth crooked and yellow from lack of care. Things have not changed from my youth. It is still the children of the poor who receive the orders to die for patriotism, valor, and the American Way.

"A lot of tension here," I say.

He takes his iced tea from the waitress and pours half a cup of sugar into it. "It'd be easier if there weren't no tourists." Then he flushes. "Sorry, lady."

I reassure him that he hasn't offended me, and I explain my purpose.

"We ain't supposed to talk to the press." He shrugs.

"I won't use your name," I say. "And it's for a magazine that won't be published for a month, maybe two months from now."

"Two months, anything can happen."

True enough, which is why I have been asked to capture this moment with the vision of an outsider. I know my editor has already asked a white Dakota correspondent to write as well, and she has received confirmation that at least one Native American author will contribute an essay. In this age of cynicism, a miracle is the most important event of our time.

The boy sits at an empty table and pulls out a chair for me. His arms are thick, tanned, and covered with fine white hairs. His fingers are long, slender, and ringless, his nails clean. He doesn't look at me as he speaks.

"They sent us up here right when the whole thing started," he said, "and we was told not to let no Indians up here. Some of our guys, they been combing the woods for Indians, making sure this ain't some kind of front for some special action. I don't like it. The guys are trigger-happy, and with all these tourists, I'm afraid someone's going to do something, and get shot. We ain't going to mean for it to happen. It'll be an accident, but it'll happen just the same."

He drinks his tea in several noisy slurps, tells me a bit about his family—his father, one of the few casualties of the Gulf War; his mother, remarried, to a foreman of a dying assembly plant in Michigan; his sister, newly married to a career army officer; and himself, with his dreams for a real life without a hand-to-mouth income when he leaves the army. He never expected to be searching cars at the entrance to a national park, and the miracle makes him nervous.

"I think it's some kind of Indian trick," he says. "You know, a decoy to get us all pumped up and focused here while they attack somewhere else."

This boy, who grew up poor hundreds of miles away, and who probably never gave Native Americans a second thought, is now speaking the language of conquerors, conquerors at the end of an empire, who feel the power slipping through their fingers.

He leaves to return to his post. I speak with a few tourists, but learn nothing interesting. It is as if the Virgin Mary has appeared at Lourdes; everyone wants to be one of the first to experience the miracle. I am half-surprised no one has set up a faith-healing station: a bit of granite from the holy mountain, and all ailments will be cured.

The light is turning silver with approaching twilight. My stomach is rumbling, but I do not want one of the hot dogs that has been twirling in the little case all afternoon. The oversized salted pretzels are gone, and the grill is caked with grease. The waitress herself looks faded, her dishwater blond hair slipping from its bun, her uniform covered with sweat stains and ketchup. I go to find Kenny, but cannot see him in the crowds. Finally I see him, on a path just past the parking lot, sitting beneath a scraggly pine tree, talking with an elderly man.

The elderly man's hair is white and short, but his face has a photogenic cragginess that most WASP photographers find appealing in Native Americans. As I approach, he touches Kenny's arm, then slips down the path and disappears into the growing darkness.

"Who was that?" I ask as I stop in front of Kenny. I am standing over him, looming, and the question feels like an interrogation, as if I am asking for information I do not deserve. Kenny grabs his camera and takes a picture of me. When we view it later, we will see different things: he will see the formation of light and shadow into a tired, irritable woman, made more irritable by an occurrence she cannot explain or understand, and I will see the teachers from my childhood enforcing some arbitrary rule on the playground.

When he is finished, he holds out his hand and I pull him to his feet. We walk back to the car in silence, and he never answers my question.

Speculation is rife in Rapid City. The woman at the Super Eight on the Interstate hands out her opinion with the old-fashioned room keys. "They're using some newfangled technology and trying to scare us," she says, her voice roughened by her five-pack-a-day habit. Wisps of smoke curl around the Mount Rushmore mugs and the tourist brochures that fill the dark wood lobby. "They know if that monument goes away, there's really no reason for folks to stop here."

She never explains who she means by "they." In this room filled with white people, surrounded by mementos of the "Old West," the meaning of "they" is immediately clear.

As it is downtown. The stately old Victorian homes and modified farmhouses attest to this city's roots. Some older buildings still stand in the center of town, dwarfed by newer hotels built to swallow the tourist trade. Usually, the locals tell me, the clientele is mixed here. Some businesspeople show for various conventions and must fraternize with the bikers who have a convention of their own in nearby Sturgis every summer. The tourists are the most visible: with their video cameras and towheaded children, they visit every sight available, from the Geology Museum to the Sioux Indian Museum. We all check our maps and make no comment over roads named after Indian fighters like Philip Sheridan.

In a dusky bar whose owner does not want to be named in this "or any" article, a group of elderly men share a drink before they toddle off to their respective homes. They too have theories, and they're willing to talk with a young female reporter from California.

"You don't remember the seventies," says Terry, a loud-voiced, balding man who lives in a nearby retirement home. "Lots of young reporters like you, honey, and them AIM people, stirring up trouble. There was more guards at Rushmore than before or since. We always thought they'd blow up that monument. They hate it, you know. Say we've defaced"—and they all laugh at the pun—"defaced their sacred hills."

"I say they lost the wars fair and square," says Rudy. He and his wife of forty-five years live in a six-bedroom Victorian house on the corner of one of the tree-lined streets. "No sense whining about it. Time they started learning to live like the rest of us."

"Always thought they would bomb that monument." Max, a former lieutenant in the army, fought "the Japs" at Guadalcanal, a year that marked the highlight of his life. "And now they have."

"There was no bomb," says Jack, a former college professor who still wears tweed blazers with patches on the elbows. "Did you hear any explosion? Did you?"

The others don't answer. It becomes clear they have had this conversation every day since the faces disappeared. We speak a bit more, then I leave in search of other opinions. As I reach the door, Jack catches my arm.

"Young lady," he says, ushering me out into the darkness of the quiet street, "we've been living the Indian wars all our lives. It's hard to ignore when you live beside a prison camp. I'm not apologizing for my friends—but it's hard to live here, to see all that poverty, to know that we—our government—have caused that devastation because the Indians—the natives—want to live in their own way. It's a strange prison we've built for them. They can escape if they want to renounce everything they are."

In his voice I hear the thrum of the professor giving a lecture. "What did you teach?" I ask.

He smiles, and in the reflected glare of the bar's neon sign, I see the unlined face of the man he once was. "History," he says. "And I tell you, living here, I have learned that history is not a deep, dusty thing of the past, but part of the air we breathe each and every day."

His words send a shiver through me. I thank him for his time and return to my rented car. As I drive to my hotel, I pass the Rushmore Mall—a flat late-seventies creation that has sprawled to encompass other stores. The mall is closing, and hundreds of cars pull away, oblivious of the strangeness that has happened only a few miles outside the city.

By morning, the police, working in cooperation with the FBI, have captured a suspect. But they will not let any of the reporters talk with him, nor will they release his name, his race, or anything else about him. They don't even specify the charges.

"How can they?" asks the reporter for *The New York Times* over an overpriced breakfast of farm-fresh eggs, thick bacon, and wheat toast at a local diner. "They don't know what happened to the monument. So they charge him with making the faces disappear? Unauthorized use of magic in an un-American fashion?"

"Who says it's magic?" the CNN correspondent asks.

"You explain it," says the man from the *Wall Street Journal.* "I touched the rock face yesterday. Nothing is carved there. It feels like nothing ever was."

The reporters are spooked, and the explanations they share among themselves have the ring of mysticism. That mysticism does not reach the American people, however. On the air, in the pages of the country's respected newspapers and magazines, the talk revolves around possible technical explanations for the disappearance of the faces. Any whisper of the unexplainable, and the show, the interviewee, and the story are whisked off the air.

It is as if we are afraid of things beyond our ken.

In the afternoon I complain to Kenny that, aside from the woman in the truck and the man he talked to near the monument, I have seen no Natives. The local and national Native organizations have been strangely silent. National spokespeople for the organizations have arrived in Rapid City—only to disappear behind some kind of protective walls. Even people who revel in the limelight have avoided it on this occasion.

"They have no explanations either," Kenny says with such surety that I glare at him. He has been talking with the Natives while I have not.

Finally he shrugs. "They have found a place in the Black Hills that is *theirs.* They believe something wonderful is about to happen."

"Take me there," I say.

He shakes his head. "I can't. But I can bring someone to you."

Kenny drives the rental car off the Interstate, down back roads so small they aren't on the map. Old, faded signs for now-defunct cafés and secret routes to the Black Hills Caverns give the area a sense of *Twilight Zone* mystery. Out here, the towns have names that send chills down my back, names like Mystic and Custer. Kenny leaves me at a roadside café that looks as if it closed when Kennedy was president. The windows are boarded up, but the door swings open to reveal a dusty room filled with rat footprints and broken furniture. Someone has removed the grill and the rest of the equipment, leaving gaping holes in the sideboards, but the counter remains, a testament to what might once have been a thriving business.

There are tables near the gravel parking lot outside. They have been wiped clean, and one bears cup rings that look to be fairly recent. The café may be closed, but the tables are still in use. I wipe off a bench and sit down, a little unnerved that Kenny has left me in this desolate place alone—with only a cellular phone for comfort.

The sun is hot as it rises in the sky, and I am thankful for the bit of shade provided by the building's overhang. No cars pass on this road, and I am beginning to feel as if I have reached the edge of nowhere.

I have brought my laptop, and I spend an hour making notes from the day's conversations, trying to place them in a coherent order so that this essay will make sense. It has become clearer and clearer to me that—unless I have the luck of a fictional detective—I will find no answers before my Monday deadline. I will submit only a series of impressions and guesses based on my own observations of a fleeting moment. I suppose that is why the *American Observer* hired me instead of an investigative reporter, so that I can capture this moment of mystery in my white California way.

Finally I hear the moan of a car engine, and relief loosens the tension in my shoulders. I have not, until this moment, realized how tense the quiet has made me. Sunlight glares off the car's new paint job, and the springs squeak as the wheels catch the potholes that fill the road. Kenny's face is obscured by the windshield, but as the car turns in the parking lot, I recognize his passenger as the elderly man I saw the day before.

The car stops, and I stand. Kenny gets out and leads the elderly man to me. I introduce myself and thank the man for joining us. He nods in recognition, but does not give me his name. "I am here as a favor to Little Hawk," he says, nodding at Kenny. "Otherwise I would not speak to you."

Kenny is fiddling with his camera. He looks no different, and yet my vision of him has suddenly changed. We have never discussed his past, or mine for that matter. In California, a person either proclaims his heritage loudly or receives his privacy. I am definitely not an investigator. I did not know that my cameraman had ties in this part of the Dakotas.

I close my laptop as I sit. The old man sits beside me. Silver mixes with the black hair in his braid. I have seen his face before. Later I will look it up and discover what it looked like when it was young, when he was making news in the 1970s for his association with AIM.

I open my mouth to ask a question, and he raises his hand, shaking his head slightly. Behind us, a bird chirps. A drop of sweat runs down my back.

"I know what you will ask," he says. "You want me to give you the answers. You want to know what is happening, and how we caused it."

My questions are not as blunt as that, but he has a point. I have fallen into the same trap as the locals. I am blaming the Natives because I see no other explanation.

"When he gave his farewell address to the Lakota," the old man said in a ringing voice accustomed to stories, "he said, 'As a child I was taught the Supernatural Powers were powerful and could do strange things. . . . This was taught me by the wise men and the shamans. They taught me that I could gain their favor by being kind to my people and brave before my enemies; by telling the truth and living straight; by fighting for my people and their hunting grounds.'

"All my life we have fought, Ms. Sunlake, and we have tried to live the old path. But I was taught as a child that we had been wicked, that we were living in sin, and that we must accept Christ as our Savior, for in Him is the way.

"In Him, my people found death over a hundred years ago, at Wounded Knee. In Him, we have watched our Mother ravaged and our hunting grounds ruined. And I wish I could say that by renouncing Him and His followers, we have begun this change. But I cannot."

The bird has stopped chirping. His voice echoes in the silence. Kenny's camera whirs once, twice, and I think of the old superstition that Crazy Horse and some of the others held, that a camera stole the soul. This old man does not have that fear.

He puts out a hand and touches my arm. His knuckles are large and swollen with age. A twisted white scar runs from his wrist to his elbow. "We have heard that there are many buffalo on the Great Plains, and that the water is receding from Lake Powell. We are together now in the Hills, waiting and following the old traditions. Little Hawk has been asked to join us, but he will not."

I glance at Kenny. He is holding his camera chest-high and staring at the old man, tears in his eyes. I look away.

"In our search for answers, we have forgotten that Red Cloud is right," the old man said. "The *Taku Wakan* are powerful and can do strange things."

He stands and I stand with him. "But why now?" I ask. "Why not a hundred years ago? Two hundred years ago?"

The look he gives me is sad. I am still asking questions, unwilling to accept.

"Perhaps," he said, "the *Taku Wakan* know that if they wait much longer the People will be gone, and the Earth will belong to madmen."

Then he nods at Kenny and they walk to the car.

"I will be back soon," Kenny says. I sit back down and try to write this meeting down in my laptop. What I cannot convey is the sense of unease with which it left me, the feeling that I have missed more than I could ever see.

"Why don't you go with them?" I ask Kenny as we drive back to Rapid City.

For a long time he does not answer me. He stares straight ahead at the narrow road, the fading white lines illuminated only by his headlights. He came for me just before dark. The mosquitoes had risen in the twilight, and I felt that the essay and I would die together.

"I can't believe as they do," he says. "And they need purity of belief."

"I don't understand," I say.

He sighs, and pushes a long strand of hair away from his face. "He said we were raised to be ashamed of who we are. I still am. I cringe when they go through the rituals."

"What do you believe is happening at Mount Rushmore?" I keep my voice quiet, so as not to break this, the first thread of confidence he has ever shown in me.

"I'm like you," he says. His hands clutch the top of the wheel, knuckles white. "I don't care what is happening, as long as it provides emotion for my art."

We leave the next morning on a 6:00 A.M. flight. The plane is nearly empty. The reporters and tourists remain, since no one has any answers yet. The first suspect has been released, and another is in custody. Specialists in every area from virtual reality to sculpture have flooded the site. Experts on Native Americans posit everything from a bombing to Coyote paying one last great trick.

I have written everything but this, the final section. My hands shook last night as I typed in my conversation with Kenny. I am paid to observe, to learn, to be detached—but he is right. So few stories tug my own heartstrings. I won't let this one. I refuse to believe in miracles. I too want to see the experts prove that some odd technology has caused the change in the mountainside.

Yet, as I lean back and try to imagine what that moment will feel like—the moment when I learn that some clever person with a hidden camera has caused the entire mess—I feel a sinking in my stomach. I want to believe in the miracle, and since I cannot, I want to have the chance to believe. I don't want anyone to take that small thing away from me.

Yet the old man's words do not fill me with comfort, either. For the future he sees, the future he hopes for, has no place for me or my kind in it. Whatever has happened to the Natives has happened to them, and not to me. Please, God, never to me.

The sunlight has a sharp, early-morning clarity. As the plane lifts off, its shadow moves like a hawk over the earth. My gaze follows the shadow, watching it move over buildings and then over the hills. As we pull up into the clouds, I gasp.

For below me, the hills have transformed into a reclining woman, her head tilted back, her knees bent, her breasts firm and high. She watches us until we disappear.

Until we leave the center of the world.

With White Deer Gone

Rick Wilber

H ands outstretched, that long, wonderful moment of fingers reaching, the ball spiraling toward them, the catch. The Catch.

If you lived in Minnesota back then, you remember it. Mankato High against Central Jesuit. State finals. In 1967. Gregory White Deer's Golden Moment.

We started the second half of that game down by twenty-seven points. Jesuit had just flat-out whipped us, running through us, passing over us, and stopping me flat.

I was terrible that day. Threw fourteen times in that first half and had four short completions and two interceptions. White Deer, our All-Stater, hadn't caught a single pass. I'd missed him three times.

But White Deer believed in me, in us.

I remember standing on the sidelines toward the end of the first half, watching the debacle, watching our remarkable season shatter before my very eyes, when White Deer came up to me and put his helmet into my face. His eyes were wild.

"You have to believe," he yelled at me over the crowd noise. "You have to know it's going to be true."

I just smiled at him. We'd grown up together, he and I, and he'd always provided my courage, my nerve, urging me on to do things I wouldn't have tried for myself. Some of them—the broken window at Mrs. McNichol's house from a baseball thrown farther than I'd ever thrown one before, the bent frame of my older brother's bicycle after I took it over that plywood ramp at full speed—had turned out poorly. But others, like being the quarterback of the football team, or having the nerve to ask Marianne Simon out on a date, had gone just fine.

But this, I thought, was different. All the believing in the world wouldn't help against that Jesuit defense. I couldn't think of a thing we could do about it.

But he could. "The Ghost Dance," he yelled at me. "You remember that?"

"Sure," I said. It was hard not to know about these things back then, when your best friend was Santee Sioux and a media favorite— the Super Sioux they called him, and nobody laughed—and you were a sixteen-year-old with a great arm who was terrified by everything he didn't know. "Sure," I said. "You've told me all about it a dozen times. Wovoka. Kicking Bear. Sitting Bull. The assassination. So?"

It seemed like no time to be getting into Indian history, much as I was caught up in it. God, I admired White Deer so much. He had a cause, a reason for being, in an era that demanded causes. His mother was white and his father full-blood, so he could live in both worlds. He chose the Native blood.

The family had a nice house in a nice neighborhood in North Mankato, and that never struck me as odd growing up. I lived just down the street, and White Deer and I were throwing footballs back and forth to each other from the start.

He always had the gift for the game, a blend of physical skills and the kind of total concentration that helped him make the tough catch in heavy traffic, take the hard hit.

And, my, he could run, those golden legs flying in the thin sun of a Minnesota fall. No one could keep up with him, and by the time we were in high school together, I always knew that if things weren't going well, all I had to do was just let it fly long and he'd go get it, time after time. Until that day, when my panicky failure had the whole team near collapse.

"C'mon," White Deer said to me, there on the field. "Me and you, pal." And he pushed me toward the tunnel that led back to the locker rooms.

"The Ghost Dance," he said. "It will make us strong. Here." And he took my hands in his and raised them up high. "Now. Dance."

And we did, with the last few seconds of the half winding down and Jesuit marching in for another score, we danced.

Legs kicking high, bent over and then standing tall, throwing our arms out, howling in the echoing confines of that tunnel, we danced.

It's all part of the local lore, now. The stories about the Dance and how the team saw it as the players and coaches came in for halftime. How it affected them. How we came storming back.

It wasn't quite like that, really. Truth is, I didn't want to do the Dance, but White Deer had me in thrall. He was a senior, older, so much wiser, more talented, a brilliant student, a golden future, scholarship offers certain to roll in. To a sixteen-year-old junior quarterback, White Deer was everything. He could have asked me to jump off a cliff with him, and I might have done it.

But all he asked me to do was dance, and then to win that game, to hand off and read defenses and to throw—oh, my, to throw. And so I did in the second half. One touchdown. Another. Another after that.

And then, in the final moments, the pass of my life and The Catch.

We were on their forty, fifteen seconds left, third down, and he ran what looked like a sideline route for a first down. I pumped, he broke for the end zone, and I let it fly.

He caught it fully outstretched, fingers embracing the ball as he fell toward the earth, both feet in bounds, touchdown, game winner, state champs.

I never saw it. I was hit just as I let go, and was flat on my back, staring at a gray sky that spit rain, as he made the catch.

Greatest play of my life, biggest moment of my life, and I never even saw it. As he was running to his pinnacle, I was falling backward, falling to the ground.

A year later my shoulder was separated for the second time, my left knee was in ruins, and football was over, the glory gone.

I felt sorry for myself until his mother called. White Deer had chosen the military instead of college, had said it was something he wanted to do, needed to do. He told me before he left for advanced infantry training that the fighting over there was the game that really mattered. I agreed, planned to do the same thing after I graduated. College, we figured, could wait.

But now he was coming home, his mother said. He'd been in a firefight in Quang Nai province, and when the choppers showed up to evac them, he'd been the last guy to back out. He'd been laying down covering fire, then finally run for the chopper's salvation, running in those bounding strides, when he stepped in the wrong place.

He lived, minus a leg, but the game was over.

We spent a lot of time together at first, but then I slowly lost track of White Deer over the years. I went off to college at the University of Minnesota, my patriotic fervor having changed to skepticism about the war. I drifted into journalism, wrote for the *Minnesota Daily,* marched in demonstrations, got caught up in the energy of the times.

And White Deer was back home in Mankato. He tried the junior college for a while, did fine, but dropped out, left for California, as I heard it. We wrote for a time, and then even that slipped away.

I heard stories about him from time to time, and even saw his name in a newspaper story or two—picketing here or staging a sit-in there. He was part of that angry group of Native Americans that spent the late sixties and early seventies reminding us all of what we'd done to their people.

And he was effective. He walked without a cane, but there was a definite limp, and he used that, I thought, to make his point about being a veteran, a hero, who just wanted his people to be treated fairly. "After one hundred years of cheating," I heard him say in one TV sound bite, "we just want fairness. That's all. Just fairness."

For him, it culminated in a violent confrontation in South Dakota. Shots were fired, people on both sides died. Gregory White Deer got fifteen years pretty much just for being there. I never heard from him when he was inside.

Then, last year, more than twenty years since the last time I'd talked with him, I saw White Deer again. He was signing books at the Oaks Mall in Santa Barbara as I was walking into the B. Dalton there to see if they still had any copies of my newest book on the shelves— an exposé of yet another Hollywood star's life. It wasn't exactly the kind of journalism I'd had in mind back at the U, but it paid the bills and then some.

I walked right by him, not noticing the long black hair, the aquiline nose, the smile.

"Robert?" he asked. "Robert MacAdam?"

And I looked, and it all came back, was all still there in its own way, the handsome face with the high cheekbones weathered now from the intervening years. But the smile was still there, the handshake firm, the friendship back in moments.

I waited until he could take a break, and then we got caught up a bit on things. He didn't talk much about the prison years, said he'd done his time, gotten an early release, and got on with life.

His mother had died while he was in prison—cancer, and his father had drifted into trouble and then drifted away; White Deer didn't know where he was.

Part of the terms of White Deer's early release was teaching the kids on the reservation, and he found himself liking that. He liked being able to teach the kids how to read, how to learn, how to find out about their own history, to help them know themselves by knowing their past.

He got back to the junior college and did fine there, and then, in his thirties, he picked up a bachelor's, followed that up with a master's, and now was teaching English at a junior college in South Dakota. Things were going well for him. He was happily married, with two kids. He was, he said, past the hard times.

And he was writing, of course. Had sold some short stories, a handful of poems, and now this book, *Rough Feather*. I bought a copy there, had him sign it, and took it home to read.

And it was a brilliant little thing—slim, taut. It started with sad honor and ended with pain.

It told the story of a dying, hungry Sioux warrior who tracks a lone buffalo for days through a freezing Dakota winter, finally kills it, and then brings the hide and meat home to his family, to find them dead, the village burned, its people slaughtered by the soldiers of Major Samuel Whitside and their deadly Hotchkiss guns, which fired explosive shells for miles at a rate of a shell a second.

A few nights later, White Deer and I met for a beer, and continued our conversation. His book was selling, his teaching position brought in a steady income. White Deer was happily married, had two young kids—he was a success story by any standards.

He and his family lived in a farmhouse outside of Mankato, just a few miles down the road, really, from the high school stadium where he'd made The Catch.

We even talked about that, about the play that still had the two of us famous in one small Minnesota town, about the Dance.

He smiled to recall that day.

"It was stupid, you know, to waste the Dance like that. It was blasphemy. I caught all sorts of hell for it from the tribal council."

"Really? You never told me that."

"I never brought it up, figured you might not understand."

"Understand what?"

"You know the history of the Ghost Dance. It offered a way out, a solution, to those poor people when the cavalry seemed to want nothing except slaughter."

"Those were superstitious times," I said, "and desperate people. Sad, to think that a dance could save them." I shook my head.

He laughed. *"They* were superstitious. How about you?"

"What do you mean?"

"Oh, Bob, that dance was something I cooked up on the spur of the moment. I had to figure out some way to get your head back in the game, to get your confidence back up. I came up with the Ghost Dance."

I could only laugh. It had meant so much to me, and now it turned out to be a sham. I shook my head. "Jesus, Greg, I never realized, it just never occurred to me."

"Well, hell, Bob," he said. "Like I said, that's what the dance was for, even a hundred years ago."

He smiled. "You know, the Ghost Dance did save those people back then, in a way," White Deer said. "It gave them something to hang on to while the inevitable happened. It gave them something to do, something tangible, real, you know what I mean? A focus, a way to take action against enemies you can't hope to defeat. It was the same thing for you, really. See what I mean?"

And I could only nod my head and laugh at myself. I'd grown up with White Deer, a couple of years older and wiser, always taking care of me. The Dance shouldn't have surprised me.

And then we went on with other things, he listening to me bring him up to date on my life.

I had things in reasonable order just then, so I could share in the warmth of success hard attained. I'd spent years getting there.

After years of working in newspapers I'd finally broken away ten years before with the first biography. Now I had my third book on the shelves, and if they were nasty little exposés, at least they were books. I'd finally realized I wasn't going to write *Moby Dick.*

There were no kids, but my wife seemed to like me, which I thought a step in the right direction after the previous two tries. I could write the books anywhere, once I'd done the research, so we spent weeks at a time at our little cottage in Scotland and the rest of the year in our Florida home.

I had discovered Scotland, I told him, during my first trip abroad, back with the first wife. Despite my last name I hadn't ever paid any attention to the place, but once I was there it seemed to resonate for me somehow. I felt at home, as if I belonged. Walking down Princes Street in Edinburgh, or hiking through the Grampians up near Pitlochry, I found a place that offered me a past, a sense of history, of belonging to something. I loved the place for that, despite the miserable weather, the poverty.

The people, their past—that echoed right through me. I started going back every year, first for a week or two and then, as the years went by, for longer and longer stretches. I made friends, good ones, and discovered more about myself each time I went. I asked him to come share it with me sometime. He said he would.

It wasn't all warm and fuzzy, of course. White Deer, gentle Gregory White Deer, had made a lot of enemies over the years; being outspoken carries a price. There were those who thought his book was trying to start a new Indian War, and told him so in long, hate-filled letters. There were those who told him that he needed to be stopped. He got phone calls late at night, death threats. It's a weird world out there.

But, for the most part, it was all a good night of getting caught up, hearing those tales that accumulate when there have been twenty lost years between friends.

And then it ended. He had a family to get back to, I had a wife. We traded addresses and phone numbers and promised to stay in touch, and then we parted, and I didn't hear from him again for almost two years.

Sally and I were in the cottage, a nice little place on the North Sea coast of Scotland, in the little village of Auchmithy, up the coast from Dundee.

The phone rang one morning about eight. It was White Deer. He was at the train station at Arbroath, the large town a few miles away. Could I come fetch him from the station? Could he stay with us a bit?

I picked him up in the morning drizzle a bit later, and found him struggling with a tragedy of immense proportions.

He had come to Scotland to get away from it for a little while, sort things through, hide, think, heal.

His wife and one of the two children had been killed in an auto accident on a frozen Dakota road. One child, the little girl, had survived.

They had all been at a meeting in Pierre, and White Deer had stayed behind as his wife left to get the children home and into bed. In the cold, with a gray sky spitting snow, something or someone had driven them off the road and down a steep shoulder into a concrete culvert.

About a half-mile from that spot, in 1874, a band of Sioux warriors had tangled with the cavalry, killing several soldiers and stealing many horses.

Two nights later the cavalry got even. The braves were gone. In the tepees were old men, women, and children. Forty-seven of them died. The small concrete marker for that "battle" is just off the road. In the winter it is mostly buried in the snowplow's drifts. The car rolled after hitting the culvert, and came to rest with the collapsed roof against the old marker.

The police said his wife might have fallen asleep, or just lost control.

White Deer thought otherwise; he figured someone had set out to drive them off the road at just that spot, the only place for miles in that prairie where driving off the road could bring injury and death.

The police, he said, admitted it was possible. But they had nothing to go on, no witnesses, no dramatic tire tracks in the snow, nothing.

It was a time of insane chaos for Gregory White Deer. Only his daughter was left, a four-year-old, staying now with grandparents back in the states while White Deer tried to make sense of this, of his life, somehow.

Was it murder, an accident, drunken hunters, or vengeful men full of hate?

Did it matter? They were dead, and there was blood on that place again, blood frozen into the soil.

He told me all this in bursts of anguished conversation over the next two days. He was thinking about the price that he felt his family had paid. He was thinking maybe it was time to leave the reservation, just get out of the struggle altogether.

He had a job offer he could take at a junior college down in Missouri. It would be calm there, safe. And the kids he was teaching on the reservation would be fine, he thought. He wasn't indispensable, there were other teachers, other writers.

I couldn't offer much advice, didn't dare to. I could listen as he struggled with it. I could make coffee. I could stay out of the way.

Mostly he slept, and went for long walks. From our cottage you can walk down a narrow road to the coastal cliffs, the rocky, torn edge of the North Sea. A footpath leads along the cliffs into Arbroath.

On the third night we walked that path in a light rain for the three miles or so into the town. White Deer's limp was heavy, as if the weight of all that had happened made the false leg even less dependable. Maybe, I thought, he was just tired.

But he insisted on walking it, and in an hour or so we came down off the cliffs and into town, to a quiet pub where they knew me. We had a few pints of Caledonia and tried to talk of other matters, of Scottish football or the lousy weather.

Mostly we managed to avoid his pain, but the tragedy was always there, of course, in the background, coloring everything, hovering behind us as we tried not to notice.

At eleven the time bell rang and we started our walk back, hunched against the cold, sharp wind that would be in our face the whole way

There is a long strand of beach there, and at the end of it the path starts climbing to the cliffs. At the first promontory, once the path has risen to the top of the cliffs, there is a small ruin, a souterrain, dug into the soil, lined with stones.

We stopped there, stood on the edge of that place, and looked out to the sea. It was late, but a lone fishing boat worked its way toward the harbor. Life in this place was still hard, still deadly, for some.

The souterrain was built by the Picts who had once ruled this land, I told White Deer. Proud, ancient warriors, they had stopped the advance of Rome in the second century. This souterrain was a lookout post, keeping an eye on the sea and the roads to the south, a place to watch for the legions of Septimius Severus, coming up from Roman Britain.

The Romans never conquered the Picts. Instead, Septimius built a fort farther south, near Edinburgh, and that place marked the edge of the empire. The Picts, hidden away in their hills and rocky shorelines, were too difficult to dig out, their land too poor to conquer.

It was, I told White Deer, the pinnacle of Pictish Scotland. When

Rome collapsed and the legions withdrew, the Picts, victorious in battle but culturally doomed, intermarried with the Scots, lost a few key battles, withdrew into the Highlands, and then, in time, disappeared entirely. There had been no Picts for a thousand years.

He shook his head, "An entire people, their culture, their lives . . ."

"Gone," I said. "There are a few archaeological sites. Some burial mounds, a shield here, a sword there . . ."

"Gone," he said.

And then he walked over to the cliff edge, stood there against the wind, raised his arms out to embrace the wind and rain, and cried out in anguish.

I wanted to help him, somehow, wanted to know how to give support, lend strength.

And so I started the dance.

I am not sure why. I didn't think about it, I just walked over to him, took his hands and raised them high, and started to dance, slowly at first, and then faster.

He fought me at first, in tears, then just shook his head, started dancing too, then, laughing and crying, went into it with increasing energy, the one knee kicking high, the artificial leg holding him steady to the ground.

I looked up at the gray sky for a moment, smiling myself, feeling the cold rain on my face, lost in the dance.

And when I looked back to White Deer, there was another one who had joined us in the dance, a vague figure in the mist, tall, thin, dressed, I thought, in worn leather, but with a small round shield on his left arm and a short sword in the right.

White Deer saw the figure, too, and raised his fist to him as the dance progressed. The figure raised the sword in return salute, and danced with us, the three of us there in the darkness and the cold rain, the shattering blows of the North Sea angry against the cliff below us, the lights of Arbroath dim in the distance.

We danced. To those who were gone, to extinction, to finality. To life. To going on. To remembering. To all that, we danced.

And then the figure was gone, the rain falling harder, the waves pounding the shore below. The fishing boat, I saw, had made it in to safe harbor.

White Deer and I didn't say much as we walked on back to the house. We didn't tell my wife about the dance, or the figure in the mist.

A few days later Gregory White Deer left, back to the States, back to South Dakota, back to his daughter who needed him, and to teaching her and the other children on the reservation how to read, to learn, to know. Teaching them to remember. He planned to let his little girl live with her grandparents until he was sure it was safe.

He promised to stay in touch. I promised to visit.

It was a strange morning when I took him to the station. Sunshine poured down, it was warm enough for shirtsleeves. I waited with him until the 125 for King's Cross came through, shook his hand, and then watched the train pull out and head south toward London and his flight home.

Then I drove to the car park near the base of the cliffs, got out, and climbed the steep path to the ancient stones of the souterrain.

I stood atop them and looked out to sea. There, a mile out from the town, was a boat, heading out to the fishing grounds.

The same one? It doesn't matter, I suppose.

And then, with White Deer gone, I walked back down to my car, put it into gear, and drove home to my wife.

Turtle Woman
Gerald Hausman

Along time ago there was a girl named Beth who lived in a country of dark woods. Beth's mother died while giving birth. Her father, a logger in that country, had been killed by a falling tree when the girl was still a child. But she had a grandmother, a solitary old Iroquois woman, who lived a life of simple seclusion by a lake in the north. After she moved in with her grandmother, all that remained of Beth's former life were a few of her father's last possessions, among them a pair of high-laced logger's boots. These things the old lady carried up to the attic and stored with a lot of other family belongings from the past.

When Beth came to live with her grandmother, she found herself in another world. The old lady enjoyed smoking a pipe on her porch, and she was often found there, puffing contentedly, surrounded by cud-chewing goats and the neighbor's children, who liked nothing better than to ask her questions about catching woodcocks, making pets of newts, and why the maidenhair fern uncurls like a party whistle in the spring.

This new world that Beth lived in was much like a dream. Grandmother, as Beth always called her, seldom lost her temper, and she kept herself and those she cared for in a gentle world of secret thought, which, in summer, was like the spiderweb that pulses in the wind and, in winter, like the glaze of ice around a birch tree when the sun catches it and makes it glare.

Beth had learned from the day her father died that nothing stays. When she looked into Grandmother's eyes, she saw that one day the scrawny boys who always visited on the porch would go away and not return and the squirrels and jays they fed would come no more. She knew this as surely as she knew that Grandmother was preparing to go on the long journey her mother and father had already taken.

One morning when Grandmother seemed weaker and more distant than she had ever been before, Beth drew away from her. The time has come, she thought. But Grandmother just pulled on the ceiling ladder that led to the dusty attic. For most of that day the old lady stayed up there stroking the soles of her dead son's logger's boots. Beth would not go up those stairs, but she heard Grandmother singing softly, and she knew this was a death song.

A day or so later, Grandmother spent several hours walking in a pine thicket near the cabin. When she returned, she told Beth, "I feel my bones are just waking up after a long sleep." Beth didn't know what to say, so she said nothing. Grandmother saw Beth draw away and said, "Child, child. Promise me that when I'm gone, you will look for me." And her ancient eyes gazed in the direction of the pine trees.

"Where I go is a good place. Someday you will meet me there, but you must not be surprised if I do not look as I do now. For after I am gone, I will be something else, just as the winter is different from the spring. When I am gone, I would like you to bury me in that apple tree in the meadow. I planted that when I was your age, and now it is the chosen place for these old bones to rest."

Just before the old woman passed away, she seemed to see into another world. Toward the end, she sang herself to sleep at night, and in the morning Beth woke up to her sudden, strange, flutelike laughter.

There wasn't a ceremony because Beth didn't know one. She carefully folded Grandmother into her most cherished blanket and carried her out to the apple tree. Then, one inch at a time, Beth hoisted her up into the first outspread branches and left her there with a poem: "Come, my friends, and dry your tears, for I will return when Christ appears."

Beth thought this little verse was something good. But she could summon no tears. There was Grandmother, asleep in the old apple tree. What difference would it make, she wondered, if Christ appeared? What could he do to bring her grandmother back to life? And even if he could, why would she wish to return? Hadn't she said she felt herself changing, turning into something?

In the time that passed after Grandmother's death, Beth saw many things in her sleep. For a while her dreams were wild and strange. One night Grandmother came to her bedside with eyes flickering like fire coals, her face like a turtle's eyelids, droopy and full of folds. Beth saw her grandmother float about the room. The old woman's feet were webbed.

When she woke next morning, Beth got out of bed and walked barefoot to the cold island of pine at the meadow's edge. Here the

woods were dense, and there was little sun to light the way. She remembered the path taken by Grandmother through the pine trees. As
she walked along, the briars caught on the hem of her nightdress.

A dark wandering it was, with Beth half asleep as she wound
uncertainly through the wet wood. Somewhere the sun was up in
the sky, warming the day. But where she walked, the woods were as
dark as a night with no moon. Finally she grew tired. Then she sat
upon a stump and listened to the faint sobbing noise of the saw-
whet owls. She felt empty inside. She had proved nothing. How far
was she from the cabin? She didn't know. Nor did she know what
time it was, for the pines grew so close they wove a tapestry of needles that kept out the sun.

She noticed that she could barely see herself. I am a shadow, she
thought, a shadow shedding shadows in the gloom, a little girl hunting
a ghost in the ghostly woods.

Then she stood up and began to walk home. That day something
terrible closed between herself and the world. Something like a door
that dismisses the sun as it closes on the day. Somehow she knew there
would be no more dreams.

Beth chose to live the rest of her life alone in Grandmother's cabin.
Time passed slowly, as it must for all who live by themselves. Day-
dreaming at the window during the long winter rains, she marked
those hours on earth that mattered only to her. When weather was
suitable, she worked the garden, cut firewood, fed goats, repaired
cedar shakes. But she lived so much by herself that after a time there
was nothing she needed or wanted; she got on with her life, such as it
was, and passed from girlhood to womanhood without a trace of regret. For it was all the same to her whether she was here or there,
happy or sad. The boundary of her world was the ring of trees that
circled the meadow.

If she tried, Beth could remember the road to town, a place to
which she was completely indifferent. There were little boys she had
once known who long ago had come to visit Grandmother. Though
they were grown now, perhaps one or two remained who remembered
her, but if they should have met, gathering wood in the forest, they
would have given no sign. For Beth's eyes held the world and all
things in it at one remove, and visitors to her part of the forest saw
only a woman whose mysterious emptiness was nothing less than for-
bidding. She was one who lived apart and liked it that way.

The years fed upon the seasons. Summers flushed into autumns,
winters melted into springs. Beth had begun to get older, and in the
lines of her face there was a softness that was not there before. There
was a melting in her, as well as the weather, that sometimes kept her

captive. Without knowing it, she slipped into that time of life when there seems to be no urgency about anything. She dreamed down the days, the seasons, until they were one to her. She was like an icicle, losing itself, one drop at a time, melting into nothing.

Nights when she slept, she did not dream. When sour wet leaves were sucked down the chimney in a sudden draft, she didn't know it. If the attic walked on itself when a strong wind came, she slept through it.

Yet there was a night, in the darkness before dawn, when a voice spoke to her. It was a voice that moved on water, a voice that came from within a cave.

"Child, have you forgotten?" the voice said.

Beth knew the voice.

"Have you gotten old?" it asked.

The voice floated on the glistening soft current of Beth's dream.

"Are you ready to meet me now?" the voice asked. Then it departed, curved in upon itself, and when Beth woke, clutching her bedclothes, she heard the rain running slantwise across the shingles.

She was sitting up in bed, staring emptily at the wall. Wasn't there something she had to do? Somewhere, in the back of her mind, waves were lapping and saying—do, do, do—like a wooden boat knocking against a dock in the wind.

She became absorbed in the rocking of the waves, rocking, rocking as she was taken back to a time in memory—to something in the attic, to a pair of old boots.

One step at a time, she climbed the ancient rungs. When her head was level with the hole in the ceiling, Beth felt something irresistible lift her into the dusty attic.

In the dim light she made out the objects of her infancy: childhood scribblings on white birchbark paper were rolled up like scrolls. There was a broken sled, a pair of sprung snowshoes. But her dead father's logging boots were gone. In their place was a pair of doeskin moccasins that cast a cone of light into the dust and decay of the attic.

Beth reached out and touched the moccasins. They felt almost warm to the touch. Then she took them and went stiffly down the ladder. On the wide plank pine floor of the cabin, crouched in her faded nightdress, Beth put on the moccasins. They were a perfect fit—and the moment they were on her feet, she felt young again, her blood sang with life. She closed her eyes. In her mind she saw a great bear with a fish in its paws. The fish slapped its tail, came free of the bear. Then a fishhawk fell from the sky like a dark bolt and took the fish in its talons. But, again, the fish flapped its tail and broke free, this time falling back into the stream where it was born. What this little moment of dreamtime meant, Beth did not know. But she saw the fish moving freely in the stream, safe from the two hunters of death.

"I am not going to die," she heard herself say, and then: "Oh, Grandmother. Oh, where . . . ?"

The voice from the water said, "Child, do you feel your bones waking?"

"Yes," she said to herself. "Yes, I do."

Then she felt so young, so perfect in her bones, that she wanted to run across the meadow. She wanted to throw her arms to the Sun Father and shout her love. And she did—she ran out into the pine trees, smelling sweetly of sunrise, and she dreamed she was a girl again, splashing in the water of the lake, swimming like the fish she had seen behind her eyelids, swimming toward the deep dawning water of the lake.

"I'm changing," she heard herself say, but it was not her voice, it was the water's. Then she was swimming under the voice. She was riding the back of a great turtle, her fingers digging into the moss of lost summers. "Hold on, child," the water-voice said as it took her from one dream to another into her next life.

Paul Bunyan Dreams

Alan Rodgers

The day Paul Bunyan turned sixty, he and his great ox Babe lay down in the cradle between two mountains. Paul Bunyan wasn't a brooder, and he wasn't much on sleeping, either, but the year was 1957, and Paul Bunyan wasn't happy anymore.

He hated what he saw when he looked out across America, and everywhere he looked he saw it—even from here in his place between the mountains he could see everything from the Rockies to the Atlantic. It was the America he'd made with his own great hands, but it wasn't what he'd meant to make, and it didn't look the way he'd meant it to, and the more he looked, the more the vision made him brood.

"I never meant it to come out like this, Babe," Paul Bunyan said.

The blue ox snorted.

"All these cities! All these farms! There's no place for woodsmen on this land."

Babe looked away without saying a word, but it didn't matter. Paul Bunyan understood what the ox wasn't saying. And he knew that Babe was right, no matter how much he hated it.

As a man lives longer than a mouse and an elephant longer than a man, Paul Bunyan's life rolls through decades the way ours roll through days. So it was that sometime in February 1958, Paul Bunyan—still brooding in the cradle of the mountains—drifted off to sleep.

He didn't sleep well. How could he have slept well, with the nation in such a state?

As he slept he dreamed. He'd never dreamed before, but he dreamed now—dreamed a nightmare dream where Thunderbird haunted him, watching fatefully from a distance always just beyond the periphery of his vision.

When Paul Bunyan turned to face him, Thunderbird would vanish.

Most people wouldn't know what to think if Thunderbird haunted their dreams that way. But Paul Bunyan knew Thunderbird, and he recognized that fretful totem hanging over his heart. Of course he recognized him! The Sioux themselves had told Paul Bunyan all about Thunderbird in 1907. And Paul had known before that, too—for when he was an infant, Thunderbird had found him in his swaddling clothes, playing jinx with trees and boulders, and swooped down on the defenseless mountain infant to prey on him as a hawk would strike a prairie dog.

Baby Paul rose to his feet and bellowed out a defiant infant challenge at the terrible god-bird—and Thunderbird turned away from his attack.

Thunderbird did not turn because he feared the fight (for Thunderbird fears nothing, not even his own death, which he has foreseen and eagerly awaits) or because he knew he was the great infant's master, for Thunderbird has no vanity, and does not imagine himself the master of those whose stature is as mythic as his own.

Paul Bunyan the infant bellowed out his defiant challenge and Thunderbird saw his bravery—and the god-bird could not help but respect and admire such bravery in one so young. And what is respect if not the greatest root of love? Thunderbird spared Paul Bunyan because he loved him. (Remember that: somewhere down inside, it is the secret of the world.)

In Paul Bunyan's dream, Thunderbird who loved him menaced him, lurking where Paul Bunyan couldn't see. Paul Bunyan tried to call to him, *Thunderbird, Thunderbird, why have you come to me?* But in his dream his throat was silent and he could not speak.

He woke up screaming, *"Thunderbird!"*

The mountains shook with the sound of his scream, but Thunderbird did not answer.

Paul Bunyan cleared the sleep away from his eyes, and saw that the world had changed again while he lay sleeping. The giant was never afraid, but what he saw that day left him shivering and terrified of things he'd never thought to fear.

Because the world had passed him by.

It was 1994, and everything Paul Bunyan had ever meant to the world was gone and changed and changed again. When he looked out across the land, he saw that there were woods again, woods and trees and mountains, virgin mountains like the ones he'd conquered as a boy.

Oh, it wasn't all like that—in the nearness of the plains everything was farmland, corn and wheat and oats for miles on end. But in the east the farms were fallen back to seed, consumed by forest, and the towns—even the cities!—were crumbling. Almost all the factories that had made Paul Bunyan feel irrelevant now lay silent—they were empty, shell-dead, manufactured carcasses, ghosts of what they'd been.

Babe was waking, too. When the blue ox looked at the land, he trembled.

"Not good," Babe said.

Paul Bunyan knew the ox was right, but he argued with him anyway.

"It *is* good, Babe," he said uncertainly. "There's a place for us now. There's work to do! Woods to cut, cities to rebuild."

The ox gestured at a city in Pennsylvania that lay seemingly in ruins. "Look again," he said. "Nobody cares."

The giant looked at the ruins, and what he saw dismayed him. "You're right," he said. "No one wants those towns. No one needs the timber in those woods." He sounded very sad. He kept looking into the east, hoping to see some sign that Babe was wrong, but there was nothing. After a while he shuddered.

His tremor made the mountains quake.

"I need a closer look," Paul Bunyan said. He started to get to his feet, then noticed the ski resort someone had built on his left arm in the 1970s—and paused. Paul Bunyan hated to break things. He was a lumberman, a builder, not a destroyer. He lifted the chalet off his arm carefully, set it back down on the mountainside as gently as he could. But being careful wasn't much use; he still pretty near wrecked the place.

Not that it mattered. The ski chalet was insured, and it was empty—it was high summer, and there'd been no one in the ski resort since the last snow melted in April.

The blue ox stood, shook away the pine woods that'd grown across his back. And followed Paul Bunyan across the Midwest.

Somewhere just past Pittsburgh a storm came up, and there was thunder. It was night by then, and Paul Bunyan thought maybe it was time to hunker down to weather the storm, but something stopped him.

Maybe it was the Thunderbird dream he'd had in the seventies that inspired him to walk into the thickness of the storm, or maybe it was just cussedness. Does it matter? East of Pittsburgh the farmland of the Midwest gave way to forest—a forest as thick and primordial as the first woods the giant and the blue ox cut when they were young.

These are woods, Paul Bunyan thought. *Woodsmen like me need woods like these.* That was no reason to be sad, was it?

But he was sad. Where the woods should have filled him with joy, they gave him nothing but dread. The promise of the thriving, teeming forest was a lie, and he knew it—he didn't know why, because he didn't understand the change that had come upon the nation, but he knew that it was nothing good that had made the people abandon their land.

The whole idea depressed Paul Bunyan more than he could say.

The giant and the ox were deep in the northeastern wilderness now, and the thunder was everywhere. Lightning struck them again and again, but it didn't hurt them because the elements of nature never could.

Thunderbird, Paul Bunyan thought. And almost as if summoned, Thunderbird appeared at the top of the sky, soaring toward them. The ancient spirit dropped through the air like a stone on wings, quickly, deliberately, until it came to a sudden stop in the air before the giant's face.

Thunderbird hung there on the wind, staring Paul Bunyan in the eye.

"Leave us alone, Thunderbird," Paul Bunyan said. "I don't feel like talking to no totems."

Thunderbird glowered ominously. He didn't go away.

"I tell you, Thunderbird," the giant said, his great, booming voice all strident with insistence, "this is not my day. I woke up today and saw the world had passed me by—I'm in a mood and I'm fit to be tied. This ain't the day to make an avocation of Paul Bunyan."

Thunderbird scowled.

"You can't imagine what this is like, Thunderbird," he said. "Go *away.*"

Thunderbird bristled; lightning flashed and blazed around them as the great totem shrieked with rage.

Paul Bunyan didn't even notice.

"Run about your business, huh? I hear they been looking for a rainstorm in Nevada."

Thunderbird shrieked again, and now he whispered—and when he whispered his voice was the rain and the wind and thunder rumbling in the distance. *It's you who can't imagine, giant.*

Paul Bunyan's hair like to stand on end when he heard that voice, but he hardly even noticed how it scared him. He was too angry. *"What?"* he demanded, shouting so forcefully that the rumble of his voice set off an earthquake in the Sierra Madre. "What do you mean by *that?*"

Your time is gone—your people have forgotten you. Thunderbird laughed, and the sky roiled around them. *You might as well be dead.*

"You *lie*," the giant said. He raised his fist and shook it at the bird. "Admit it!" he demanded. "Admit you lied!"

I never lie.

"You're wrong!" Paul Bunyan said. "I'd like to know who you think you are, mister! I'd like to know where you get off!"

Thunderbird fell silent for a long moment—then opened his great wings and sailed into the sky. Paul Bunyan shook a threatening fist after him, but the totem ignored it.

The rain eased; the wind died down.

Paul Bunyan stood in the dying rain for the longest time, shaking his fist after the soaring totem and swearing printable oaths. Maybe he thought Thunderbird would return to face him if he found a challenge angry enough to vex him, or maybe the giant was only venting spleen.

Either way, it took Paul Bunyan the longest time to notice that Babe was trying to get his attention.

The blue ox had been trying to get Paul Bunyan's attention for a while, in fact—almost from the moment Thunderbird had appeared to them.

"Paul?" Babe said.

The giant wheeled around angrily to face the ox. *"What?"* he demanded.

"He knows."

Paul Bunyan scowled. "What do you mean? What does he know?"

The ox didn't answer right away, and when he did answer he chose his words carefully, answering the giant's question with a question of his own. "Where are they?"

"Where are who?"

Again, the ox hesitated. "They're gone."

"Make sense, Babe."

The ox snorted. "They're gone, Paul. He's lonely."

And suddenly it came to Paul Bunyan just exactly what it was the great blue ox was saying. Dark veins swelled along the sides of his vast face; his eyes bulged wide. He tried to respond, but all he could manage was a sputter.

"Just like you, Paul."

Paul Bunyan bellowed angrily and stomped off into the hills.

The ox didn't follow him. Babe knew when it was best to leave well enough alone.

■ ■ ■

When Paul Bunyan came back he looked shaken, even wounded—as though something the ox had said had hurt him to his core.

"What's your point, Babe?" the giant asked.

"No point at all," the ox said defensively. He was lying, of course; they both knew that. But what did it matter? There wasn't any point in saying more.

The rain started in again just before they reached the Poconos. It started out gentle—easy summer rain like a cool shower drizzling down from God—but it didn't stay that way. The force of the downpour grew steadily, and kept growing. Now it was a heavy rain; now driving sheets of water like an ocean falling on the land. When the deluge grew too intense for either the giant or the ox to see where they were going, it suddenly relented—and now the stinging spray became a heavy rain of fat wet drops. Lightning flickered back and forth across the sky; Thunderbird whispered in the clouds.

"He's come back," the giant said. "I knew he would. I said he'd come back, didn't I?" He hadn't said anything like that, and they both knew it. But the ox held his tongue.

"Thunderbird!" the giant shouted. "Here, Thunderbird!"

Now the totem circled above them like a vulture wheeling over its dying meal; now, slowly, slowly, he descended to hover before the giant and the ox.

"You're like I am, aren't you, bird?" Paul Bunyan asked. He raised his hand, reached up—touched Thunderbird's beak.

Seven bolts of black lightning smote him as he touched it. Paul Bunyan didn't flinch.

"I cleared this land," Paul Bunyan said. "Then the farmers came with diesel plows and planted everywhere. Then there was nothing left to do."

Those farms are forests now, Thunderbird said. Thunder sounded all around them; lightning crackled fiery in the air. *The world is never done. There's always more to do.*

"I know that," Paul Bunyan said. "It bothers me."

Thunderbird looked at him steadily, measuring the giant's heart.

The giant shrugged. "I thought I made a difference," he said. "I thought I made my country! And now it's like I made nothing at all."

Thunderbird cawed mournfully; lightning blasted a great hole in the mountain, sundering the forest that grew on the mountainside. When the air was clear, they stood in a smoldering clearing half a mile wide.

"It wasn't like that for me," Paul Bunyan said. "My people *loved* me. I was their hero!"

Thunderbird's ebony eyes went wide with indignation. He screamed again, enraged, and once again their surroundings trembled.

But now there was nothing to destroy.

"Oh," Paul Bunyan said. And the melancholy came over him again, and he felt like he might cry, and because the giant could not bear to have anyone see that, he hung his head in shame and turned to walk away.

Thunderbird circled above him three times, then descended to perch upon the giant's shoulder. Thunderbird is great, and Thunderbird is mighty, and someone once told a tale that nothing but the night could ever carry him. Maybe that's true. But if it is, then Paul Bunyan is greater than the night—and is it any wonder? Paul Bunyan is a mountain made into a man; his shoulders dwarf the hills.

"Leave me alone, Thunderbird," Paul Bunyan said.

Thunderbird didn't go away. Instead he flapped his wings and shrilled as thunder sounded in the distance.

The blue ox looked up at Paul Bunyan worriedly.

"It isn't time, is it, Babe?" the giant asked.

Babe shook his head.

The giant sighed. "You're right again, Babe. You're always right." He sounded disgruntled and depressed.

They wandered north till now they walked among the Adirondack Mountains, and the Adirondacks were emptier and more abandoned than the Sierra Nevada had been the day that Paul was born. The giant found himself a crook between two abandoned hills and lay back to rest his eyes.

Thunderbird still perched on his shoulder. He flapped his wings three times as Paul Bunyan settled into the ground, but he didn't loose his grip on the giant's collarbone.

Not for an instant.

"Lay down beside me, Babe," Paul Bunyan said, "and tell me what you know."

The blue ox hunkered down beside the giant, but he didn't say a word. After a while they both fell back to sleep.

Neither of them dreamed this time. Maybe Thunderbird dreamed. Who can say? Thunderbird is an enigma. It may be that he did not even sleep.

When Paul Bunyan woke again, the world had changed all over. Places that should've been cold were warm, and places that should have been dry were wet. He looked north and saw the Kansas wheat-fields stretching to the Arctic Ocean; he looked west and saw the deserts and the prairies turned to gardens. Some crazy people out in California had filled Death Valley with a lake.

Thunderbird was still with him, perched on his shoulder. When Paul Bunyan looked to see what he was doing, the god-bird blinked three times, but he didn't say a word.

"I don't see the people," Paul Bunyan said. "Where are the cities? Where are the towns?"

Thunderbird grinned; there was a cruel look in his eye. *You'll never learn,* he whispered on the wind, and maybe he was right, because Paul Bunyan couldn't imagine why he'd say such a thing.

The ox Babe grunted, nodded south and east. Paul Bunyan looked in those directions—and saw the ruins of Boston and New York. There wasn't much to see, but they were there if you knew to look for them—broken and eroded, the cities' foundations grown over with ivy.

"It's the end, isn't it, Babe?" His voice broke up a little when he said those words, and maybe he cried. There's no way to know for sure; Paul Bunyan would never admit if he ever shed a tear. And if he did, the totem and the ox would've looked the other way. "The last of them are gone. All my people, dead."

The ox grunted. Shook his head. "Look again," he said. "Look deep into the woods."

And to his amazement Paul Bunyan saw that there were people scattered in cabins all across the land—living like Indians deep in the woods. And those were farms, way out there on the plains, weren't they?

"What's the world coming to?" Paul Bunyan asked. "What use is a woodsman in a place like this?"

Thunderbird laughed, shaking the sky.

"Cut it out," Paul Bunyan said.

Babe was giving him that cold-eyed look again, like he was still ignoring the obvious. But Paul Bunyan was damned if he knew what that could be.

"I hate this," Paul Bunyan said. "I'm going back to sleep."

Thunderbird screamed, sky broke open.

No!

"You can't run from the world forever, Paul," Babe said. Paul Bunyan's eyes went wide with astonishment. Babe never talked like that! So many words! When the blue ox spoke he measured his words sparingly, as though each one of them cost him more than it was worth. But not this time. "Things are always changing. Live long enough and you have to find a new place for yourself. Some people have to do that every year."

The giant knew the ox was right, but he argued anyway. Of course he argued! He was *Paul Bunyan!* He was a myth made live, a giant of a man with a place and a purpose that was his and his alone, and there was no way he could change and still be who he was.

"I can't," Paul Bunyan said. "I was *meant* to be a woodsman. How could I walk away from my vocation?"

You have no calling now, Thunderbird whispered. *The world forgets you. No one else will care if you forget it, too.*

"No," Babe said, "that's wrong."

"What do you mean?"

But Babe didn't have the words to answer. He shrugged—which is a strange and ungainly thing for an ox to do—and sighed. "Beats me," he said.

The ox climbed up onto his feet. After a moment he wandered west to take a drink out of the lake that used to be Death Valley. Before the dust could settle behind him, Thunderbird took wing and followed him.

When he was high in the air over Lake Erie, Thunderbird looked back over his shoulder and called back to the giant. *The world moves on,* he whispered. *Sometimes you have to follow it.*

Paul Bunyan tried to argue with him—he was a myth, damn it, not a man, and legends don't bend to sway in the wind—but it wasn't any use, because Thunderbird was already too far away to hear. And after that, what else could the giant do? Paul Bunyan climbed to his feet and hurried out across the land.

He got to Death Lake Valley just a moment after Babe.

It's What You Need

Pamela Sargent

I was sitting near a stream, not knowing how I got there. Above me, the pines were murmuring among themselves, as if they knew something I didn't. Maybe they knew who I was and why I was there.

A bow was in my hand, and a tomahawk in my belt. I had possessed another weapon once, one with a long metal barrel and a handle of wood. I got up and adjusted the quiver near my waist, then began to walk downstream.

My thoughts grew more clear. I remembered my clan first, then the name of my people. My clan was the Bear, my people the Ganeagaono, the People of the Flint, the Mohawks, one of the Nations of the Hodenosaunee. I could not find a name for myself.

My bow felt solid as I gripped it, but my feet were treading air. I looked down. My moccasined feet trod the ground, but as I moved, the pine needles under my soles were still, the dirt undisturbed. I followed the stream until it widened into a small pond, and walked along the northern bank, leaving no footprints in the mud behind me, until I came to a beaver lodge.

One of the beavers swam toward me under the water, rose to the surface, slapped the water with his tail, then crawled out to sit down next to me. "Haven't seen a man that looks like you for a long time," the beaver said.

"What do you mean?" I asked.

"That kilt, those leggings and that buckskin shirt—haven't seen clothes like that lately. Hair's different, too. You don't see men shaving their heads and wearing scalplocks too often, at least not near here. Nowadays they *worry* about getting bald." The beaver picked up a stick of wood and chewed at it with his long front teeth. "Nice moccasins, though. You'd have to pay a lot to get a pair like that around here."

I looked down at my footwear. My wife had worked the deerskin with porcupine quills before sewing on the beads. "My wife made them," I said, but couldn't remember her name. That wasn't so strange, since I couldn't remember my own name, either.

"How long have you been dead, anyway?" the beaver asked.

"I don't know." Somehow I wasn't surprised to hear that I was dead. It explained why I could look contentedly at the clear waters of the pond and stream without wanting to drink, why I could recall the taste of food without feeling hungry. Despite the way I felt, fit and whole, I didn't really have a body.

"Judging by your appearance and those weapons," the beaver said, "I'd guess you died a while ago."

"I had a rifle once," I said, remembering the name of the weapon with the metal barrel.

"Apparently they didn't bury it with you. Probably gave it away to the mourners with your other belongings."

"Another warrior could have used it," I said. "We were using both rifles and bows by then, and the rifles were more deadly." I was beginning to recall my death. "Now I remember." I let out a laugh. "I was leading a raid on an Ouendot village to the north. We attacked, but they were ready for us, and captured me. One of their men had shattered my lower right arm with his war club in the hand-to-hand fighting." I stretched my arms, grateful that a ghost did not have to carry his body's wounds. "They couldn't adopt me with such an injury—I would have been useless on the warpath. So of course they had to put me to the torture."

"Perhaps they didn't bury you properly afterwards," the beaver said. "That might be why you're still wandering around."

"But they showed me the greatest respect," I replied. "I couldn't have asked for more courteous captors. In return, I was all they could have wished for in a victim. More curses and filthy names fell from my lips that day than most men speak in a lifetime—I wasn't going to play the coward for them, or beg for mercy. I sang for them even as they were cutting the flesh from my body. I didn't die until well into the night, so you can't say I disappointed them. They got their fill of fun and ceremony from me. Their chiefs ate my heart themselves." I could feel myself swelling with pride at how I had met my end. "They must have interred me with the proper rites—they wouldn't have honored me that much and then left my spirit to wander."

"I suppose not," the beaver said, "but here you are, distracting me from more important matters."

I frowned, trying to remember more. My body had been taken back to my own home; memories of haunting a feast for the dead were coming back to me. "My brothers, the men of my war party, attacked the Ouendot again. They avenged my death and carried my body back to my own village." My mouth watered as I recalled the smells of corn soup, cooked meat, and a sacrificed dog; I had enjoyed the food at that feast even while being unable to eat it.

"Well, your own people would have buried you properly." The beaver set down his stick, now stripped of its bark. "Yet here you are, wandering aimlessly about."

"I'm not the only ghost who lingered," I said. "I can recall a lot of other spirits coming with me to join war parties from time to time. We'd follow the living into battle. I felt—" The word to describe my feeling eluded me.

"Nostalgic," the beaver offered. "Longing to recapture the old days."

"And I always come back for the Feasts for the Dead. So do a lot of other ghosts, from what I can tell. Why, just last winter—" I had followed a few hunters, partly for fun and partly to help ward off any evil spirits that might cross their path. But no other ghosts had joined me, and no evil spirits had shown themselves. I had gone to be with the women when they later danced for the dead, and had seen no ghosts I knew, only the spirits of those who had died during the past year.

I sat there thinking. The beaver fidgeted, as if impatient to get back to work with his brothers and sisters. "Something is wrong," I said at last. "It seems that other ghosts stay near the living for a short while and then go on their way, while I keep coming back."

"How long has this been going on?" the beaver asked.

"I don't know."

"What were you called when you were alive?"

"I don't remember. Not that it matters now. My clan would have given that name to someone else after my death, so it isn't really my name anymore." I sighed. "Maybe if I went on the warpath one last time, took part in one last raid with the living, just to—" Suitable words were eluding me again.

"Just to get it out of your system," the beaver murmured.

"Yes."

The beaver sighed. "Well, you're not going to find a war party around here."

That was true. I knew that even as he spoke. My people had given up war long ago. Too much was coming back to me; all my fighting, even as a ghost, had been futile in the end. We Long House people had fought among ourselves before the great chief Deganawida brought our Five Nations together in peace, but we had made war on other peoples before the white men came. Instead, we might have done better by making a peace with the Ouendot and turning all our strength against our true enemies. Perhaps my death hadn't been so heroic after all. Being drawn back to the world of the living again and again might be my punishment for a useless death. I wasn't sure what angered me more—that the whites had taken most of what was once ours, or that all of us hadn't died fighting against them.

"A hunting party, then," I said to the beaver. "If I can't go on the warpath, then to hunt would be—"

"And what will you do after that?"

"I don't know."

"Probably forget everything again," the beaver said, "before you come to yourself in the land of the living and go wandering off to another Feast for the Dead or a White Dog Festival. I'd better come with you, at least until you get your bearings. Not that I don't have better things to do, but somebody has to look out for you." He suddenly began to grow, becoming a burly, bucktoothed man clothed in a thick fur coat. "It'll help if I take on a human guise. People don't often notice spirits of any kind these days, but when they do, they seem to prefer those who appear in human form. It's as if we have more authority that way. The only animals a lot of people want to talk to now are their pets."

"I wouldn't mind some company," I said. "I have the feeling it's been a while since I talked to anyone."

"Then come along." The man-beaver glanced back at his lodge, as if already missing it, then led me away from the pond.

Something was pulling at me. The man-beaver had dropped behind me, allowing me to take the lead. Was one of the living summoning me? Had someone cast a spell to bring me back? Somehow I didn't think so. Calling on the spirits of the dead could be dangerous, even for an experienced medicine man.

We walked for a while until we came to a wide trail with a black surface. Up ahead, four men were standing near a metal wagon on wheels.

We approached until we were standing no more than a few paces from them. They didn't see us at all, but I was prepared for that, remembering now that even people at Feasts and Dances for the Dead, who knew we were among them and who expected us as guests, didn't really *see* us. Even those in the medicine societies never seemed to get a really good look at us. People were getting less and less observant as time went on. About the most I could hope for was that one of these men might sense my presence somehow.

"A hunting party," I said to the man-beaver. "Maybe a war party." The men were all sturdy young fellows with black hair and sharp brown eyes, looking as if they might be almost too well-fed to move quickly along trails on foot. I gestured at the metal wagon and recalled a word I'd picked up somewhere not long ago. "A tank."

"A pickup truck," the man-beaver said. "And these guys aren't warriors or hunters. My guess is that they're on the way to the casino."

"The casino?"

"They're opening a casino near here. Bingo, roulette, whatever. Your people'll make some more money."

"From games?"

"From gambling. Don't look so long in the mouth about it. White folks will be the ones losing money."

"It isn't the same as going on the warpath," I said.

The man-beaver scowled. "It isn't the same as being unemployed and on handouts, either."

One of the men had been fiddling with the insides of the metal wagon. He put down the top, the others climbed inside, and the wagon rolled away along the trail. By now it was getting dark, and the man-beaver muttered under his breath about finding a place to stop.

We left the black trail and followed a smaller trail with deep ruts until, through the spaces between the pines, I saw some longhouses in a clearing.

"A village," I said. Had a stockade been standing around the long wooden buildings, I might have thought that I was in my old home.

"A children's summer camp," a voice said behind me. "And the season's over, so nobody's around."

I turned. A young doe was standing amid the pines, gazing at us steadily with her soft dark eyes. "They open it up again," the deer continued, "for deer-hunting season. Some hunters come up and rent the place then."

"Is that why I'm here?" I asked the man-beaver. "To join a hunting party?"

"Not likely," the deer said before the man-beaver could reply. "The season doesn't start for another month." She stretched her neck to peer more closely at me. "You look like one of the Hodenosaunee, the Long House people."

"He is. He's a Mohawk," the man-beaver told her. "He's also a ghost."

"I can see that for myself." The deer sounded vexed. "I can also tell he must have died a long time ago."

"The Ouendot tortured me to death, but I mocked them with my last words," I said proudly.

"Don't talk to me about torture," the deer said. "How would you like to be field-dressed by some hunter who doesn't know what he's doing? You should see some of the bozos we get around here these days, getting tanked up on beer and running around the woods firing at anything that isn't wearing a piece of bright orange cloth. Then some idiots shoot one of us and end up puncturing the stomach and ruining the whole carcass before they've hardly started dressing it."

"You're prey," I said. "Somebody's always going to hunt you."

"But they don't even show us the proper respect. Oh, you get some who know what they're doing, who aim at you properly and get off a clean shot, but there seem to be fewer of them these days. A fine choice people give us—we can get shot, or too many of us can starve to death instead."

"Are the winters getting that hard?" I asked.

"It isn't the winters, it's the crowding. More and more people, fools who can't even hear the words of the noisiest forest spirits, just have to build their houses on unspoiled land. Deer don't have to go far to wander into somebody's backyard nowadays."

"And people call us an ecological problem," the man-beaver muttered, "just because we dam up a few streams."

I searched myself, but could find no memory of speaking to animal spirits while I was alive. My palavers with them as a ghost hadn't been lengthy, either, as I now recalled. But I had exchanged words with other animal spirits from time to time, and couldn't remember any of them being as irritable as this deer or as grumpy as the beaver.

"Might as well stop here for the night," the man-beaver said.

"Do spirits need sleep?" I asked. This was something else I couldn't remember.

"Of course not," the man-beaver replied. "But people dream at night, and send their souls wandering outside their bodies, and if you're not sitting somewhere quietly so you can see what's going on, how are you going to get into their dreams and tell them things they should know? Not that many of them pay much attention anyway."

"I'll keep you company," the deer said. "I don't have that much to do until hunting season starts."

I turned around and saw that the deer was now wearing the form of a woman with long black braids, large dark eyes, and a deerskin dress that reached to her ankles. "You can keep a deer's form if you want," I told her. "I don't mind. Not that you aren't a fine-looking woman."

"I didn't do this for you," the woman-deer said. "It's so there's a chance of getting at least a little attention if I get into anyone's dreams. Not that people mind if animals talk to them in their dreams—it's just that they don't take talking animals very seriously."

The man-beaver let out his breath. "They don't take much of anything seriously."

We walked over to one of the longhouses and sat down in front of the door. A lake lay ahead, its surface still; Gaoh, spirit of the winds, was resting tonight. The pines all around the clearing were whispering the gossip of the day, but my companions were silent. Maybe they were waiting for some wandering spirits to come by, but I sensed that they also didn't feel like talking to me. How could I blame them? A ghost who can't remember much doesn't have a lot of stories to tell.

"Sometimes I think we'd be much better off," the woman-deer said at last, "if people suddenly disappeared from the world."

The man-beaver said, "I know what you mean." So did I, since I was remembering having felt the same way about white people. But such useless thoughts had not made those settlers vanish, and maybe these two animal spirits were wishing that my Long House people would disappear along with everyone else.

Had this world become so cruel that even the animals could no longer endure living among us, that even the gentlest wished for our end? It was enough to make me want to forget the world of the living for all time.

I got up after a while and wandered among the nearby trees. The truth was that I felt like pissing, and as soon as I had that thought, I felt as if I had already made water. It's the way of spirits, to feel a bodily desire and then have that longing satisfied at once. By now I wasn't so anxious to follow parties of warriors or hunters. I was remembering that the excitement of following warriors had faded a long time ago, and my animal companions had dampened some of my desire for the hunt. Why, then, was I still drawn back to the world, thinking that I wanted to be on the warpath before recalling that I had given that up?

At the lakeside a few geese were resting, black heads tucked under their wings. One looked up, fluttered her wings, then flapped her way to my side.

"Shouldn't you be farther south by now?" I asked.

"We're heading there," the goose said as she began to preen herself. "Autumn was a bit warmer than we expected, so we're not exactly rushing. Anyway, you'd be surprised at how many geese don't even bother to fly south anymore."

"Why is that?"

"They'd rather settle down on a golf course, or lay their eggs near some decorative body of water in one of those suburban industrial parks or office complexes." The goose stretched her neck and hissed. "Freeloaders, that's what they are, living among people instead of with other flocks. A lot of them have even forgotten the old migratory routes." This goose seemed as irritable as the woman-deer and the man-beaver.

A loud sigh from a pine tree distracted me. A spirit, a female form with slender limbs, was caught in its branches.

"Now there's a troubled soul," the goose muttered in her hoarse honking voice, "so distressed that she can't even see where she's going." I watched as the wraithlike spirit struggled, freed herself, then drifted away.

I knew then that I would have to follow that spirit.

I lifted from the ground, flying over the trees. The goose flew at my side. The spirit led us to a small brown cabin not far from the long-house; it stood at the crossroads of two blacktopped trails, at the edge of a cluster of shabby buildings decorated with lighted symbols. The spirit quickly disappeared inside the cabin, and I followed her through a half-open window, the goose alighting behind me.

A woman slouched in a chair, eyes closed, one hand around a glass. It came to me that she was drunk, and that her drunkenness had addled her spirit during its travels. I had seen drunks before during my times among the living, when I had come back to find my people herded into reservations. Drink had been the only solace for too many of them.

"I should have known," the goose said. "I've seen her spirit bumbling around in the night before, but she refuses to listen to me. She's one of your people, you know. Maybe you can talk some sense into her."

I gestured at the woman's tangled light brown hair. "How can she be one of us, with that hair?"

"Her father was white, for one thing. And, for all we know, she might have an ancestor or two that were white captives adopted by the Hodenosaunee. Inheritance can sometimes be a trickster." The goose settled on the floor, tucking her legs under her and constricting her neck. "I was going to put on a human shape, but it's just too damned much trouble. She probably won't talk to us anyway."

The goose was wrong about that. The woman suddenly opened her eyes and looked straight at me. "Who are you?" she said.

"I'm a ghost," I admitted. "I've lost my name."

"What's that damn bird doing in my house?"

"You could show a little more courtesy," the goose said. "Treat me rudely, and I may decide to shit all over your rug."

"She doesn't mean it." I shot a look of warning at the goose. "She's just mad at everything. All of the animal spirits seem angry now. Seems people have forgotten how to placate them."

"People are wiping them out, that's why," the woman said. "Some animal spirits aren't around these days. Know why? Because they're extinct. And the endangered animal spirits are even bitchier than that goose. You'd be pissed off, too, if your friends were threatened or sick or disappearing all over the place." The woman gulped from her glass. "What do you want, anyway?"

"I'm not sure." I forced myself to look into her bloodshot blue eyes. "I saw your spirit wandering around, looking lost, and felt I had to follow it here." I motioned at the glass in her hand. "You're drunk."

"You're right about that, brother."

"Whiskey's poison to our people."

"This isn't whiskey." She showed me her teeth. "It's vodka."

"Whatever it is, you shouldn't be drinking it." I drew myself up to my full height. Maybe that was why I had come among the living, to be a vision warning people to give up drink. "It was the Creator who sent a vision to the prophet Handsome Lake long ago, and told him that the Hodenosaunee must refrain from strong drink. I know our people didn't give Handsome Lake as many followers as the other Long House Nations did, but you have to admit he was right about that."

I had remembered that much of the past, and right when I needed it. The trouble was that I was also recalling other visits, when only those lost to drink had been able to see me, when I had looked for war parties and found only drunken brawlers. I had come to fear that only those flooded with strong drink could see me at all.

"Don't talk to me about Handsome Lake." The woman took another sip from her glass. "Him and his prophecies, telling men that the mothers of their wives were the root of much evil, that meddling women were the cause of much trouble. Handsome Lake was a sexist."

I grew large with rage. Handsome Lake might have had his faults, but he had given the Hodenosaunee a new way to live even while keeping the best of our old customs. "You have no right to say that," I shouted, "you, who are rotting your soul with drink. Give it up, woman! I am a ghost, I've seen the souls of drunkards in the next life, where Hanegoategeh, the Evil-Minded One, eternally mocks their weakness. Is that where you want to end up?"

She looked frightened now, eyes wide, hands shaking. She set down her glass and sagged against the chair. "I've tried," she whispered.

"Swear to give it up," I said firmly.

"I will," she said, and then passed out.

"You didn't accomplish very much," the goose said.

"What do you mean?"

"She'll forget she ever saw you by morning. The only time she ever talks to any of the spirits is when she's plastered, and she always forgets what we say. Alcoholics often have blackouts, you know. What she needs is a good twelve-step program, not a vision."

"I don't know why I came back," I said. "All I've found are angry animal spirits, and the only human beings who can see me are drunks." Maybe that was why some of my people still drank—because it was the only way they could hear the spirits who had once spoken to them.

"Go back, then," the goose said. "Stay with the dead, where you belong. You don't have to hang around here." She hopped up to the windowsill, slipped under the sash, and flew away.

I was sitting on the roof of the cabin. I didn't remember crawling out there, but had nowhere better to go at the moment, and still felt that something other than a drunken soul had brought me here. The buildings near the cabin were hidden in the darkness, their lights having gone out.

I could now see evil spirits below, lurking near the trees beyond the cabin. They were small beings with distended mouths and bulging eyes, and I knew that they were waiting to enter the house and torment the woman inside. Strong drink often gave them a gateway into people's souls. I wondered if I could ward them off, not that it would make much difference. They would come back the next time drink got the better of the woman.

"Go away," a voice said below me. "I won't let you inside. I'll sit here, and you won't get past me."

I got up and crept to the edge of the roof. A young girl was below, sitting on the steps that led up to the cabin's front door. "Try," the girl muttered, "just try. You won't get in."

The spirits gibbered and chattered, the girl chanted something at them, and then they disappeared among the trees. Perhaps tobacco had also helped to ward them off, because I could see now that the girl was holding a pipe from which a thin stream of smoke rose.

Then she looked up. "You can come down," she said. "You don't have to sit up there."

"You can see me?" I asked, surprised.

"Of course I can see you."

I leaped from the roof and landed in a crouch. "You're a ghost," she said. "I've seen others, once in a while, and spirits, too. Those in

the woods are the worst, and they usually don't stay in the forest—
they go everywhere. I've even seen them in town and along the Thru-
way. They get inside people who can't even see they're around."

I sat down next to her, and she passed the pipe to me. "I don't
really smoke," she went on. "I mean, I don't inhale or smoke cigarettes or anything. It's just that burning tobacco seems to help keep
the evil spirits away from Mom."

"Mom?"

"My mother. She gets loaded a lot."

"I told her to stop," I said, then peered at the girl more closely.
Her black hair was cut short, her eyelids were painted with a sooty
black substance, and she wore a thick woolen covering with sleeves,
but something about her made me think of my wife as she had been.

"If she doesn't stop getting faced, I'm going to move in with Dad. I
haven't told her that yet, but I'm going to. Maybe then she'll quit."

"She saw me," I said, "but she was drunk. It isn't that hard for
some drunks to see me, but hardly anyone else does. I was surprised
that you could see me."

"I've always seen the spirits," the girl said, "and listened to them,
as long as I can remember. But you can't tell other people about that,
or they think you're crazy. They had me on Thorazine a couple of
years ago, and it was awful—every time I went walking in the woods,
it was like I was blind and deaf. So I finally stopped taking the stuff.
Now I just don't tell anybody what I see."

"You ought to join a medicine society," I said. "They could use
somebody like you."

"I don't know much about it. Mom doesn't hang with other Indians anymore. She keeps saying that being a Mohawk and marrying
one messed her over. I think that's partly because she's mad at Dad
for leaving her. He lives in Brooklyn—he's a construction worker."

"Ah," I said. More memories were coming back to me, of being
suspended in the air, following other men along a metal beam far
above the ground. I had lingered for a while near a band of high-steel
workers. That had been as enjoyable as following a hunting party—
maybe better. Doing such work took some of a warrior's courage.

"Can I ask you something?" the girl asked.

"Yes."

"Do you know why you're here?"

"No." I sighed. "I keep coming back among the living. I don't
know why. All I seem to find is sorrow, and even the animal spirits are
unhappy now. There's no purpose in it, returning here over and over,
having to remember everything I've forgotten from earlier visits."

"Maybe you're just not real good at being a ghost," the girl said.

"That could be the answer, that you just don't have much of an aptitude for being dead." Her eyes narrowed as she gazed at me. "But I don't think that's it. Maybe I summoned you. I've been wanting something for so long without knowing what it is—maybe that's what brought you here."

I felt her longing even as I heard it in her words, and felt that countless other souls were speaking through her.

"I think we need a vision," the girl whispered. "I think you keep coming back because you know we need one, and then you find out we're not ready for it yet."

"Do you really think so?" I asked.

"Well, I don't know for sure, but isn't it better to think so? It could be true. It's sort of like being on a vision quest, except you're trying to become a vision instead of looking to have one. Maybe you're not much of a vision yet, but you could grow into the job later on." She was silent for a while. "I think a lot of people could use a really good vision now, not just us."

Some other spirits were watching us from the trees. They were spirits of the dead, but I couldn't recall seeing any of them when I was among other ghosts. They vanished before I could get a good look at them, but I had the feeling most of them didn't dwell with the ghosts I knew.

"Did you see those ghosts?" I asked.

"Sure did. Some African spirits, and one that looked Chinese, and a couple of guys who looked Russian."

"Haven't seen them before," I said. "Maybe it's time we got together."

"Lots of luck," the girl said. "You better hope they're not as prejudiced as a lot of people who are alive." She smiled at me then. "But you should try. At least it'll give you something to do while you're waiting to be a really great vision with a lot of good medicine."

The girl's name, she told me later, was Juliette. Since I didn't have a name, she gave me one, a chief's name—Shoskoarowaneh, the Great Branch. It seemed to fit my new purpose, reaching out to other spirits while waiting for the time the living I was hoping to shelter needed the vision I might bring to them. Whether this is the Creator's purpose for me, or one I've come to by myself, doesn't seem to matter.

I think a lot of ghosts had given up, that they had decided to forget the living. I think that forgetfulness helped to bring much trouble to the world. Now more of them, along with me, are beginning to remember, but I hope they don't forget again.

I come back every year and go to the Feast for the Dead with Juliette. Every year a few more ghosts come with me. Maybe someday
more of the living will be able to see us. Juliette's mother can't, now
that she's staying sober, but she's stopped telling her daughter that
she's crazy for talking to spirits. I go to the Feast for the Dead, and
visit with some of the animal spirits to tell them I'll try to get people to
look out for them more, and then I go back to the Feast for the Living
that we ghosts celebrate now. It's a new custom, honoring the living
and hoping things work out for the world in the end. It's what you
need.

Unto the Valley of Day-Glo
Nicholas A. DiChario

T he day Mother Who's Afraid of Virginia Woolf? killed Father The Outlaw Josey Wales, they were arguing again about the pre-Reddening game of Major League Baseball. Mother's position was, as usual, supported by the Tribal Bible. It was in fact Dizzy Dean, not his brother Daffy, who suffered a broken toe during the 1937 All-Star game. Although Father accurately identified Dizzy's real name as Jay Hanna Dean, and Daffy's real name as Paul Dean, and both baseball players did in fact pitch in the same game in which said injury occurred, Father refused to attribute the broken toe to Dizzy.

Mother, incensed (as Father knew she would be, for it was his common practice to infuriate her on the finer points of the game), grabbed him by the neck and began to shake him mercilessly, until plumes of dust gathered around them in the hazy, reddish morning sunlight.

I yawned, and decided I could make do with a short nap, for soon Mother and Father and I would inspect the dead bodies of our tribespeople for insects and red worms suitable for eating, and it was good for the eyes to be well rested for the intricacies of such an endeavor.

As soon as I returned to the hut and began to doze, I heard Mother's O'gi'we, the Tribal Death Shriek:

"AIYEEEEEEEEEEEEE-YICK-YICK-EEEEEEEEEEEEEEE-oh—"

It was a shriek I had heard often enough. The horrible soil storm that had decimated our tribe from forty-seven to three—the now nearly extinct Gushedon'dada tribe, named after the Jug-shaking dance of our Iroquois Indian ancestors—had kept Mother shrieking for quite some time.

I dashed out of the hut.

Mother, on her knees in the dry dirt, cradled my limp father in her arms. "Ohhhhhhhh, Danny," she said to me. "He is dead! He is dead!"

"Are you sure?" I knelt beside Father and investigated for his pulse. Nothing. Father displayed a rather relieved, purple expression upon his face.

"I have killed him. I have killed my beautiful husband." Mother began to weep.

Father The Outlaw Josey Wales believed in the value of oral history, partly, I think, because he pretended he could not read whenever Mother cited an irrefutable fact from the Tribal Bible. In any case, he often told the tale of the Reddening, which went something like this:

Hed'iohe, the Creator, gave the Earth to the North American Iroquois Indians at the dawn of time. He then decided to take a long nap. When Hed'iohe awoke, He discovered that the white and black and yellow-skinned tribes had taken over the Earth and were abusing it to no end.

So Hed'iohe decided to turn the crafty inventions of the whites and blacks and yellows against them. Hed'iohe conjured up the carbon dioxide and methane and other anthropogenic gases from their fossil-fueled industries and began to slowly bake the oddly colored earth people under the ozone layer. Droughts occurred. Horrible fires decimated great cities. Billions of Earth people died agonizing deaths.

Eventually the great oven Hed'iohe created became so hot that the sky and the earth burned red and the water boiled to nothingness, and all of the white and black and yellow-skinned tribes perished (not possessing the secret ability of internal sweat), leaving only the red people to tread upon the overheated planet Earth.

"History," Father always liked to say whenever he told the story of the great Reddening, "repeats itself."

His meaning, of course, was obscure.

Here is another tale Father The Outlaw Josey Wales used to tell before Mother Who's Afraid of Virginia Woolf? strangled him to death:

There is a valley that glows brightly, called the Valley of Day-Glo, where all the colors of the pre-Reddening Earth can be found. Flowers are in constant bloom there. Trees reach up to the sky like tall pillars of hard muscle. Water flows freely. Fruits and vegetables flourish. In the Valley of Day-Glo, Father used to say, "death becomes life." But this valley is hidden under a great glass dome somewhere beyond Seneca Indian territory, where no man or woman dare travel.

To be perfectly honest, none of us Gushedon'dada ever believed a word Father uttered. Mother had too often undermined his authority on matters of baseball trivia, and although he was much admired for his ability to separate a rat's head from its body with nothing more than his teeth and jaws, this practice gained Father more fear than respect, which might have been his intent all along.

"We must take your father to the Valley of Day-Glo." Mother sounded gravely determined.

"What?"

She slapped me across the face. "You heard me, idiot. We must take your father to the place where death becomes life. We must bring the eldest male Gushedon'dada back to the land of the living. Without him our tribal line shall perish forever."

Mother had a knack for making me feel minuscule. "But, Mother, there is no such place as—"

"Don't say another word! Would you insult your father's spirit before his body has even become cold? You are a larger coward and failure than I ever dreamed possible. I am the eldest Gushedon'dada now, and you must obey me."

I contemplated the consequences of breaking Gushedon'dada tribal law while there remained but two of us in the tribe. If I let Mother go without me, eventually she would die alone, and so, I imagined, would I. But what chance would we have of making it alive through Seneca territory to the mythical valley beyond?

"Father is dead," said I. "Even if the Valley of Day-Glo existed, how would we transport him there with any dignity or grace?"

"I shall drag him," Mother said proudly.

"I cannot allow it."

"Try and stop me, eunuch-boy!"

"Mother!"

"I killed him. He is my burden. Fetch me some sticks."

And so I did.

True to her word, Mother Who's Afraid of Virginia Woolf? fashioned a harness and a makeshift sled out of sticks and twine and rat skins from our hut. She lay Father The Outlaw Josey Wales upon it, treating him with more kindness and dare I say respect than I ever witnessed during his lifetime.

Mother and I sat down together and ate our final rodent in silence. The eunuch-boy remark was uncalled for, thought I, and I was angry at circumstance. Out of all the Gushedon'dada, Mother was my least favorite, as I was her least favorite. The irony that we should be the only surviving Gushedon'dada I am sure came as a blow equally crushing to Mother as to me, and perhaps this was why she was so intent upon bringing Father, a man she was never all that crazy about to begin with, back from the dead.

When we finished our meal, Mother pulled on her favorite pair of Wrangler stone-washed jeans, her Puma sneakers with the Velcro straps, and her most comfortable T-shirt with the strange inscription *Esprit* emblazoned across the chest. She wrapped the Tribal Bible and the Tribal Jug in a gunnysack and slung it over her shoulder, stuck her gold hatpin in her Chicago Cubs baseball cap, strapped herself into her harness, and began walking northward without so much as a glance in my direction.

I sighed heavily and followed, carrying only the clothes upon my back: a magenta button-down oxford shirt, a pair of navy blue Levi's Dockers, and my favorite penny loafers. These articles of clothing amounted to all my earthly possessions, after losing everything in the great soil storm. I glanced back at the hut and the rocky ridge and the dead bodies of our tribespeople that I was sure never to see again, mourning only that which I had mourned for as long as I could remember: the days ahead.

The landscape shone strikingly barren, littered with dirt and rock and swirling dust, broken by an occasional fissure in the rutted earth.

I entertained only one hope for the journey ahead, the hope that Mother and I would indeed discover the Valley of Day-Glo, thus proving Father right at long last, and I suppose if I had nothing to live for prior to the remote possibility of knocking Mother down a peg or two, this was better than nothing.

Unable to remain silent, I said, "I am accompanying you on this journey, Mother, specifically so that I may see the Seneca Indians skin you alive and leave you skewered on a stake to dry in the sun like the curd you truly are, even if it means that I must lie skewered beside you." I was not trying to be cruel without a purpose, mind you. Father had been dead almost two hours, and I thought Mother might be missing him.

Mother stopped, looked at me with glassy eyes, and kissed me on the cheek.

Already Father was beginning to rot. He was deoxygenating, his purple discoloration now spreading throughout his blood vessels. His muscular contraction had hardened his extremities into quite a stiff little package. His skin had become translucent, his lips pale, his fingertips blue.

Although I found it difficult to mourn a man who stank so horribly bad, I shall always remember fondly Father's ceaseless determination in annoying Mother, which in my opinion kept him young at heart and alive up until the moment Mother strangled the life out of him.

"You win some, you lose some," Father used to say. In my estimation Father's final record was something like 5,649 to 1 in his favor, for even though Mother vis-à-vis the Tribal Bible had always proved him wrong, he had never lost his life until now.

On our journey, it would be my responsibility to trail ten paces behind Mother Who's Afraid of Virginia Woolf?—now the eldest Gushedon'dada—as she carried the Tribal Bible and the Tribal Jug, and of course Father, her death burden, leaving me to snatch flies for dinner as the insects landed upon Father's decomposing body. I had become quite an accomplished fly snatcher. So many of our tribe having died in the soil storm, it became necessary for me to cull as much sustenance as possible from our dearly departed.

Flies are the first insects attracted to the dead, followed by the dust beetles who feed upon the flies, followed by the ants and the winged cockroaches who feed upon the beetles. When a body is at the height of its foul odor, it will attract rats and scavenger birds. The Gushedon'dada feed upon all of these things.

Death becomes life.

We traveled northward along the dust plains, following a path that would eventually lead us directly into Seneca territory.

It did not take us long to run into a disheveled tribe of Independents. They numbered less than a dozen, bleary-eyed and skinny, dressed in tattered clothing from which all color had long since been sandblasted. They stared at us through sunken eyes.

Mother shirked her harness and removed the Jug from her gunnysack, warning me with a look not to interfere. She placed the Jug in the dirt and began to step slowly around it, left arm extended, right hand at her chest. One-two-three-four she stepped, back straight, neck stiff, head held sharply in the direction of her extended arm, legs crisscrossing. One-two-three-four, turn, step, step, step. Around and around the Tribal Jug she danced.

I had never seen the Jug-shaking dance performed by one individual. Father had always performed it with Mother. It was a sad sight to see Mother jugging alone, and I was hurt she hadn't asked me to accompany her, for I knew the steps well enough.

When Mother finished her dance routine, she introduced our tribe, the now nearly extinct Gushedon'dada, named after the Jug-shaking dance, and she explained that we were the only two remaining tribespeople after the great soil storm had decimated our tribe from forty-seven to two (failing to point out that she had killed Father). Then she picked up the Jug and began the ritual shaking of it, a complicated arrangement that involved a thorough jostling above the head, behind the back, and between the legs. When Mother completed the shaking, one of the men from the other tribe, the leader no doubt, stepped forward. "May we inspect your Jug?"

This was indeed a good sign, an indication that they might accept Mother's offer of mutual nonaggression. In other, more prosperous times, Mother and I might have been dead meat. But the Senecas were conquering all of the Independent tribes these days, and as of late it seemed an unspoken bond had developed among the remaining Independents.

Mother placed the Jug in the dirt and beckoned the leader forward. He approached the Jug, looked at it briefly, and finally knelt in the dirt for a closer look.

"This is an Igloo water cooler," said Mother. She removed a pamphlet from her gunnysack and handed it to the leader. He unfolded it and began to read, glancing from Jug to pamphlet, from pamphlet to Jug.

"Pressure-fit lid with molded-in easy-grip ball handles," he read. "Seamless, easy-to-clean plastic liner. Drip-proof, recessed spigot. Polyurethane insulation keeps drinks icy cold. Great for camping and picnics."

"Yes," said Mother. "Model number four-three-one, with extra UV inhibitors to resist cracking, peeling, and fading caused by the sun. As you can see, it is still a very pretty blue color. We have kept the Jug extremely well preserved."

"The Gushedon'dada are known to be a very meticulous tribe." He stood and handed the pamphlet back to Mother. "Is this the infamous asexual boy named Broadway Danny Rose we have heard so much about?"

Mother nodded. "I am afraid so."

"My sympathies. We are the Gadages'kao, the Tribe of the Fetid Banks."

"Ah, yes, the Gadages'kao. I have heard of you. Descendants of the Mohawks, correct?"

"That is correct." The leader motioned his people to sit. They spaced themselves unevenly in a semicircle and sat cross-legged behind him. They sat as rigid as ancient stones baking in the sun. Mother and I and the leader remained standing. Our meeting had not yet become informal.

Mother said, "It was my understanding that long ago the Gadages'kao had made the journey to Seneca territory to become part of the Seneca League of Nations."

He nodded. "That is also correct. But we are now officially renegade." He did not elucidate. It would have been rude to question him further, but I was extremely curious. The Gadages'kao leader eyed my rotting father. "You carry the dead one to attract food?" he said, his eyes brightening a bit.

"We carry the dead one upon a sacred quest," said Mother, "unto the Valley of Day-Glo."

There came a murmuring from the semicircle of Gadages'kao. The twinkle of hunger I'd seen in the leader's eyes flashed into disbelief and, if I might say so, something of horror. He breathed deeply. "Have you any idea what is going on in Seneca territory? Have you not heard of the preposterous mega-city they have established? The overpopulation, the starvation, the disease, the impending revolution?"

Mother shook her head. "None of this matters to us. Our journey is not politically motivated."

"When it comes to politics, the motivations of those who claim neutrality make little difference."

Mother nodded. "This is true."

The Gadages'kao leader shrugged. "May we inspect the dead one?"

Mother hesitated. "He is my husband."

"I have a wife who is quite accomplished at forensics. She might be able to help you better preserve his body for the difficult journey ahead."

Mother nodded and stepped away from Father, taking me by the arm and pulling me back with her. Whether she reached out to me for support, or whether she simply wished to show the Gadages'kao that the only two remaining Gushedon'dada stood all for one and one for all, I did not know. For whatever reason, it felt good to stand arm-in-arm with Mother. As much as I hated her, I had always hoped the stubborn old woman and I could become friends.

She leaned close to me and whispered in my ear, "Don't do or say anything stupid and maybe they won't kill us."

The gaunt woman who was the leader's wife knelt beside Father.

She much resembled Father, thought I, this wife of the Gadages'kao leader, with her tightly drawn skin and flat chest and skeletal chassis.

"Recently dead," she uttered, unwrapping the bundle within which Mother had secured Father, wrinkling her nose at his frightful stench. I noticed that some of Father's skin had paled, and some had turned a red-purple color.

"Hypostasis," the woman said. She pressed her fingers over a large purple spot near Father's lumbar region, and the purple slowly turned white. "Not dead twelve hours yet." She continued to feel Father, and Mother tensed beside me.

"What's she doing?" Mother whispered. "Trying to challenge me for his body?"

"Don't overreact," I said.

"We'll lose the old fool if we're not careful."

"I detect congestion of the basal and posterior areas of the lungs." The wife of the Gadages'kao leader put her hand directly upon Father's crotch. "We still have some muscular rigidity, although many of the joints and bones have been broken due to the woman dragging him so inefficiently."

Mother clenched her fists. I grabbed hold of her wrist.

"Cause of death appears to be violent . . . of a suspicious nature. I don't see any wounds, that is to say no breaches through the entire thickness of the skin, but noting the irregular lividity patterns around the neck, I'd say strangulation would be an educated approximation." She stared directly at Mother. "How would you speak to that, woman? Would you agree?"

Mother yanked her wrist out of my grip—"Let me go, eunuch-boy!"—and charged at the wife of the Gadages'kao leader—two giant steps—and leapt on top of her. They tumbled to the ground in a puff of dust, Mother on the back of the Gadages'kao leader's wife, her legs wrapped around the woman's waist, her hands clutching the woman's impossibly skinny neck.

"Gawk! Gawk!" cried the woman, clawing for Mother's eyes.

A large smile creased the face of the Gadages'kao leader. The others in the semicircle jumped to their feet, barking and hollering and casting down bones. They pointed at the two women rolling in the dirt.

"Care to place a wager?" the Gadages'kao leader said to me. I could do nothing but look at him stupidly. "Suit yourself," he said, reaching into his sack and tossing some trinkets on the pile.

In the meantime, Mother had gotten the upper hand—indeed, she had never lost it—by placing her opponent into a head lock and squeezing the woman's larynx with her free hand.

Mother yanked something out of her Chicago Cubs baseball
cap—a golden glitter—her hatpin! She raised it high above her head
and stabbed at the woman's throat. A squirt of blood jetted forth.

"Gurgl-et—gurgl-et—gurgl-et," said the wife of the Gadages'kao
leader. Suddenly she was not moving around so much. The woman's
eyes bugged out, and she collapsed in the dirt.

Mother rolled off the slack corpse, gasped to fill her lungs with air,
and shrieked:

"AIYEEEEEEEEEEEEE-YICK-YICK-EEEEEEEEEEEEEEE-
oh—"

I found myself so astonished that I could not move a muscle.
Mother glared at me as if to say, *Not one word, eunuch-boy!* I marveled
at the purity of her hatred for me.

"Ha! Ha!" shouted the Gadages'kao leader. Fortunately he had
wagered heavily against his wife. He collected several bones and put
them in the sack at his waist. "I knew you could take her," he said,
helping Mother to her feet. "You should be ashamed of the boy,
though, he didn't even show enough respect to place a bet."

"Don't worry," said Mother, brushing the dust off her *Esprit*
T-shirt. "I'm plenty ashamed of him as it is."

The Gadages'kao leader suggested we honor his dead wife and
Mother's dead husband by sitting for the Wainonjaa'ko, the death
feast. He and his people carefully unpacked their Tribal china, an imitation Royal Doulton pattern with a blue-lace design, and everyone
sat in the cross-legged position, plates upon laps, for a meal of flies
and mashed winged cockroach. Because of my failure to place a
wager, I did not receive a plate, nor was I allowed within the dining
circle, even though I had contributed several flies to the meal. So I sat
with Father The Outlaw Josey Wales and the late wife of the Gadages'kao leader—who I learned was named Alice Doesn't Live Here
Anymore—while the others spoke of the Great Reddening.

Mother told the Gadages'kao Father's tale of Hed'iohe, the Creator, who gave the world to the North American Iroquois red men at
the dawn of time. She also told of Hed'iohe's great anger and retribution concerning the ozone layer and the droughts and horrible fires
that decimated the white and yellow and dark-skinned tribes. The
Gadages'kao leader said that although he had not heard the tale of the
spirit Hed'iohe he would add it to his oral history, and he could contribute the tale of Sagowenota, the spirit of the ocean tides, to the oral
history of the only two remaining Gushedon'dada:

"At the beginning of time, after filling two-thirds of the land with all the great waters of the world—waters stocked plentifully with fish and sea plants for the benefit of the Iroquois Indians so that they would always have a generous food supply—Sagowenota took a long nap. When He awoke He found that the dark and yellow and white-skinned tribes had conquered the red men, and were abusing His vast contribution to no end.

"Much disturbed, Sagowenota began to warm the temperature of His waters. In no time the shifting currents began to interrupt the breeding patterns of His fish, thus beginning the extinction of all His wonderful water creatures. The elevated temperatures also destroyed His plants and coral reefs by disrupting the normal processes of photosynthesis.

"But this was not enough. Sagowenota wished to punish the whites and darks and yellows for all their insurrections, so He melted many of His polar ice caps, flooding all the land, and then offered His wild waters to the Great Spirit, who drank and drank until the Earth became a dustbowl."

Mother nodded. "I wonder if Sagowenota and Hed'iohe were in cahoots," said she. "It seems as if it would have taken more than the efforts of any one spirit to accomplish genocide and precipitate the collapse of an entire ecosystem."

"An astute observation," said the Gadages'kao leader. "It is logical that if the two spirits had napped and awakened at approximately the same time, they would have helped each other destroy the defilers of their creations. And who's to say there were not several more spirits irritated with the men of the pre-Reddening Age, spirits who would have gladly volunteered their services."

Everyone agreed on this point.

After Mother finished her mashed winged roach, she tactfully broached the subject of the Gadages'kao's status as a renegade tribe. The Gadages'kao leader shook his head mournfully, and his tribe fell somber.

"In the beginning," began the leader, "we were certain that joining the Seneca League of Nations was a wise decision. We, the Gadages'-kao, were a small tribe with little more than twoscore members when we excavated our 7-Eleven convenience store. Now, as you can see, we number less than half that. Granted, a 7-Eleven convenience store is not much—some automobile window-washer, a rack of Bic lighters, blister packs of keychains, some insulated travel coffee mugs, etcetera, etcetera—nothing at all like a K mart. But the Senecas wanted it. We dug in and fought bravely for a day and a half, but to continue our defense would have meant the extermination of our tribe."

"Aren't you facing a similar fate now that you have gone renegade?"

"When the Senecas appropriated our 7-Eleven convenience store, they allowed us to maintain our possessions which had become tribal artifacts—the imitation Royal Doulton china, for instance, and our Tribal Bible." The Gadages'kao leader reached into his sack and removed a volume that I could not identify from my position beside Father and Alice Doesn't Live Here Anymore. It was a hardcover book. He handed it to Mother.

"Although at the time our defeat was honorable and the terms of our surrender acceptable to us, when we reached Seneca territory we learned of their true purpose. They would annex our tribe into the League of Nations, and in so doing extract an indoctrination taxation and take from us all of our tribal artifacts."

Here the Gadages'kao leader took a very large breath. The others frowned and shook their heads.

Mother paged through the Gadages'kao Tribal Bible. It would have been rude of her to do otherwise. There was an extended hush while the Gadages'kao allowed her to peruse its contents without distraction. Mother said, "May I show your wonderful Bible to my worthless son?"

The Gadages'kao leader muttered, "I suppose this would be permissible," and Mother handed the volume over to me. It was an oversized book entitled *The Microwave Cookbook,* with colorful pages of exquisitely prepared meals. There was one recipe for low-cholesterol swordfish filets that looked scrumptious, calling for green onions, lemon grass, and fresh jalapeño peppers, topped with a lightly seasoned coconut sauce, all such ingredients supposedly abundant during the pre-Reddening Age.

I was dreaming of how perfectly transcendent it would have been to just once in my life have had the opportunity to wrap my mouth around such a taste sensation, when suddenly an eerie sound cut across the barren plains: "caw-caw-caw-caw-caW-cAW-CAW-CAW-CAW-CAW-CAW—"

The Seneca War Cry!

I think we all must have seen them at the same time, a band of women warriors charging across the plains, bearing stainless-steel knives and Louisville Slugger aluminum baseball bats and .22-caliber Ruger pistols and Remington twelve-gauge pump shotguns.

The Gadages'kao leapt to their feet and ran for it. Mother grabbed my arm and said, "Sit still! Give me the Bible." I handed her *The Microwave Cookbook* and glanced up at the Senecas closing in on our position. In no time at all the Seneca women were upon us. They blew past us like the wind—"CAW-CAW-CAW-CAW-CAW-CAW-CAw-

Caw-caw-caw-caw . . ." a pack of wild primates, a flash of Lady Levi's and assorted bandannas, suspenders, boots, scarfs, and imitation jewelry. The mighty Seneca death heralds, the S'hondowek'owa.

True to their name, the S'hondowek'owa wasted no time in dispensing their particular brand of justice to the miserable Gadages'-kao.

I witnessed the silvery flash of stainless steel in the waning sunlight as it cleaved into unresisting flesh. Aluminum Louisville Sluggers crushed skulls and snapped bones. Ruger .22-caliber pistols cracked and echoed and cracked and echoed, blood spitting from the miniature holes punched into their helpless victims. There came the heavy *POOM-POOM-POOM* of twelve-gauge shotguns (although the deaths of the Gadages'kao were at this point redundant). All of this to the "CAW-CAW-CAW" of the women warriors.

The Gadages'kao never screamed or cried. They must have welcomed death to some extent. As Mother had mentioned earlier, to go renegade was asking for trouble, and one could only surmise that death was a kinder alternative than life to the Gadages'kao.

I shivered beside Alice Doesn't Live Here Anymore as the S'hondowek'owa went about desecrating the bodies of the Gadages'kao. The women warriors stomped on bloody corpses and ripped out entrails. Those S'hondowek'owa armed with cutlery butchered the organs of the dead, and all the others began feasting on raw meat.

"Now I understand," said Mother. She stuffed *The Microwave Cookbook* into her gunnysack.

"What?"

"The old ways," said she, flipping her Chicago Cubs baseball cap onto her grayish-reddish hair. "Our pre-Reddening, pre-Industrial ancestors of the Golden Age believed that by ingesting the blood and organs of their enemies, they could steal their spiritual power."

I nodded. "The desecration of the bodies. The cannibalism. The Senecas are attempting a full-scale revival."

I reached out to Father to steady myself. He felt cold and hard beneath my hand. "You win some, you lose some," he seemed to be saying from behind his mask of death, in his old familiar way. But no, he shook his head and opened his death-glazed eyes, and then he spoke:

Hey, Danny Boy, what's going on in the land of the living?

"Father?"

This may come as a shock to you, but you can't win or lose anything once you are dead. Take my word for it. I'm not looking to gain anything anymore.

I glanced at Mother to see if she had heard Father's wisdom. Apparently she had not. Perhaps the S'hondowek'owa had brought with them my insanity. "Father, have you gone to the Spirit World?" I said, or perhaps I communicated my thoughts to him in some other-worldly, spiritual way.

All I know is that I am not going anywhere fast. There is no place to run, nothing here from which to escape. When you are dead, you are perfectly happy to stand in the place where you are.

"Father. The Valley of Day-Glo—does it truly exist? Can you see it from your unique vantage point?"

Father smiled, and then his face once again stiffened in death. I reached over and closed his eyes.

"When the S'hondowek'owa come for us," said Mother, "let me do the talking."

And come for us they did, swarming like grand and deadly winged cockroaches, never quite landing in one place, while Mother Who's Afraid of Virginia Woolf? and I sat side by side in the rising dust, choking on what could be our last breaths. They circled so closely that we could feel their heat and smell on them the blood of the Gadages'-kao. At one point I thought I heard Mother declare needlessly, "Don't move a muscle, eunuch-boy!"

One of the S'hondowek'owa warriors stepped forward. She was a husky woman with a shaved head, her teeth sharpened to fangs, a Remington twelve-gauge shotgun slung over her shoulder. She wore a black pleated skirt and a blazing fuchsia blouse. Her biceps bulged beneath the flimsy material. What a frightful sight. I was so horrified I could not shut my eyes.

She stepped closer to me, blood dripping from her fangs onto the toes of my penny loafers. Her shadow hovered over me, and I imagined it pressing down against my chest so that I could not breathe. She grabbed the front of my shirt and hauled me to my feet.

The other S'hondowek'owa began to chant some indiscernible, rising keen. With her free hand, and faster than my eye could follow, she whipped a knife out of a hidden sheath and sliced my Dockers slacks open from fly to waist with nothing more than a flip of her wrist. The keening grew louder, and some of the women began to whoop at the sight of my newly exposed anatomy.

Mother toppled over, guffawing.

The S'hondowek'owa fell silent.

They observed Mother rolling in the dirt, laughing hysterically. One of the women warriors drew a bead on Mother with a Ruger .22-caliber semiautomatic pistol, but the woman who held me suspended in midair signaled her to hold her fire.

My assailant lowered me to the ground. "What do you find so

amusing, old woman?" I was thinking very much the same thing as I gasped for air.

Mother got control of herself and began to speak. "You are about to rape a eunuch-boy!" said she, and roared with laughter once again.

A look of incomprehension crossed the woman warrior's face. She scrutinized my skinny body momentarily, and delivered a swift kick to my chest, which flattened me out on the ground. "You are incapable of sexuality?" she asked me quite pointedly, leaning over and examining my male member, as if it might answer for me.

I wheezed and rubbed my chest where the flat of her foot must have put a permanent indentation. "I don't see where that is anyone's business but my own."

"Ha! Ha!" she called from deep in her belly. "This must be the infamous asexual boy named Broadway Danny Rose of the Gushedon'dada we have heard so much about." And the entire S'hondowek'owa joined her (and Mother) in hardy laughter.

I could feel a rush of anger rise within me. Mother had no right to make me an object of ridicule. I sat up, as if this might purchase me my dignity, but alas, this seemed only to generate further amusement. "Stop laughing, all of you. What's so funny?"

"He's a disgrace to the Gushedon'dada," said Mother, wiping tears of laughter from her eyes. "And he is our only surviving male."

The S'hondowek'owa shook their heads in sympathy. "The sexual dysfunction of the males must be the most dishonorable way for a tribe to perish," said my attempted rapist. "If you like, I shall slay the both of you this very instant and forgo the traditional torturing and desecration of your bodies."

Mother, already upon her knees, bowed low. "What a gracious offer. But I must shame our people once more and beg for mercy."

"We will hear your plea," said the woman warrior, sitting cross-legged in the dirt, arranging her pleated skirt neatly over her lap.

The other S'hondowek'owa gathered around us—Mother and myself, Father The Outlaw Josey Wales, and Alice Doesn't Live Here Anymore—in a tight circle, but remained standing, as if at any given moment they might be called upon to slay and devour us, which was in fact a distinct possibility. The death heralds watched me with interest, as if they might detect some behavior indicative of my asexuality.

"When my husband died," said Mother, motioning to Father's stiff and malodorous body, "one can only imagine the tragedy of losing the last true male Gushedon'dada." The S'hondowek'owa nodded their agreement, glancing disapprovingly at my exposed manhood. I gathered my pants around my midsection and stared back at them incredulously. "But there is a greater tragedy that clings to my husband's spirit as fiercely as the red worm clings to the lips of the dead."

"And what is that?" inquired the rapist. She had a remarkably lilting voice. She scratched at her bald, pimply head.

"My husband's spirit is haunted by a quest unfulfilled. You see, when my husband died, we were journeying to the great territory of the Seneca Indians and the League of Nations. It had always been my husband's dream to travel to Seneca territory before his death, so, upon his final breath, my worthless son and I vowed to complete the journey in his stead, so that his spirit might become one with the spirit of the Seneca and allow his soul to rest in peace forevermore. My worthless son and I would gladly accept your offer of a quick and painless and honorable death, if it were not for the vow sworn upon the death of the last true male Gushedon'dada."

The great, husky woman sat silently for a moment, the twelve-gauge shotgun perched upon her lap, her finger poised disturbingly over the trigger. I noticed her staring at me. She licked her lips.

"Because we have enormous sympathy for you, due to the disgrace you must suffer because of your infamous asexual son the Broadway Danny Rose, the S'hondowek'owa agree to escort you and your worthless son to Seneca City, the land of the League of Nations, at which point your husband's spirit quest will be fulfilled and his soul will rest in peace forevermore, and the fate of the remaining Gushedon'dada will then be decided by the S'hondowek'owa. Let it be understood that you shall be our prisoners until, or if, it is decreed otherwise."

"You are kind and just beyond measure," said Mother.

The rapist motioned with the barrel of her shotgun toward the dead bodies. "Who is the other dead one?"

"She is Alice Doesn't Live Here Anymore of the Gadages'kao."

"CAW-CAW-CAW-CAW-CAW-CAW-CAW-CAW-CAW—" came the death cry.

The band of S'hondowek'owa fell upon the corpse of poor old Alice—stomping, gouging, biting, and beating her into a bloody pulp. Mother and I had all we could do to crawl out of the mess uninjured, dragging Father along behind us.

I discovered myself trembling. Mother looked at me with what might have been compassion. She reached out and squeezed my hand. "The days ahead will not be easy," she said. "Be strong."

These would be the last words she would speak to me until some days later, when our destinies were due to collide with the revolution.

Mother and I were forced to travel separately.

The S'hondowek'owa bound my hands behind my back and forced me to walk with my Docker slacks undone, so that I had to insert my fingers into my rear belt loops and walk bow-legged in order to remain modest. As I walked, the S'hondowek'owa spat upon me, pinched me, and ridiculed me. At night, exhausted and humiliated, I was often poked and prodded and not allowed to sleep.

I thought a lot about Mother during the long days and nights of our journey. She was quite an intelligent and remarkable woman, really. Her handling of the Gadages'kao affair had almost certainly saved our lives. Although the slaying of Alice Doesn't Live Here Anymore had been brutal, if Mother had lost the contest or allowed Alice to live, the hungry and desperate Gadages'kao undoubtedly would have killed us.

The S'hondowek'owa would have tortured us to death if Mother had not laughed like an idiot at my expense, and then her creative fib about Father's dying wish guaranteed us safe passage to Seneca territory, one step closer to our final destination, the Valley of Day-Glo.

And the trip to Seneca City could not have been easy for Mother, either. One evening the S'hondowek'owa forced Mother to perform the Jug-shaking dance while they laughed and jeered. They also made her perform the Jug-shaking ritual, after which they took our most treasured tribal artifact, the revered Igloo cooler, smashed it against the rocks, peppered it with .22-caliber bullets, and pumped twelve-gauge shotgun slugs into it. What minuscule blue shreds of it remained, they tossed into their evening fire, along with *The Modern Book of Baseball*—our Tribal Bible—and the Tribal Bible of the Gadages'kao, *The Microwave Cookbook*.

Yet, during all this barbarism, I never once saw Mother flinch or shed a tear.

One night Mother and I were laid to sleep close enough so that I could hear the low murmuring of her raspy voice. I remember distinctly Mother reciting from memory several verses from our recently burned Bible:

"A first baseman's glove should be no more than twelve inches tall and eight inches across, with no more than a five-inch web. . . . Rule number one-hundred-sixteen states that all players must wear a polycarbonate alloy shell-type batting helmet. . . . In the same year Babe Ruth hit sixty home runs—the pre-Reddening year of 1927—the Venezuelan Federation of Amateur Baseball was formed. . . ."

At which point I imagined I was actually observing one of these exciting pre-Reddening baseball contests, and I believe I fell fast asleep for the first time in many nights.

■ ■ ■

Father The Outlaw Josey Wales was treated with the utmost respect. The two S'hondowek'owa women placed in charge of Father carried him silently and efficiently. At night I was always laid to rest beside Father because—so I was told by my captors—my asexuality made me as good as dead to the tribe of the Gushedon'dada.

Between the harassment of the S'hondowek'owa and the few minutes of sleep I stole each night, I found myself observing Father to see if he might have a few more words of wisdom for me. His skin had turned a slightly greenish hue, and he stank like spoiled meat. His rigor mortis appeared to be completely relieved as he lay flaccid. His facial features were barely recognizable, and gas blisters had begun to form under his flesh.

Once Father rolled over and spoke to me:

Danny Boy, allow me to tell you a secret about death. In the land of the dead, nobody is right or wrong because nothing matters anymore. Every question I have asked so far has been answered with one of the following remarks: "Who cares?" or "What's the difference?" The answers to all of one's questions here are questions, and yet there really are no questions worth asking because nobody cares about the answers.

"Father," said I, or perhaps I thought it or communicated it in some other worldly, spiritual way, "you are giving me a headache of massive proportions."

Who cares? he responded, chuckling softly. *What's the difference?*

"Did you happen to recognize anyone there in the land of the dead? Have you run into any of our recently deceased tribespeople?"

I don't know. Nobody has a face in death. Nobody has a voice, either. Once you are dead you automatically develop a higher, or perhaps a lower, form of communication. You never have to work your jaw or throat or vocal cords, and you never have to listen to anybody if you don't want to, but on the other hand, one no longer may indulge in the pleasure of listening to the sound of one's own voice.

"Father—the Valley of Day-Glo—does it truly exist?"

Who cares? What's the difference? Who cares who cares who cares?

He then rolled over and returned to the land of the dead.

Let me tell you about my meetings with Dewutiowa'is, my attempted rapist, in the order in which they occurred:

Late one night, after the embers of the evening fire had all but died, and I was beyond the capability of sleep, she came to me, her eyes flashing in the light of the moon, her breath heavy. She stared at me for the longest time, and I, bound and helpless, stared at her, wondering why she had come out to look at me after everyone else had gone to sleep. Did she see me as some sort of aberration? Did she want to sink her fangs into me? What was running through her savage mind? At some point my wonder turned to restless dreams, and I woke to the sound of cutlery being sharpened on stone, and a hot, dry wind in my face.

The following night Dewutiowa'is came to me again. After staring at me for some time, she whispered, "What is wrong with you? Don't you find me attractive?"

She knelt in front of me and unbuttoned her fuchsia blouse, releasing a musky animal odor.

"Look at these breasts." She pressed them together and thrust them forward.

"They are most impressive," said I, although I saw nothing more than lumpy shadows in the moonlight.

"Of course they are, you useless asexual."

She returned her breasts to her blouse and walked away.

On the third occasion, Dewutiowa'is approached me during one of my rare moments of sleep. She kicked me in the head and I woke with a start. She sat cross-legged, with her lap very near my head.

"My name is Dewutiowa'is," said she.

I was so neatly tied, I could not see her unless I stretched my neck into a horrible position. I did so only long enough to learn that she wore no underpants beneath her black pleated skirt.

"It is an ancient Indian name," she continued, "from the pre-Reddening, pre-Industrial, Golden Age of our Indian ancestors. It means 'Exploding Wren.' "

Ah, thought I, so Mother was indeed correct. The Senecas had adopted the ways of our ancient ancestors. This did not bode well for the future of the post-Reddening Indian race, nor did it bode well for me and Mother.

"You may speak your etymology," she said.

"My name is Broadway Danny Rose, also derived from the pre-Reddening Age, based upon a 1984 black-and-white Woody Allen film about a downtrodden talent agent who inadvertently gets into trouble with gangsters. Mia Farrow plays his love interest who—"

"That is enough."

We sat together quietly for quite some time, listening to the wind whistle across the dark, empty landscape.

Finally she spoke. "Why do the Independent tribes fear the ways of our Indian ancestors, yet cling to the ridiculous pop culture of the extinct Honio'o? You worship their artifacts, study their books, name your children after their ridiculous moving picture shows, which you have never even seen. To what purpose?"

Although Exploding Wren's questions did not seem to be uttered in anger, I became afraid to answer. A discussion about the Honio'o—the pre-Reddening whites and yellows and dark-skinned tribes, a topic of much dispute between the Senecas and the Independents—could easily be the death of me. Alas, I felt compelled to answer candidly:

"The Independents believe that we all must actively integrate such words of wisdom and such objects and rituals as remain from the pre-Reddening Honio'o into the cultural habits of the post-Reddening Indian tribes, so that the horrible deeds that provoked the great Indian spirits to destroy the yellow and dark and white-skinned men will never be duplicated in ignorance by the surviving tribes of North American Iroquois Indians. If we lose the history of our conquerors, it will always be possible for us to be conquered again, this time, perhaps, from within."

"Everything you treasure, everything you hold dear, is Honio'o. This is blasphemy. As long as we raise the Honio'o above the Indian, we live in danger of incurring the wrath of the spirits again. We must let the Honio'o die. We must return to the ways of our ancestors, to a time long before our people were infected by the disease of the Industrial Revolution. We were a great nation in the pre-Reddening, pre-Industrial, Golden Age."

The Golden Age.

Dewutiowa'is was of course referring to the time when tall trees filled the mountain ranges and sparkling rivers coursed through the earth and thousands of wild animals ran free, and the sun, Ende'-kagaa'kwa, the brilliant orb, shone like gold in the daytime sky. This was a time long before the Honio'o tried to fix, with more chemicals, the damage their chemicals had already caused.

"The Independents have always maintained our tribal heritages," said I. "We derived our tribal names from the ancient language. We still perform many of the ancient rituals. The Jug-shaking dance, for instance, during a performance of which you so rudely chided Mother, was practiced by our ancestors during the Golden Age. Our tribe often performed the annual harvest thanksgiving ceremony, the Gane'owo, even though there has been no such thing as a harvest of green corn or squash or tobacco or red apples for years and years and countless years."

"Ha! You Independents know nothing of the *true* rituals."

"If you are referring to cannibalism and the desecration of dead bodies, we would rather not know. And I should like to point out that the great S'hondowek'owa warrior women are all wearing clothing excavated from the Honio'o discount and department stores."

"We wear them to disguise our true intent."

"True intent? What true intent?"

Dewutiowa'is grunted. She looked beyond me then, into the black of night, as if she were imagining great and mystical things, golden things. I had not originally pegged Dewutiowa'is for an idealist, or an ideologist. Now I feared she was both.

"This land was once a vast river valley," said she. "And the Great Spirit sowed five handfuls of seed in the rich soil of His creation. From the seed of the Great Spirit came the Five Nations of the North American Iroquois Indians—the Mohawks, Oneidas, Onondagas, Cayugas, and—strongest of all—the Senecas. The Senecas ruled over all the land with an iron fist, and when the Honio'o tribes sailed in their ships from the faraway place called Europe and began to steal our land and establish their settlements, the Senecas protected the five families and avenged the loss of life and land with great savage justice.

"But the Honio'o kept coming. They seduced the weaker tribes with rum and useless gifts and false promises, and while the Iroquois spirits slept, the Senecas could not keep the Honio'o down, though most of us died trying. In the end, there was nothing to do but succumb to their villainous treaties. But the spirits awoke, and gave back to the Iroquois Indians what was rightfully theirs."

I shook my head. "It is true that the Honio'o were cruel and unjust. But we have survived them. Is that not enough?"

"The proud tribe of Senecas, like our spirit-protectors, have no tolerance for the bitter and scheming Honio'o ways. It would do the Independent tribes well to learn from our sacred ancestors!"

Her voice had risen sharply. I detected the soft footfall of an approaching S'hondowek'owa sentry. Dewutiowa'is crawled away into the darkness.

A gangly woman with large toes came up to me and warned me to shut up or I might discover myself toothless. I nodded and closed my eyes and did not sleep.

Exploding Wren returned the next evening.

"Why do you think you are not a sexually functional male?" she asked. "You are not a *true* asexual, after all. I have seen that you do possess sexual organs. Technically speaking, you are impotent, correct? Do you suspect that this is a biological defect or an environmental anomaly?"

I was at a loss for words.

"Allow me to conjecture: You were raised in a warrior-dominated tribal society. Born male, you were expected to hunt, kill, suffer, die, all of this silently, never being allowed to show your anger or your sadness. At all times you were required to maintain a bold, brave, and dominant public appearance. You were at all times required to demonstrate to your elders that you were focused, logical, controlled, and obsessive in your goal orientation. But you, Broadway Danny Rose, were a sensitive, creative, physically as well as emotionally fragile child, and, if I may say so, a pretty little asthenic boy. You lacked the strength and dexterity of your fellow male Gushedon'dada as well as their mental resolve, and so you became fearful of your inner-child, of revealing your weaknesses to the scrutiny of a tribal community that would not accept your inferiority. Your fear turned into self-loathing, repression, depression, and, in the ultimate act of avoidance and isolation, you became something defective, not a person at all, but a *thing* that had gone wrong—an 'asexual'—and the burden of responsibility for your own actions was suddenly lifted, and you became not someone who had failed in the eyes of your people, but someone failed *by* the people, or by the system as it stands, a victim of your own rigid societal maxims."

"By any chance, have you been speaking with Mother Who's Afraid of Virginia Woolf?"

"I am merely suggesting that your impotence may be nothing more than a subconscious act of rebellion, the repression of rage and resentment taken to extremes. With the proper guidance of a female skilled in the arts of sexual gratification, well—how shall I state this delicately?—who is to say you might not be converted to normalcy?"

I thought that Exploding Wren might try to prove her theory while I lay bound and helpless before her, for she leaned over and kissed me upon the forehead and reached for my loins, but the first hint of the day's new sun began to glow against the horizon, and Dewutiowa'is slipped quietly away before the early march to Seneca City was to renew, leaving me to ponder her psychological hypothesis in the reddish haze of morning.

But my mind grew preoccupied with the dead.

Danny Boy, said Father, *I have been developing a list of things I would have liked to explore during my lifetime. Number one: What were some of my wants, rather than my needs? Number two: What was the source of my self-esteem? Number three: What special gifts had been bottled up inside me that I might have been able to share with my loved ones? Number four: I wish I would have been more ambitious, more of a journeyman, and more of a loner. Number five: I really should have loved myself more. Number six: I would have liked to experience more grief, more empathy, and less actual self-centeredness.*

Now, of course, all these points are moot. Nothing matters over here in Deadsville.

"Father, don't leave me. Things are tough. I could use your company." But he retreated into death.

Oh, Father, in your deathly wisdom there lay great sadness and great joy. I wished with all my heart that nothing mattered in this Earthly realm. I envied you your death, where no victories prevailed, for lack of meaning, for lack of fate, for lack of life, in the land of Who Cares? and What's the Difference?

Shortly after dawn, as we marched through dry wedges of hilly terrain, a bullet passed directly through the skull of the S'hondowek'owa walking next to me, and she toppled over into my legs, knocking me to the ground.

Shots strafed the campsite.

"Mother! Mother! Where the heck are you?"

The S'hondowek'owa took up their guns and cutlery and Louisville Sluggers, and Dewutiowa'is barked out orders to her troops.

A war cry—no, several war cries—issued forth from the surrounding plains . . .

"UG-O UG-O UG-O UG-O UG-O UG-O UG-O UG-O UG-O—"

"HSSSSSS HSS-HSS-HSS-HSS-HSS-HSS-HSS HSSSSSSS—"

"It's an ambush!" cried Mother. She crawled up beside me.

"Who? Why?"

Another war cry: "MEEEEEEE-OW MEEEEEEEE-OW MEEE-EEEE-OW MEEEEEEE-OW—"

"Have you truly learned so little over the years? Don't you recognize the war cries of the Gako'go, the tribe of the Gluttonous Beasts; the Adodar'ho, the tribe of the Snaky Heads; the Ono'gweda, the tribe of Cattails?"

"Mother, I was never a warrior, you know that. Why must you continuously throw my failings up in my face?"

"Because your failings continue to slap me in mine."

More gunshots rained down upon the hot, dry terrain. Mother yanked the hatpin out of her Chicago Cubs baseball cap and stabbed at the twine binding my wrists. Finally the knot snapped, freeing my swollen fists. I had no time to dwell on my pain, or the bloody remains of my wrists, for the battle raged on.

What happened in the next few moments came to me in mostly a blur. There was tremendous dust, shouts echoed, gunshots kissed the air, bullets raked the land, feet pounded on hard, dry earth, aluminum baseball bats clanked as warriors clashed, death cries and screams of agony rang out.

And then Mother was on the back of a S'hondowek'owa, her deadly hatpin lashing down to puncture the jugular vein of one of the women warriors assigned to carry Father The Outlaw Josey Wales. The other guard turned on Mother, kicked her in the ribs, and took aim with her Ruger .22-caliber pistol.

I could stand idly by no longer.

I leapt without ceremony (that is to say, I bellowed no war cry, for I am ashamed to admit I knew not our tribal call to arms, and even if I did, I was too terrified to verbalize it, and in fact my ignorance might have saved my life, for the S'hondowek'owa warrior never saw me coming).

I tackled her, simultaneously stumbling as my trousers fell to my ankles. She squashed my head between the ground and her ample buttocks, filling my mouth with dirt. The realization of how quickly and easily I might be killed froze me in place, as did her massive weight.

But Mother Who's Afraid of Virginia Woolf?, as always, came to my rescue. She threw herself into the fray, biting, scratching, stabbing with her hatpin, in a performance worthy of a mighty S'hondowek'owa.

Still, Mother was no match for the strength of her opponent. Gouged and bloodied as she was, the Seneca woman tossed Mother aside as if she were no more than a winged cockroach.

I rolled over, dizzy and gasping for breath, and spat the dirt out of my mouth.

The woman warrior approached Mother, squeezed the hatpin from her grip with one hand, and with the other began to strangle her.

I saw the Ruger lying in the dirt. I snatched it off the ground and pushed myself up. I had never used a gun before, but during the past few days I had certainly seen them used often enough by the S'hondowek'owa. The plastic grip felt hot in my hand. I pointed the weapon at the woman and quickly yanked the trigger.

One would have thought, with my close proximity to my intended victim, coupled with my intended victim's enormous girth, that it would have been impossible for me to miss, but operating a Ruger .22-caliber pistol proved to be a trickier affair than I had imagined. As I pulled the trigger, the gun jerked sideways in my hand and I missed badly to the right.

The S'hondowek'owa stopped strangling Mother and turned her

attention to me. I was so frightened of both the woman and the gun—or what either of them might do at any given moment—that I could not shoot again.

She laughed and stepped toward me, leaving Mother coughing and choking upon her hands and knees. "Put that gun down, you pitiful asexual, before you hurt yourself. Ha!"

Laugh at the eunuch-boy, will you? I closed my eyes and fired and fired and fired—*bang bang bang bang*—until the Ruger no longer banged, but clicked and froze, announcing that I had run out of bullets. The smell of scorched gunpowder rose to fill my nostrils. Only then did I open my eyes to find the woman prostrate in front of me, her blood wetting the dirt, and Mother lying facedown with her hands over her head.

"Stop shooting, you idiot. Are you trying to kill me, too?"

For the briefest of moments, I wished that I had not spent every last round of ammunition on the S'hondowek'owa.

Ah, but there was no time to ponder possibilities. Bullets continued to spray the battlefield. Mother was already wrapping Father into his tattered blankets. She lay him upon the makeshift sled in which she had originally dragged him across the plains, and strapped him in.

Suddenly, out of the rising dust, three armed and crouching Indians approached us, rifles at the ready.

Mother reached down, grabbed her hatpin, and clutched it behind her back. I readied the Ruger in my hand, even though I had emptied the clip.

"Who are they?" I asked Mother.

"They are Adodar'ho, Snaky Heads."

"Ah, yes, I see." They wore purple bonnets with fluffy golden-colored ear flaps, and perched atop each bonnet was the openmouthed head of a cobra baring its fangs—a cloth head, most naturally. The Adodar'ho, so legend had it, had unearthed an entire warehouse full of these bonnets years and years ago, from which they had derived their tribal name. This was my first opportunity to witness the famous Snaky Head bonnet. (It was assumed that the caps were promotional items associated with the nickname of some popular pre-Reddening Honio'o sports team, or the marketing symbol of an AMF bowling ball, or the logo of some rock group phenomenon for which we currently have no record.)

"Quickly, come this way," one of them said, beckoning us, his cloth cobra bobbing atop his head. "It will not take long for the Shondos to regroup. We have struck and now we must run."

"What is going on?" inquired Mother. "Have the Independents joined forces against the Senecas?"

"Yes. The revolution has begun in Seneca City, and is spreading outward." He made a thespian's sweeping gesture.

"Where are we going?" said Mother.

The Snaky Head stamped the butt of his gun in the dirt. The gun, as far as I could tell, was a small-caliber, lever-action Winchester rifle. "Look, old woman, what's the difference where we are going? We are rescuing you from the Shondos. Isn't that enough for you to know?"

"An ill-conceived rebellion can lead to conditions far worse than anyone could imagine in an oppressive regime. Besides, my son and I have undertaken a sacred quest to discover the Valley of Day-Glo. We intend to bring my late husband back to life." Mother motioned to the collection of ragged flesh and bones that used to be her living husband. "Thank you for your kind offer, but I think we shall continue upon our journey to Seneca City."

"That is ridiculous. You have no idea what is happening in the mega-city even as we speak. The Senecas are under siege. There is rioting in the streets. Violent death everywhere—"

"We must go," snapped one of the other Adodar'ho, a slim, nervous-looking fellow. "We have no time to argue with fools who wish for death."

But the first Snaky Head said, "They have a right to know." He leaned upon the barrel of his rifle. "Old woman, the revolution has been brewing in Seneca City for many moons. Starvation and epidemics have ravaged the population. Inadequate housing facilities and sanitation, intolerable noise pollution, and poverty like you wouldn't believe have become rampant plagues upon the city's tribes.

"The Senecas took all of what the Independents had once claimed as our wealth, all our holdings and tribal artifacts, either by force or by taxation or by trading promises of prosperity they could not keep, and then they went about destroying everything."

"Yes," said the nervous-looking Snaky Head. "The Senecas have been destroying tribal artifacts in an attempt, so it would seem, to intentionally collapse the economy."

I thought about how the S'hondowek'owa had used our Tribal Jug for target practice, and how they had burned *The Modern Book of Baseball* and *The Microwave Cookbook.* And I thought of what Dewutiowa'is had said to me about the evil Honio'o and how we must let them die or suffer the wrath of the great Indian spirits of an age and then another age gone by. Had the Senecas established their great mega-city only to lure the Independent tribes into their League of Nations, abscond with their wealth, and destroy all that remained of the Honio'o? Based upon their distorted principle of cultural cleansing, would they purposely collapse the entire economic structure of the post-Reddening Indian Age by destroying the Honio'o artifacts that had become our most valued treasures?

"Of course, social disorder was bound to follow," said the first Snaky Head. "So the Independents have risen against the Senecas. We have raided most all of their armories and storage facilities, and today, while the Seneca hierarchy is in chaos, the revolution remains organized, armed, and angry."

"We three Adodar'ho," said the nervous one, "are part of an ambush squad positioned on the outskirts of the mega-city, deployed specifically to intercept Shondos returning from missions on the plains. Lucky for you we attacked before the Shondos reached Seneca City. At the first sign of rebellion they would have cut you to ribbons!"

He made slashing motions with his rifle, almost striking the squat little Adodar'ho behind him, who had yet to breathe a word, and the other one, the first Snaky Head, told him to forgo the waving of his rifle for fear someone might get hurt accidentally.

"Great Adodar'ho," said Mother. "We could not begin to humble ourselves enough to thank you for our rescue. But we are honor-bound to my late beloved husband to escort his body unto the Valley of Day-Glo, whereupon he might be resurrected from the dead."

The first Snaky Head sighed. "Many errors of judgment have occurred in moments of great sorrow. But a vow is a vow. At least allow us to escort you to our outpost. From there it will be a short march for you to the ruined mega-city."

And so it was decided.

We quickly gathered Father and whatever belongings we could salvage from within the immediate area, including two clips for the Ruger .22-caliber semiautomatic pistol I now possessed. I also discovered a small piece of twine that I strung through my belt loops and tied off at the waist, in order to keep my Dockers from falling, and a couple of bandannas to wrap around my bloodied wrists.

Just before we were to make our getaway, Mother knelt beside the woman she had slain with her hatpin, and cried:

"AIYEEEEEEEEEEEEE-YICK-YICK-EEEEEEEEEEEEEEE-oh—"

Then she turned to me, and motioned to the woman warrior I had riddled with bullets. Until I looked into Mother's eyes—the eyes of a hardened killer—it had not occurred to me that I too had taken a life. But indeed I had. I knelt down beside my bleeding victim. I could not look at her lifeless form, but I knew she was there. Mother came over and knelt beside me, took my hand in hers, and together Mother Who's Afraid of Virginia Woolf? and I delivered the Tribal Death Shriek. It was the feel of the shriek deep in my throat—not the immobile red female body at my knees—that told me I had committed an irreversible atrocity. And yet I remained cold inside, and distanced from my act.

The Adodar'ho urged us to make short work of our ritual, for we had already delayed too long.

As we rose and I turned my back upon the S'hondowek'owa for whose death I was responsible, I felt strangely capable and justified in my homicide, and in a way that troubled me only in that I seemed untroubled, I stepped forward into the vast unknown.

I, Mother Who's Afraid of Virginia Woolf?, Father The Outlaw Josey Wales, and the three Snaky Heads traveled through the windy swirl of soil toward the Adodar'ho outpost bordering Seneca City.

Without ceremony—for she no longer possessed our Tribal Jug with which to perform the Jug-shaking ritual or around which to perform the Jug-shaking dance—Mother introduced us as the only two remaining Gushedon'dada.

"Ah," said the nervous-looking one, pointing the muzzle of his Winchester at me. "So, this must be the infamous asexual boy named Broadway Danny Rose."

Mother hushed me with one of her deadly looks. It surprised me that even after having killed, thus bringing me either up or down to Mother's level, I feared the old woman no less, and the old woman still did not fear me.

The leader of the Adodar'ho introduced himself as the movie *Mildred Pierce.*

"I do not believe I am familiar with the etymology of your name," said Mother.

"My name is derived from the pre-Reddening 1945 film of intrigue, murder, and misplaced affection," said Mildred Pierce, "starring Joan Crawford as a successful restauranteur, Zachary Scott, and a young Ann Blyth. I am surprised you have not heard of it. It was a four-star, thumbs-up, critically acclaimed picture that netted Joan Crawford the Oscar for Best Actress."

"I am humbled," said Mother.

And suddenly I liked this fellow named Mildred Pierce with the cloth cobra perched upon the crown of his head and the fluffy golden flaps dabbing at his ears.

At some point during the hike, when the wind howled fiercely and we were all forced to walk hunched over, with our heads down, to protect our faces from the swirling sand, Father entered his body again.

What's happening? he said.

I answered, or communicated to him in some otherworldly, spiritual way, "We have escaped from the S'hondowek'owa, and the Adodar'ho are guiding us to the outskirts of Seneca City."

Ah, the Snaky Heads. Don't trust them to protect you for too long. They are an incompetent and easily distracted people.

"The leader seems to have a good head upon his shoulders."

There is an old saying: Never trust a Snaky with a good head, for the two shall soon be parted.

"Father, I must know, does the Valley of Day-Glo truly exist?"

We, the Gushedon'dada, made our tribal fortune a generation ago upon the excavation of the only K mart our people had ever discovered. This occurred before Mother and Father were married. Mother was given credit for the find, and it is a shame that the tribe did not know the true story of the discovery before the great soil storm claimed their lives. When I asked Father about the Valley of Day-Glo, he related to me what had really happened all those years ago upon the discovery of our tribe's one and only buried treasure:

The Gushedon'dada excavation scouts discovered a rock and hill formation that appeared not altogether natural, so the tribe made camp and began to dig. We dug for three days. I knew there wasn't anything under that mound. I could tell. Don't ask me how I knew. It was a very strange experience. But I remember one morning waking to the sound of the K mart calling to me from over the ridge, two or three soil swirls away—"Attention K mart shoppers! Attention K mart shoppers!" So I got up and walked over to the spot from where I was sure the K mart announcement had called to me, and I began to chop at the ground with my pick. The others thought I was crazy. They dug and dug at their rock-and-hill formation for two more days without any success, and the next morning, when once again I began chopping at my spot, a few others came over to help. By the middle of the afternoon we were all working at my site. The very next morning we struck the roof of the automotive department of our tribal fortune.

"But, Father, how is it that Mother is given credit for the find in our tribal history if you were indeed the one responsible for discovering the K mart?"

Because I was a young man then, said Father. If Father could have drawn a deep breath he would have sighed heavily.

Things mattered to me then. Things made a difference. Your mother was the most beautiful woman in the tribe. All of the young braves wanted her for a wife, but she kept turning them down. Your mother was a hopeless perfectionist with an inflated sense of self-worth.

"I see some things never change."

She wanted the ideal husband, and she would have gladly died without one if she could not get him. So when they asked me how I knew where to dig, I said, "Who's Afraid of Virginia Woolf? told me to dig here." Of course she could have denied it, but she wasn't sure how to react at first, and before she knew what was happening, there was a huge tribal dance and feast and she was being praised and honored by everyone, even the chief. So when they asked her how she knew where to dig, she told them it came to her in a dream. That was the end of her search for the perfect husband. She owed me big-time, and she was afraid if she didn't marry me I would spill the beans. You know, I never mentioned that incident to anyone until now, and I never would have.

"Father, that was an ingenious ploy."

So it would seem.

I hesitated. "Ah, yes, I see your dilemma. Mother felt trapped by your conspiracy, so as time went by she became more and more vindictive. This is why she treated you with such hostility for so many years."

Bingo!

"But why did you live such a lie for so long, Father? Didn't it hurt you to be treated so poorly?"

Love.

I nodded, not at all understanding. "I have never been in love."

I know. I always loved your mother. That is the one thing I would miss if anything mattered over here in the land of the dead. I would miss loving your mother.

"Sometimes, dear Father, I wish I could feel love."

Let me ask you something. Are you out of breath? For the last ten years of my life I felt like I was always out of breath, and I hated it. Now that there is no such thing as breathing, I would welcome my old familiar shortness of breath. I would also like to hiccup again.

"Father, what has any of this to do with the Valley of Day-Glo?"

Father chuckled but refused to answer. When he fell silent, I knew he had abandoned his body, leaving me to ponder the story of our tribal fortune.

Abruptly it came to me!

The reason Mother believed so thoroughly in the Valley of Day-Glo was because Father, years and years ago, had been right about the K mart!

Was this Father's way of telling me the Valley of Day-Glo truly existed?

Should I believe, too?

■ ■ ■

When we reached the Adodar'ho outpost—a loose construction of wattle and bones woven together with the hides of various rodents— Mother whispered in my ear, "Be prepared to make a run for it."

It seemed to me that all we were doing lately was running for it. "What's wrong this time?"

"Don't be such a putz. Someone has been tracking us. I'm not sure who or why. Just be ready to run for your life, although why I even bother worrying about you is beyond my comprehension."

The man named Mildred Pierce entered the tiny ramshackle hut first and held the door, which fit badly, so the rest of us could follow. The unfit door made me think of what Father had said to me not more than a few hours ago about the Snaky Heads, how they were an incompetent and easily distracted people. If nothing else, an ill-conceived door was proof of that.

Before I entered the outpost I tried to glance inconspicuously over my shoulder to see if we were indeed being followed as Mother had warned, but the reddish glow of sand and sun and the sloping plains seemed undisturbed.

The nervous-looking Snaky Head and his squat companion closed the door behind us.

Inside, I took a moment to blink and adjust my eyes to the darkness. There was barely enough room for all of us to fit, including Father. The decorating surprised me. The Adodar'ho had made an obvious attempt to create a warm and pleasant atmosphere, with three wooden chairs (all of different sizes) placed around a small four-legged table, a wall hanging of yellow and brown branches tied together to form a petite replication of what might have been a tepee, and some curtains that I assumed had been stolen from one of the Seneca storage facilities. The curtains had probably first been stolen by the Senecas from one of the Independent tribes who may have unearthed a Sears or Domesticans warehouse or perhaps even a K mart, which made me think about the day our tribal fortune had been excavated, and the lie Mother had been living under for so many years. I wondered how and when I might be able to use this great untruth against her, for this was indeed a "trump card" as Father would have called it, referring to Hoyle's rules of euchre, a game of pre-Reddening playing cards that Father had traded to an Independent tribe for rat skins and mashed winged roach after the soil storm had decimated the Gushedon'dada from forty-seven to three, and we could no longer find a fourth to fill the required number for a euchre game.

In any event, the hut boasted only one opening—a door, no windows—so the curtains lay tacked to the wall for no apparent reason other than to create the facsimile of a swooshing fabric smile.

The squat Snaky Head offered his chair to Mother, and the neurotic one stood with his back to the door.

"Tell me something," said Mildred Pierce, glancing at me. "Do you believe the incapacity of your phallus is the cause or the effect of your loss of power as a male?"

"I have never really thought about it."

"Well," said Mildred, "it is our protrusion that makes us men, that gives us strength, just as it is the womb that is the center of a woman's vigor."

"Listen, power never meant anything to me." I was growing tired of defending myself. At least among my own tribe I had not been required to explain my asexuality. "I think being powerless is an advantage. Nobody expects great things from you. And here's another thing. I can never be controlled by my phallus, nor can I be manipulated by women. For me, there is no such thing as performance anxiety. Here's the way I look at it. If you have a protrusion, you can be easily yanked around by it. Not me."

"The boy never had a lick of power," said Mother. "It has nothing to do with his protrusion, or lack of protrusion."

I was just about to elucidate that in my case not being rooted in the male gender role had allowed me to cultivate patience, kindness, contentment, and so on, and my asexuality had opened the doors of self-awareness, when the door of the Adodar'ho outpost crashed inward, smashing the nervous-looking Snaky Head and his squat companion to the ground on top of Father The Outlaw Josey Wales.

Sunlight spilled into the hut. The blast of a shotgun bludgeoned through the opening, followed by Exploding Wren herself, a terrifying, black-skirted, fuschia-topped, red-faced warrior, crying "CAW-CAW-CAW-CAW-CAW—"

Mildred Pierce, of course, was dead. The twelve-gauge slug had blown apart his neck, thus fulfilling Father's prophecy that a Snaky and his apparently good head would soon be parted.

The two screaming Adodar'ho on the ground could not extricate themselves from underneath their ill-conceived door. Here the nervous-looking one, out of sheer panic, pulled the trigger of his rifle, and I watched a bullet splat through the palm of his squat friend, and then I saw Mother grab her shoulder as if she'd been struck.

Dewutiowa'is pumped her shotgun, and the plastic casing that had contained the deadly slug that killed Mildred Pierce popped out and plinked me in the eye. Therefore I did not witness the next two slayings, although I heard the earsplitting blasts and felt the slugs thump heavily into the ground and vibrate beneath my toes. I looked over with my good eye at Mother Who's Afraid of Virginia Woolf? and decided she could not have been badly injured for she had managed to pull Father out of the line of fire.

Dewutiowa'is slung the shotgun over her shoulder and came over to me, squishing on top of the bloody Snaky Heads. "Are you all right?" she said, inspecting my eye.

"It just stings a little."

"I'm sorry. It doesn't hurt too much, does it? I don't think the casing has done any damage to the eye."

"No, no, no, think nothing of it."

Dewutiowa'is kissed me gently on the eyelid. "Listen, I overheard what that numbskull Snaky Head said. I want you to know something. Your phallus has nothing at all to do with your power as an Indian. What determines one's power is will and determination, nothing more. The will comes from the center, the heart." She touched her fist to her chest. "Not from the sexual apparatus."

"Please," said I, "you're embarrassing me in front of Mother."

Mother, in fact, stared with an expression of disbelief at nothing in particular, and I felt a sudden chill at the absent look upon her face. She was huddled over Father's body. There on her shoulder I noticed a streak of bright red blood.

I turned to Dewutiowa'is. "How far are we from Seneca City?"

"No more than a half-day's journey."

I turned to Mother. "It is time to tell her the truth. Dewutiowa'is may be the only one who can help us now."

Mother continued to kneel in silence. She brushed back Father's frayed hair. Suddenly she looked wistful, as if she were remembering some tender moment.

"Dewutiowa'is, it is true we are on a quest, as Mother told you, but our quest is to discover the fabled Valley of Day-Glo. Mother wishes to bring Father back to life. To be perfectly honest, I do not even know why. She says it's because Father is the last true male capable of siring Gushedon'dada offspring, but I don't think that's exactly true, for Mother is long past her childbearing years, and I could not imagine her allowing Father—dead or alive—to sleep with another woman. I think she is feeling guilty, for it was Mother, in a fit of rage, of unleashed hostility, for reasons I have only just recently learned, who strangled my poor father to death. Whatever her reasons, the quest was genuine and honorable, even if we did not know whether the Valley truly existed. It seemed the right thing to do for the last two surviving Gushedon'dada, rather than to sit and wait for death."

Dewutiowa'is remained silent, looking at Mother with what might have been pity.

"Does the Valley of Day-Glo exist?" I asked her. "And if so, can we bring Father to the Valley and return him to life?"

Dewutiowa'is furrowed her brow and stepped over to Mother. "Old woman," she said. Mother looked up with somewhat vacant eyes, from under the bill of her Chicago Cubs baseball cap. "For the sake of your courageous son, I forgive you your deceit. I also forgive you the slaying of my sister warrior which I witnessed from afar, which was not in self-defense, for which I should most certainly skin you alive and expose your open nerve endings to a grainy sandstorm."

She returned to me—*squish, squish, squish*—on top of the bloody Adodar'ho. "Your killing of my sister warrior, courageous Broadway Danny Rose, was in self-defense and there is nothing to forgive. I will answer your questions. The Valley of Day-Glo does in fact exist, in a manner of speaking, and we can bring your father to the Valley of Day-Glo and, in another manner of speaking, bring him back to life."

"Mother!" I said. "Did you hear the good news?"

Much to my surprise, Mother's expression did not vary. She gently rocked her dead husband in her arms.

Dewutiowa'is said, "Before I can guide you to the Valley of Day-Glo, I am honor-bound to desecrate the bodies of these enemy Adodar'ho, and feast upon their internal organs. I hope you understand."

"Of course. You don't mind if Mother and I wait outside?"

"Not at all. Make yourselves comfortable. This should not take long."

So Mother and I dragged Father out of the ruined hut, where we waited in the bright red sun for Dewutiowa'is to mutilate the bodies of her victims and feed upon their remains.

Mother sat trembling. Perhaps, at long last, the stress had been too much for her, the stress not only of this journey, but of a lifetime of fear and hidden resentment and stifled emotions. I could no longer hate her. Perhaps this had been Father's intent all along. I did not know, and I was not about to ask him. I hoped that he was enjoying this moment with Mother. Even in the land of Who Cares? and What's the Difference?, a brief interlude of love might somehow bridge the gap between life and death. That would be nice to know, as it is a path that I, and all who live, must someday travel.

Chop, chop, chop. I heard Exploding Wren carving up her snack. I wondered exactly what she had meant by saying that the Valley of Day-Glo existed "in a manner of speaking," and that Father might be brought back to life "in another manner of speaking," but upon these details I did not dwell.

Instead I sat down next to Mother and inspected her wound, only to discover it a more serious injury than I had originally assumed. What I thought to be a scratch was quite obviously a smear, probably from Mother's own hand, and I was now certain that the bullet had lodged itself in her shoulder. The bleeding had stopped, however. I tore off a piece of my shirt sleeve and removed the bandannas from around my wrists, and while Mother sat motionless I wrapped the cloths around her shoulder and under her armpit and tied them off.

I then curled my arm around her to give her what comfort I could, even though she seemed oblivious to my efforts.

Mother Who's Afraid of Virginia Woolf?, now wounded, a rather disturbingly cold and stiff specimen, and Father The Outlaw Josey Wales, a blistered greenish horror who nonetheless gave the near life-like appearance of a puckered, gelatinous mold, could not look away from each other, these two outrageous lovebirds. Who could have possibly foreseen that their relationship would blossom after Father's death?

I told Mother that everything was going to be all right, and that I would take care of things from now on, and see to it Father was taken care of. I assured her that soon our quest would be fulfilled, one way or another.

This is what I saw of the Seneca's great mega-city:

Lots of smoke. Black smoke, gray smoke, pasty white smoke. Everything, all of its structures, all of the inadequate housing facilities, of which Mildred Pierce had forewarned us, were either burned or burning.

Indians lay dead everywhere, gutted, stampeded, bodies mangled, skulls crushed, some of the Independents even scalped, a ritual that our pre-Reddening, pre-Industrial North American Iroquois Indian ancestors used to perform regularly during the Golden Age. The wounded moaned to themselves, against their will it seemed, perhaps aware that they could so easily be killed by friend or by foe, for mercy or for malice. And in between the buildings all ablaze and the horrible human suffering, what Seneca and Independent warriors remained continued to melee in small parties of three or four or five, looking to bludgeon or shoot or stab to death their enemies, or to hide until the killing stopped and it became clear who, if anyone, would stand to claim victory.

Dewutiowa'is had said she would guide us to the cave that led directly unto the Valley of Day-Glo, the only entrance to the legendary land of which Father had described, and, true to her word, in her single-gleminded way, she maneuvered us through the mayhem, as if she knew a safe and abstract route only through time, avoiding the perilous reality of space.

Perhaps what amazed me most of all was Dewutiowa'is herself, who appeared to be untouched by the demise of Seneca City, *her* city, and the suffering of her people. These S'hondowek'owa were truly unique warrior women, thought I, a breed apart.

It was I who now dragged the death burden of Father The Outlaw Josey Wales, and held Mother's hand, actually pulling her along as I tried to remain focused on Dewutiowa'is so that I would not feel my exhaustion, or despair, or terror.

Oh, fear!

How easily it could overwhelm me if I but gave it the slightest measure of my mind. But Father kept my thoughts sufficiently obscured:

You had better be afraid, he said to me. *How lucky you are to have fear.*

"Lucky? I think I could die from fright."

That is how you know you are alive. Fear is a great teacher, a great motivator, and best of all you can really feel it knocking at your door. Nothing knocks at your door when you are dead. I would give anything to be afraid of death. But now that I am dead I care nothing about it at all.

"I am also afraid for Mother."

Ha! Lucky you, again! You are not only afraid for yourself, but you are afraid for someone else. Listen, don't worry about the old bag. She will be fine.

Dewutiowa'is moved slowly, cautiously through the city, taking long respites for which I was entirely grateful. To travel with haste, said she, would only attract unwelcome attention, and we did not want to look as if we had somewhere to go, for during a fierce battle people tended to follow people who looked as if they had a purpose or a destination, or they tended to kill them. We wanted neither company nor death.

Dewutiowa'is assured us the fighting had become sparse enough now that with careful navigation small skirmishes could be avoided. And perhaps she was right, after all, for at one point when my legs trembled and I thought my shoulder muscles would snap from the strain of the harness, Dewutiowa'is raised her hand and we came to a halt, and there on a ridge far below us stood a company of five Oniat'ga, the tribe of Rancid Meats, guarding the entrance of the cave that Exploding Wren assured us was the cave that led unto the Valley of Day-Glo, and we had reached our destination, so it would seem, without incident.

"Now," said Dewutiowa'is, "we have only to defeat the Oniat'ga and the Valley will be ours."

I saw the gleam in her eyes. "No more killing," I said. "I have been witness to enough death already. I will not be the cause of any more. If we cannot get past the Oniat'ga without killing them, then our quest ends here."

Dewutiowa'is muttered her disapproval, but in the end she did not complain. I began to think that perhaps she had fallen in love with me, Broadway Danny Rose, the useless asexual.

We settled in and remained hidden, resting and munching on some provisions Dewutiowa'is had procured from the Adodar'ho outpost, not, she assured me, any portions of which she'd carved from the Snaky Heads themselves.

There in the dirt, Dewutiowa'is sketched out a plan that might gain us entry into the cave.

"Mother, aren't you excited?" said I. "The plan is a good one, is it not?"

She did not answer. I hoped that if she was going to be of no use to us, she would at least not cause us undue difficulty.

Was this how Mother used to feel about me?

"Help me!" I cried, as I limped along the trail, dragging Father behind me, with my arm wrapped around Mother.

The five Oniat'ga whirled about and aimed their rifles at us. Crouching, they stepped behind some strategically placed boulders.

I noticed Dewutiowa'is then, above them, on the ledge over the mouth of the cave. She had circled around and climbed up the outcrop from behind. I knew I had already given her all the diversion she would need to carry out the first part of her plan, for as soon as the Oniat'ga turned their backs to the cave, Dewutiowa'is lowered herself into the darkened mouth.

"Don't shoot! We are allies! We are Independents! My name is Broadway Danny Rose of the Gushedon'dada, and this is my dead father, The Outlaw Josey Wales, and my mother, Who's Afraid of Virginia Woolf?, who has been seriously injured in the revolutionary battle."

Two of the Oniat'ga slunk out from behind their boulders and approached us, scanning the area for any sign of the enemy, too late to detect the presence of Exploding Wren.

Neither of the Rancid Meats spoke to us. I remembered Mother once telling me in her typical scolding manner of a tribe that sulked to the point of not uttering a single syllable (many of them sulked for an entire lifetime without ever speaking), and I thought that the Oniat'ga might in fact be this sulking tribe. I wished Mother were her old self again. Oh, what I would have given for a crisp slap across the face, one of her lovely scowls, and a harsh defamation of my character such as "Eunuch-boy! Have you learned nothing in all your years! Of course these are the sulking Oniat'ga!"

But alas.

"My mother has been shot. Can you help her?"

The Oniat'ga led us directly into the shelter of the cave, where two of them laid down their bolt-action rifles and began to handle Mother. They retrieved medical supplies from a darkened corner, and quickly and efficiently removed the bullet, which most fortunately was not deeply set, from Mother's shoulder with nothing but a shiv and a spoon, then cleaned the wound and changed the dressing. Mother, silent and expressionless throughout the entire procedure, was the perfect Oniat'ga patient.

Meanwhile, the other three guards resumed their positions just outside the mouth of the cave.

The best part of Dewutiowa'is's plan, as far as I was concerned, was the simplicity of my role. I had only to confront the Oniat'ga outside the cave, allow them to take us in as Dewutiowa'is hoped they would, and then she would take care of the rest.

Which she did most efficiently.

Her initial attack came so swiftly out of the shadows that the first Oniat'ga, a huge beast of a man with tufts of hair clinging to his chest and back, never saw the second one fall, never saw the large rock descend upon the base of his companion's skull, knocking the poor fellow senseless. When he turned at the sound of his fallen friend, seemingly wanting to shout but then perhaps remembering that he was Oniat'ga and could or should not, Exploding Wren drove her fist into his squared chin, dropping him like a stone giant.

Unfortunately, the other Oniat'ga heard this large one crash to the ground.

But off we ran!

Dewutiowa'is picked up Mother, tossed her over her shoulder, and dashed into the deep black pit of the cave.

Blinded by the darkness, with Father in tow, I followed Dewutiowa'is by the sound of her footfalls and her hushed voice, "This way! This way! No—this way!"

The Oniat'ga shot at us, their gunfire cracking and echoing in the surrounding caverns, but in stopping to shoot they had allowed us to elude them.

Dewutiowa'is halted, and caught me as I stumbled into her arms. "Sssssshh," she whispered. "They are listening for us."

And indeed I noticed the Rancid Meats were no longer shooting, and the caves had turned deathly quiet.

"Offshoots," whispered Dewutiowa'is. "There are scores of them to choose from in only the short distance we have run. That should keep them busy for a while."

Dewutiowa'is knelt on the path and began to dig at some loose dirt. I took this opportunity to adjust Father's harness more comfortably about my shoulders.

More scuffling came from behind us, and some dull light.

"Flashlights," said Mother, the first word she had uttered since the debacle at the Adodar'ho outpost, and my heart filled with joy at the thought that Mother might be recovering from her injury and melancholia.

My eyes had adjusted to the darkness well enough to identify the objects Dewutiowa'is had unearthed—a large hiking pack, and some sort of unusually shaped helmet. She quickly brushed the dirt off these items, strapped on the backpack, turned to me and placed the helmet upon my head, and adjusted the strap of the helmet under my chin.

She said, "With this hard hat, you will be able to follow closely behind me, and shed light upon the cave path ahead. I am tightening the lamp bracket . . ." She turned a knob on my helmet, flipped a switch, and the light upon my hat illuminated a vast portion of the cave in front of us. "If I tell you to turn off the light, simply flip this switch down." She touched my fingers to it. I nodded. The footsteps behind us drew closer. "We must move quickly. The light is bright and the Oniat'ga might see it." She lifted Mother over her shoulder again—Mother did not argue or even try to move on her own—and off we jogged.

Through the limestone caves we scurried, caves formed during the time of groundwater, explained Dewutiowa'is. We passed long stretches of crystal clusters and white flowstone. In some sections of the caves, beautiful speleothems had precipitated on the cave walls and ceilings. Stalagmites scattered about the cave floors posed constant obstacles.

Soon I was panting, and feeling frighteningly enclosed. I shivered from the fear. But onward, ho! The Rancid Meats, being persistent, sulking Indians, were not likely to give up on the hunt once they had detected our trail.

"Bathtub," said Dewutiowa'is, stopping suddenly, indicating a low spot in the underground cavern filled with water.

"Might I suggest we follow that offshoot to the left?"

"We could, but the Oniat'ga will be more reluctant to wade through the pool."

"We are reluctant too, are we not?"

"But we are prepared." Exploding Wren reached into her backpack, dug out two slim tubes of plastic she called transparent body suits, and unrolled them. We climbed into the plastic suits and zipped them up to our necks. She then waded into the pool, holding Mother above the water, and I did likewise with Father, harness and all. I felt the water swirling around me, up to my knees, hips, waist, chest, and I began to fear that the bathwater would surely climb above my head and drown me, and my arms ached, and I was certain I could not take one more step against the resistance of the cold water, but then the pool began to slope upward again, and as we climbed out of the bathtub I nearly collapsed, hopelessly exhausted. Sensing now that we could put some much-needed distance between us and the Rancid Meats, Dewutiowa'is insisted we carry on, so we stripped off our transparent suits and forged ahead.

Shortly thereafter we came upon a "squeeze," an extremely confining Z-shaped passage that required us to belly up against the cave walls in order to cut through to another main artery. The sharp stones nicked our skin and left us all slightly gashed and bleeding—except, of course, for Father, who could no longer bleed. But at least we had made it through the squeeze, and upon doing so, Dewutiowa'is finally allowed us to stop and rest.

Dewutiowa'is removed something she called a carbide lamp from her backpack. She lit the lamp and told me to switch off my headlight and remove my hard hat. I gladly obeyed. It seemed easier to breathe without this weight pressing down upon my brow.

"I am very familiar with these caves," she said in her lilting voice. "I have visited the Valley of Day-Glo many times. Do not be afraid."

"It seems to me that if we keep going down, as it appears we have been doing since the very beginning, we shall discover the center of the Earth, which is a strange place to find a valley of any sort."

"I can assure you, this is the strangest valley of any sort you shall ever see."

"If I live to see it." Not a joke, although Dewutiowa'is chuckled, and scratched at her pimply brow.

"I am well prepared for cave survival." She came over and planted a hard kiss upon my lips.

"*Hmph,*" I said.

Under the soft glow of her carbide lamp she unpacked some nourishing provisions. I was so hungry I did not ask anything about the crunchy treats. I attempted to enjoy their salty flavor and block from my mind the Senecas' penchant for cannibalism. After all, these were dire times.

I crawled over to Mother and held her hand; it felt icy cold. I noticed that I was cold, too. It surprised me how chilly the caves had become. Dewutiowa'is handed me a small wool blanket from her hiking pack, and I wrapped it around Mother's shoulders. I tried to feed her some of our provisions, but she would not eat.

Although Father had told me not to worry about Mother, how could I not?

Soon we were foot to path again. Mother still required to be carried, for she could not make her legs move, and when I asked her to recite her name and tribe, she seemed confused and her speech was slurred and her eyes had glazed over, so Dewutiowa'is threw Mother over her shoulder. I found it easier to transport Father in such a manner as well, so I left behind the cumbersome harness once and for all.

Eventually the tiny, confining pathways began to widen, and the four of us broke through onto an open ledge overlooking a vast cavern, and far below, in the center of the cavern, shone a brilliant globe of bright white light. I switched off my headlight. So stark and spectacular an essence emanated from the shining globe that I forgot all about my fear of heights and knelt down on the edge of a steep declivity and stared into the eminence as if it were the exposed heart of Man. Perhaps it was. I felt godlike momentarily, as if gazing down upon the sun from a heavenly mantel.

"Be careful on the ledge," said Dewutiowa'is. "The light can be hypnotizing."

She helped me to my feet and we began our long descent toward the Valley of Day-Glo. It seemed as if the faraway light gave me strength. I could look at nothing else as we wound our way down the rocky pathway, and yet my steps fell sure and confident. Father The Outlaw Josey Wales was no longer a burden to me. There was only light in my mind, a light that spread throughout my entire body, and the wonder of the Valley, and the mysteries of what treasures lay inside.

Neither of us spoke, even when we reached the level of ground upon which the Valley lay sprawling, and the huge dome towered over us like an impossible serendipity. Perhaps we had both fallen victim to the hypnosis of which Dewutiowa'is had forewarned.

Silently we marched along the cavern floor, moving closer to the remarkable globe of light. Inside it, steep hills spotted the landscape, thick with green grass; dark brown trees with leaves of rich amber stood tall, like sentinels; rows and rows of bright red, orange, yellow, and blue fruits and vegetables twisted and turned along the hilly terrain. All of this under the huge glass dome.

We walked directly up to where the glass met the cavern floor, so that the tips of my loafers were centimeters away from something I had never before seen, touched, smelled, tasted, or felt between my toes: grass. And suddenly a new definition of time and space and distance revealed itself to me, as I might have been six million kilometers away from the Valley rather than mere centimeters, for the grass and all the other treasures that lay beyond were no more mine now than they had ever been. I stood at the threshold of the Valley as a carrion might stand in prayer over a wounded man.

There was a door, or hatch, sealed shut just to our left. Above the door a plaque read:

DAY-GLO PROJECT
2041

"Welcome to the Valley of Day-Glo," said Dewutiowa'is, setting Mother gently down upon the ground.

"How? How did they do it?" I dropped Father at my feet, and shed my cumbersome helmet.

"We do not know how the Honio'o did it. We studied it for quite some time."

"Why did you study the Valley? I thought you abhorred everything about the Honio'o."

"We studied it because we planned to destroy it. We tried everything. We tried beating it down with our baseball bats, but we couldn't even scratch the surface. We tried blasting it with our shotguns. We tried dropping huge boulders on top of it from the ledges above. We even tried digging under it, but it appears to be constructed in a completely global fashion. We studied the globe so that we might find a way to obliterate it before the Independents learned of its existence. We did not want the Valley preserved as a monument to the Honio'o."

"You would have destroyed it the way you have destroyed all of their other artifacts."

"Yes."

"The way you have destroyed the economy."

"We had no choice."

"You knew all along the revolution was coming."

Dewutiowa'is nodded. "We seeded it."

"So of course you did not care about the fall of Seneca City, or the violent deaths of your people."

"We were all prepared to die to rid us once and for all of the evil

Honio'o. With the economy collapsed, and the artifacts of the white and yellow and dark-skinned tribes destroyed and otherwise rendered valueless, out of the death and struggles of the Iroquois, after a generation or two or three, a new order would emerge, stronger, prouder, and based solely upon the culture of the Indian race."

I reached out to the glass dome and rested my hand upon it. It felt hard and warm to the touch. "You would have killed the only innocent life that inhabits this planet."

"For what it's worth," she said, "I did not agree with the destruction of the Valley of Day-Glo, and eventually our sachems decided to let it stand. I was glad we could not penetrate it."

Dewutiowa'is came up behind me, grasped my shoulders, and turned me around. "Friend Broadway Danny Rose, the politics surrounding the revolution and the revolution itself are already part of this planet's history, and we can do nothing to change them. The important thing now is your quest. In order for your father to become one of the living, we must leave his body here and travel to the far side of the Valley. But if you look upon the rocky ledges above us, you will see there are still two Oniat'ga upon our trail. If we leave the body, they will surely reach it and desecrate it before any miracle of life can occur, and then they will continue to track us and try to kill us, and since they are armed with rifles and we no longer have the cave walls to protect us—"

"I know," said I, reaching up and gently stroking her chin. The past was indeed the past. How fond I had grown of this burly woman.

"You are a strong man," she said, holding my hand.

"No."

"To do what one must do to survive is the only true measure of strength." She strapped on her shotgun.

"Be careful," I said.

She motioned to the Valley. "The light will be in their eyes." She drew her knife and gripped it between her teeth, and ran back up the pathway. I watched her pick her way through the rocks for a while, and then I turned my attention to Mother, who sat motionless in front of the beautiful Valley, staring as if she could not see it. I reached out and massaged her clammy neck.

"In the pre-Reddening year of 1993," said Mother, "the first woman radio announcer for the game of baseball was hired by the San Francisco Giants. The Honio'o had been playing baseball for well over a hundred years, but no woman had ever announced a game. A few years later, the league disallowed the chewing of tobacco by baseball players. It was a strange time in the history of the game. It was almost as if the league was trying to make the game more feminine. I wish that I could have been more feminine during my life, but I really couldn't. There was no time or place for femininity after the Reddening. The spirits Hed'iohe and Sagowenota never gave a thought to the women when they created their new world. What a shame."

Mother's words trailed off so that I could barely hear them. "Mother? Are you all right?"

But it was Father who answered.

Son, do not worry about my lovely wife any longer. She is coming with me.

I turned to Father. His flesh barely clung to his bones. He looked like a chewed and regurgitated piece of meat. His teeth knocked together. If he smelled horrendous, I could no longer detect it, or no longer cared.

Who would have thought that she could not survive without me? I wish I could have lived to enjoy this revelation. But of course now it does not matter and I do not care about anything.

He paused. I nodded. What could I say?

Danny Boy, I was just thinking about something interesting. Wouldn't it be nice if during our lives we could always feel detached from the world and uninvolved in our own existences, as I feel now in death— and then in death, after we have gone through all the struggles of our lives and made all of our irreversible choices, in death we could relax and enjoy our feelings for the rest of eternity? I wonder if there is anyone here I could talk to about that? Of course no one would care. That would be a problem in implementing any sort of plan.

"Father, how did you know the Valley of Day-Glo existed?"

I heard it call to me, just as the K mart called. Except it called to me in a vision rather than a voice. Little did I know it was my death calling me. Listen, whenever you hear a strange voice in your head, or a vision comes to you unbidden, and it tells you to do something, run the other way. It is your death calling you.

"Is that what you are, Father? My death?"

His face twisted into an obscene smile, and then he vanished into death.

I turned to Mother. She was gone, too. She lay slumped over, her eyes still staring blankly at the Valley of Day-Glo. Quite beyond my control, my body shook with grief.

I went over to Mother, closed her eyes, lifted her limp body, and lay her next to Father. I straightened her *Esprit* T-shirt and fixed her hair under her Chicago Cubs baseball cap, and then I took the gold hatpin she was so fond of and held it between my hands while I wailed the sacred O'gi'we, the Tribal Death Shriek:

"AIYEEEEEEEEEEEEE-YICK-YICK-EEEEEEEEEEEEEEE-oh—"

I slipped the hatpin into my pocket—something by which to remember my dear mother—and gazed at the brilliant orb that was the Valley of Day-Glo, the new Ende'kagaa'kwa, wherein lay all the miracles of nature. "Oh, great Valley," I prayed, "can you possibly save them both?"

I heard Dewutiowa'is approach me from behind, and felt her hands grasp my slumped shoulders.

"I am sorry about your mother. Now we must travel to the far side of the Valley," she said. "More Oniat'ga are coming, but they are a day's journey behind us, and they will be too late to prevent any miracle of life that may occur here."

I did not ask her how she had learned this information about the approaching Oniat'ga. I did not want to know. She carried two more rifles with her, the rifles of the dead Oniat'ga, I presumed.

I rose to my feet and spoke:

"She was my mother, Who's Afraid of Virginia Woolf?, named after a 1966 film starring Elizabeth Taylor and Richard Burton, based on an Edward Albee play. Taylor's performance as Martha, a wild, screeching bitch, was arguably her best character portrayal in a storied career as an actress.

"He was my father, The Outlaw Josey Wales, named after a 1976 Western film starring Clint Eastwood as a farmer turned Confederate soldier during the Civil War, determined to avenge the deaths of his family members, who were mercilessly slain by renegade Union soldiers."

I paused to take a deep breath. "And I am Broadway Danny Rose, the last remaining Gushedon'dada."

Now I was ready to go.

I did not know why we had to leave the bodies of my parents behind. I decided it was part of the miracle process that no living being could be present for the resurrections, if there was in fact such a miracle awaiting them. Regardless, I felt in my heart that an end had come to many things, and whether a miracle should occur had no particular bearing upon my existence from this moment forward. I knew no other way of life now but to carry on.

As we walked outside the Valley, Dewutiowa'is described to me many of the fruits and vegetables that grew inside. Bright red tomatoes. Figs, vines of grapes, orchards of apples, mulberry, and peach trees.

"Is there anyone alive in the Valley to harvest all of these wonderful foods?"

"Yes. We have never seen the Honio'o, but we know that at least some of them are alive to take in the harvests. We also know that they are responsible for the miracles of life that you will soon witness."

There were pretty little birds flying everywhere. Dewutiowa'is described them as tiny hummingbirds of shocking yellow, sparrows the color of tree bark, blue jays, and cardinals.

"Do you see those tall green stalks?" she said. "Maize, just like you would find in the Golden Age."

On the other side of the glass, a large body of water stretched for kilometers on top of kilometers, and as we walked outside its sandy shoreline, I lost all track of place and time. I had never before seen a vast body of water. It lulled one to sleep, it took one away to an indefinable area of the mind, and I thought that the ocean, as Dewutiowa'is called it, must surely have been a metaphor for death during the pre-Reddening Age.

Eventually the ocean gave way to a huge tropical rain forest, matted with dark, wet soil rich in nutrients. Amazon trees rose to the height of at least forty meters. Dark green moss and thick rows of ferns and rubber-tree plants grew wild and free.

And then we came upon a sprawling botanical garden. Flowers of every shape, size, and color dotted the rolling hills inside the glass dome, and there were little flying insects everywhere. Dewutiowa'is called them bees. Ah, yes! I had heard of bees, all sorts of bees, bumblebees, queen bees, wasps, etcetera, etcetera. They used to pollinate the flowers when flowers lay in the woods and the grassy fields and even in small gardens of personal ownership.

I had no idea how long or how far we had walked, but finally, as we stood gazing at the colorful nature, my legs collapsed from sheer exhaustion.

"I cannot take another step."

Dewutiowa'is sat beside me. "That is all right. Get some rest. We have reached our final destination. Now we need only await the miracle of life."

When I woke, I discovered I had fallen asleep in Exploding Wren's arms. I felt very safe there, so we cuddled for a while, neither of us speaking. I stroked her strong shoulders and she held me tightly and I kept my eyes closed, reluctant to let go of my dreamless slumber.

"How long have I been out of it?"

"About a day."

"That long?"

"I slept too," she said.

I sat up. "The miracle?"

"Has occurred."

"Mother? Father?"

Dewutiowa'is nodded behind her toward the Valley of Day-Glo. I rose to my feet and went over to the glass dome. I pressed my fingers against the transparent barrier. My heart pounded inside my chest.

There, in the botanical garden, resting atop the tender soil, lay my parents. Already they had begun to take root. Vines and grasses curled around their extremities. The tiny bud of a flower poked out of Father's armpit. Mother appeared to be laced in tiny white lilies. "Death becomes life," said I, "in the Valley of Day-Glo."

And it was true. Nowhere else upon the entire reddened planet Earth could something be planted, and out of it grow life.

Life.

"We discovered the miracle by accident," said Dewutiowa'is. "One day when we were dropping huge boulders from the high ledges in an attempt to crack open the glass dome, one of our tribesmen lost his footing and fell to his death. Because of our precarious positions in the upper rocks, we could not retrieve his body for several hours. When we were finally able to send a party out in search of him, we could not locate his remains. A day later, another war party working this end of the Valley noticed that the fallen man had been planted here, in the botanical garden.

"So we experimented. We left a few of our elderly dead around the entrance hatch and waited for the Honio'o to emerge so that we might ambush them and gain entry into the Valley. But they must have been able to detect our presence, even though we were hiding. So we left other dead bodies and returned to the city, and when we came back the next day, we found them buried here."

"It is so beautiful," I said. "My mother and father are alive. They are growing."

"The Seneca sachems held closed council to discuss the burials, and after our medicine man consulted the spirits, the sachems decided we should abort all our efforts to destroy the Valley of Day-Glo. We felt that the Honio'o were honoring our dead, and for the first time in the history of Man, they were showing proper respect to the North American Iroquois Indians. Although all their culture deserved to be destroyed, we would let the keepers of the Valley live, and use the Valley as our new burial ground."

I knelt down and rested my cheek against the glass dome. "They used to cry," I said. "The Honio'o. They possessed tear ducts, and when a loved one perished, they would shed water through their eyes, and then they would feel better."

"Have you not heard the tale of Niganega'a, the spirit of little waters and medicine powder?" she said softly.

"No."

"When Hed'iohe began to bake the white and yellow and dark-skinned tribes, and Sagowenota began to destroy His oceans, of utmost importance became a way to save the North American Iroquois Indians from the rapidly changing hazardous environmental conditions. So they called upon Niganega'a, the spirit of the little waters and medicine powder, who suggested this:

" 'With my medicine powders I will change the little waters inside all of the Iroquois red men, so that they will be able to conserve their bodily fluids during the baking process by producing very little urine and exceptionally dry feces. Then I will raise their body temperatures so that they might conserve even more water. From this day forward I will lower their metabolic rate to reduce their need for water, and I will eliminate their sudoriferous glands and ducts and give them the gift of internal sweat, so that they will always have a supply of water in their bodies and never suffer dehydration and only take a drink of water as a luxury. My medicine powders will also allow the nostrils of the Iroquois to open and close at will to keep out the deadly choking sands, and allow their nasal cavities to moisten and cool the air they breathe. And their eyes shall adapt to the bright red light and their bodies to the anthropogenic gases. All of this I will do so that the North American Iroquois Indians may survive the wrath of the spirits.'

"And with this, Niganega'a released His medicine powder into the air, and the little waters inside all of the Iroquois red men were forever altered, and the yellow and dark and white-skinned tribes, the Honio'o, who could not survive the deadly effects of their own industries, perished in a most agonizing fashion."

"I wonder if leaving us waterless was such a good idea," I said. "Niganega'a might have left us some tears with which to cry. That was how the Honio'o would release their great emotional stress. I think watering was a very important cultural practice for the Honio'o."

Dewutiowa'is knelt beside me. She wrapped her strong arm around my shoulders. "In the pre-Reddening age, there was plenty of time for such things as watering. Here, now, in our world, there is only time for survival or death. In the Valley of Day-Glo, death may become life, but outside, life becomes death very quickly."

I detected a note of urgency in her tone. She stood and moved away from me. I heard her loading slugs into the chamber of her shotgun. She unsheathed her knife and began to sharpen it upon a nearby stone.

I heard a voice echo through the huge cavern—a war cry! One of the Independents. I could not tell which tribe. Apparently the Oniat'ga had obtained reinforcements. This did not bode well for the Senecas. They were surely defeated.

I stood beside her. "You sacrificed your life for me. You knew they were coming. Why didn't you leave? Why didn't you try to escape?"

"It would not have mattered. Shortly there will be no place for a Seneca Indian to hide. We will all be tracked and killed. Better to die facing the enemy than with your back to them."

"So we shall make our last stand here," said I. "This is as good a place as any to die."

"You are not going to die."

"What do you mean?"

"When the Independents are within firing range, I shall force you out into the open at gunpoint with your hands bound behind your back. This will prove to the Independents that you were indeed my prisoner, and that I have chosen to die an honorable death and not take the life of an innocent captive. You will be safe. Then, if I am lucky, my own death will be quick and painless."

The voices drew closer, echoing eerily off the surrounding cavern walls. War cries. Death shrieks. The enemy closed in. Dewutiowa'is appeared completely undaunted. A breed apart she was, yes, definitely, and I admired her so. And I thought, What is the difference between us?

I reached into my pocket and pulled out my mother's hatpin. "I would like you to have this."

Dewutiowa'is looked confused for a moment, making me think she had never before received a gift of any sort, and therefore knew not what to do with mine. She could not look me in the eyes, but took the hatpin from me and stuck it into her black-pleated skirt at the hip. She arranged the bolt-action rifles near at hand between the rocks, and positioned herself behind two boulders.

More shouts. Gunshots now. The Indians fired rounds of ammunition into the air as they wailed their call to arm.

"They have much cause for celebration," said Dewutiowa'is. "It appears they have routed my people, and now they have discovered the legendary Valley of Day-Glo. This day shall be remembered by the Independents for many years to come."

I reached into my rear pocket and withdrew my Ruger .22-caliber semiautomatic pistol. The gun was loaded, and now of course I knew how to use it. One had only to close one's eyes and squeeze the trigger. I also possessed an extra clip. "I will stand and fight."

"You have an opportunity to survive. You must take it."

"Survival, my good woman, means nothing. I realize that now. Once you reach the land of the dead, I have come to learn by means I cannot begin to describe to you, one discovers that nothing matters at all."

Dewutiowa'is watched the Independents descend the cliffs and ledges and begin to circle. "You have surely lost your sanity."

"I am in full possession of my mental faculties."

She aimed one of the .30-06 bolt-action rifles she had taken from the Oniat'ga, pulled the trigger, and the shot rang out, shocking my ears. She jerked the bolt and a shell kicked into the air and she fired again, and again, and then tossed the rifle aside. It clattered among the rocks. She picked up the other .30-06 and took aim.

"I must tell you something," she said. "When I was a child, and my grandmother was alive, she used to tell me stories. Some of the stories she told me were secret stories."

She fired. This time I heard an Independent scream.

"One day she told me something and made me promise to remember it forever. She told me that I had another name, a name other than Dewutiowa'is and Exploding Wren. She told me my name was A Woman of Paris."

"*A Woman of Paris*! A classic Charlie Chaplin film from the pre-Reddening year of 1923! A drama about an innocent country girl who travels to Paris to become the lover of a rich philanderer."

Dewutiowa'is squeezed off another shot. "Of course I knew it was blasphemy to carry such a name, but the more I tried to forget it, the more I remembered it."

The Independents fired at us. A volley of shots pinged off the surrounding boulders. We ducked behind the rocks. Dust and slivers of stone flew.

"I always hated my grandmother for that. When she died, I spat upon her grave. Now I forgive her. I believe she was foreshadowing my death."

Dewutiowa'is stood and fired two more rounds, then tossed aside the last Oniat'ga rifle. "Your moment has arrived. If you do not go now, I fear your fate shall be sealed with mine." She took up her shotgun. "Unfortunately, a shotgun is a close-range weapon."

"Woman of Paris," I said. She turned to look at me. I stood beside her and held the Ruger out in front of me. "I shall stand beside my companion in battle. I have made up my mind."

"I love you," she said, showing her fangs. She turned once again to face the enemy.

I positioned myself behind her, watching the Independents close in. There were too many of them to count, hopping from boulder to boulder, some of them wearing blue jeans and windbreakers, others wearing Fila body suits, others outfitted in corduroys and plaids. They barked and hollered and shot at us. Their bullets ricocheted off the rocks and the glass dome, the place of miracles. When they noticed we had ceased to return fire, they became bolder. A few stepped out into the open and crouched forward. One broke from the pack and dashed toward us, screeching, waving a maroon-colored Louisville Slugger aluminum baseball bat. Dewutiowa'is stood out from behind her rock and fired her Remington, blasting him to a bloody pulp only a few meters away. But more came, fanning out in front of us.

I knew that it was time for me to die. I took a step back from Dewutiowa'is, aimed my Ruger in the general vicinity of the approaching enemy, and closed my eyes.

"AIYEEEEEEEEEEEEE-YICK-YICK-EEEEEEEEEEEEEEE-oh—" I cried, and fired!

Blast-blast-blast-blast-blast—ten shots in all, as fast as my finger would allow me to pull the trigger.

I opened my eyes, released the first clip, reached into my rear pocket and grabbed the second, jamming it into the butt of my gun, knowing at any moment a bat or an ax or a bullet might end my life.

And then I saw her, Dewutiowa'is, Exploding Wren, A Woman of Paris, dead at my feet, a victim of my own blind fury. I had plastered her with a full complement of .22-caliber bullets.

The Independents swarmed our position among the rocks in a mad rush. I screamed and dropped the Ruger. They fell upon me, raised me upon their shoulders, and began to chant, "DAN-NY! DAN-NY! DAN-NY! . . ."

"Dewutiowa'is!" I cried. But in the crush of bodies I could not see her. I could only imagine her indelicate form riddled with bullets discharged from my own gun, her remains trampled, her internal organs ripped from her belly in the same manner in which she had dealt death to so many of her enemies.

"DAN-NY! DAN-NY! DAN-NY! DAN-NY! . . ."

"Oh, Dewutiowa'is," said I. "I love you, too."

So the good-for-nothing asexual became a war hero.

You win some, you lose some.

This is the story of my heroic struggle, as told to me by a stranger several days after the fall of Seneca City:

Mother and Father and I fought bravely for the Independents during the revolution. We were attacked by a small party of mighty S'hondowek'owa warrior women. Father was mortally wounded, Mother injured, at which point I singlehandedly fought off our attackers and, with what strength yet remained to me, hauled Father, not wanting his body desecrated, and Mother, seeking medical attention for her wound, to the Oniat'ga outpost.

We were surprised inside the cave by the attack of yet another mighty S'hondowek'owa warrior, who tried to kill us, but, finding herself outnumbered, took Mother hostage in a desperate attempt to gain whatever victory she might claim. I would not allow Mother to be taken prisoner, so I bravely gave chase through the caves, once again dragging Father's body along with me for fear it might be mauled should it fall into the hands of the enemy.

I am given credit for clearly marking our trail so we could be tracked through the caves by the Independent warriors—ah, at last a truth, although I performed no such service intentionally—thus leading the Independents to the legendary Valley of Day-Glo, the most sought-after treasure in the history of the post-Reddening Indian Age.

There at the Valley, after an exhausting hunt, I too was ambushed and taken prisoner by the S'hondowek'owa warrior woman, thereafter learning that the wound to my mother and the physical and emotional ordeal had proved too much for her to bear, and she had succumbed to death.

When the final battle began in front of the botanical garden, I awaited my opportunity to appropriate one of the enemy's guns—in this case a Ruger .22-caliber semiautomatic pistol—and then pumped the filthy Shondo full of lead, thus avenging the deaths of my parents.

In a matter of days the new order was established and the Seneca League of Nations dismantled. I was given a seat upon the Independent Council as a military and philosophical adviser, and a presidency as the last remaining Gushedon'dada.

The Senecas were successful in only one area: collapsing the economy. In so doing, however, they precipitated the rise of a cash-based economy established by the Independent Council as an emergency measure to stabilize social order and generate entrepreneurship and industry.

Father The Outlaw Josey Wales had been right all along. "History," he had said over and over again, until he had made a hopeless nuisance of himself, "repeats itself."

I thought often of Dewutiowa'is.

What really happened during our final battle at the botanical garden, outside the Valley of Day-Glo? I could not believe that I had aimed so poorly I had accidentally killed her. Could she have purposely leapt into the line of my fire? That would have assured her a quick death at the hands of the man she loved, rather than a horrible, agonizing finish devised by the enemies she so hated. But to intentionally end one's life would have been considered an unforgivable act of cowardice to a mighty S'hondowek'owa warrior woman. Could she have known that to create the illusion of my killing her would not only save my life but make me a war hero? Is it possible that Exploding Wren loved me that much?

Dewutiowa'is once said that if one has an opportunity to survive one must take it. She also said that survival was the only true measure of strength. Perhaps she was right, after all. Perhaps I was a strong man all along, and just never knew it.

Often, in those early days of the new order, I traveled to the Valley and sought Father's sage advise, but he had not spoken to me since Mother joined him in death, and I could only imagine that the two outrageous lovebirds had renewed their kinship. Or perhaps Father had been working diligently on the project he had once discussed with me that would allow people to pursue lives uninvolved in their own existences, so that in death they might relax and enjoy their feelings throughout all eternity. Or, most likely, Father had become so deeply rooted in nothingness, in the world of Who Cares? and What's the Difference?, that he no longer had the inclination to speak.

In front of the Valley of Day-Glo, on the very spot where the final battle occurred, a stone-cutter of Gako'go descent sculpted a statue of me.

There I stood in granite, pistol in hand, dressed in my Dockers and penny loafers and the tattered remains of my button-down oxford shirt, my foot atop a fallen S'hondowek'owa warrior woman, the only woman I have ever loved.

AUTHOR'S NOTE:

The Iroquois words and names used in this story are from the original Iroquois language, and have been translated by many scholars before me, well versed in Native American culture. I thank them all for their contributions (especially Arthur C. Parker) and for keeping alive a rich and colorful chapter of American Indian history.

GLOSSARY

Adodar'ho   Snaky-headed.
Dewutiowa'is   Exploding wren.
Ende'kagaa'kwa   Brilliant orb (the sun).
Gadages'kao   Fetid banks.
Gako'go   Gluttonous beast.
Gane'owo   The harvest thanksgiving ceremony.
Gushendon'dada   The jug-shaking dance.
Hed'iohe   (originally *Hodianok'doo Hed'iohe*). The Creator.
Honio'o   White man (liberally used in this text to include all
   non-Indian people).

Iroquois League of Nations:

Ganeagaono   Mohawk, Flint people.
Gueugwehonono   Cayuga, People of the Mucky Land.
Nundawaono   Seneca, People of the Great Hill.
Onayotakaono   Oneida, Standing Stone people.
Onundagaono   Onandaga, People of the Hills.
Niganega'a   Medicine powder (little water).
O'gi'we   Death chant.
Oniat'ga   Rancid meats.
Ono'gweda   Cattail (a marsh plant).
Sagowenota   Iroquois spirit of the river tides.
S'hondowek'owa   Death herald.
Wainonjaa'ko   Death feast.

Afterword

This project began as an off-the-cuff remark I made to Brad Linaweaver that *Tatham Mound* was my favorite of Piers Anthony's novels. Brad's reply was "Why don't you suggest to Piers working on an anthology together?"

This was at a party—a really great outdoors party—at a convention sponsored by the Orlando Area Science Fiction Society, and as chance would have it, Owl Goingback was in a nearby conversation and overheard Brad's comment. Within a few minutes we had come up with submissions guidelines, a thematic framework, and a title. Brad offered to contact Piers on my behalf, and a few months later Piers called to say that Tor Books wanted to publish the project.

We took more than a year to make story selections, an unusually long period for an anthology. Several tribal newsletters and journals helped publicize our call for stories, and we placed listings in the sorts of publications often read by professional writers. The response was overwhelming: hundreds of submissions and more than a million words in manuscripts. Selecting the best wasn't easy; we could easily have published a volume twice this size, and we appreciate the patience the writers showed in allowing us time to make our selections.

There are five stories here by authors making their first professional sale. Publishers and editors alike take great pride in discovering a new author. Almost any publisher can figure out the advantages of publishing a best-selling author like Piers Anthony. Beth Meacham, our editor at Tor, encouraged us to seek out new authors for this project. Tor has a long and outstanding record of finding strong new authors, and we are pleased to have helped continue that tradition.

Editors at publishing houses rarely receive public credit for the books on which they work. This is a practice I'd like to see changed, particularly when the publisher's editor is as helpful and as essential to the quality of a book as Beth has been to this project. Both Piers and I wish to thank Beth for her fine help and support.

So, how did I come to be interested in Native American culture? It's always been a part of my life, a part of growing up on a farm in northern Alabama, in the foothills of the Appalachian Mountains where the Creek and the Cherokee lived. I suppose I was about six when I took an oddly shaped rock back to the house to show my parents. It was an arrowhead, they said, and told me stories of the peoples who had lived on the land in earlier times. That was important to me, knowing that the land had a history and that I belonged to the land.

Things change. The family sold the farm and I had to move. The field where I found the arrowhead is now a tract of upper-middle-class housing. I don't go there so much anymore. There isn't much of what I valued left there for me to go back to.

I think this is one of the great shortcomings of our modern society: a lack of a sense of place, roots upturned and strewn aside, individuals and cultures displaced with little consideration for what is being discarded.

The pow wow I attended in April 1993, at the invitation of Owl and his family, was much different from what Piers correctly describes as the state of far too many such events. "Plastic medicine" as Owl calls it—commercial shows held in civic centers, with not much emphasis on spirituality. Owl's pow wow was in a remote part of north-central Florida, well away from population centers and tourist trade. There was no admission fee asked, not even a collection plate passed around during the blessing, just people gathered to share good spirits and to be a part of the celebrations—all of this underneath a clear, bright sky, surrounded by a circle of trees, removed from the turmoil of change. The evening was very special, and I thank Owl and his family very much for having honored me with their invitation to share it with them.

As for this book, whatever truths are in it, I think that they are there for all peoples. To quote the teachings of Jim Audlin, the spokes of a wheel all meet at the center, but the path along each spoke is very different. You'll find many different and unusual spokes represented in these stories. As Piers puts it much to the point, there are things here to entertain, and things to think about as well.

Richard Gilliam

About the Authors

MERLE APASSINGOK was the captain of his high-school Problem Solving team that made educational history by becoming the first school to win two national academic championships in one year. He lives on an island in the Bering Sea and is the striker (harpooner) for his family's whaling boat. He was seventeen years old at the time he wrote this story.

JAMES DAVID AUDLIN is the Northeast Regional Chief and Tribal Council Chief of the Free Cherokees. His writings, as Chief Distant Eagle, appear frequently in a variety of Native American publications.

JACK DANN has been a frequent nominee for the Nebula and World Fantasy awards. His more than thirty books include *Junction, Starhiker*, and *The Man Who Melted*. Jack's most recent novel, *High Steel*, was written in collaboration with his longtime friend Jack C. Haldeman II.

NICHOLAS A. DICHARIO is a discovery and frequent coauthor of Mike Resnick, appearing in many of Mike's anthologies, including *Christmas Ghosts* and *Dinosaur Fantastic*. In just a few years as a professionally published author, Nick has been a Hugo, John W. Campbell, and World Fantasy Award nominee.

ROBIN M. DINNES is a gemologist who lives in Cowee, the gem-mining area of North Carolina. She is currently working toward a Masters in English, concentrating in Creative Writing. This is her first published story.

ESTHER M. FRIESNER is the author of such novels as *Majyk by Accident* and *Yesterday We Saw Mermaids;* her short fiction has appeared in many anthologies, including Jane Yolen's *Xanadu*. Esther's anthology, *Alien Pregnant by Elvis,* offers a satirical look at tabloid journalism, featuring stories by many of SF's best-known authors.

OWL GOINGBACK is a traditional storyteller whose many speaking appearances have brought him wide recognition. His fiction has appeared in such diverse anthologies as *Confederacy of the Dead, Grails: Visitations of the Night,* and *Quest to Riverworld.*

ED GORMAN is best known for his novels *The Autumn Dead* and *A Cry of Shadows,* and for his many outstanding short stories. His anthology appearances include *Lovecraft's Legacy* and *Monsters in Our Midst;* his short story "The Face" received the Golden Spur Award from the Western Writers of America. Ed, in partnership with Martin H. Greenberg, is the publisher of *Mystery Scene Magazine.*

GEORGE GUTHRIDGE is a professor of English and Eskimo education in the University of Alaska Fairbanks system. A Nebula and Hugo Award nominee, he has sold more than fifty science fiction stories. His latest novel is an offbeat western called *The Bloodletter.*

GERALD HAUSMAN, whose books include *Turtle Island Alphabet: A Lexicon of Native American Symbols and Culture* and *Tunkashila: From the Birth of Turtle Island to the Blood of Wounded Knee,* lives in Tesuque, New Mexico, in an adobe house that he built in 1977.

GABRIEL HORN is a writing instructor at St. Petersburg Junior College in Florida. His books for children include *Ceremony in the Circle of Life* and *The Great Change.* His autobiographical novel, *Native Heart: An American Indian Odyssey,* was published in 1993 and was widely hailed by critics.

ANNA KIRWAN-VOGEL's first novel, *The Jewel of Life,* gained her much critical acclaim, as did her short story "Jaguar Lord" in *Xanadu.* Her poetry has been widely published, including an appearance in the anthology *Mother Earth, Father Sky.*

BRAD LINAWEAVER is a screenwriter and essayist whose short stories have appeared in more than two dozen anthologies, including *Confederacy of the Dead* and *Psycho-Paths.* His nonfiction writing has appeared in a distinctively unusual group of magazines, ranging from *Famous Monsters of Filmland* to *National Review.*

JAY LITTLEHAWK, a poet and martial arts expert, lives in Central Florida, where he frequently performs as a fancy dancer at area pow wows.

BILLIE SUE MOSIMAN is the author of five novels, the most recent of which, *Night Cruise,* was nominated for an Edgar Award from the Mystery Writers of America. Her short stories, totaling more than sixty-five, have appeared in many leading magazines and anthologies, including *Psycho-Paths* and *Phobias.*

This is R. K. PARTAIN's first professional sale of a story. Keith lives in northern Alabama, near the traditional lands of his Cherokee ancestors.

MEREDITH RAYMOND is a student at the University of Hawaii, and has been published in such periodicals as *The Magazine of Fantasy and Science Fiction.* She is the daughter of her coauthor, George Guthridge.

MIKE RESNICK is the author of almost forty science fiction novels, among them *Santiago, Ivory, Soothsayer,* and *A Miracle of Rare Design.* He has been nominated for eight Hugo Awards, and won that award in 1989 and 1991. A busy and popular editor as well, Mike has some twenty anthologies to his credit, nearly all of which have received outstanding reviews.

CAROLINE RHODES worked as a forensic toxicologist for three years for the Arizona state crime lab in Phoenix, before leaving to found her own forensic consulting company. This is her first published story.

ALAN RIGGS is a historical researcher who lives in Central Florida. This is his first professional sale.

ALAN RODGERS's career includes the novel *Pandora* and a Bram Stoker Award for his novelette "The Boy Who Came Back from the Dead." "Paul Bunyan Dreams" is dedicated to his writing teacher, the late Cherokee author Tom Sanders (Nippawanock).

KRISTINE KATHRYN RUSCH has compiled an astounding number of awards and nominations in the first four years of her career, including a World Fantasy Award. In addition to her several novels and many short stories, she is the editor of *The Magazine of Fantasy and Science Fiction.*

WILLIAM SANDERS lives in Tahlequah, Oklahoma, where he is an active member of the Nighthawk Keetoowah Society, the most conservative religious-ceremonial group of the Oklahoma Cherokees. He is the author of fourteen published books, including his popular Taggart Roper series of mystery novels.

PAMELA SARGENT is the author, most recently, of *Ruler of the Sky,* a historical novel about Genghis Khan told from the points of view of the women in his life. She has won a Nebula Award and a Locus Award, and has been a finalist for the Hugo Award. She is part Mohawk, and lives in upstate New York, near the home of her late Mohawk grandmother.

LAWRENCE SCHIMEL is a poet and short-story writer whose work has appeared in nearly one hundred anthologies and periodicals, including *Grails: Visitations of the Night, The Saturday Evening Post,* and *The Wall Street Journal.* He is twenty-two years old.

STEVE RASNIC TEM's novel *Excavation* received excellent reviews, but he is best known for his more than two hundred short stories, including appearances in *Psycho-Paths* and *Monsters in Our Midst.* Steve is an important member of Colorado's growing literary community.

DEBRA WHITE PLUME coordinates the master's program in Lakota studies at Oglala Lakota College. Her story "Mother Called It Daddy's Junkyard" first appeared in the Winter 1993 issue of *Tribal College Student* magazine.

RICK WILBER's short stories and poems appear regularly in both mainstream and genre publications. His anthology appearances include his much-praised short story "Bridging," in *Phobias.* He is a professor of journalism at the University of South Florida and the author of the textbook *Magazine Feature Writing.*

JANE YOLEN is the author of more than 140 books, many of them for children and young adults. A past president of the Science Fiction Writers of America, she is also the editor-in-chief of Jane Yolen Books. Jane's work has won numerous awards, including the World Fantasy Award, the Mythopoeic Society Award, the Kerlan Award, and the Caldecott Medal.

May Belle Highway
She was like that
Back so far ago
Always more than others
Her energy even when
asleep it lingered over
and near hear waiting for

her to rise once more an
begin again. Always an
almost starting over — renewing
what was around — Her
Painting the turquoise bench beneath
our bottoms as we squirmed
to keep up with her. up an out
she stirred us
as if out of her
boiling roiling
pot.

Under neath the house dark with
damp
my hand goes up in side the box
but I can reach nothing
as it drips   on me   it's
Just on me I will have to
go back up and try to
wrench the water back in it's
place   I don't want to
be back up under here again
The black widow house is
Probably full to bursting
But maybe she will let me go
Like I did her others in Yogurt
& cottage cheese containers. Flinging

them up and out over the
humbug sides of the road.
The containers will offer them
Some protection till they make
a new home or die in the
sun. It gets hot up
there but still there is a chance.
Sometimes I place their egg
sacks with them. If I see them
But that was some time ago
I do not take that time
anymore. Like the tea ceremony
It is just in paper now.
A slim book or a reference to slow
down watch the water spill
into and then boil up
when I'm up underneath and
everything is almost dry

The goblin Night has come and gone.

No dark orchard
No long walk home
    down the Rialto

I'm so faraway
    from there
        so faraway

all of us not even close
    to there